FIRELIGHT AND WOODSMOKE

Pierre-Edouard loved this great stretch of land; he felt at home here, in his fields. He knew them by name, at least those which belonged to the Vialhes. Here the piece called Longue, with its old nut trees; over there, next to Caput Hill, the Peuch field; further on the Malides — a crop of wheat; further still the Perrier patch and finally, right at the end, hidden by the White Peak, the Big Field, sown with rye . . .

The slope was so steep that everything had to be done by hand, but the yield justified the labour. With fifteen hectares, eight cows, a dozen ewes, two goats and three sows, the Vialhes were among the more substantial landowners in the commune.

Claude Michelet was born in Brive in Limousin in 1938. He still lives on his land at Marcillac, close to Brive, where one of his six children now farms with him. He is the author of a trilogy about the people of Saint-Libéral which begins with *Firelight and Woodsmoke* and many other works, including a biography of his father, Edmond Michelet, who was a minister in General de Gaulle's government.

ALSO BY CLAUDE MICHELET

Applewood

Scent of Herbs

Firelight and Woodsmoke

CLAUDE MICHELET

Translated by Sheila Dickie

PHŒNIX

A PHOENIX PAPERBACK

First published in Great Britain by Orion in 1993
This paperback edition published in 1997 by Phoenix
a division of Orion Books Ltd,
Orion House, 5 Upper St Martin's Lane,
London WC2H 9EA

A CIP catalogue record for this book
is available from the British Library.

Printed and bound in Great Britain by
Clays Ltd, St Ives plc

To Bernadette

The People of Saint-Libéral

Il y a deux choses auxquelles il faut se faire, sous peine de trouver la vie insupportable: ce sont les injures du temps et les injustices des hommes.
                                        Sébastien Chamfort

There are two things to which we must adapt, lest we find life unendurable: they are the injuries of time and the injustices of man.

PART ONE
The House of Vialhe

1

THEY abandoned the sunken path and the shelter of the thick brambles. The east wind burst in their faces, seared their cheeks and lashed their bare legs; cold prickly tears appeared like pearls between their clenched eyelids.

The three children crossed towards the far edge of the plateau and slipped between the juniper bushes. The snow squeaked beneath their steps, stuck to the nails of their clogs and gave them huge, heavy white soles; they stopped frequently, knocked their feet together to shake off the frozen blocks, then trotted on.

The eldest led the way; he walked without hesitation and as fast as the undergrowth, snowdrifts and rocks would allow. Behind him came a young lad, his hand outstretched behind him, holding a little girl firmly by the hand. Her face was reddened with cold, she was sniffing noisily and almost running to keep up.

'There it is,' pointed out the eldest. They were approaching a juniper bush.

The thrush was stiff, frozen, hard as stone. The wind gave it the appearance of life, making it revolve on a necklace of horsehair hanging from a low branch. The snare must have trapped it early in the morning, at the hour when the pale sun broke between two clouds of snow. Attracted by the black laurel berries neatly arranged in a little trench of pressed snow, it had pecked up to the fatal fruit, in front of which Léon Dupeuch had placed the noose. At twelve years old, Léon was already a creditable trapper. His snares deceived even the wiliest hare.

'It's a lovely little songster,' he said, unhooking the bird. 'With the others that makes seven, and they're worth at least fifteen sous each. That makes . . .'

3

He hesitated, his brows furrowed, then, discouraged, he turned to his companion.

'Five francs twenty-five,' said Pierre-Edouard Vialhe, puffing himself out a little.

Pierre-Edouard Viahle was considered one of the best pupils in the village, and the schoolmaster was sure he would get his school certificate one day. He was only ten and a half, still plenty of time before he would have to face that exam, but he was preparing for it already.

'Blimey! How do you do it?' groaned Léon jealously. 'I don't understand all those numbers!'

Pierre-Edouard shrugged his shoulders. 'Hurry up, it's late; we must get back,' he said, examining the sky.

'We're going to get into trouble,' whimpered his sister, and suddenly, without a sound, began to cry. She regretted having insisted on following them.

'You're just a little girl, Louise!' Léon had teased her. 'What use would you be to us up there!'

'I'm nine and I am *not* a little girl. I want to go!'

'All right, come,' her brother had said. He was kind, was Pierre-Edouard; he almost always did everything she wanted. But this time it would have been better if he had not given in to her demands.

She was frightened and cold. What was she going to tell her mother as an excuse for this escapade? First of all their parents did not like them to leave the village; secondly they wouldn't like to know that Louise and Pierre-Edouard were with Léon Dupeuch. Although Léon was good fun, they said he was not well-bred; that he would rather be out in the wilds than in school; that everything he found – even a stray hen – became his property; that his poaching would lead him to prison one day – and above all, that his parents were worthless.

No one really knew where they'd come from, they weren't from this region. They had been seen arriving eight years ago, from the area of Brive, more than thirty kilometres away. Strangers . . . Tenant farmers on one of the solicitor's farms, they cultivated three hectares after a fashion: two cows, six sheep, a pig and some poultry. They lived poorly, spoke little, and did not join in the community life of Saint-Libéral-sur-Diamond. Therefore, no one trusted them.

'We must go,' insisted Pierre-Edouard.

'Hang on! Let me get my trap ready for tomorrow. In weather like this, other birds are bound to come down from the north; my father says the cold spell will last as long as this moon.'

'I know, Grandfather told me that, too. Come on, let's go – it'll be dark, they're bound to punish us!'

Without hurrying, Léon delicately attached a new circlet to the middle of the juniper branch, which he curved down to the ground and held there with a big lump of frozen snow. The ring of horsehair was at just the right height. If a bird put its head through, it was done for. The slightest shake would free the branch and the victim would be suspended, without even having swallowed the bait.

Léon got up at last, and blew on his numbed hands. 'I hope the wind won't get up again and bring more snow, that will spring the whole thing. You crying again?'

Louise sniffed fiercely, pulled her cloak tight around her and took her brother's hand. 'Hurry up,' she urged. 'They're bound to have called us in by now.'

Pierre-Edouard agreed, and began to step out. They were not far from the village; they could make out the columns of smoke, down there on the side of the hill. At any other time they would have reached it in less than a quarter of an hour; they only had to zigzag down between the trees to rejoin the path and the first houses. But the snow made rapid progress impossible. In places the wind had driven it up to fifty centimetres deep; elsewhere the frost had solidified the long streams of water which poured in torrents from the moorland. There were many tricky spots which they had to negotiate with care, making progress difficult and slow.

It had been bitterly cold for a fortnight. It had come all of a sudden, without warning.

'You see, mon petit, it's to finish the century,' Pierre-Edouard had been told by his paternal grandfather. 'It

5

hasn't been a very good one. It's dying as it lived, meanly . . .'

It had all begun on 10 December, a Sunday. The wind, which until then had kept the humidity of the west, had veered round to the north. It didn't stay there long, just long enough to change the colour of the clouds, which threatened snow now, instead of rain. And then, as suddenly as it had quit the west, the wind shifted to a full easterly, and settled there. The thermometer at the Mairie had registered minus 10° that Sunday, then minus 12° the next day, and eventually, on Tuesday, minus 16°. That was when the snow arrived; not a single flake melted on the frozen land. Since then it had held, frozen to the heart, during several awful nights. 'There'll be more!' declared Grandfather.

Pierre-Edouard stumbled, almost went sprawling, and let go of his sister's hand.

'We'll be told off,' she repeated between two hiccups. She was still crying silently, and two long candle-drips of mucus flowed down to her chapped lips.

'Blow your nose!' ordered her brother. 'No, perhaps they won't have noticed today . . .'

He had taken a risk, agreeing to this escapade with Léon. Normally he would never have dared to vanish for so long, and go so far; he had too much respect for his father's belt, that terrifying thong of leather which whistled as it swept down on his bare legs and thighs.

But today was different. First of all it was Sunday, and then it was Christmas Eve; the adults were preparing for the celebration supper after Midnight Mass and the next day's holiday. With a bit of luck, no one would have noticed their disappearance.

They had left at about two thirty, and had immediately climbed towards the vast plateau which dominated the village. Passing close to the source of the Diamond – the stream which ran down to Saint-Libéral, springing from a cave on the side of the hill – they could not resist the temptation to break the huge ice stalactites which hung from its vault. Then they set off again, each sucking a delicious candle of ice, so cold that it stopped your breath and burned your tongue.

The climb through the wood had warmed them up and their cloaks seemed too hot, almost unnecessary. Already Léon had pushed back his hood and undone his muffler. But an icy blast greeted them on the plateau. Up here there was nothing to stop the wind; only the path bordered by hedges and some clumps of bushes gave intermittent shelter.

Pierre-Edouard loved this great stretch of land; he felt at home here, in his fields. He knew them by name, at least those which belonged to the Vialhes. Here the piece called Longue, with its old nut trees; over there, next to Caput Hill, the Peuch field; further on the Malides – a crop of wheat; further still the Perrier patch, and finally, right at the end, hidden by the White Peak, the Big Field, sown with rye.

The boy also knew to whom the other fields belonged, the position of each boundary; he knew everyone who worked there, landowners and tenants, and whether they paid in money or kind. Almost all lived in Saint-Libéral, and almost all had other strips of land spread across the hillside to which the village clung. Down there the Vialhes owned more meadows and woods, and also a nascent vineyard and a big plot for vegetables, set on the open escarpment, exposed to the rising sun and well protected from late frosts. The slope was so steep that everything had to be done by hand, but the yield justified the labour. With fifteen hectares, eight cows, a dozen ewes, two goats and three sows, the Vialhes were among the more substantial landowners in the commune. Only the solicitor and the château had more land, and perhaps some of the leased farms belonging to people from Terrasson, Objat or Ayen.

'We'll get told off,' said Louise once more.

'Your sister's just like my jackdaw!' joked Léon. 'She always says the same thing.'

Pierre-Edouard did not rise to the bait – not because of the comparison, which he did not mind, but because he did not want that ugly bird introduced into the conversation.

7

Everyone knew that the only sentence the Dupeuchs' jackdaw could repeat (ad nauseam) was 'Pig of a priest! Pig of a priest!'

'A disgrace!' said Grandmother Vialhe. 'That's why you shouldn't associate with the Dupeuch boy, my dears.'

Pierre-Edouard knew perfectly well that it was not Léon but his father who had taught the bird this vulgarity, but it was still an irritating subject. Pierre-Edouard went to catechism classes, and Mass, and would soon make his First Communion. Léon didn't do any of that and prided himself on it, an attitude which upset Pierre-Edouard; embarrassed him, too, for it gave his parents good reason to forbid him to see his friend.

'We won't be there before dark!' admitted Pierre-Edouard.

The shadow was advancing quickly, densely. It was climbing up the valley, already drowning the village. Up there on the plateau it was still almost daylight, but the wood into which the children had plunged was growing darker minute by minute.

'Stop crying, you! We'll get there,' he said, shaking his sister.

'It'll take ten minutes,' declared Léon, 'if that.'

They were right in the centre of the wood when the howling transfixed them. It seemed to come from the plateau – more exactly, from the spot where Léon had stretched his last snare, close by the White Peak. The cry, long and wavering, echoed again.

'A wolf,' breathed Léon. 'My God, a wolf!'

'Quick, quick!' whispered Pierre-Edouard. 'We must run. You be quiet!' he ordered his sister.

She was not saying anything; besides, she was paralysed with fear.

'No,' said Léon. 'Just the opposite, we must make a noise. My father told me that. Make lots of noise. It'll be frightened of us!'

His voice was barely audible.

'Run,' insisted Pierre-Edouard. And he leapt down to the left through the snow.

Another howl reached them and this one did not come from the plateau; it rose up from the valley, flowing out of the darkness and echoing on the sides of the hill, an interminably long cry, which froze their blood.

'Quick, quick!' stammered Léon. 'Let's run *and* make a noise. They're there, they're after us! They've smelt us! Make some noise, Pierre, make a noise, for God's sake.'

'What with?'

'Talk, talk loudly,' begged Léon in a whisper.

'I don't know what to say,' murmured Pierre-Edouard. However, he raised his voice and stammered out his last geography lesson.

'La Corrèze; administrative centre Tulle, other towns Brive and Ussel . . . La Corrèze is a region which . . . which is part of Limousin. It is irrigated by three rivers, the Dordogne, the Vézère and Corrèze. It, it . . . I don't know any more!'

'Go on, go on,' begged Léon. 'They're coming!'

They reached the path as a fresh howl rose from the plateau and impelled them on their way.

'Say something! We're not near the houses yet, they can still eat us!' gasped Léon.

'Throw away the thrushes! That's what they can smell,' ordered Pierre-Edouard.

'You must be mad. I've got more than five francs' worth!'

'Throw them away, I'm telling you,' insisted Pierre-Edouard, shaking him, 'otherwise they'll get us!'

'All right,' groaned Léon. He opened his rucksack without slowing down, drew out fists full of birds, and threw them over his shoulder.

'Talk, Pierre-Edouard, talk!'

'Hail Mary, full of grace, the . . . Oh, I can't any more, it stops me running,' sobbed the boy.

'The Lord is with thee,' piped up Louise. She sniffed and, still crying, continued in a high-pitched tone: 'Blessed are those . . .'

At last they arrived at the first house in the village, but they went on running, right to the church square.

'Bye!' shouted Léon, crossing to the alley which led to his place.

Pierre-Edouard and Louise slowed down, drew breath, and walked to their home at the end of the main street, on the way out of the village. After blowing their noses, they slid quietly into the comforting warmth of the cowshed.

The milking had already been done and the animals were ruminating. They could make out their father, tying up a calf in the darkest corner of the barn, where the feeble glow of the paraffin lamp hardly penetrated.

'Where have you been?' asked Jean-Edouard.

'Over there . . .' said Pierre-Edouard, attempting a vague gesture. He took a fork and rearranged the straw.

'Go in,' he whispered, to his sister. 'Say that you were here with me. And I'll come in soon, with Father; Mother will think we've never left him.'

'And before that, where were we?'

'Playing in the square, sliding on the overflow from the wash-house . . .'

Louise pushed open the double door and slipped between its two wings into the main room. The dog, flopped down as close to the hearth as possible, his nose in the dying embers, turned his head towards her. His eyes shone golden, reflecting the flames, and he gently wagged his tail. Seated on the wooden settle, grandfather was delicately peeling chestnuts.

'There you are, poppet. Come and give me a kiss.'

She went up to him, placed her chapped lips on his rough, prickly cheek and settled beside him; she was still shivering.

'You're cold?'

'A bit. Where's Mother?'

'She's seeing to the pigs.'

'And Grandma?'

'Gone to the grocer's. She wanted to take you, but you weren't there.'

'And Berthe?'

'With Grandma.'

Berthe was only seven; she was much too little to follow the big boys. Good thing she wasn't with us, contemplated Louise; we wouldn't have been able to run, and the wolves would have caught us. She shuddered at the thought.

'Have you caught a cold? Where have you been?'

'I was with Pierre-Edouard . . . Hey, will you roast me some chestnuts?'

'Here,' said the old man. He bent down towards the hearth, moved aside the warm cinders with his fingertips, and revealed some fifteen chestnuts roasted in their skins. 'I knew you'd want some.'

He took several steaming nuts, rubbed them between his clasped hands so that the charred, cracked skin fell off, and stretched them out on his palm to the little girl. The wall-clock struck six as Jean-Edouard came in, his son behind him.

'Have you heard the news?' called out Jean-Edouard, approaching the fire. 'The wolves have come!'

'He's made Pierre talk!' thought Louise, and her throat felt dry. Punishment was imminent.

'Who said so?' asked the older man.

'Go out into the yard, you can hear them!' Jean-Edouard took down the paraffin lamp and lit it. A harsh, white light replaced the gentle warm glow of the fire. 'Delmont came to find me in the byre,' he explained. 'He's just met the doctor, who saw one on the way back from Ayen; it crossed the road right in front of him. Then we heard them.'

'How many?'

'At least three. Two on the plateau, towards the peaks, and another sounding off towards Yssandon. I bet they're coming from the north. With this cold it's not surprising.'

'Three, that's nothing,' said the old man. 'Remember '78, in February, there were at least fifteen prancing around us every night, even after gobbling up Marjerie's dog at Perpezac!'

'I know, I know, but I thought things had calmed down since the big round-up two years ago – no, three; it was

'96. We're going to have to do something about them, I don't like those animals.'

Steps sounded outside and then the tap of clogs against the steps. Grandmother entered, pressing her grand-daughter close to her.

'You know?'

'We know,' said Grandfather. 'You're not going to tell me that three wolves curdle your blood. You didn't hear any more?'

'No,' she agreed, taking off her woollen cloak, 'but the little one was frightened. Go and warm yourself, darling, there's no danger now. Go on.'

Louise glanced at her sister. Berthe was sucking a stick of liquorice given her by their grandmother. She breathed in long, wet slurps.

'I heard the wolves!' she crowed. 'I heard the wolves and you didn't, so there!'

Louise shrugged her shoulders and munched a chestnut. One day, one day, she'd tell that little brat that she had not only heard them, but had almost been devoured, and Pierre-Edouard and Léon too! For after all, their adventure on the plateau and White Peak was a much bigger thing than going to the grocer's and back! She stuck out her tongue at her sister and popped in another chestnut.

Pierre-Edouard was struggling painfully against sleep. Already the myriad tapers which surrounded the crib seemed like a gigantic single sun, an enormous warm sphere. Beside him, among the thirty catechism-class children, a few were already asleep, supported against each other on their benches. They wavered, leaned forward, sat up suddenly and then resumed their slumber.

Pierre-Edouard rubbed his eyelids and envied his sisters, who had stayed at home in their grandfather's care. They must be asleep; he pictured them in bed, and dozed off for a few seconds. The scraping of chairs being pushed back awoke him; everyone else was standing up for the Preface. He rose with a jump, and calculated in his head that he would have to endure at least another half hour of the service – ten minutes to get to the end of this second Mass, and, if everything went well, about twenty minutes for the third and last Mass of Christmas Night.

Three Masses was really too many; especially as the first one had been sung, and the sermon had lasted an eternity! The priest always took advantage of the big feast days, when parishioners filled the church, to give his flock a good telling off, for, according to him, they did not visit the House of the Lord often enough. He addressed himself mainly to the men, who preferred to spend their Sundays at the bar, or hunting, or – mortal sin – at work, rather than in the glorification of God.

Pierre-Edouard did not like this sort of scolding; he felt himself on the side of the men. Admittedly, his father did not go to Mass every Sunday, far from it, and nor did his grandfather, but at least they kept Easter. They were not like some others who never practised their faith, never even entered the church for funerals.

He turned round, looking for his father in the congregation. Of course he was there, in the third row, with his mother and grandmother. In front, in the pew reserved for them, stood the squire, his wife, two daughters and their governess. He saw, too, the doctor's wife, the solicitor and his family, the baker's wife and children; all the familiar faces of the community.

He was suddenly aware that his father was frowning in his direction, and hurriedly looked to the front. This was no time to step out of line.

He hardly dared believe in the fabulous luck which had enabled them to return from their expedition without damaging consequences. However, the slightest mistake might reveal that he did not have an easy conscience. He loved his father, but he feared him. He was intimidated by his great bulk, his burliness, his enormous hands and stern face intersected by a thick black moustache. And then, he seemed so old – not as old as Grandfather, but almost. He didn't know his parents' exact age, and did not remember ever having had the courage to ask them.

He realised with pleasure that the second Mass was

drawing to a close, and Father Feix was already restarting the prayers at the foot of the altar.

'The little fellow's asleep,' said Marguerite as she collected up the plates. They had all just celebrated the Eve of Christmas with a hearty meal, except of course the two girls, whom nothing and no-one could wake. Head on the table, Pierre-Edouard was sleeping beside his plate on which a small piece of white sausage lay congealed.

The men rose, went over to the hearthside carrying the tobacco-pot of red stoneware; they rolled their cigarettes which they lit with tapers.

'Did you talk to the others?' asked Grandfather.

At sixty-nine, despite a lifetime of work on the land, seven years of military service and a year at war, despite the rheumatism which bowed him to the earth, Edouard Vialhe controlled the fate of his farm and his family with a heavy hand. Nothing escaped him; although he found it more and more difficult to do his share of the work, he kept an eye on every detail.

Only son of Mathieu-Edouard and Noémie Vialhe, he had inherited from them the basis of the existing property: eight hectares, gathered together patiently by a whole line of Vialhes who, from generation to generation, had handed on the land, the knowledge, and the Christian name Edouard as their heritage. To his eight hectares he had been able to add one more on his return from military service, and his wife Léonie had brought two good hectares of grazing as part of her wedding settlement in 1859. Born the following year, their only son, Jean-Edouard, had been a great help with the farm work, and above all had made a good deal in marrying Marguerite when he was twenty-eight. Ten years his junior, pretty as a jenny wren, her dowry had included four hectares of excellent land.

The only complaint one could make was that their daughter-in-law had three children; to think, that fat-head Jean-Edouard did not know how to cast his seed more wisely! One day those three kids might quarrel and divide the land. God forbid that an old man should live to see such a destruction of their assets!

'Well, did you talk to them?'

'Yes, we're going to hunt them down.'

'When?'

'Tomorrow.'

'Tomorrow's Christmas,' protested his mother. 'Couldn't you make it a day of rest?'

'Listen,' argued Jean-Edouard, 'we're not going to let the wolves settle in this country again! I have children and I have animals. Everyone in the village is agreed on tomorrow, they'd even prefer to go right away. Anyway, the mayor has decided.'

'That rascal!' grumbled Grandmother. She did not really mind that the leading citizen of the community was totally indifferent to religion; it did not matter to her that the mayor would eventually burn in hell. But he had dragged her son on to the local council – that she could not forgive!

Secretly she was very proud of his role, but she refused to admit that a free-thinker like the mayor could also be open-minded enough to invite Jean-Edouard, a man who went to Mass at least three times a year, to sit with him in council. She always feared he was up to no good; that the mayor and those other republican atheists might lead her son into a trap. She was not aware that the mayor had chosen Jean-Edouard as his deputy firstly because he knew how to read and write, and secondly because he was an excellent farmer, who would co-operate in getting a buying syndicate off the ground, one of his long-term ambitions.

'He may be a rascal, but he's a good mayor,' cut in the old man. 'Come on, let's get to bed.'

Everyone rose and Marguerite, helped by her husband, undressed Pierre-Edouard in front of the fire. He did not wake, even when she slipped on his nightshirt which had been warming by the flames, nor when she laid him in the big bed where his two sisters were already asleep.

2

JEAN-EDOUARD swallowed the last mouthful of bread and homemade pâté of his morning snack and emptied his glass of wine. Then he carefully wiped his knife on his thick black corduroy trousers, closed it and slipped it into his pocket.

'The wind's still in the east,' warned his father from his seat opposite on the other side of the fireplace. 'You'll have to approach them through the château pinewood, otherwise they'll outwit you.'

'I know. Anyway, there's nothing to say that they're still up there. They travel, those animals . . .'

He left the hearth and plunged into the darkness of the room, not considering it necessary to light the lamp. He opened the drawer of the dresser, fumbled in it, found the box he was looking for and took from it a fistful of cartridges, then returned to sit by the fire.

'What are you waiting for?'

'Jeantout and Gaston. They're supposed to pick me up.'

The daylight was slowly sharpening; the clouds, thick and low, lingered on the edge of the plateau, hiding the peaks. The door banged, and Marguerite entered.

'You're still here?'

She had come from attending to the cows, and the smell of the byre floated into the room with her. She put down the milkpail on the table.

'Help me put the pig bucket on the fire.'

He rose, grasped the enormous pot full of kitchen waste mixed with turnips, bran mash and water, and hung it on the chimney hook.

'I thought you were going on this hunt,' she repeated.

'I am going. Look, there they are,' he said, catching sight of his neighbours through the window. He slipped on his heavy hunting jacket and took down his gun.

'Try to be back by midday, won't you? It *is* Christmas,' she reminded him. 'And . . . take care.'

About fifteen men were grouped in front of the Mairie, stamping about in an attempt to warm their feet. Jean-Edouard and his companions joined them, shaking hands.

The village was waking up and from all the cowsheds, those opening on to the main street and its seven side alleys, came familiar sounds: the low mooing of cows calling their calves, the hiss of milk on buckets, the raking of forks on flagstones, cries of famished pigs, clucking of poultry already scratching about on the dung heaps, gentle plaints from ewes and goats.

Houses were opening up with a great banging of shutters and heavy whorls of smoke rose from the chimneys; the air smelled of fires re-lit, of cut wood and dried broom. The bedroom lights in the inn came on one by one, and in the big saloon downstairs some customers were already seated at tables: three pedlars trapped by the snow, a wood-merchant and a mattress-maker. Only a few still slept: those in professions needing no animals, and shopkeepers, who would not be opening up on Christmas day.

The church clock was showing two minutes to eight when the squire appeared at the end of the main street. Muffled up to his ears, his gun on his shoulder, he was stepping with care on the frozen snow. Behind him, holding back four good-sized dogs with great difficulty, came Célestin, the man-of-all-work at the château. The squire mingled with the group, shook hands and joked.

'Time, it's time!' he trumpeted. 'His worship the mayor is late, he's been overdoing the celebrations.'

Jean Duroux was a good-looking forty-year-old, with a cheerful disposition and easy manner, who revelled in his role as Lord of the Manor. He had been born here, and was on friendly terms with all the men of his age.

Son and grandson of ships' chandlers, the death of his father had left him heir to the château, with ninety hectares of good land and forests surrounding it, and to property in

Brest, Rouen and Paris. Not lacking for money, he considered it an unnecessary bore to try to make any more. His days slipped by pleasantly, surrounded by his wife, his two daughters, the governess, Célestin and several servants. Twice a year he assembled his household, loaded them all on to the train at Brive or Terrasson, and left for two months in Paris or Biarritz.

There was only one shadow on his happiness: his name lacked any trace of nobility. He cleverly repaired this deficiency by introducing himself as Jean Duroux de Saint-Libéral; great was his joy when, on arriving in Paris or Biarritz, he heard them announcing Monsieur de Saint-Libéral!

Who was ever going to check up that Saint-Libéral-sur-Diamond was a country town in the lower Corrèze, and that he, Jean Duroux, was only one among the 1092 citizens of the commune who could claim that title? He would have been shocked to find that at the markets of Tulle, Seilhac, Brive, or Turenne, all the men used the same strategem, not out of boastfulness or vanity, but simply to give an address and show their origin.

The people of Saint-Libéral ignored his little deceit; if he was The Squire to them, someone from another world, they all agreed that he was not stuck-up.

'You've got a new rifle,' remarked Jeantout, who had been eyeing the weapon since the squire had arrived.

'Oh yes,' admitted the owner, drawing the double-barrelled gun from his shoulder. He held it out, turned it over, then broke the barrels. 'Nice piece, isn't it? It's the best there is at the moment; I bought it in London. Look, hammerless, Anson and Deeley system, twelve-bore, central percussion of course. Three breech bolts, choke-bore on the left barrel, English shoulder-piece. It's a little heavy, perhaps, but nevertheless a wonderful thing! Best of all I can use cartridges with B powder – no more smoke, and unrivalled power. As to the coupling . . .'

They drank in his words, and if the technical terms went over their heads, it only served to demonstrate just how old-fashioned their own rifles were. The most modern were only some Lefaucheux with exposed hammers and pin-fire cartridges. A few still sported muzzle-loading flintlocks, and they all used black powder, of which the most minor inconvenience was that it gave off a thick cloud of smoke on ignition.

'It must have cost something,' murmured one of the admirers.

'A bit . . . Fifty louis.'

The amount left them speechless. A thousand francs for a rifle! The price of three good cows! Crazy!

'That's impossible,' blurted out Jean-Edouard incredulously. He could not begin to understand how someone could lay out a sum like that for a rifle, however beautiful it was.

'Well, I wouldn't like it,' joked Jeantout. 'I wouldn't be able to take aim. With the big hammers at least you can frame the target,' he said, bringing his old gun to his shoulder and tracking an imaginary partridge across the sky.

But no one was listening to him; they were deflated by the enormity of the price. When the mayor arrived he found them reverently passing from hand to hand the weapon which Jean Duroux had kindly lent them.

'Beautiful gun!' It was his turn to admire. He felt its weight, put it to his shoulder, then handed it back to the owner, whistling quietly when he was told its price.

Antoine Gigoux had been elected mayor at the age of forty-two, and had fulfilled his mandate for more than twenty years. He managed the community with the same care he devoted to his farm. Affable to all, he exercised, when necessary, the good-natured but firm authority of a paterfamilias. He climbed the steps of the Mairie and raised his arm to call for silence.

'Before leaving, I would remind you that hunting is forbidden when snow is on the ground. So, no games. I don't want to hear gunshots after hares mistaken for wolves . . . Only aiming at a wolf is allowed, or possibly a fox. And also, to do it properly, I should have permission from the préfecture, but I'll take that responsibility. Tulle's a long way off, the prefect won't hear us! Right, we'll get into groups, how many are we?'

He counted quickly and then pointed to the village policeman: 'Octave, you take five volunteers, good shots, and go to the sunken roadways. Put three on the cutting and three on the Coombe. Get a move on, you're not tired out already! The rest of us will beat across the peaks and the plateau with the dogs. If all goes well and if they're still up there, we should get a fair shot by about eleven o'clock. Let's go, and don't fire at each other!'

'And don't shoot at my dogs, either!' advised Jean Duroux, stroking his animals.

'Your dogs have never seen wolves, have they?' asked the mayor as they started off.

Jean Duroux could not protest at the familiar 'tu' the mayor used in addressing him; they would make fun of him if he did. But he could not adopt the same familiarity, because he was so much younger than the mayor; so he attempted to maintain his superior position by an exaggeratedly affected way of speaking. The forced informality of his manner did not deceive anyone, least of all Antoine Gigoux.

'Not seen wolves, my dogs? See here, my friend, you remember our hunt three years ago? I already had Trompette and Tambour then, and there was no holding them! The two others are younger, but they are very keen after foxes.'

'And what are they called, Bugle and Fifi?' quipped the mayor.

'Of course not! Their year letter was A, so that one is Ardent and . . .'

'And the other is Angry,' suggested a joker behind his back.

'And that one is Aramis,' continued Jean Duroux, ignoring the laughter.

He adored guns, hounds and hunting and could talk forever once he started on one of these topics. They listened willingly enough, for no one could deny that he was one of the best hunters in the area, perhaps even in the whole region, a dog-handler without equal and a crack shot.

'Yes,' he continued, 'this cross of fox-hound and Poitou dog is really a success. Just look at that neck, those solid hindquarters, the stance! And wait till you see them point or spring . . .'

All the hunters were grouped around him, and measured their pace to fit his.

'You haven't got that other one any more?' asked one of them. 'The big fellow with mournful eyes, like a beaten wife, who almost tripped over his own ears?'

'I expect you're talking about Faraud, my deerhound? Yes, I've still got him, but he's almost blind – fifteen's a lot for a dog. I miss him, there was none better after hares.'

They left the village and plunged into the pinewoods, up the steep pathway beside the château, which they could see perched higher up the slope. It overlooked the town and the whole valley from its sheltered position on the south-facing cliff. From up there you could see almost ten kilometres on a clear day; you could make out the Monédières, the foothills of Cantal, and the greater part of the Vézère valley in the foreground.

The castle had been built at the beginning of the century by a distant cousin of Marshall Marbot, on the remains of a medieval stronghold. Not very imposing, more like a large family house than a château, it owed its title to its position and the size of the estate, rather than to its architecture. Solidly fashioned from blocks of light sand-stone, its side wing looked like a keep from the distance; capped with a solid roof of slate and enhanced by a series of terraced gardens, it was very attractive.

Grandfather Duroux had bought it for a song in about 1825. The proprietors, who had been forced to retreat to Paris at the time of the White Terror of 1815 and 1816 – particularly threatening in this area – had never dared to return to face a population whom they considered implacably hostile. They did not realise that no one wished them the slightest harm. The blaze of anger shown by the villagers was nothing but a flash in the pan, as ephemeral as the fistful of agitators who came from Périgord to unleash reprisals, which had been truly bloody. Once those wanting revenge had left in search of other victims, the village had returned to its habitual calm, and no one even thought of going to break the casements or empty the cellar of the uninhabited house for ten years.

Grandfather Duroux had not mentioned this to the vendors, and had paid a derisory sum for the entire estate. This masterly stroke, known to all, assured him of unquestioned esteem in this rural environment, where money was scarce. Those who knew how to buy or sell at maximum profit were always respected.

The prestige of the new proprietor had flowed down to his descendants, and guaranteed Jean Duroux the respect due to the richest man in the commune. Only a few older people, like the mayor, the priest, the doctor or even old man Vialhe, treated him a little lightly, but all the others deferred to him.

Jean-Edouard shivered; the cold was winning. He was startled to find himself dreaming of a blazing fire and a good bowl of hot wine.

He had arrived at one of the posts designated by the mayor a quarter of an hour ago, and had placed himself beside a huge chestnut tree, leaning up against the enormous trunk. He could make out the immobile silhouette of Jeantout thirty paces away, and further off that of Gaston. Ears pricked, he waited for the howling of the dogs which would herald the start of the drive.

The wolves must still be up on the plateau, for he had seen no sign of them in the snow during his long trek from the town. Besides, wolves had well-marked paths for climbing to the plateau or coming down from it, possibly as many as five or six, which they alternated according to the wind. What always amazed Jean-Edouard was that the hares, foxes and even wild boar followed almost the same tracks. An undeniable imperative seemed to draw them back, generation after generation.

'Good God,' he thought, 'what are they doing? They must have had time to get up there by now!'

He pictured the hunters emerging at the other end of the plateau and fanning out in extended order after releasing the hounds. The right-hand group would comb over the White Peak, the fields and chestnut groves that surrounded it; those on the left would be beating over the Caput Hill and the whole stretch of plateau where the Vialhe fields lay, in all three good kilometres' walk to reach the cutting which he was guarding.

This cutting, the remnant of old iron workings, bit into the plateau as if hewn by a giant axe-blow, thirty metres long and forty wide. Not a single tree remained undamaged in that hollow. Every one without exception had been struck by lightning, some several times over. Fireballs flashed into the cutting at each storm, attracted by the red iron-ore in the soil.

Jean-Edouard still recalled the terror which had nearly driven him mad when he was still just a boy, minding the flocks with Jeantout and Gaston. One stormy day they had rushed to shelter in an old half-collapsed mine tunnel, where they endured, dumb with terror, for half an hour whilst the lightning crashed incessantly around them. He still remembered the monstrous thunderbolts which ricocheted from rock to rock before exploding in huge showers of dazzling sparks. Cowering in their hole, the three boys had thought that the priest's frequent threats might have come true: they really were in the depths of Hell.

'What the devil's keeping them?' he grumbled. Now he was not only freezing but longing for a smoke, and there was no question of that. You might as well fire a shot to warn the wolves they were expected!

The little troop of beaters topped the crest of the White Peak, then descended towards the chestnut grove which began at the foot of the steep escarpment.

The White Peak and its twin, Caput Hill, still bore the traces of the espaliered vines which had covered them to their summits twenty years earlier. The thick bed of snow could not blot out the undulations in the earth formed by the thousands of ridges where vines had once grown.

Their raised profile was silent witness to the dirty white earth, full of flints, heavy with impenetrable chalk, a geological curiosity isolated in this plateau of good red soil; the peaks had rejected any other crop but vines. Ever since the phylloxera infection had ravaged and destroyed the French vines, it had lain fallow, supporting nothing but juniper, box and Spanish broom.

Before the attack of the American disease, the vines on the peaks had guaranteed a considerable income to the majority of farmers in the village. Every time they returned to these places, long since uncultivated, each felt a weight of sadness, arising from the many failures which had rewarded their attempts to replant with American vines.

The soil rejected them. It alone was to blame. This vine was impervious to the parasite, and developed properly when planted in other fields of the commune. Its wine was found to be drinkable. Of course, it was not as good as the old one, far from it: it lacked strength, bouquet, dignity; it was neuter. But it was a good cropper and the young vines grew well.

Here, the plantations of Riperia or Rupestris wilted mysteriously during their first year; they vegetated, produced puny shoots and sickly leaves, then died. No one had succeeded in keeping one of these vine stocks alive for more than three years. Tired of slaving away in vain, the men had gradually abandoned cultivation on the slopes. The walls of the hundreds of terraces, no longer maintained, soon succumbed to the pressure of the earth; rainstorms scoured out gullies and frost insidiously undermined them. Split open and collapsed, the terraces failed to retain the soil; up till then it had been preserved by the painstaking work of men, who carried back up baskets full of the earth which trickled down each winter.

Since then the peaks had been barren, and the children of the village could not understand why those places had such unlikely names as High Vineyard, Beautiful Vines, the Trellises, or Low Vines . . . For nearly twenty years these designations had been meaningless, and already new names were developing: Quarry Meadow, Stonefield, Turnstones, the Junipers . . .

Just as the beaters reached the chestnut groves, one of them called out to Jean Duroux. Célestin still followed him, holding back the dogs with more and more difficulty.

'Here!' cried the man, and was immediately surrounded by the rest of the band.

There was a trail. It led from the steep escarpment which plunged from the very edge of the plateau to the valley across woods and rocky scree.

'A young one,' commented Jean Duroux, 'not more than two years old. By the way, I'd like to know whose children have been playing around here. Have you seen? Three kids, and not very old by the size of their clogs.'

'I noticed the footprints,' said the mayor. 'I expect it was Séraphine's kids who came through here; they're into everything.'

Séraphine lived two kilometres away, in a tumbledown cottage at the place called Calvary. The widow of a farm labourer who had died four years ago, she had somehow survived since then, thanks to the warm welcome most of the local farmers gave her. To save her the shame of begging, she was given work according to the season: some fleeces to wash in the Diamond, hemp to be dressed, linen to rinse in the stream. Wielding her sickle, she joined in the harvest; the farmers turned a blind eye to the stalks she sometimes forgot – there had to be some ears of corn for her kids to find when they went gleaning . . . Lively as squirrels, they were out of doors in all weathers, picking up a forgotten turnip here, a few chestnuts there.

'They're brave, those kids,' commented the squire. 'Good, this animal is heading right into the chestnut trees. I'll let the hounds go, but first I'd like to know where the other two are.'

'Here!' called one of the hunters, who had followed the trail up to the wood.

They joined him.

'That one's a big old wolf,' explained Jean Duroux. 'Not young, that animal, look at his pads! He's coming from the same direction and heading the same way. Look, the young one has caught up with the older one's trail, and he doesn't like it! See how he's peed on it to try to mask the smell! You know what I think? We'll find the she-wolf's tracks a bit further on. It's time for her to come on heat, I bet that animal has lost her mate and she's calling the male.'

They entered the dark chestnut grove. The hounds wailed mournfully at the end of their chains.

'Peace, my beauties, peace! Be patient.'

At last they found the third trail.

'And here's our little hussy,' announced Jean Duroux. He stroked his dogs and then released them. They sprang away, mad with excitement.

'Perhaps we should get into line?' suggested the mayor.

'If you think so,' conceded the squire. 'Listen, I don't want to disappoint you, but the hunt's over.'

They looked at him, waiting for an explanation. No one doubted he was right; they simply wanted to understand.

'That female is out searching, she may be fifty kilometres from here by now,' explained Jean Duroux. 'Look, see her tracks, she's running hard. No wavering, straight ahead, and I'll bet she crossed the wood at the same pace. She's heading for the Forest of Cublac and she must have left the plateau by way of my acacia copse.'

'And why didn't she wait for the others? She was calling them, right enough!'

'Yes, but this isn't her patch, she's only here by chance. I tell you, she's recently lost her mate − no territory and doesn't know where to settle down. Well, she won't get a chance here! Now, if we were dealing with a pair and their cubs, with a bit of luck we'd have been able to find them here; the wood's quiet, full of game, they could stay here several days. But with a baggage who's asking for it . . . Let's go on anyway. We'd better tell the others, they must be freezing down there on guard!'

*

Jeantout and Gaston, blue with cold, had joined up with Jean-Edouard. Cross at having waited around for nothing, they were smoking furiously as they hopped from foot to foot to warm themselves a little.

'I'd like to know what they're playing at, up top! They should have been here by now!' fumed Gaston. 'The wolves certainly aren't there, so what are we waiting for!'

'They'll come soon,' said Jean-Edouard, clapping his arms energetically round his body. The yapping of the hounds suddenly reached them.

'Damn! To your positions!' shouted Jeantout, tossing away his cigarette.

He dashed off, followed by an even more furious Gaston.

'Never seen the like! What kind of work is this! They've had a little chat with them, those wolves, before chasing them?'

He stumbled on a root and measured his length.

'Damn and blast!' he muttered as he got up. 'Oh hell,' he said, looking at his snow-covered clothes and rifle.

Chilled and disheartened, he shrugged his shoulders towards his two companions, who tried to stifle their wild laughter. At that moment the animal emerged ten paces from him.

They mayor and the squire were advancing side by side when the hounds belled.

'So, you and your explanations!' threw out the mayor.

'My dear fellow, you don't know my dogs,' said Jean Duroux with irritating calm. 'Listen to Trompette, can you hear him?'

'Yes, and with our walking pace and guns over our shoulders, we've let the beast go. Bravo! I'll remember your lectures on wolves!'

'I hope so! See here, my friend, what you lack is a good knowledge of the canine race. I would remind you that wolves and foxes are part of that noble family, and dogs too, of course, not forgetting jackals and coyotes, but that's beside the point . . .'

'And so what?' groaned the furious Antoine Gigoux.

'Well, good old Trompette isn't going for a wolf, but a fox. Difference in size, isn't there?'

'It's a fox he's put up?'

'Of course, what do you think it is! With the noise we've been making since we found the tracks, no wolf would have stayed around. This fox is from round here; he'll just go to ground in some bushes, hoping that we'll pass by without getting wind of him, but with Trompette he doesn't stand a chance. I hope the marksmen on guard don't miss him.'

'Unless they've gone home,' muttered the mayor. 'We've certainly taken long enough to make ourselves heard!'

'Yours! Yours!' yelled Gaston. 'Shoot, dammit! There! There!'

Jean-Edouard raised his gun, but he could see nothing.

Then suddenly he spied the fox, which made a half-turn at full speed and climbed back up the side of the cutting. He fired, and the cloud of smoke hid his target.

'Again! Again!' urged Gaston.

But the animal was long gone; they caught a glimpse as it reached the crest, ran along it for a second and then disappeared into the coppice.

'And you, why didn't you fire?' shouted Jean-Edouard.

'I don't intend to blow my head off. Look at this. It made you laugh when I fell, but look at my gun barrels. Stuffed with snow, they are! That happened to my father once; he took a shot and almost blew his brains out with it!'

'Did you hit it?' asked Jeantout.

'What do you think? It was too far! And him telling me "Yours, yours!" and not telling me where, the silly ass!'

'Oh, well, the others will laugh. Look, there are the dogs. By God, how they point! They can't track in this snow, they're scenting on the wind.'

'I should have had Duroux's rifle,' mutterd Jean-Edouard. 'It's no good with my old pop-gun . . .' He was annoyed, and looking for excuses. 'It's true,' he insisted, 'he was more than forty metres away. And you, you had to go and try to break your neck!'

'Sorry; I did it on purpose, of course! And you, if you can't see properly, you should get some spectacles!'

'Come on, you two, leave it be!' said Jeantout. He winked in the direction of Jean-Edouard, clumsily mimed the incident of the fall, and let out a shout of laughter under the wrathful eye of Gaston.

LÉON got up as gently as possible, taking great care not to rustle the hay. He slid out of the warm hole where three little shapes slept huddled together, muffled under an old coverlet.

He knew very well what was going on in the house; he was the oldest, after all, and he had understood immediately when he saw the doctor arrive at about nine o'clock in the evening: this New Year's Eve would see one new member to increase the Depeuch family. But for that, the only bedroom in the house had had to be cleared.

Their closest neighbour, called on by the doctor to help out, had suggested to Léon that they should settle down by the hearth in her house, but the boy hated that woman; he found her more disagreeable and ill-tempered than an ailing sow. Rather than accept her offer, he preferred to take his three little sisters to the stable. There he took care of them. He hollowed out a nest in the big stack of hay which had been put ready for tomorrow's feeding time, in the area which separated the two cows from the ewes. The little ones had immediately fallen asleep, reassured by the animals' quiet breathing.

Léon half opened the barn door and listened. He remembered the last birth, two years earlier, and knew that the baby would be there when his mother's groans died away. But it was impossible to catch the slightest sound above the howls of the tempestuous wind and rain.

It had been bucketing down since the day before yesterday; the rain was unusually warm for the time of year, and had drowned all traces of the snow. The town was now saturated with water, and the Diamond rose hour by hour, swelled by streams from the plateau and slopes. They said the miller had been forced to take hasty refuge in his own loft; but then he did live at the bottom of the valley.

Léon closed the door and the barn returned to complete darkness. He felt his way towards the pile of hay and settled down in the warmth; he had made up his mind to wait for the birth, to stay alert for as long as was necessary. Five minutes later he was asleep.

'Here's another one who won't end up in the priesthood!' cried the doctor, dangling the tiny child at arm's length. He held the chubby, shining body by the feet and smiled as he observed the furious grimaces of the baby, who was yelling at the top of its voice.

'Wash her,' he ordered, passing the child to the neighbour. 'And you, get rid of that for me,' he said, pushing an armful of bloodstained linen towards the father.

Then he bent towards the mother, who was still spreadeagled across the bed. With a long caressing stroke he soothed her; her belly was still contracted and tense, yet it relaxed beneath his massage.

'If all women gave birth as easily as you . . .' he murmured, pressing gently on the abdomen. 'Wait, I'll deliver the afterbirth and then it will be over.'

At sixty-five, despite thirty-eight years in practice, Doctor Fraysse still felt a great joy – and even a sense of wonder – at each birth. God knows he had seen enough of them, and all sorts!

Since he was an excellent physician, the mothers gladly forgave him his familiarity – he addressed them with the intimate 'tu' from beginning to end of the birth. And if some husbands were occasionally shocked, the squire for instance, he explained with a smile. 'It is possible, dear friend, that you got her in that condition by saying "vous" to her; everyone to his own taste and methods. For my part, I need intimacy to finish your work; believe me, this is not the most attractive stage, I need tenderness and trust. I need to speak gently to your wife, or to bawl her out if necessary. And that's not possible with: "Madame would it please you to, if I might ask . . ." But if it really worries you, I can do without you. And now my friend, let's go, just us two, and see how this little fellow is getting on. And don't worry, all will be well, you listen to me.'

He had adopted this custom of using 'tu' in the field hospital to which he had been posted during the war.* There, in the tents, when they bought him cartloads full of wounded, he searched and probed, wielded scalpel and saw on the crushed bodies, and he noted how pain and labour were alike in many ways – the same anxiety, the same rattle in the throat, the same convulsions, panting breath and sweating, the same waiting for relief. And in both cases, the same comfort brought by a friendly calm voice, a fatherly gesture, a caress.

'It's over,' he said, placing the placenta in a basin. 'There you are, my dear, everything's all right. You've been very brave; I'm going to bind up your stomach with these two towels and then you can rest. Not sleep, you understand. You remember, don't go to sleep straight away; you must watch in case there's any serious bleeding. But don't worry, I'll stay a while; I'll have to do the dressing for your daughter. By the way, what is she to be called?'

'Mathilde,' murmured the mother.

'Lovely name. Here, Emile, hold your wife up while I fix these towels for her. And I must say, you know, between us, five is quite a lot, isn't it? I would very much like not to have to come back next year . . . But that's your business.'

'I would have liked another boy,' said Emile, as he replaced the pillows.

'Bah, you'll get sons-in-law!'

'Well, yes . . . Say, would you like a glass of punch? It's all I can offer you.'

'Fetch something to eat as well,' suggested his wife in a weak voice. 'You forget that it's time to celebrate the New Year!'

'My God, that's right! A new century, too!' exclaimed Emile.

'Yes, by heavens!' cried Doctor Fraysse, feeling in his

---

* The Franco-Prussian War, 1870–71

waistcoat pocket. He took out his watch. 'Half past midnight! There's my first customer this century! Well, that must be celebrated! And I shall provide the toast! Emile, you slip over to my place, they'll be bringing in the New Year. 1900 – that's quite something! Tell my wife to give you a well-filled basket and a bottle of champagne. Ask for a bottle of Bordeaux for your wife too, that will revive her. And don't forget to tell them to wait for me, I'll be there within the hour. What's the matter?' he demanded, when he saw the father's look of dismay.

'I can't,' said Emile, 'I'd never dare go and ask for all that. We've already kept you from the celebration . . . No, no, I can't!'

'No, we can't accept that,' his wife reiterated, 'we'd be too ashamed. We're not well off, we could never repay you, so . . .'

'Oh in God's name, you two make me tired! Madame Lacoste, have you finished with that little girl?'

'I'll bring her to you,' called out the neighbour, who was finishing bathing the baby in the next room.

'Did you hear what I asked Emile to do?'

'Doctor, I'd rather you and Madame left now . . .'

'Give me that child, I'll deal with her. Slip over to my place, since this big ninny is making a fuss. Go on – and get the basket well filled, I'm so hungry I could swallow a whole bullock raw!'

'Don't go, Germaine!' begged the mother. 'You know we can't repay him.'

'That's enough from you, you should rest. Go on, Madame Lacoste, you must always do what the doctor says! Hurry up. And remember to tell them to wait for me!'

The dog barked as it heard the neighbour returning, then recognised her and calmed down. Léon woke with a start and listened. It was still raining. He nearly fell asleep again, then suddenly noticed he was not in his own bed. He gently pushed aside one of his sisters who was snuggled up against him, got up, and felt about to retrieve his clogs.

The damp cold gripped him as soon as he reached the yard. He ran to the house and flattened his ear against the door. Nothing, no more groans; the baby had been born. He pressed the latch, pushed first on the top half of the stable-door, and hesitated a minute.

'Come in!' said his father.

The light surprised and dazzled him. For a brief moment he did not recognise the room; the doctor's big hurricane lantern spread an unaccustomed brightness, illuminating all the dark recesses never revealed by the family's oil-lamp with its thin wick.

He saw then the food and bottles on the table, and wondered where the devil his father could have got them from – surely not from the chest or cupboard? He knew their contents too well.

Eventually he noticed his mother through the open door. He went towards her hesitantly; he hardly recognised her either. He was accustomed to her looking fat and weighed down; now she seemed quite slight and thin.

'At least look at your little sister,' said his mother.

He glanced in disappointment towards the cot; he would have preferred a brother. Three sisters were too many already.

'Here, come and eat with us!' cried the doctor.

Léon treasured the astonishing memory of that first night of the century all his life; the first thing he described to Pierre-Edouard when he met him next day was this remarkable New Year Party.

'And I even drank champagne, I did!'

He had to explain to his friend what the champagne was like – its taste, colour, the strangely-shaped bottle and the curious cork which could not be put back once it had been pulled out.

'The doctor told me that it was done specially so you can't re-cork the bottle, so you have to drink it all up! That's what I did with the doctor and Ma Lacoste. My father didn't want to drink any.'

'Why not?'

'He was too ashamed.'

'And was it good?'

'It's prickly and full of bubbles which make you burp . . . And of course it's expensive. My father told me it might be worth more than ten francs a bottle! It made him ill! And on top of that, you know, the doctor didn't want to be paid for his work.'

'Who was sick?'

'No one, he just came to get my sister born. He said it was free because it was his first customer of the century. That's something, that is!'

The birth of Mathilde Dupeuch filled all the conversations in the village during the following weeks. Since Madame Lacoste had been a privileged participant in this famous party, she recounted all the events of New Year's Eve.

She did not like the Dupeuch family, so she transformed their poverty into misery and the doctor's gesture into the munificence of a lord. She managed it so well that many finished by believing that Dupeuch had begged the doctor to take pity on them. They had not thought much of him beforehand; now they despised him.

Despised, but envied too, for the town council had decided to honour the first-born child of the century by opening a savings account for her, with a deposit of fifteen francs. Many were convinced that Emile would drink it away before she was three months old; that was pure slander, as everyone knew he was an abstemious man.

On top of that, the solicitor's wife proposed herself as godmother, since Emile was one of her tenants; she also added ten francs to the account and had a whole heap of clothes, which had once belonged to her daughters, carried over to the Depeuchs'.

Then a letter from the préfecture announced that, as Mathilde was the first-born of the century in the whole département, the general council had voted unanimously to deposit fifty francs in the newly-opened account.

Emile, pale with shame at being the focus of the whole community and the subject of whispering which weighed heavily on his conscience, became convinced that all this generosity was simply aimed at showing up his poverty.

Poverty alone he could bear. What else could he do, since he was responsible for others? He worked, he didn't drink, he had owed no one anything before that cursed night. True, he earned little, very little; but the few sous which enabled him to support his family were the result of his own work, and they weren't dying of hunger. None of them had ever gone begging.

But his pride prevented him from accepting all these gifts passively; to preserve his honour he should have offered the donors something in return; perhaps not the equal amount, but at least the best part of the value received. It was impossible. He realised that for the rest of his life, whatever he did, the community would remember him as the man who had been fed by his kids, the one who had accepted everything and given nothing in return . . .

Léon bumped into his father's dangling legs when he entered the barn on the evening of 16 January. Emile had been dead for two hours.

By his side lay the savings book, torn to pieces, the pile of clothes given by the godmother, and an unopened bottle of Bordeaux.

'And what's to become of the five little ones?' asked Marguerite, putting down the soup tureen in the middle of the table.

Jean-Edouard made a dismissive gesture; they had discussed it at the town council, and no one had found a solution.

'She'll just have to go back home!' pronounced old Léonie. For her the matter was plain; she had always said that Dupeuch was good for nothing. He had simply confirmed that by destroying himself, like a heathen.

'The solicitor is letting her keep the farm,' announced Edouard. 'He told me this evening. With Léon, she can manage: they only have two cows to look after!'

'You should have told me,' remarked his son. 'At the council meeting we did want to make a collection . . .'

'That's the limit!' cried his mother indignantly. 'With

all the money the little one got, just for being born! And the solicitor's wife is her godmother!'

'And also,' continued Edouard, with an irritated look in his wife's direction, 'the doctor is going to take on Léon to work in his garden, which will give him a few sous.'

The old man began to eat his soup, noisily sucking in the thin slices of soaked bread, then wiping his moustache on his lapel. 'He is strange, the doctor. He's saying everywhere that it's his fault . . .'

'What's his fault?' asked Jean-Edouard.

'The business with Emile.'

'And how could it be his fault?'

'We'll find out sooner or later.'

'Perhaps the little one looks too much like him,' commented the old woman ironically, without raising her head from her plate.

She was bringing up an old piece of gossip from twenty years ago. At that time the doctor was still unmarried, and some rumours had been attached to him. It was said that he had shown marked attention to certain female patients, and two or three had even boasted of having received – and refused, of course – unmistakable advances.

Finally the doctor heard the story and laughed about it, as if it were a good joke. He considered the matter so banal – and silly – that he had never felt the need to silence this slander, which was repeated from time to time. 'Especially in the spring!' the doctor was convinced. 'I have a few patients who need a good dose of extract of water-lily root, it's excellent for soothing the over-heated . . .'

'You be quiet!' ordered Edouard. 'The children are listening! What tales you're telling again! With a wife like his, do you think he needs Amélie Dupeuch! That little scrap, thin as a rake and smelling of the cowshed! Just be quiet!'

'Well, why did he say that it was his fault?' insisted Jean-Edouard.

The old man shrugged.

'Well, I know,' said his daughter-in-law. 'Yes, it was Germaine Lacoste who told me . . .' She fell silent,

37

hesitating because of the children. Then she thought it would be good to keep them in the picture; forewarned, they might later avoid repeating the same mistake (even the sin) of the Dupeuch family.

'Yes,' she recommended. 'Germaine had a good look, she was at the birth – the child was marked by bad luck, just under the left breast, a patch like a crescent moon . . . And besides, she'll be blind; she opened her eyes straight away!'

'And so what?' remarked Jean-Edouard mockingly.

'Well, she *has* brought bad luck with her. Already her father . . . But it is to be expected that it would happen like that, you remember the Chasse Volante . . .'

'Oh yes,' murmured her mother-in-law, 'that one in March, about the 25th, that would be just the right time . . .'

They all remembered, even Pierre-Edouard. That evening, the sound of the flight had woken him; a terrible sound, full of cries and howls which fell from the sky. It had passed over the village, and the wails had echoed so close that he had rushed to his parents' bed. Then his mother had explained that he was hearing the cries of all the condemned souls of the village; they returned to circle above the cemetery, cursing those who did not pray for their sins to be forgiven, and she had recited her rosary immediately.

'That's all nonsense!' protested Jean-Edouard violently.

'Don't say that,' commanded the old woman, 'your wife is right! That evening, if the Dupeuchs had been praying instead of . . . they wouldn't have had this punishment nine months later! And the mark on the little girl is the result – it's the sign of mortal sin, and a bad omen!'

'Nonsense!' insisted Jean-Edouard. 'And besides, why should that be the doctor's fault, eh?'

'You know he doesn't like salt to be put in the water for the first bath, nor a piece of blessed boxwood. He says it's dirty! Well it may be, but it's the only way to guard against bad luck. That's why it's his fault!'

Jean-Edouard served himself a generous helping of

cauliflower with bacon and looked at his father, but the old man would not take sides.

'Rubbish,' repeated Jean-Edouard. 'The next flight of game-birds I hear, I'll go out and bring one down for you with a shot from my gun!'

'You wouldn't do that!' begged his wife.

'I will if you go on reciting all that nonsense in front of the children. It's only good to frighten them, they're old wives' tales!'

'That's what the teacher told us,' said Pierre-Edouard in a small voice. Caught in the crossfire, between two beliefs, he did not know where to position himself; he was hesitating before publicly choosing which camp to join.

'And what did he tell you, that teacher?' interrogated his grandmother.

'Well . . . It was just after the last . . . Chasse Volante, that time in the autumn . . . He said we . . . shouldn't believe that they were the souls of the damned . . .'

'There you have it!' cried the old lady in triumph. 'He doesn't believe in God or the Devil!'

'Let him speak,' murmured Grandfather. 'Tell us, mon petit, what the teacher said?'

Pierre-Edouard looked anxiously at his mother, then at his grandmother, and held himself ready to dodge the blow he felt was imminent.

'He said they were birds flying by, wild geese and – something else, I don't remember any more what, he talked about a route.'

'The heathen!' muttered Grandmother. 'Birds! Honest birds can't see at night! It's only birds of ill-omen, like tawny owls and barn owls, which fly and call at night! Anyway, even if they were birds, they'd still bring bad luck. But they're not birds!'

'Yes, they are,' cut in Jean-Edouard. 'I've been told they're birds too, and I believe it.'

'Who told you?' questioned his wife.

'The squire. He knows about these things, he does!'

The two women were silenced: one could not accuse the squire of being a heretic. He accompanied his wife to Mass

39

every Sunday, except when he went hunting or fishing; he kept Easter, and he invited the priest to dine at the château twice a year, on Corpus Christi and on 15 August, the feast of the Assumption.

'Well, he's wrong!' insisted the older woman. 'You mark my words, you'll see other misfortunes happening because of that baby.'

Father Feix had been priest in St Libéral for thirty-five years. He understood perfectly the mentality of his parishioners, their vices, faults, and good qualities, for he was the son of peasants who kept a smallholding in a neighbouring village. He was strict with himself, and did not compromise when he felt the authority of the church he represented was in danger. His moral code was inflexible and he guided his flock with a firm hand; when he passed judgement, which he did only after long reflection and prayer, none dared to contradict him openly.

So he had forbidden his congregation to patronise the grocer's shop belonging to Jean Latreille. Since losing his wife, Jean had been living openly with a little servant girl; he was old enough to be her father! Ma Eugenie's bar was off limits as well, for her bed was open to all; forbidden, too, were the Saturday night dances the Chanlat couple organised at the inn. The sort of dances they did there could only corrupt the young, by exciting lust and impurity.

Despite this narrowness of outlook, Father Feix knew he was supported and loved by all his faithful flock. Certainly an anticlerical tendency, originating in the towns, had been developing in the village for some time. But it had not come to open warfare, and the few atheists in the community were neither insolent nor malicious; moreover, all paid him the respect his position merited. Only those whose dissolute life he had openly condemned turned aside as he passed and kept their hats on their heads. But the others – the mayor, for example, the doctor and the two teachers, man and wife – never refused to speak to him when the occasion arose.

Emile Dupeuch's suicide deeply saddened him and, but for his cassock and responsibilities, he would have been among the first to offer his support to the family of the deceased. But the sinful manner of the death called for perpetual condemnation; he therefore allowed two weeks to pass before visiting Amélie Dupeuch.

Despite the bitter cold of this month of February, he found her in the little garden behind the house. She was planting onions with the help of Léon. He knew that Amélie was a good Christian. During her husband's lifetime she had attended Mass as often as possible, made sincere confessions, and had had the two children born in the village baptised, even though her husband had been indifferent in religious matters. She had apologised for the jackdaw and its insulting call; she had also apologised for Léon, who modelled his attitude on that of his father, and cultivated a condescending contempt for all that holy stuff. Thank heavens that Emile had been tolerant; it hadn't mattered to him if his wife practised her religion, as long as it did not interfere in any way with the daily work.

The priest advanced down the line of digging, stopped and smiled sadly.

'Well, my poor Amélie, what a misfortune, what a misfortune! I would have liked to come earlier, but you know how it is . . .'

She knew. She understood the penalty for suicide. Emile had been buried like a dog, and besides refusing a religious ceremony, the priest had publicly expressed his total disapproval and indignation. If he had come earlier someone might have thought that he was absolving the sin. At the same time, to avoid exacerbating the situation, Amélie had refrained from visiting the church.

'After all,' he continued, 'time heals all . . . With regard to that, I hope to see you at Mass again soon. Another thing, I spoke to that good lady Madame Lardy; she's still prepared to be godmother to your little girl. Of course we shall have to do that as quietly as possible, you do understand, don't you?'

She understood. During Emile's life their situation had

41

forced her to be modest and discreet. By destroying himself her husband had prevented her from ever escaping this position; she would always be the widow of the man who had committed suicide, and her children the orphans of the one who hanged himself.

'And then,' continued Father Feix, 'you'll have to send me this boy now, to learn his catechism. You don't want him to stay a heathen. You'll come, Léon, won't you?'

'No, I won't come! Never!' growled the child.

'Don't speak to the priest like that,' said his mother sharply. 'You'll go to catechism classes as of Sunday!'

But she knew very well that he would do no such thing, and no one could force him to give way. Since he had become head of the family, Léon took his role seriously and kept his own counsel. She needed him too much to run the risk of striking him. He was only twelve years old, but when he knocked against his father's legs that evening he became as hard and cold as a man toughened by a half-century of ordeal and affliction.

'You will do what your mother asks, won't you?' repeated the priest.

'I'll do what I have to do,' said the lad, without lowering his eyes. He spat between clenched teeth, turned round and continued his work.

4

PIERRE-EDOUARD Viahle sat the examination for his school certificate on 11 July 1902. He needed all his strength to face this test, for he was paralysed by fright and discomfited by his Sunday suit.

Of the five candidates defending the honour of the community of Saint-Libéral-sur-Diamond that day, he was the one who was expected to do well. And knowing that so many hopes rested on him did not help to calm him. He was scarcely able to enjoy all the marvellous treats which accompanied this expedition: first of all a journey in old Lamothe's horse-trap, then lunch in a restaurant.

The five candidates climbed into the conveyance, accompanied by their master Monsieur Lanzac, who was taking the place of parents busy with their work, and settled down for the journey to the county town. Pierre-Edouard and his friends were familiar with this stretch of fifteen kilometres; they had all walked to market in company with their fathers. But only Jacques Bessat and Edmond Vergne could boast – and they made the most of it – of having ridden in the old rattletrap before.

Jacques was an old hand; his grandparents lived in Ayen, and he went to see them several times a year. As for Edmond Vergne, not only was he familiar with the great trek, he could also outline the programme for the entire day, including the menu awaiting them at the restaurant: noodle soup, sausage and pickled pork with lentils.

It was no credit to him that he could play the fortune-teller, for this was the second time he had sat for the certificate. His father worked in the post office at Saint-Libéral and was determined that his son should win this diploma, which would open the door to an administrative post.

43

Pierre-Edouard was greatly impressed by old Lamothe's dexterity as he guided the horses, two magnificent beasts with huge hindquarters, shoulders heavy with muscles and hooves larger than soup plates, topped by shining well-brushed hair on their pasterns. But he could not really enjoy the journey; he could not manage to forget that every turn of the wheels brought him closer to the formidable test.

With an anguished expression, he surveyed the country-side. All around was the same destruction as at Saint-Libéral, everywhere the same carnage – rows of peas fallen and plastered in mud; cereal and fodder beaten flat to the ground, as if crushed by giant feet; fruit trees torn down with leaves already wilted, their fruit still green but dull and withered.

All around men, women and children were busy; here raking yellow, dusty hay, which still smelled of water and the beginnings of mould; there harvesting with difficulty the mangled ears and crushed straw of cereal crops; in other places, trying to gather up a few remnants of peas and some plums spared by the hail.

It had been a year of storms. The first had come at the end of April, proving Grandfather Vialhe once more correct, for he had predicted it from the month of March onwards: 'Look at the birds, they're building low: that's a sign of storms.' And truly the magpies were not construct-ing their nests in the tops of the poplars or the oaks, but rather halfway up, and sometimes even in the big blackthorn bushes, two metres from the ground.

After some warning rumbles at the end of April, the heat built up throughout May; a damp, suffocating mugginess. Every evening the thunderstorms grumbled in the distance, turned, rolled away and broke over the mountains of Auvergne or Cantal; the nights were full of flashes. In the morning the sun emerged, looking washed out, from a dirty haze in which threatening blanched clouds of cumulo-nimbus were already discernible.

Once June arrived they should have attacked the hay and scythed it, despite the constant menace which hung over them from midday onwards. On the morning of the 12th it rained, the warm drops of the tail-end of a storm, which made the earth steam and filled the atmosphere with a thick and unhealthy humidity.

Everyone felt the threat growing; animals and humans alike were irritated by the stings of horse-flies and, despite the heat of the long days, the hay was not drying well.

On Midsummer's Eve a dark cloak of cloud unfurled over the whole valley of the Vézère, pushed along at a great pace by a boiling, turbulent wind. The village was spared this assault, but they could see the columns of rain hanging like long, black twisted ropes from the clouds.

However, this deluge was not enough to change the weather, and the next day they were all aware that the storm was still imminent. They sensed it, they felt it lying in wait, just beyond the horizon. It gathered its forces for almost a week; it broke each evening, distant but oppressive.

In the fields and meadows they struggled against the weather: exhausting days without rest. The men rose two hours before dawn to mow and harvest; the women, the old men and children busied themselves turning the hay and binding the sheaves.

During the hottest hours, when the draught cattle could no longer bear the pace of work or the temperature, they gathered the burning sheaves and packed them into stacks, and collected the hay into pot-bellied heaps which were later loaded onto the carts; in the evening, when the animals had been rested, they could drag the towering heaps to the haylofts, which were as hot as ovens.

On Monday the 30th, the sun rose with a copper glow. Already in the west the storm clouds were swelling with iridescent outcrops, burnished by a warm, constantly shifting wind. There were no preliminary rumbles, nothing; a dense silence in which the slightest everyday sound, the swish of the scythes or the creak of the carts, sounded menacingly loud. Towards midday the crickets fell silent, the hens took refuge in the barns, and the myriad swallows suddenly left the sky empty.

At St Libéral, they waited. A presentiment, a fear, kept the men at home. Standing at their thresholds, they surveyed the gigantic cap of bronze clouds with darkened edges which topped the peaks. They were ready for the worst, but the magnitude and suddenness of the attack took their breath away.

A thunderclap of incredible violence exploded above the village. At the same time a shower of sparks set the plateau aglow in the area of the cutting, where the ore-bearing ground always attracted thunderbolts. Almost at the same moment, as if released by the ribbon of lightning, the clouds of hail vomited their load. Real pebbles of ice, as big as a fist, fell with a roar like a stream in spate, and the noise was such that it overwhelmed the sound of the bell which the perspiring sacristan was swinging with whirling arms to frighten away the storm.

In a few seconds everything was white. A cat, mad with fright, fled from some cellar and sped along the main street in search of shelter; half-pound hailstones knocked it to the ground, battered it, buried it.

The hail pelted down for three long minutes. It broke everything, flayed the trees down to the sapwood, reduced the vines to skeletons, overturned and hammered all the crops. In the village only the thatched roofs withstood this unprecedented assault, which cracked the more substantial coverings of slate; at the Vialhes' they later counted a hundred and eighty Travassac slates which had been broken like glass in the mutilated roof, despite being nearly as thick as a man's finger.

The cumulus clouds moved away eventually, but were immediately replaced by an opaque stormcloud, heavy with rain and iridescent with electrical charges. Darkness enveloped St Libéral, and in every house people grouped themselves around the holy candles they had lit at the first clap of thunder.

After the hail came flood and fire. A dazzling flash of light dodged among the spouts of water, caught the edge of the Peyrou barn with one of its claws, and set it alight in a few seconds. The building, laden with hay still warm from the fields, blazed like a bundle of dry broom, spouting thirty-metre flames towards the sky. Peyrou himself had to be held down by his son-in-law to prevent him throwing himself into the furnace. The old man wanted to untie his beasts; they were found later, four cows and six ewes, burnt to death.

The pandemonium lasted for an hour, and then the devils of the air moved on. At last the silence returned, and the alarm bell echoed, dismally throbbing through the coolness.

Peyrou's barn was nothing but a heap of smoking embers, and it would have been useless to waste time trying to salvage any debris. In contrast, all around were flooded cellars, roofs torn off by the wind or split open by the fall of trees or the weight of hailstones. The drumbeat of the village constable, calling them to arms, mingled with the alarm bell.

One by one, silent and haggard, all the able-bodied men gathered in the square. Even the priest and the squire offered their labour to clear the rubble, empty the basements, work and go on working until night fell, so as not to remain inactive in the face of such a catastrophe.

It was not until the next day that the men dared to go out to the fields, and the destruction was such that more than one cried silently, alone, in the middle of his plot of devastated maize or tobacco. For some it spelled ruin; complete, with no hope of recovery, the end of a life dedicated to the land. In one single hour this thunderstorm was going to push them out of the village, forever. They would have to escape, disperse, some towards Terrasson, some to Brive or Tulle, but all of them towards a town which would perhaps offer them a chance to survive.

The Vialhes' property was severely affected, but by luck some of their lands were untouched, for the hail had fallen in a narrow corridor; certainly everything had suffered from the water-spouts and the wind, but the losses were more easily recovered than elsewhere.

To provide for the most needy, the mayor requisitioned all the craftsmen – the masons, carpenters, thatchers and slaters – and directed them to the most urgent repairs. He was a peasant himself, so he knew that the farmers would have to save what they could of the crops still standing; and they had to work fast, for mildew threatened. Furthermore, there could be other storms.

The horse-trap quickly climbed the last long slope before the descent into Ayen. Pierre-Edouard sat with glazed eyes and felt the panic seize him – he was no longer able to recite the seven-times table. He saw he was lost, almost ready to give in to despair.

'We'll soon be there,' warned the teacher. 'Remember my advice, now!'

Pierre-Edouard had not forgotten it. Firstly, well presented work with perfect handwriting; no spots or rubbings-out, careful punctuation and, when necessary, well formed, graceful capital letters. Then, modest behaviour, decorum: no hands in pockets or fingers in noses, stand up straight to answer questions, clasp the hands behind the back to relax the voice and not constrict the breathing; always think before answering and beware of this sort of trap: 'So, you are certain that the revocation of the Edict of Nantes took place on 18 October 1685. You're sure?' Or again, 'You have just told me that six times seven are forty-four?' After having reflected with mature consideration: 'Yes' or 'No, sir'.

Finally, and this was one of the secret weapons revealed by their teacher, never hesitate to make some mention of Alsace and Lorraine, whenever the opportunity arose. It was quite easy, especially in history or geography. There was nothing to prevent them, for instance, speaking of the real – or provisional – frontiers of France, and of her natural and historic frontiers. Nor was it forbidden to recall that Alsace had been linked to France by the Treaty of Munster in 1681, and that Lorraine had been French territory since 1766.

Pierre-Edouard remembered all that, but he was still searching for the seven-times table when they arrived at the district capital.

First they had to solve a problem of area, a silly rigmarole about one hectare and twenty ares of land to be divided among three heirs: two-fifths to the eldest, one-and-a-half fifths to each of the other two. Pierre-Edouard managed it very well, and nothing showed in the copy he handed in of the unorthodox way he achieved it.

In fact, at home he was used to calculating area in strips of ten square metres, not in hectares or ares, so he naturally converted; one hectare equals 10 strips, twenty ares are worth 2 strips: 12 strips altogether. The rest was obvious.

In history and geography there was no question about Alsace and Lorraine, but about the reign of Henry IV and the Aquitaine Basin, and it would hardly have been sensible to make any allusion to Strasbourg or the course of the Rhine.

Then, by a stroke of luck – or their master's perfect knowledge of the programme – the dictation offered was one of those they had studied three weeks earlier. Pierre-Edouard immediately recognised the text by Victor Hugo, remembered the pitfalls, and only made one-and-a-half mistakes.

Later, when it was all over and they were seated on the terrace of the restaurant waiting for the results, he showed the rough copies he had carefully kept to the teacher, and anxiously awaited the verdict.

'Well, my boy, if you didn't make any mistakes in copying out, you will have your certificate. Very good; very, very good.'

An hour and a half later the results were published, and Pierre-Edouard approached the notice-board with trembling steps and dry throat. But he did not know where to look for his name, and it was the teacher who announced to him that he was first among the candidates from St Libéral, and third in the district. It was more than a success, it was a triumph!

Edmond Vergne had also passed, but only just. As for the others, it was a débâcle . . .

When they returned to the village, the teacher insisted on

accompanying his pupil right to his home, and seeing them pass you could not tell who was prouder and happier, the teacher or the pupil!

Grandfather Edouard was alone, seated in front of the house; since the thunderstorm, he had been tortured by rheumatism. All the rest of the family was harvesting the wheat in the Malides field, up on the plateau.

'Well, there it is!' said Monsieur Lanzac. 'Pierre-Edouard passed, and passed well. I'm very proud of him!'

The old man looked at them and then made a movement which amazed his grandson, who knew how painful it was for his grandfather to hold himself upright: he got up. His wrinkles deepened in a smile, and Pierre-Edouard could hardly believe his eyes when he noticed that the old man's eyelids were edged with tears. And his astonishment grew when he spoke, not in patois, which had always been his customary language, but in French, the French which he only employed in exceptional circumstances.

'No, no,' he assured them, 'I'm not going senile, it's nothing . . .' He swallowed his saliva and gave a faint smile: 'You know, you are the first of all the Vialhes, the first ever, to get a diploma . . . Me, I don't know how to write, and can hardly read. And you, you have a diploma, a real state diploma! Wait a minute . . .'

He went limping into the house and they could hear him rummaging in his bedroom. He returned carrying three glasses on the tips of his fingers and a bottle of ratafia under his arm. He put them all down on the bench, sat down, plunged his hand into his waistcoat pocket and took out a napoléon worth twenty francs. When he held out the coin, his grandson shook his head. He could not accept such a large gift.

'Yes, yes, take it, it would give me so much pleasure. It's for you, you deserve it. Go on, take it.'

Pierre-Edouard stretched out his hand towards the shining napoléon which lay on the calloused palm among the dark wrinkles. When he touched the skin, dry and hard as old leather, Edouard Vialhe closed his fist and shook his grandson's hand slowly.

'The first of all the Vialhes . . . You're a man now. We shall drink your health and your teacher's, and he shall dine with us tonight. We have had enough misery these past few days; we must make ourselves a bit of happiness.'

Pierre-Edouard took off his Sunday clothes, slipped into his everyday wear, and climbed up towards the plateau singing to himself.

He announced his news from as far away as possible, and his cry of joy was echoed by his mother, grandmother, and sisters. As for Jean-Edouard, he leant on his scythe, regarded his son and whistled his satisfaction. He too was flushed with pride.

But there was work to be done, and it was a long time till nightfall. When Marguerite heard that the teacher would be there for dinner she held out her bundle of withies to her son: 'You take over for me here, we must receive him properly!'

Pierre-Edouard worked until dusk. He followed his father, step for step, and tied up the sheaves with practised movements. First of all he gathered the swathes cut by the scythe in to his chest and made a round-bellied heavy sheaf, which he bound with a fistful of damp rye straw. Then, turning the sheaf onto the ground, he pressed his knee onto its creaking stomach and with both hands twisted the withy, making sure that it held by slipping the ends under the belt of straw. His sheaves were as fine, heavy and thick as those made by a full-grown man.

His sisters gleaned behind him. Finally, at the end of the procession came his grandmother. She gathered the sheaves into stooks of thirteen, arranging them head to head in a cross with four arms; each arm of three sheaves overlapped and the last sheaf capped them to protect the whole. And everywhere on the plateau, there was the same patient persevering labour.

Jean-Edouard often stopped to draw the grindstone from the box lined with damp grass which hung at his belt and re-sharpen his scythe. The steel sang under his strokes.

When at last they stopped, darkness already covered the

whole valley. The teacher was waiting for them, sitting in front of the house with the old man. The table was laid, the air was fragrant with chicken broth and goose preserved with mushrooms.

'No, it's impossible,' said Jean-Edouard. 'Besides I already said no to Monsieur Lanzac, and that was only yesterday evening!'

'I know, I heard that he was dining with you,' affirmed Father Feix, 'and I suspected he would suggest some sort of plan of his own . . .'

Jean-Edouard passed his finger along the edge of the blade. He had just been sharpening his scythe and preparing to set off for the plateau when the priest arrived.

'You must understand,' insisted Father Feix, 'your lad is a brilliant fellow, a good, well-behaved boy, you have no right to squander his talents. Remember the parable of the talents? God will ask you one day what you made of your son.'

'I need my son. He works like a man, and if you think we can do without workers, after this last disaster!'

'I know, but it wouldn't cost you anything! I guarantee you that I'll come to some arrangement with the bishop, so that you don't have a penny to pay.'

'Oh, yes, and that teacher, he wants to make arrangements with some school inspector or other! I'm going to tell you straight, no disrespect intended, you seem to me just like recruiting sergeants! It's no! The boy is not going to a seminary, nor to any kind of school in Tulle. He'll be staying here; that point is settled! Look here, just ask my wife what she thinks about it!'

'Well, you too, Marguerite; you're of the same opinion?' asked the priest.

The young woman had just come from seeing to the pigs. She dried her hands on her apron and came nearer.

'Yes, Father,' she said, blushing just as she used to do when she stumbled over her catechism in class, 'I agree with Jean-Edouard. We don't want all these arrangements, we need the boy too much.'

'But you're only thinking of yourselves, aren't you? And him, his future, what about that?'

'He doesn't want it either,' said Jean-Edouard. 'He has no desire to be a teacher, nor a priest!'

'But it's not a question of making a preacher out of him! I am simply saying that concentrated study at the seminary would do him a great deal of good. And if, later on, he wanted to turn to the priesthood . . .'

'Monsieur Lanzac said exactly the same thing, only it wasn't a question of ending up as a priest, but as a teacher!'

'You're not going to compare the institution which I'm suggesting to you with some lay school, where all Christian ideas are forbidden!'

'The result's the same,' interrupted Grandfather, who had just dragged himself to the doorstep. 'You want to take our boy away from us. That's not good what you're doing there, not good at all!'

'Well, what use is his school certificate to him?' shouted Father Feix angrily. 'It's pointless to push him this far if you're then going to stop him!'

'He can use it to say: "I have my diploma",' retorted the old man. 'The point is that he can read, write, count, walk with his head high! And you think that's not enough? Why do you want to add other diplomas, which will turn his head and make him forget his father and mother? And his land! No, no, I don't want this boy taken away from me and spoiled in your towns. He too is a Vialhe, an Edouard, an eldest son, and you want to deprive him of his land? And the farm, what would become of it without him? Give it to the girls? Never! The land has belonged to the Vialhes for more than a century, and it's going to stay like that!'

'Well!' sighed the priest, 'you are all consummate egoists. I am disappointed in you, Marguerite; yes, most of all in you . . . And Grandmother, what has she to say about it?'

'The same as me,' cut in the old man. 'And I'd like to see her say anything different!'

'Well, I can see that you're all in it together; I won't go on. But you'll regret it one day. You'll say: "Ah, if only we had listened to the priest!" But it will be too late! Well, too bad; *I* shall have a clear conscience!'

Father Feix mopped his streaming brow and departed with a flourish of his cassock.

Pierre-Edouard now emerged from the house. He had heard everything and feared at one point that his parents would give in. He had no desire to leave the house and village to go to these distant schools they were proposing to him. School was finished. He was thirteen years old and had his certificate; he felt a man now.

Father Feix nodded to several old ladies who were gossiping under the lime trees in the square, and went into the presbytery. The heavy door banged shut behind him.

He was in a very bad mood, and angry with himself for falling into the temptation of wrath once more, coming within a fraction of succumbing to it. Of course he had managed to control himself in front of the Vialhes, but it would have taken very little to make him explode, and offer some thoughts which had little to do with Christian charity.

He poured himself a large glass of his own infusion and forced himself – as a mortification and despite being very thirsty – to drink slowly. He lived modestly and soberly, and kept the wine from his small trellis for Sundays and Holy Days. In the high season he prepared a refreshing and invigorating drink based on the leaves of the ash tree; in autumn he made a light wine from apple juice, and in winter he drank water.

He mopped his brow and neck, which were dripping with sweat, unbuttoned the neck of his cassock, turned back his sleeves and went out in the little garden. Here the heat was unbearable. The plot was encircled by walls which stored and reflected the sun's warmth; it only cooled down late in the evening, and the rows of vegetables needed watering every day.

He quickly returned to the presbytery, appreciating its coolness, and settled himself in a rattan chair to continue reading his breviary. But he had to make a great effort to banish all traces of anger from his mind; this anger had laid siege to his thoughts for months, and the slightest irritation brought it to the attack.

But how could he remain passive in the face of the madness and scandal shaking the whole country, threatening the Church and the Faith? Thanks to the generosity of the squire he had a subscription to the newspaper *The Cross*, and read it from the first to the last line. He also kept himself informed on events in the region by reading *The Cross of Corrèze*, which the solicitor's wife gave him. So he was well-informed, and from the first he had followed the rise of atheism and freemasonry with disquietude. Neither his congregation, nor the village in general, had really been affected by this disease, but he had nevertheless felt a certain change of attitude amongst some parishioners.

The mayor, for example, was more proud and self-confident than ever before, and pinned back the ears of his electors by recounting, for the thousandth time, the story of his interview with the President of the Republic! If you believed him, Eric Loubet and he had become inseparable friends! They mayors' banquet must have taken place almost two years ago, but Antoine Gigoux never ceased to tell of its splendour. And as time passed he skated over the fact that he had been only one of more than 20,000 mayors privileged to be received by the President . . . The priest forecast that in a few more years he would be saying that he had lunched with him tête à tête!

Father Feix was not jealous of the aura now surrounding the first citizen of the community, but he deplored the infatuation, not to say devotion, centred on Antoine Gigoux. He was indisputably popular, so it was easy for him to direct the municipal administration in a modern and dynamic way. With the help and wisdom of Jean-Edouard, he had started a buying syndicate, where most of the farmers came for their supplies.

Already there was a rumour that the council were going to organise a market, to take place twice a month in the church square. Father Feix had been told that the soundings of cattle dealers, street-traders and pedlars had been favourable, and only the cost of installing a weighing machine for the animals was holding up the start.

The priest was wary of this innovation. Certainly it would bring some money into St Libéral and everyone would feel the benefit of that, but there was a risk that it would radically change the way of thinking in the community. Moreover, and worst of all in his view, all this was being done for the glory of the Republic – that Republic which was revealing its true nature as the months passed. It was the face of the Antichrist.

He had been indignant first about the law concerning congregations, then scandalised by the unjust case brought against the Assumptionists in the previous year. Since then he had boiled with anger. And how could he calm down! The last elections, on 6 and 20 May, had fostered the atheistic aims of the government, rather than putting the brakes on them. Now they had the power to continue their campaign against the Faith until the end of their term of office. Since the Republican faction held 367 out of 587 seats they could do anything, and they were making the most of it!

Not content with defeating men like Barrès, the Socialists had just chosen a leader worthy of themselves, the renegade Emile Combes; further encroachments on the power of the Church were to be expected, for he had a malicious hatred of it. It all stank of decay and decomposition; like the treason and immorality spread by that horrible Jew Dreyfus and all who supported him!

Father Feix often reproached himself for falling into pessimism and despair; so, as soon as he felt the flame of the second virtue dying, he hurried to revive it – with prayer, of course, but also, he had to admit, with a burst of anger which propelled him, still raging, out of the presbytery. Then he went on his rounds among the faithful and exhorted them to resist and fight on.

But there too, what disappointments, what disillusion! To his way of thinking his parishioners lacked fire, passion and spirit. He found them too passive, too soft. Only a few women supported him, but the others, all the others, continued their humdrum lives without taking sides; not against him, but not with him, indifferent. So the mayor could influence them as he pleased, helped by the teacher, who passed *La Petite Republique*, that dreadful rag full of lies and slanders, all around the village.

Even the squire was spineless; he did not want to quarrel with anyone, took care not to reveal his opinions openly, and kept friends on both sides. He wanted to stand for election to the *Conseil Général*, so he reconciled chalk and cheese to arrive at this goal. As for the solicitor – careful not to annoy any of his clients, he smoothly played down his political position; even if he secretly shared the priest's concern, in public he played the role of Pontius Pilate.

Doctor Fraysse was a free-thinker who spoke frankly, and the priest almost preferred his mocking attitude to that of his lukewarm, faint-hearted supporters. The doctor did not conceal his opinions, and seemed to be highly delighted by the turn of events. He counted the blows of the combatants and amused himself freely by reading out articles from the *Petit Journal*, but he was never malicious. The priest even forgave his recent greeting: 'Ah, tell me, what are they doing to you? If I were in your place I wouldn't put up with it!' Basically the doctor was not a threat; he was not an ally, but not an enemy either, rather an honest irrelevance. He jokingly gave his judgement on a dispute which did not affect him. Besides, since Father Feix had never expected his support, he was not disappointed in him.

He did not feel the same about the Vialhes. That family was slipping away from him, he could feel it. Jean-Edouard was getting out of hand, taking over authority, restrained only by old Edouard's grasp. But the latter was in his decline, his physical pain, his age, relegating him to a secondary role. Of course he still directed the farm and the family with his voice, but the real owner, the master, was now Jean-Edouard. His capabilities won him the respect of all: it was he who used the first fertiliser, he who boldly established a plantation of a hectare of walnut trees on the plateau, he who, it was said, was soon to own a mechanical reaper; he, finally, who managed the buying syndicate.

Jean-Edouard was not really in opposition to the priest, not yet . . . He respected religion, went to church at Easter, but more and more he kept his distance. The proof was in the way he had been received an hour ago! Jean-Edouard had dared to compare the Church's behaviour with that of the teacher, what a sorry state of affairs!

And after all, wasn't that the best solution: to send little Pierre-Edouard, who was so talented, to study seriously at a seminary? Wasn't that the only way to foster his intellectual and moral development? And most of all, wasn't this the opportunity to score a point against the anti-clerical movement, and reassert his shaky authority in the village?

But the Vialhes had refused his offer; even Marguerite had rejected it. Luckily, they had also refused the teacher's tempting but underhand proposition. Perhaps all was not lost . . .

He closed his breviary and immediately reproached himself for allowing his thoughts to stray in this way, so far from spiritual meditation. But wasn't the aim of his work to strive to protect his flock? To guard them against the attacks which he knew assailed them from so many directions?

5

JEAN-EDOUARD finally decided to buy a mowing machine in April 1905, having thought about it for a long time. He had planned the purchase years ago, but had to postpone it as a result of several bad harvests.

After the catastrophic storm of June 1902, he was unable to recoup the losses caused by the hail; the accounts showed a deficit in the years which followed as well. A late frost in the spring of 1903, and again in 1905, destroyed practically all the vegetables and fruit, which provided a substantial part of the farmer's income in a normal year. They had coped, but there was no question of making new investments.

In the community, the shortage of money was reflected in the buying syndicate, and it had taken all Jean-Edouard's persistence to prevent its closure. But the number of subscribers continued to diminish. In three years twelve farmers had left the village, compelled by force of circumstance to seek work in the town. Luckily the fortnightly market had developed rapidly, and the country folk came from far and wide to buy and sell in the market-place of St Libéral. It was a great comfort to Jean-Edouard and the rest of the town council, and it also brought prosperity to the tradesmen.

For the Vialhes, Grandfather's increasing demands added to the difficulties caused by the capricious weather. The old man could no longer move without terrible pain and effort; his attacks of rheumatism were so severe that they often had to call out Doctor Fraysse, or his colleague, the young Doctor Delpy, who was to take over the surgery and clientele before the end of the year. At two francs fifty a time, with potions and other medicines on top, it came to ten francs nearly every visit.

Jean-Edouard never begrudged his father the cost of the care he needed. His father had worked his time; from now on he had a right to rest, and nothing would be spared to see that he enjoyed it as much as possible. He kept himself informed about the work on the farm, made them take him to the looseboxes from time to time to see the calves or the sheep; he worried about the condition of the soil and the growth of the fruit trees.

On the day of the first market he had wanted to get to the square at all costs. There, gripping his walking stick in one hand, the other on his grandson's shoulder, he had slowly made the round of the rails where the cows and calves were tethered. He was very proud that his son was one of the architects of this creation; very proud, too, to tell several old acquaintances from nearby villages that his son had the best yields in the community, thanks to his knowledge and use of fertilisers.

But Jean-Edouard knew his father was rapidly weakening. It now took both his wife and Marguerite to get him up in the morning, and it was seldom that a week passed without a visit from the doctor. Because of all this he had been forced to delay buying a reaper. Yet it had become essential; his father could not work any more, his mother and Marguerite were kept busy looking after him and the animals. Jean-Edouard had only himself and his son to count on.

At sixteen, Pierre-Edouard was a fine young man. Tall and well-formed, he could work almost as well as an adult, but he still did not have quite the staying power or work output. The periods of heavy work were becoming harder. At forty-five Jean-Edouard was still at the height of his strength, but he could see ahead, and knew that his power and endurance would fade and decrease. Occasionally, after a day of reaping or harvesting, he would feel a stabbing pain shooting through his kidneys, an indication that his body was rebelling against such arduous work.

He endeavoured to take on a farm labourer, a sturdy, honest man, but it was no use. Those who were looking for a job preferred to work in the town, and the others plied for hire in the farms on the plain near Brive, Larche or Terrasson, where the work was less strenuous than on the slopes of St Libéral. Only a few day-labourers stayed in the village, and he didn't want them at any price. He could not do with them pottering about, demanding their pay each evening; they got drunk straight away and took two days to sleep off their wine. Besides, he did not want men like that sitting at his table, looking at his wife, and at Louise too.

Louise was turning into a really beautiful girl. She would soon be fifteen, and already had the manners and affectations of a young lady, which worried her father a little. She was lively and coquettish and just as proud of her little breasts – hardly bigger than nuts! – as Pierre-Edouard was of his shadow of a moustache!

Brother and sister had a close relationship which allowed them to understand each other's feelings without speaking. They never quarrelled but always supported each other, uniting in adversity. They excluded their little sister completely from their secret conversations – after all, she was only twelve, cried for no good reason, and was completely spoiled by her grandmother. Besides, Berthe often told on her older brother and sister, happily reporting their actions and movements, and more than once had got them into real trouble with their parents by doing so.

Jean-Edouard's anger was uncontrollable the moment he thought that someone was contesting his authority. He had submitted to his father until he was forty, and he intended to impose *his* will for as long as he could. He was head of the family, master of the land, the leader, who thought and acted for the Vialhe household, and no one ever questioned his decisions. So no one reacted when he announced, during supper on the evening of 23 April, the plan for the following day.

'I'm going to Brive tomorrow, it's market day.'

Louise glanced at her brother, requesting his help. She was dying to go to Brive with her father. She still did not know the town which her brother had talked about so often. He had all the luck!

Pierre-Edouard had already been to Brive twice with his father – once in 1904, for the onion market which took place in August, and another time for the 'King's Market', the most important one in the area, which took place each year in the week of Epiphany. And he had talked to his sister about all the splendours of the great city, and the marvels of the journey by train.

Best of all, he had had the luck to see petrol-driven cars motoring along during the journey; he jauntily assured her that he was not afraid of them! But she thought he was showing off a bit, because their father had also spoken of these encounters, with quite terrifying descriptions! He was sure that these machines would never come into the country, for the noise and the flames surrounding them would make the cows go dry, madden the sheep, and drive the pigs wild. Despite this, Louise was prepared to suffer these distressing experiences for the sake of finally getting to the great town.

'Please, father, may I go with you?' she ventured to ask.

'You stay here to help your mother and look after the livestock. Pierre-Edouard will accompany me!'

It was still pitch dark when they set out, and St Libéral lay silent and asleep. They had a good two hours' walk to the station at La Rivière-de-Mansac; the train passed there at 6.10, coming from Terrasson. It would get them to Brive three-quarters of an hour later, after connecting with the villages of Larche and St Pantaléon.

They were just reaching the last houses when a silhouette started out of an alleyway.

'Is that you, Léon?'

'Good morning, Monsieur Vialhe. Hi, Pierre!'

'You're going to the market at Brive?'

'That's right.'

'Well, we'll go along together.'

In contrast to Pierre-Edouard, who was still coasting through adolescence, Léon Dupeuch was a man, and few people realised that he was only eighteen. He was stocky and rugged, with a deep voice and a thick black moustache which accentuated his stern features. Through his confrontation with death at too young an age, he had acquired a cold look and the maturity and cynicism of an old man, mixed with harshness, icy humour and a curt manner.

After his father's death he had buried two of his sisters, one after the other. Tuberculosis, said the doctor; a curse, whispered the women, who remembered the mark Mathilde bore. This last child was not blind at all, contrary to all predictions; she was now a little scrap of a girl, five years old; the only person, they said, who knew how to make Léon laugh. He never forgot to bring her back some treat from each of his journeys.

Two years ago he had been taken on as a scout by a cattle-dealer from the village of Malemort, a place on the other side of Brive on the road to Tulle, as well as still keeping busy with the meagre smallholding belonging to the solicitor. His judgement was infallible. At a glance he could estimate to the pound the weight of a calf or cow on the hoof; although he had earlier been confused by calculations, he now knew what should be offered for an animal, almost to the centime.

His work consisted of hurrying among the lines of animals as soon as the bell announced that the market was open, to spot the beasts he wanted and to enquire the price. He immediately offered a much lower amount – or, worse still, shrugged his shoulders, disclaimed any interest in buying, and hurried towards other clients. In this way he gauged the mood of the market and the tenacity of the stockmen, and he had a marvellous knack of casting doubt into the minds of sellers.

Once he had finished his tour of the market he began the circuit again, still just as blasé, just as haughty, and on his heels came the buyer, more agreeable, more flexible and a tiny bit less mean. He was a faithful pilot fish for a shark in a blue overall, indicating by a secret look which prey seemed easy to take . . .

But he could also be a formidable seller when he offered a lot of heifers bought by his employer in Seilhac or Treignac, or bullocks acquired in Turenne. He haggled over every sou of the price, fought over each centime, and often displayed such strength of character that even his own employer admired him – and *he* was a real skinflint!

Léon was paid by the head – bought or sold – and made a good living, but he knew that the majority of the inhabitants of St Libéral saw him as a complete scoundrel. The farmers instinctively distrusted cattle-dealers, and that was what he was in the process of becoming. There was really absolutely no doubt that, the way he was going, he would be his own master within five years, for he had shown proof of his skills.

On top of that, many could not forgive him for still being an incorrigible poacher, just as he had been in his youth. Everyone knew that he was laying snares, but no one had ever been able to surprise him doing it. It was understood that he hunted without a licence, but to catch him red-handed . . . The village policeman and even the gendarmes from the Ayen force had all tried and failed!

Finally, everybody disapproved of his power over women – and in this particular matter his fame spread beyond the village. You could imagine that he fascinated them with his cold-blooded stare, like a viper. Certainly he was far from having as many conquests to his name as he was credited with, but there too he had a certain savoir-faire.

Strangely enough he had remained friends with Pierre-Edouard, though they seldom met; sometimes their paths crossed by chance, or, like this morning, they met on the same road. Then a sort of brotherly understanding revived between them, with a hint of mutual admiration – the younger admired his elder's experience, and the latter valued the cheerfulness and erudition of his friend. But both knew that the Vialhe parents would not have liked these chance conversations, however rare they might be.

They kept going at a good pace for an hour, and none of them considered it necessary to talk during that time. Jean-Edouard had nothing to say to this fellow Léon, whom he distrusted; Pierre-Edouard did not dare say the first word. As for Léon, he kept quiet, as was his custom. Nevertheless it was he who broke the silence.

'Tell me, Monsieur Vialhe, is it true, this story about the railway?'

'They're talking about it . . .'

For those whose business it was to talk about it *were* talking! Jean Duroux took his role seriously, since he had been elected general councillor. It was thought that he was going to stand as candidate for the legislature. He let the rumour spread without confirming or denying it.

On the other hand he had got it into his head that the railway should pass through St Libéral, and he was doing everything possible to achieve this aim. He wanted the line leaving La-Rivière-de-Mansac to climb up to Brignac; from there it should ascend to Perpezac-le-Blanc, then reach St Libéral before turning away towards Ayen and Juillac. The villages it would pass were far from agreeing to this ambitious project; even before the route of the line had been settled, they were talking about woodlands cut in half, farms broken up and fields and pastures destroyed.

Cliques had formed, and even within the inner circle of the town council of St Libéral you could reckon with two factions. Antoine Gigoux himself hesitated over which party to join. He had recently been re-elected, and it was known that this would be his last term of office, but he wanted to finish in a dignified way so as not to damage his son's chances – it was no secret that he hoped for the succession.

As for Jean-Edouard, he was one of the warmest proponents of the project. If one day the railway came to the village, he would be able to consign to it all the fresh vegetables and fruit which he now had to deliver to the wholesale market at Objat. Moreover, he would be able to get to Brive or Tulle in a reasonable time. But he did not have very high hopes; politics was behind all that, everything depended on politics. Jean Duroux tried his best to keep in with the deputy, and even with the prefect, but no decision would be taken before the next electoral campaign, and it promised to be hotly contested!

Jean-Edouard often wondered when this stupid quarrel between Church and State would at last stop. He was fed up with being the target of both sides. The fact that he went to Mass three or four times a year earned him sarcastic comments from some of the anti-Church faction in the village – there were not many of them, but they grew increasingly vociferous – and his membership of the town council, which had a left-wing mayor, attracted public censure from Father Feix. He would not quickly forget the dreadful scene the priest had made when he had first been re-elected as vice-chairman.

'You're an ally of those barbarians and Freemasons! You approve of the dissolution of parishes! You're hounding poor monks who have been chased out of their monasteries! You are lining up with those who demand accounts from us, it's despicable! Your duty as a Christian is to resign!'

What the priest could not begin to understand was that Jean-Edouard, like the majority of men in the community, had very little interest in a quarrel which he didn't really understand. He did not feel concerned about the ins and outs of these laws, these decrees, these expulsions. From his point of view, none of it was worth fighting over. Besides, in the village there were only a few hardliners who tried, in vain, to whip up opinion against Father Feix. Apart from this handful of trouble-makers, no one wished the priest any harm at all. They knew he did his work well, that he was poor – he gave away all he received – and they respected him.

But he was asking for more, the poor man! He was calling the faithful to arms; he clamoured for their support, practically demanded that they loudly condemn the attitude of those up there in Paris who had the responsibility for governing the country.

It was really senseless; people had quite different things to worry about, and more serious ones too! They were not going to get mixed up in a dispute which hardly affected them, certainly not just to please him!

Of course, by means of sermons, visits and discussions,

the priest had succeeded in convincing many women. And that, quite frankly, was displeasing! Jean-Edouard had been forced to speak severely to his own mother and even Marguerite, to stop them filling his ears with this rubbish. To make matters worse, he had recently had to put some idiot in his place, a silly ass who felt secure, surrounded by fellow drinkers on the terrace of Ma Eugenie's bistro, who thought it was clever to stand in his way and bray. He didn't play the donkey for long! Jean-Edouard had shot him into the middle of the road with a boot to his backside and once there, stretched him out for the count with a single backhander. All the same, he didn't want to have to lay hands on his wife to get some peace and quiet.

'Well, do you think it'll come, this railway?'

'You bet!'

'So then you'll pass your time scouring all the market places!'

'You have to look for the money where you can find it . . .'

'Maybe, but you're not going to get hold of mine!'

'Well, I'm showing a lot of beautiful heifers at the market. They're five months in calf, and I'm sure you'll find the one you're looking for among them,' countered Léon, solely for the purpose of discovering the reason for his neighbour's journey to Brive.

Jean-Edouard gave a quick laugh; what an obvious trap!

'You're still a bit young to catch me out! Keep your old goats, and spare your tongue too! Come on, walk faster, or we'll miss the train.'

The market was not yet open when they sat down at a table outside Gaillard's bistro, but Guierle Square was humming with a thousand sounds: the lowing of worried cows, the cries of calves separated from their mothers, the squeals of pigs, the shouts and oaths of men.

The bistro was directly opposite the market-place, and Jean-Edouard and his son noticed Léon, twenty paces away in the bay reserved for cattle merchants. He was busy with his animals, combing them, brushing their hair first one way and then the other, preparing them.

Jean-Edouard noted that they actually were very fine heifers. They were classic examples of the Limousin breed, well-covered, with plump hindquarters, and their light red coats shone from the damp brush Léon was wielding with energetic strokes.

These animals would be resold for at least 325 or 330 francs each, which really put them out of his reach. Besides, it was obvious that the beasts had been specially brought on – they hadn't put on all that meat by eating hay, more likely artichokes and barley-meal! They were in too fine fettle to be put out for the winter, as whoever bought them would soon find out . . . Put to grass, those heifers would lose twenty kilos in a month!

And finally, maybe they were in calf, but could you prove that it was five months? With those traders you could expect anything; they were ready to sell their mothers and fathers so long as they made a profit!

But if Jean-Edouard distrusted the cattle-dealers, he was even more suspicious of the salesmen for agricultural machinery. Confronted with the dealers he felt an equal, and was quite capable of detecting the faults and good points of a beast; the animals presented no difficulties for him, and he conducted negotiations without ever losing his grip on the situation. But the machinery salesmen had him at their mercy.

They were not offering a familiar commodity, but instruments with mysterious workings. Lacking technical knowledge, he had to accept as Gospel whatever they confidently asserted, for they were initiated into these mysteries.

Jean-Edouard knew nothing about these machines. If, for example, he did understand how the horse-driven threshing machine worked, the one the contractor brought to St Libéral each year in the high season, he was still incapable of starting it himself; even less of repairing it, should it break down. The same went for the mowing-machine he wanted to buy.

His choice had been made since the last King's Market. That day he had compared the models and prices at great length, but he knew his judgement was based on a few superficial details – colour, or the shape of the seats! – rather than on mechanical criteria. He was confused by the complexity of the machines; he felt vulnerable, and wary of the traps the salesmen might lure him in to.

Nevertheless, he forced himself to hide his worry and to stroll about. Followed by Pierre-Edouard, he sauntered through the machinery park, stopping in front of a vine-grower's cart, looking at a drill, fingering a harrow, to return eventually to the mowing-machine. He slowly walked all round it, pretending to be passionately interested in the crank-head, the pinions of the big gear wheel, or the blades of the cutting-bar.

'So, have you made up your mind this time?' asked the salesman, coming up to him. He recognised the customer who had questioned him for more than an hour at the last King's Market.

'Possibly . . .' admitted Jean-Edouard. 'But I would like to be sure that it cuts well, and won't break down . . .'

And what he had dreaded actually happened: the salesman immediately launched into a long and detailed explanation, loaded with technical terms and barbarous names.

'And look, with this gearing, the wheels drive the transmission shaft, on top of which is a disc-crank which, in turn, by the motion of the driving-rod, gives an alternating movement to the blade which slides along the cutting bar . . .'

Jean-Edouard nodded in agreement, and turned to his son.

'Do you understand?'

'Yes, it's not complicated,' declared Pierre-Edouard. He hesitated, a little frightened by his audacity, and asked: 'If you want to regulate the cutting height, how do you do that?'

'Quite simple,' the salesman was delighted to reply. 'You just have to operate the trimmer, here. Look, here, you have a screw which slides in this groove; with that you can raise or lower the blade.'

'And to take out the blade, you use that too?'

'That's right. I see you're mechanically minded.'

Pierre-Edouard blushed with pride. It was true that this machine fascinated him, and no less true that he understood perfectly how it functioned.

'And you say you could fit a board to it for the sheaves?' murmured Jean-Edouard, who felt excluded from the conversation.

'Yes,' explained the salesman, still addressing himself to Pierre-Edouard. 'Look, you fix the board here and hold it in the high position by means of this pedal; the stalks fall there. When you think the bundle is thick enough, you release the pedal, the board drops, the sheaf slips off and all the followers have to do is pick it up. But if you prefer, we have real reaping and binding machines,' he finished, turning to Jean-Edouard.

'No, no, that would definitely be too expensive for us. Even your mowing machine . . . How much does it come to now?'

'The same price as last time, three hundred and sixty-five francs.'

'It's much too expensive!' declared Jean-Edouard.

'Not at all; it's *not* expensive! You have here one of the best machines currently available! We pride ourselves on several decades of experience, and have won the premier prizes in all the exhibitions of Europe and America! Just ask around, everyone will tell you that the McCormick reapers are the champions.'

'Sure! You sell them, you're not going to tell me anything different! Come on, give me fifteen francs off and we can go on talking, okay?'

'Impossible, I'd lose by it!'

'Go on,' persisted Jean-Edouard. 'Fifteen francs, what's that to you!'

He felt at home again. Now that it was a question of price rather than mechanics he could fight on equal terms, and he made the most of it. He knew that the dealer would not lower his price, but he was sure he could get some other concessions.

The discussions became long and bitter, and threatened to break down. Jean-Edouard was encouraged by a group which had formed around him, and felt honour-bound to beat the salesman down. But the latter knew that his reputation was at stake. At last the moment arrived when Jean-Edouard sensed that his opponent would not give ground in front of witnesses.

'Good, let's go and settle it over a glass,' he said wearily. 'And you, you wait there for me,' he threw at his son.

He returned a quarter of an hour later, and Pierre-Edouard knew straight away that he had won.

'Well there it is,' said his father, in high spirits. 'She's costing me dear, but I got him to give me a spare blade. Also, he's going to deliver it to the house, and then he'll show me how to start it. And to top off the bargain, he's giving me two litres of oil for the gears! You see, you must always bargain. Now, this machine, is it true that you understand how it works?'

'Yes. You know, it's not at all complicated.'

'Obviously!' replied Jean-Edouard. He was firmly convinced it was very complicated, but there was no need for his son to know that.

There was a crowd to watch the machine working, one month later. Almost all the men of the village, and some of the women too, were squeezed together along the edge of one of the Vialhes' meadows, not wanting to miss a single moment of the show.

Once more, the salesman turned to Pierre-Edouard with the necessary explanations. The young man listened to chapter and verse, made him repeat several details, mentioned some of the problems which could arise – like meeting a mole-hill or scraping the blade badly – and hoisted himself into the seat. He was confident, but still felt very excited. He looked at his father, whose job it was to lead the animals.

Jean-Edouard stood firm between the two cows, the

goad under his arm; he gave an appearance of calm which he was far from feeling. He was worried that some incident might make him appear ridiculous in everyone's eyes. He knew that his purchase had inspired jealousy. Some of the men, especially the older ones, were convinced that this engine could never produce such good work as a scythe in expert hands; others insinuated that the grass would not regrow so well after a machine had been over it.

It was all nonsense; they had said virtually the same things when he had spread the first phosphate fertiliser – some of them had even predicted that he would scorch all his land with it. He knew that the reaper did good work; he had seen two of them in operation on the plain at Larche, and had been able to judge the quality of the cut. But it remained to be proved to the sceptics that he, Jean-Edouard Vialhe, could do just as well as the big landowners on the plain. He looked questioningly at his son, and saw that he was ready. Taking a step forward he called to the animals.

The experiment would have been a disaster if it had not been for his great experience with cattle. The team panicked at the unaccustomed noise clacking away at their backs, and almost bolted; it was only by pressing against the cows' horns and calming them with his voice that he succeeded in controlling them.

As for Pierre-Edouard, he did not turn a hair, but simply knocked the big tufts of grass out of the way with his whip; if they were cut too fast, the blade was in danger of getting jammed.

Gradually, the animals slowed down as they got used to the noise; at last they found the right pace. Behind the reaper appeared a long ribbon of cut grass jumping with grasshoppers.

Jean-Edouard went up to the end of the meadow and stopped the animals. Already the curious neighbours were swarming along the break opened by the cutter, and all they could do was nod in admiration and exclaim in astonishment. Followed by his son, he walked along it in his turn to inspect the work.

What a marvel! A regular cut, flush with the ground, one metre-twenty wide; a long swathe cut in a few moments which a good scytheman could not have lined up in less than twenty minutes!

He looked at his neighbours, and knew that his demonstration had succeeded. Even his fiercest critics, those who had been poking fun and nudging each other three minutes earlier, were won over, convinced; they all knew, consciously or otherwise, that they had been present at a great event. From now on, thanks to machines of this sort, the work on the land would never be the same.

'Well,' asked the salesman, advancing towards Jean-Edouard, 'are you satisfied? Is that all right?'

'Yes indeed! You'd have to be hard to please not to like it!'

'Say,' added the dealer, lowering his voice, 'if by any chance you have the slightest problem, let me know straight away. Yes,' he insisted, as he saw Jean-Edouard's look of astonishment, 'two or three of your neighbours are interested in this reaper, and I think ... Well, your machine should be a credit to the brand name, okay?'

'You don't waste much time, do you?'

'Say what you like, agricultural equipment's the future. The time will come when you won't be able to do a thing without it.'

'That would surprise me, the price you're selling it at!'

'You'll see, you'll see ... Good – anyway, when you next come to Brive, drop in and see me. I'll give you a few blade sections, and a set of cogs to replace any that might get broken on the stones.'

'You'll *give* them to me?'

'But of course! I tell you, I want this reaper to go like clockwork. You're the first buyer in this area, I owe you that.'

Jean-Edouard nodded his head. Yes, once more he was the first in the area. By using fertiliser he had already amazed everyone. Today he had raised himself to the ranks of the leaders in farming, thanks to this machine, and he would have to do everything to keep that position.

'Okay,' he said. 'I'll keep an eye on it.'

'And above all, listen to what your son says. He has a feel for machinery, that lad.'

'I know,' cut in Jean-Edouard, somewhat drily. 'But as you say, he's only a lad.'

6

PIERRE-EDOUARD set the plough down sideways on the headland, the strip left at the end for turning; stopped the animals with a word, and looked back. He could be proud of his work. He had begun ploughing the morning before and the field of nut trees looked good. The furrows were perfectly straight and of even depth, worthy of a master ploughman, and Pierre-Edouard knew his father would be satisfied, even if he wouldn't say anything.

The field was really superb and rich with promise: the rows of young trees were encircled by a shining brown wave of ploughed soil. One day, in twenty years' time, it would be a fertile plantation where you could pick walnuts by the cartload.

'Are you dreaming?' called out Louise, who was spreading manure thirty paces from him.

He shrugged, and moved towards her.

'If you won't let me take a breather, at least let the beasts have a rest!'

'I'd like to get back down before nightfall, that's all.'

'Oh yes, and I know why,' he said teasingly. 'But if father found out about it . . .'

'So what, I'm not doing anything wrong!'

He shook his head with a knowing look and returned to his team. At his command the animals turned on the headland, lined themselves up on the unploughed land, and resumed their slow march. They knew Pierre-Edouard well: for several months it had been he who had commanded them.

His father's time was more and more taken up by municipal responsibilities; since a good number of the local inhabitants seemed to have gone mad, someone had to try to make them see reason. And this had been going on for more than a year, since September 1906 to be exact.

From the beginning of the electoral campaign, the deputy standing for re-election had taken over the planning of the railway track as if it were his idea, cutting the ground from beneath Jean Duroux's feet. The squire, a good sport, had supported him, weighing in with all his influence as a general councillor to bring the plan to fruition, but it was whispered that he had retired from the electoral contest on the promise of a seat on the senate . . .

Once re-elected, the deputy had to put his promises into action, show that he was a man of his word, and since then, the village had been in a fever of excitement. The critical mission of talking round the opponents of the scheme had fallen to Jean-Edouard, who also had to control the absurd demands of the landowners affected by the route of the railway, and keep them within reasonable limits. This thankless task made him more enemies than friends.

Already the 'anti-train' lobby had completely broken off negotiations; they maintained that the railway, and especially the navvies and the railway yard which would come with it, would corrupt the whole community. Several older people were of this opinion, including a handful of women cunningly indoctrinated by the priest – who was to be pitied, for it was obvious that he was campaigning for a lost cause.

A final quarrel had taken place between Father Feix and Jean-Edouard in December 1905, when the priest, devastated at the separation of Church and State, had rushed to Jean-Edouard to demand his resignation. He was beside himself with rage, and had gone so far as to say that all those who supported this government, whatever their status, were liable to be excommunicated. Jean-Edouard had shown him the door. Since then neither he nor his son had set foot in the village church, and to make their point they had since celebrated Easter at Yssandon or Perpezac. But the priest and his little band of allies hardly bothered Jean-Edouard. They did not own any land affected by the line, and so offered only verbal opposition.

In contrast, almost all the landowners affected by the

route were fighting a fierce campaign to secure the maximum compensation. Moreover, they had succeeded in getting the whole area on their side by appearing to show that they were fighting for the good of everyone, and that if they gave in, nobody would have any protection from the designs of private companies.

During the preceding spring the company had sent one of the engineers to obtain their permission. The poor fellow had not managed to get a single signature! It might have been possible to initiate procedures for compulsory purchase, but the outcome was uncertain; moreover, this could take years, constantly delayed by litigants who would enjoy running from one law court to another.

To crown it all, the general mood of the country was frankly hostile at the beginning of the year, which led the authorities to proceed with extreme caution. The whole wine-growing area of the Midi was in turmoil, and nothing should be done to inflame tempers and to incite the people of Corrèze to imitate the Midi. Certainly the farmers of Perpezac, St Libéral or Ayen had no real reason for espousing the wine-growers' cause. The battle being fought further south was not theirs, and they had very little in common with the wine-growers, but you had to reckon with a tendency to revolt which lay dormant in every countryman. It was therefore important to proceed with caution.

To avoid all risk of discontent, the company changed its tactics and brought its alternative plan into effect. The original route had the merit of being the shortest and most logical, but the inconvenience of running slap into this block of landowners; so they threw that in the bin and decided, with the agreement of the Ministry of Bridges and Roads, simply to follow the lane which already curved between all the towns and villages the railway wished to reach. It was much further in kilometres and involved some ridiculous bends, but when the sums were done, it worked out less expensive than the inflated compensation which the rebellious landowners demanded.

There remained one difficulty; the road was not wide

enough. They would have to increase its breadth by several metres, and to do that they would once more have to win over the wayside landowners. These proprietors were not in such a strong position, and could not count on popular support. They could not decently invoke the sacred rights of ownership, nor complain of their fields being divided; the road had passed that way for centuries, and no one had ever complained of any inconvenience from it. Nevertheless, someone had to persuade them to give up the few square metres needed to put down the rails.

The company, on its guard after the first setback, asked each commune concerned to appoint a mediator to be responsible for collecting signatures. So it was that Jean-Edouard, accompanied by an engineer and a surveyor, launched into the campaign for authorisation.

Here there was opposition from a quarrelsome fellow who refused to let them cut down a couple of stunted oaks or three crooked chestnut trees, there an indignant farmer deprived of a metre and a half of grazing; elsewhere the protests of workers who stood to lose the tip of a vegetable plot, or half a row of vines.

Jean-Edouard had to reassure each one that compensation would be paid, and that it would not be trifling. Often the engineer and surveyor had to take measurements and put in poles to show exactly where the route would pass, to demonstrate it more clearly than on the paper plan; so once again it was a long, troublesome business.

In more than six months, not a week had passed without the engineer arriving to fetch Jean-Edouard so that he could smooth out some disputed point. However, these trials were coming to an end; almost all the landowners had now signed, and the two or three stubborn ones who needed a lot of coaxing would eventually give in too.

Already, teams of specialists were marking out the ground plan. If all went well, the building-yard would open before the end of the year.

Pierre-Edouard stuck his whip in the ground, slipped between the cows, which were damp with sweat, and unhitched his plough. Night was coming on, and it was high time to go down and take care of the animals. Today his father had again gone off, grumbling, to try to overcome old Treilhard's resistance; he was refusing to let the track cross his land on the pretext that it would cut him off from a spring, which was pure invention. Pierre-Edouard knew full well that if his father had the misfortune to suffer another setback, the slightest delay or smallest mistake would cloud his temper. Even at eighteen, he still dreaded a parental scene. The era of slaps or the belt had passed, but the bitter comments which had taken their place were not to the young man's taste.

For the moment he accepted the criticisms without comment, even if they were unjust, but he had a feeling that the day would come when he would stand up to his father. Already he was as tall as his father and almost as strong, but he still confined himself to passive defence; the more Jean-Edouard raised his voice, the more he kept quiet.

Louise did not hesitate to answer back, but all she usually gained from it was a couple of smacks. As for Berthe, she was still a sly one, with a marvellous knack of diverting her father's or mother's admonishments towards her older brother and sister.

He moved to the animals' heads and set off down the path to the village. Despite his good advice, Louise had already left half an hour ago. He was worried about her. He loved her dearly, and for several months had been seriously troubled on her account; but she did what she wanted!

Louise pushed the rebellious lock of brown hair back under her scarf; it was always escaping and falling in her eyes. She patted her dress to brush off a few stalks of hay, confirmed that her clogs were clean, grasped the can of milk and went out.

She climbed back up the main street and crossed the square. Already her heart was pounding and her mouth was dry. She pushed open the door of the inn and went in.

He was there, as he had been every evening for the last six months.

'Well, little Louise, always on time!' teased the inn-keeper's wife.

She agreed with a smile.

Every evening held the same fascination. She would go in, hold out the milk, and she had less than two minutes to look at him. She watched him in the big mirror which decorated the corner of the room behind the bar. She could see him between a bottle of gentian bitters and a flagon of plum brandy.

He was always there, moving slowly around the billiard table; calculating his shots, thinking, hesitating, and then playing. She guessed whether he had won the point or not from the sound of the balls.

Tall, slim and well-dressed, he smoked small cigars, which he raised to his lips with a charming air of refinement, allowing her to admire his hand, a delicate white hand with long supple fingers and immaculate nails. Sometimes he gently stroked his small black moustache with his forefinger, especially when he was considering which combination to play. His face was then tense with concentration and his dark stare became more definite, more penetrating beneath his folded lids.

One evening his eyes were attracted to the mirror and met hers; the memory of this meeting still made her blush every time she thought of it.

She knew everything about him. She had gleaned her information here and there, with the patience and care of a spider, and she guarded it like a treasure. He was an assistant surveyor and had been lodging at the inn for six months. It was he who often came with the engineer to fetch her father to win over an opponent. It was he who was now busy marking out the line.

From her father she had learned his name, Octave Flaviens, and his age, twenty-five. From the innkeeper's wife she knew where he came from: a town in the north, Orléans. From one of the servants she discovered all his favourite dishes; he didn't like leeks but adored creamed carrots! Thanks to the second servant, who looked after the bedrooms, she knew that he read *Le Petit Parisien*, and big books as well; that he received very little post and, unlike many others, had never tried to kiss her. If he had, Louise would have forgiven him and slapped the little slut!

Yes, she knew all about him. She lived with him, breathed in time with him, walked in his footsteps, slept with him. But she had never spoken a word to him, and was nowhere near doing even that!

It was enough to come each evening to deliver the milk, to open the door and see him.

Jean-Edouard dipped the ladle into the soup tureen and made a sign that they should pass their plates up. He filled them and then looked at his mother.

'And father?'

'That's all right, he's already eaten.'

Old Edouard was steadily losing strength and rarely left his bed now. But occasionally he had a fancy to sit by the fireside or, if it was fine, in the sun outside the door. Then he was supported as far as the settle or the bench where he remained, murmuring and sighing, feebly moving his huge hands which were now useless, quite deformed and stiffened by arthritis. He did not complain; he was waiting.

'Did old Treilhard sign?' asked Marguerite.

'Yes, but what a cunning old fox he is! He wanted to make me believe he was being cut off from his spring!! What a joke, the spring's on the other side! All the same, if I hadn't been there he would have fooled the engineer and his spear-carrier!'

Louise trembled; she hated her father speaking of Octave like that. Octave was *not* a spear-carrier; he was an assistant surveyor, a professional! But her father always appeared to be making fun of him. He probably found him too distinguished, too handsome.

'If he's conceded, is it finished, can the line go through?'

'Yes; the Deschamps and the Moulys have signed as well, they were the last.'

'So you don't need to get involved in it any more?'

'No.'

'All the same, the mayor can't hold a candle to you! Basically, you've done his work!'

'Better that job than the one that's coming. From now on, I just wish them luck . . .'

'And who'll deal with it?'

He made a dismissive gesture and did not reply. He had completed his task, and was satisfied that he had managed it well, but he knew that many held a grudge against him. He was accused of betraying the country folk by siding with the company. Some people would never believe that he had not been paid an inflated price for the few square metres which he, too, had been forced to give up. Of course it was not true; he had received no more than his due. But that did not prevent malicious tongues from insinuating that he had banked a small fortune!

He knew all the lies that were being told behind his back. From now on he would have to take a back seat for the sake of some peace, let his part be forgotten, and let the other members of the town council worry about the problems. And there would be plenty of them!

Now that the work could begin, the urgent business was to lodge and feed the dozens of workers who would occupy the town — it was said there would be more than a hundred! Dormitories, canteens and bars would have to be provided. All that would bring a lot of money into the community, but also a lot of trouble for those in charge of organising it.

Already, before anything had been decided, Jean-Edouard knew that the mayor was being accused of favouritism. One of the carpenters in St Libéral was his brother-in-law, and it was whispered that he had exclusive rights to the work. Other rumours insisted that if the station was sited next to the bar and grocery store belonging to the Delmonds, that was because their cousin Gaston was a member of the town council . . .

All this was idle gossip, but Jean-Edouard knew that some people were taking advantage of the situation, and that this malicious nonsense would leave its scars. If he wanted to follow Antoine Gigoux as Mayor one day – as time passed, he became more and more convinced that Gigoux's son, who also wanted the office, was a total pudding-brain – he would have to drop into the background for a while; devote his time to his farm and the syndicate and nothing else. The day would come when everyone would feel the benefit of the train and he would be thanked for playing the role of mediator who had made the route possible. On the other hand, they would find it more difficult to forgive allegedly corrupt officials, and even the most scrupulous administrators would have great difficulty in ridding themselves of that defamatory label.

He cut himself a thick slice from the ham, then pushed it back into the middle of the table.

'You say you'll be finished by tomorrow night?' he asked his son.

'Definitely.'

'Good, then while you're finishing the ploughing, I'll do the sowing. Is the drill up there?'

'Yes.'

'You, you'll come with me,' he decided, looking at Louise. 'We'll take Grey and Saddleback, it will do them good.'

Besides the two old working cows, Red and Ribbon, they had trained a pair of young animals. They were strong and very hardy but still a bit lively, too nervous and fearful to plough comfortably. Grey especially was wayward, like a goat; she sometimes tried to go off on her own, forgetting the yoke – as strong as an ox, she would side-step a metre or two, pulling her companion with her. She was not yet ready for the plough, which demanded a perfectly regular and straight walk. On the other hand, a day pulling the drill would calm her, accustom her to his voice and signals.

'Saddleback is missing a shoe,' warned Pierre-Edouard.

'My God, couldn't you have told me earlier?'

'I told you when she lost it, last week.'

'You told me! You told me!' shouted Jean-Edouard . . . Yes, now he remembered, and was furious at having forgotten. 'And now what? Why didn't you take her to be

83

re-shod? I have to tell you everything! Huh, if I'd worked like that for my father!'

Pierre-Edouard held his peace. He was not in the wrong, and knew it; it was not his job to decide when to take the animal to the smithy. He had done his duty by warning his father; the rest was not his business.

'All right,' conceded Jean-Edouard, 'we'll go and get her shod at daybreak. Bloody hell! It's a bit rough when I have to think of everything round here!'

Jean-Edouard snuffed out the candle and slipped between the sheets, which were already stiff with cold; the temperature was already so low, for mid-November, that a severe winter was expected. He crept towards his wife, appreciating her warmth. Marguerite murmured a little as she felt her husband's icy feet against her calves, and really shivered when he hugged her.

'Are you asleep?'

'No.'

They were obliged to whisper in each other's ears to prevent the two girls hearing their conversation. The house only had two bedrooms, a communal living room, and a loft. When Pierre-Edouard was fourteen they had to give him a corner of his own; it was not proper to let him continue to sleep in the same room as his sisters and parents. So he had his bed in the living room; the grandparents had the first bedroom, Jean-Edouard, Marguerite and the two girls the second. A screen separated the beds, but it was not enough to stop sounds travelling.

Jean-Edouard continued to feel cold, however much he pressed against his wife, who was snuggled up in a ball.

'You know,' he said, 'I'm glad to have finished with all that business of the signatures. Are you listening to me?'

'Yes, yes.'

'Now all we have to do is wait and prepare ourselves . . .'

'Yes . . . Tell me, do you really think there will be so many people?'

'Perhaps even more! Believe me, it will bring fantastic opportunities, and it will last! Just consider — we're in a position halfway between La Rivière and Ayen; all the workmen on the track will gather here, and for a long time!'

'How long?'

'The engineer told me we could count on two years. According to him, the line should be open at the end of 1909. Trust me, it'll bring prosperity to everyone with a bit of go. If we get busy, we can make any amount of money — and honestly. Money no one can begrudge us. We'll give Louise a proper dowry and find her a good match. I'd be pleased with a fellow like Léonard Bouyssoux.'

'The Bouyssoux from the Heath?'

'Yes.'

'He's old . . .'

'No he isn't! He's not even thirty. Best of all, he's an only son, and Heath Farm is magnificent . . . Well, we'll talk about it later.'

'I'd have thought he was older than that.'

'And so what! I was a good twenty-eight and you hardly eighteen when we got married, and it's good, isn't it?'

'With us, it wasn't the same. And you say we should sow at least twenty strips of potatoes?'

'Yes, and haricot beans, broad beans and cabbage, and you must raise as many chickens and hens as you can, and then I'll buy two extra sows . . .'

'And are you sure you can sell all that to the men on the line?'

'Yes.'

'You're really sure?' she persisted.

It was his secret; he had not talked to anyone about it and still did not want to reveal it, even to his wife. One day, when accompanying the engineer to La-Rivière-de-Mansac, he had made the acquaintance of the steward who worked for the company, a man burdened with the taxing job of feeding an army of famished labourers every day.

He had quickly seen how he could turn this meeting to

his own advantage. A man who had so many stomachs to satisfy must always be on the look-out for assorted supplies. Jean-Edouard tested the water.

'And where do you buy your produce – let's say vegetables, for instance?'

'Where I can find them, mon ami! And it's not always easy, believe me, I have to chase around! A ton of tatties here, five hundredweight of beans there – if you knew the time it takes me! Look, when I began to work for the railway building-yards, in the '90s, I started on the section of the main line between Uzerche and Brive. Well, believe it or not, I had to get potatoes sent from the Seine area! Yes, no means of making my living from thereabouts, unless I spent all my days traipsing round the farms!'

Jean-Edouard listened, fascinated.

'If you like, I'll provide them for you, the tatties . . .'

'And why not!'

'You'd take several tons?'

'Of course!'

'And beans?'

'Everything that's edible and not too expensive.'

'So cabbage, too?'

'Naturally.'

'And meat?'

'Yes, pigs or barren cows.'

He could hardly believe his ears. It was providence that had set this man in his path!

'Do you really mean it?' he persisted.

'It's as real as the train that's coming through your way.'

'Let's shake on it. I'll grow it and you buy it.'

'Mind you, I buy at wholesale prices.'

'Understood.'

'Well, let's shake on it, then.'

Their hands had touched; that was worth the same as a signature.

Since then he had been designing his plan of cultivation. The fellow wanted provisions? He should have them!

'Answer me,' repeated Marguerite, turning to him. 'You're sure we're not going to grow all that for nothing?'

86

'I know what I'm doing!'

He placed his broad hand on his wife's hip and pulled her towards him.

'We could never manage to hoe and weed all that,' she insisted, 'and to lift all the potatoes, think about that too?'

'Don't worry,' he said, tightening his embrace.

PART TWO

The House Divided

7

THE opening of the railway construction yard turned life in the village upside down, to the jubilation of its opponents. But revenge had a bitter taste for Father Feix and his few sympathisers; what use was it to have predicted all the disasters which were now unleashed on St Libéral? What good to say 'I told you so!', for the enemy was within!

It had come in the form of more than a hundred workers, whom the community were responsible for housing. And as soon as dormitories and canteens had been built on the edge of the village, they were literally swamped every evening by a motley crowd of bellowing and bellicose men divided by region or race: Italian navvies, men from Brittany and the Auvergne to place the sleepers and carry the rails, team leaders from Paris or Lyons. Added to these main groups were a certain number of men taken on locally; also two Poles accompanied by a woman — they lodged, all three together, in a sort of shepherd's caravan — and finally a huge Senegalese, who terrified the children.

As soon as they finished work, this whole mass took over the two bistros in St Libéral, invaded the bar at the inn, laid siege to the shops, fought, got drunk, whistled and called after the women and girls, and created a shocking din until the early hours.

Saturday nights were the worst; the village belonged to the newcomers, and the young people from round about were virtually barred from the dances at the inn.

The Chanlat couple, hustled and barracked, overcome by the activities and the arrogance of the strangers, resigned themselves to seeing their establishment turned into a dance-hall. Some of the Parisians made fun of the hurdy-gurdy and barrel-organ, and told them bluntly that these were as dated as ox-drawn carts; they should keep up with the times. The old folk-dances gave way to the fashionable *java*.

But although a whole host of men wanted to dance, there were not enough partners for them. There was no question of the local girls sullying themselves with the strangers; only a few not very respectable women of doubtful reputation were content to be passed from arm to arm – like Ma Eugenie, whose bed never had time to cool down! Added to these four or five hussies were the two inn servants and the Polish woman who, they quickly discovered, was the sister of the two jabberers, and the consoler of all the unmarried men. That was definitely too few women for the hundred lively fellows quartered at St Libéral, and even if a certain number of them sometimes went down to Brive or Terrasson on a spree, there were still too many left without dancing partners. It was unusual for the dances to end without fisticuffs.

The village policeman was completely powerless – and also extremely angry, since four laughing Italians had dispatched him, little drum and all, into the middle of the village wash tank. He warned the mayor that henceforth he would not set foot outside his house after six o'clock in the evening. The village therefore became accustomed to regular visits from two policeman from the Ayen force. They arrived at a trot, let themselves be seen, paraded about the square, let their mounts have a breather, inquired of Antoine Gigoux how things were going, and then went home again. But they were never there on Saturday evenings, about ten o'clock, when the first blows were struck in the big hall of the inn or outside in the square.

To this constant din, the brawling and shouting that disturbed the life of St Libéral, was added another no less serious scourge. The workmen had hardly been there a week when not a single hen was safe outside a firmly shut henhouse guarded by dogs! Usually all the hens were left free to peck around outside the buildings, and so the farmers' wives blamed foxes for the first disappearances, but they quickly realised that these thieves had broad shoulders – unless Reynard had lost two paws and learnt Italian . . .

Their raids made huge gaps in the winged tribes of the region; even geese and turkeys disappeared without trace. The band of Italians —with a good percentage of French mixed in – were very well organised, and did not stop until they had cleaned up everything. These vultures even managed to wipe out all the guinea-fowl, a very shy bird, by trapping them like partridges, either by laying snares or with vicious hooks concealed in a piece of cooked potato!

The people of the community, disheartened by such an accumulation of irritations, at first avoided all contact with the invaders; many regretted having opted for the railway-line. But very soon many also realised the benefits they could derive from this mass of consumers. Of course, the workers had their canteens, but they were not above supplementing their normal fare; their fowling raids were proof of that.

By tacit but unanimous agreement, there was a sudden rise in prices. A dozen eggs jumped to one franc forty, a litre of wine to seventy centimes, and a bottle of plum-brandy was worth up to four francs. To make up for their losses from pilfering, the farmers' wives offered a pair of young chickens at six francs, and demanded the same price for a couple of ducks. Thus, as Jean-Edouard had thought, everyone profited from the railway-yard; but for a long time he remained the only one to have planned ahead on a grand enough scale to transform a small business into a great enterprise.

Since the village had been taken over every evening by workers in festive spirits, there was no question of Louise going to deliver the milk to the inn. For now the inn overflowed with drinkers; their salacious comments, not to mention evil propositions, prevented any nice girl from going near the place. Certainly she was prepared to brazen it out and shut her ears for the sole joy of looking at the handsome Octave Flaviens for a brief moment, but she had to accept her mother's decision and allow Pierre-Edouard to replace her.

She did not even attempt to plead her cause, certain that to persist would arouse suspicion. It was, of course, impossible to breathe a word to her parents of the emotions which this young man had awakened. She had therefore to show extreme prudence, without which, she knew, the drama could become a tragedy. The Vialhe household were not about to allow a chit of seventeen to fall head over heels in love with a stranger, an outsider!

Naturally, Pierre-Edouard had known for a long time what was going on, but he had never spoken to her openly about it; he simply let her know by a few remarks that he was not deceived. But he would keep quiet; and she was not worried about him. On the other hand she distrusted Berthe; the little one had a sharp eye and a mind quick enough to interpret the slightest sigh.

Curiously, although Louise had remained an adolescent for a long time, as though her body were tentatively searching out the most beautiful shapes, Berthe became a woman in a few months, and only her childish behaviour betrayed her fifteen years. She had already been whistled at by several of the louts who hung about the main street even in broad daylight.

Louise merited such demonstrations of admiration too but, unlike Berthe, she took no pride in being noticed. Her beauty, style and daintiness were not for street fowl: they could peck around beneath her feet, they did not exist. Only Octave counted.

She continued to love him with a silent and patient love. A love which grew stronger and more idealised day by day, until she convinced herself that it was too great, too beautiful, too pure not to be returned! She could not imagine that the young man could be indifferent to her attention; no, he remained silent and reserved out of discretion.

She was convinced that he was suffering as much as she was from their separation, and she was deeply affected when it became impossible to see him every day. She lived through a dreadful week while she pondered the best means of re-establishing their meetings. At the same time she undertook a novena to seek aid from Saint Eutrope, the patron saint of the parish.

The saint heard her – at least Louise believed so – for the innkeeper's wife let it be known that she would prefer to receive her milk in the morning than the evening. Louise saw in this a sign from heaven, a sort of miracle; God was blessing her love! In fact, Madame Chanlat was monopolised every evening by the swarms of drinkers, and had no time to deal with the milk. Swept along by a whirlwind of glasses to rinse, beermugs to fill, measures of rum to pour, she forgot to boil the milk two evenings in a row; it curdled and had to be given to the dogs. So she wanted to have it in the morning. At dawn the inn was peaceful; only the customers who slept at the establishment breakfasted quietly in the corner.

Louise cleverly questioned the servant, found out what time Octave ate, and suggested to her mother, quite innocently, that she should save Pierre-Edouard the trouble of delivering. Marguerite saw no objection to letting her take over the job again at that time of day.

With her heart thumping, quite pink and glowing with happiness, Louise pushed open the door of the inn, went in, and almost let go of the milk-can. He was there! He was no longer far away at the other end of the room, in the corner by the billiard table, but there, standing at the bar. Alone, completely alone in the huge saloon, he was breakfasting off a bowl of coffee into which he dipped a slice of buttered bread as big as a hand.

They looked at each other intensely for several seconds and she knew, quite definitely, that he was pleased to see her again. She searched for something to say, found nothing, and simply nodded to him.

Then he spoke. He did it with such ease, so naturally, that she felt all her shyness evaporate. They spoke to each other from the first as if they had always known each other, as if they were continuing a conversation which had started months ago.

'Well, Mademoiselle Louise, so you've come back to see us at last? Do you know that I missed your evening visits very much?'

'I did too, but . . .'

'Yes, I know; from six o'clock on, this inn turns into a real slum; you're right to avoid it. Your father is well, then?'

'Very well, thank you.'

He nodded, drank a mouthful of coffee, and glanced in the direction of the kitchen to make sure they were still alone.

'Tell me,' he continued, lowering his voice, 'don't you think this is a funny way to do things? It's good to see each other for two minutes a day, but wouldn't you like to meet somewhere quieter? I'm sure we've got lots to say to each other . . .'

'Of course . . .' she murmured, suddenly frightened by the speed with which this first real meeting had developed. Accustomed to being quiet, to waiting, she felt herself at a loss, out of her depth. Even in her wildest dreams she had never dared to imagine she would one day experience such an adventure.

'What are you afraid of?' he persisted, 'your parents? They wouldn't stop you from talking, surely?'

'That depends who to . . . And they would never want me to meet you, I know that.'

'Well, they won't find out about it, so there!'

'Listen,' she suddenly decided, 'every afternoon, I look after the animals on Combes-Nègres, there . . .'

He considered this, then smiled. Since he had been doing the surveys for the line he knew the village inside out.

'Yes, I know, that's the meadow on the slope just beyond the path down to the mill; the stream flows through it.'

'That's it,' she whispered. 'Look out, here's Madame . . .'

'Oh, Louise! Have you been here long?' asked Madame Chanlat as she came into the saloon.

'No, no, just arrived this minute,' Louise assured her without turning a hair.

She forced herself not to look at Octave, to feign complete indifference. She somehow knew that from now on she would have to hide this intrigue, to lie, to deceive, to pretend, all day long.

Pierre-Edouard straightened up, leant on his hoe and breathed out. He was aching all over. Despite that, he was still a good fifteen metres ahead of his father. He turned his tool upside down, stuck the handle in the earth, rested his behind on the flat steel and rolled a cigarette.

He and his father had begun hoeing the potatoes three days ago, and already the first rows looked different; the tops of the plants were magnificent, rich, a deep green. You felt they were full of life, but two hectares, that was really an awful lot of hoeing! And as if that were the only task to be completed! No — besides this huge area laid down to potatoes, his father had also planted out innumerable leeks, cabbages, lettuces and onions, sown interminable lines of carrots, broad beans and haricot beans, four strips of lentils and the same of turnips!

Almost all the land on the plateau was planted with crops like these, as well as their field called The Gardens, on the slope by the village. Only the Long Piece and the Big Field were given over to cereals. At least those did not require any work, for the moment . . . But the rest! He would not forget this spring in a hurry.

The outstanding event, the one he would always remember, was that Saturday in May when he came of age. From now on he was eligible for military service, and he was proud of it.

This promotion helped to dim the haunting memory of the ridiculous exhibition he had been forced to make of himself. He saw himself once again in the great hall of the Mairie in Ayen, just as naive and awkward as Jacques Bessat, Edmond Vergne and his other friends from the village. They were all even more frightened than they had been on the day they had sat their examination together.

'Right,' Jacques Bessat had cried, unbuttoning his shirt. 'After all, they can't cut them off.'

But his heart was not in it, and his remark only raised a few thin giggles among the dozens of young men crowded in there.

'Get on with it! Are you scared of catching cold?' bellowed the fat, apoplectic warrant-officer.

'Have you seen his ugly mug, looks just like my backside!' came an anonymous whisper. 'If he keeps still, we won't be able to find him among all our bums!'

This joke corresponded exactly to their image of military life and galvanised them: they larked around and teased each other as they undressed. But once they were naked they all looked at each other with a false air of confidence; none of them dared to check openly, by comparing, whether or not their organs seemed a normal size and shape. And they did not know what to do with their hands.

They were weighed, measured, examined, questioned. Pierre-Edouard had filed in front of the authorities, shown his feet (not at all flat) and his teeth (in good condition). He had also stated, and proved, that he knew how to read, write and count, and that he had his school certificate. He noticed that the mention of this diploma resulted in a satisfied nod from the non-commissioned officer who was making notes.

He heard himself declared fit for service, dressed again in a hurry and at last found himself outside, where he was set upon by the pedlars of cockades and ribbons, of fanciful military-style caps and paper flags. Already Jacques Bessat and Edmond Vergne were decked in various bits and pieces, and shouting some ribald song to which they only knew half the words. No matter, their hearts were in it!

Then they joined a group of happy conscripts, squeezed into an enormous cart hired for the occasion, and rattled off in the direction of Tulle; a bottle mysteriously appeared from nowhere and circulated from mouth to mouth.

They disembarked outside the préfecture during the course of the afternoon and, still bawling, began a tour of the bars. Later, after quite a few glasses, they arrived at the door of a brothel and entered it as an occupying force; to see what they could see! But only three of the dozen dared to follow the women, the others assuring each other in loud voices that, no, really the ladies were too ugly. As for Pierre-Edouard, he was obliged to make a hasty exit in search of air; the last four brandies had been too much for him . . .

Much later, towards midnight, they met up again in the cathedral square, where they 'sang' a hymn before setting off in procession for the Corrèze. They had thrown plenty of stones into the river, tried unsuccessfully to push a huge charabanc into it too; then the group had separated, scattered, and disappeared into the night.

So the St Libéral conscripts began their journey home. They had a thirty-five-kilometre walk ahead of them before reaching their beds; Pierre-Edouard arrived home just as his father was coming out to see to the animals.

'I'm okay!' he called. Then he staggered as far as the barn, where he curled up in the straw and slept until evening.

'The chores won't get done by themselves!' yelled Jean-Edouard. 'You won't get to the end by standing there with your nose in the air.'

'I'm doing my bit, it seems to me!' retorted Pierre-Edouard.

He slowly lit his cigarette so as not to give the impression of knuckling under too quickly, then took out his knife and carefully scraped the blade of his hoe, on which the red sticky earth had built up.

'Not finished messing about yet!' railed his father, within an inch of exploding.

Since the beginning of the year Jean-Edouard had been in a sombre mood. First of all he took it badly when many blamed him for what had happened since the yard had opened, even though he had expected it. To listen to all those loud-mouths in the village, you would think he was responsible for the behaviour of the workmen. And then there was a great deal of jealousy; he was reproached for not having shared his idea of large-scale planting to provision the canteens of the company.

It was true that he had kept his secret well, even going so far as to buy a large quantity of his seed from a merchant in Objat, and not from the syndicate in St Libéral, despite being its chief founder. So he avoided alerting the others; they did not see him acquire such a weight of seed.

Then he had sown and planted everything as discreetly as possible and avoided talking about his work with his neighbours. Of course they had understood in the end, when the plants came up, that Vialhe was on to a big thing. By then everyone had seen what a huge opportunity the yard offered; but they were too late, at least for this year, to compete significantly with his production. He expected to be copied the following year, but for that he already had a plan, and just thinking about it made him laugh to himself.

But these small sources of satisfaction were not enough to cheer him up. What had put him in such a bad mood was the amount of work he had undertaken: he was worried that he would not be able to carry it through successfully. He and his son were far from finishing the hoeing of the two hectares of potatoes, and already all the other plantings needed the same attention. If they didn't get it, the results would be of poor quality, not to say rotten, and the loss would be obvious. And that was what they were smirking about in the village.

He tried to set the whole family to the hoeing, but Marguerite was tied to the house by the care his father needed, and could only leave it in short bursts. That left the two girls; they came sullenly, preferring to spend their time looking after the animals. Anyway they didn't get much done and complained all the time, especially Berthe, who often contrived to stay at home, saying it was to keep her grandmother company – and it was true that Léonie was growing weaker . . .

Since he had given up his practice, Doctor Fraysse could at last devote himself to those hobbies which forty-five years of professional life had prevented him pursuing. On market days, when the patients flocked in, he still sometimes helped his young colleague. Occasionally he was called to a difficult labour, or to treat a few obstinate old men who refused the attentions of the new practitioner and threatened to waste away if they were not cured by the 'real doctor'. But apart from these few cases, which allowed him to do some of the work he still loved, his time was his own and he made good use of it.

Late in life he had discovered a real vocation as a gardener, and out of the neglected patch in front of his house he had created a garden worthy of admiration. He was not content to grow vegetables in profusion, but joined beauty and utility by interplanting flowers between the rows of carrots, cabbages or leeks. His gladioli, zinnias, lupins and blue hydrangeas were the most beautiful in the village. As for his roses, they had furnished the ground for a cautious reconciliation, even a sort of friendship, with Father Feix. It was the old priest who had taught him the art of pruning and grafting the buds.

He could indulge in fishing too, his great passion. From now on he was free to spend a whole day, his fly-rod in his hand, wading up the Diamond, aiming his fly expertly at the foot of the big alder trees, where the trout hid among the roots. He was a fine fisherman, and amazingly knowledgeable about the habits of the salmon family; he would never have let anyone else concoct all the different sorts of artificial flies which he used according to the weather, the temperature and the season. It was a great joy to him to prepare a collection of flies – wet or dry.

He was an enthusiastic botanist, and his retirement allowed him to undertake the construction of a herb garden, something he had dreamed of since his youth. He collected the multitude of species which abounded in the region and classified them with great care, and added to them a collection of medicinal plants, a professional idiosyncrasy which greatly amused his young successor. These herbs, weighed and measured to the exact gramme, gave great pleasure to several old patients who preferred an infusion of poppies, juniper or yarrow to the medicine prescribed by Doctor Delpy.

He relished every second of all these pastimes, as well as the game of billiards he played against Antoine Gigoux every night at the inn. He was not one to be scared away by the invasion of the establishment by the railway men. He even took a certain amount of pleasure, tinged with nostalgia, in plunging into this rowdy atmosphere of Gauloises and coarse laughter, which reminded him of certain memorable evenings in his student life.

Besides, this daily visit enabled him to keep himself up to date with everything that happened in the community; the progress of the work, the health of several old acquaintances, the marriages and births.

Often, between sips of gentian bitters, he and the mayor would recall past times, vanished friends, those who had left. The teacher frequently came up in their conversation. He had retired about a year earlier and returned to his native Ussel; his departure was mourned by everyone, and deprived the two players of an agreeable partner.

A young couple fresh from college now occupied the school, and they were applying modern educational methods which lacked the paternal friendliness of the well-loved former teachers. Previously, when Monsieur Lanzac or his wife heard the children speaking dialect to each other, they merely interrupted them and suggested they use French. And when a pupil, at a loss for words, spoke of the 'burn', the 'cloggie' or the 'shippon' they would gently reprove him; 'Say the stream, the cobbler, the cowshed; that way everyone will understand you, even northerners!'

Now there was no question of the children getting away with such linguistic aberrations; the new teachers pretended not to understand the dialect, and fought against its use at every turn.

The mayor was delighted with their zeal, and equally appreciative of their political militancy. The doctor was less enthusiastic.

'They're too fanatical for me. Especially him; his political opinions are too blatant!'

'They're not fanatical, they're socialists!'

'And so what? So am I!'

'Oh! You . . .'

'Exactly! But I never mixed up my profession with my politics! I looked after everyone; Royalists, followers of General Boulanger, anarchists — even the good nuns! And I never tried to make them change their opinions. Whereas your two young ones, they manage to get politics into arithmetic!'

'Who told you that?'

'Come on, it's an open secret, everyone's talking about it! No, believe me, if you let them go on like that, they'll be more tyrannical than the priests, and that's saying something! You know me, I approved when we broke the power of the clergy; I hope I don't have to fight any secular despots in the future . . . Go on, it's your turn to play, and if you win this point, I pay for the game. But I think I'm safe . . .'

That afternoon in May the air was sweet, just right for a stroll. Doctor Fraysse set off down the path to the mill, walking slowly, on the look-out for a rare plant.

It was quite by chance, because his eye was drawn to a magnificent growth of stinking hellebore in the shade of the hedge, that he noticed Louise and Octave about thirty paces away.

They were seated on the other side of the meadow at the foot of a chestnut tree, ignoring the animals which grazed not far from them. The young people must have been speaking in low voices, for the doctor could hear nothing. He noted merely that they were sweetly holding hands, so he smiled and went his way without a sound.

It was only later, when he thought over the encounter, that his conscience troubled him. He knew Jean-Edouard well and regarded him highly, but he also knew what his reaction would be if he learned that Louise was letting the young assistant surveyor flirt with her.

As a good paterfamilias, Jean-Edouard kept his girls on a short rein and saw that no young fellows came hanging about around his house. Besides, everyone knew that neither Louise nor Berthe would be married to the first comer, such was the reputation and standing accorded by his land and livestock. They would make good marriages, and it was almost certain that, at least for the elder one, her father already had a plan in mind. There was no doubt that Octave Flaviens did not feature on the list of possible future sons-in-law! His situation was respectable but no more; worst of all he was a stranger to the area – and a townee to boot! – so the doors of the Vialhe house were definitely closed to him.

The doctor knew all this; he was fond of Louise, whom he had delivered, and the young Flaviens was likeable. He often played billiards with him, and although he found him rather lightweight, a little colourless, he judged him to be honest, hard-working and well-bred. So he worried about the future of these two young people.

His anxiety grew as the days passed, for several times, and without setting out to look for them, he saw the two lovers sitting in the same place, each time just as quiet and reserved. And it was this modest behaviour which made him realise that Louise's and Octave's feelings went far beyond a simple flirtation. Truly, if Octave were a commonplace seducer, he would have already arrived at his goal and achieved the conquest, or else Louise would have sent him packing long ago.

The doctor considered the matter, hesitated, weighed the pros and cons, then came to a decision and positioned himself one day on the path which Louise took to guide her animals to the grazing. As he had expected, the girl soon arrived behind her flock, chivying cows and ewes when they browsed too long on the edges of the path.

'Good day, Doctor!' she cried as soon as she saw him.

'Good day, Louise. Well, you're growing more and more beautiful. Almost a woman, aren't you?'

She blushed, smiled, and made to continue on her way.

'Wait,' he urged, 'leave the animals, they won't do any damage. You see, this is embarrassing for me, but I must speak to you, and please don't take it amiss. What I want to say is – Listen, Octave is a good boy and you're a good girl; I think it's charming that you meet each other. Don't deny it, I've seen you together . . .'

'We're not doing anything wrong!' she defended herself vehemently.

'I know. Anyway, that's not the problem. What you have to understand is that I have seen you. Of course, I haven't told anyone. But suppose someone else discovers you and tells your father all about it? He'll see red, you'll lose your good reputation and your Octave will have to leave at the double and think himself lucky if your father doesn't thrash him! Have you thought of all that?'

'We're not doing anything wrong,' she repeated, 'and it's not nice of you to spy on us!'

'Good God, you idiot girl, I don't give a damn what you do! What are you thinking of, you silly goose! I'm talking to you to save you trouble. Consider the gossip there'll be in the village if others get to hear of it!'

'We want to get married!' she raged back.

'You've spoken to your father about it?'

'No.'

'Why not?'

'He doesn't like Octave, and then . . . Well, he's got other plans for me,' she admitted, her eyes full of tears.

'Has he told you about them?'

'Not him; my mother has.'

'Who is it?'

'Léonard Bouyssoux.'

'Oh yes, him from Heath Farm . . .'

He knew the young man in question, and prevented himself from adding that he considered Léonard an absolute fool. Whatever Louise's plans were, Léonard Bouyssoux had the best chance of getting her to bed. Next to him, Octave did not count, at least in Jean-Edouard's eyes. She would doubtless be Bouyssoux's wife within two years, so it was pointless to tell her what he thought of her future husband . . .

'And you, of course, don't want that?'

'I'm going to marry Octave, and no one else!'

'Well, that's not my business. All I want you to understand is that you must take more care. Don't spoil everything by letting some gossip surprise you with jealous scandal-mongering. That's all I wanted to tell you, the rest is none of my business.'

He moved away and cut across the meadow to return to the village. It was then that he noticed Octave, concealing himself clumsily behind a clump of bushes. He ought to have gone to talk to him, but he shrugged his shoulders and continued on his way.

8

LÉONIE Malcroix, young Doctor Delpy's housekeeper, could not resist the pleasure of relaying the news. The story had been doing the rounds for some time, but no one had been able to guarantee its authenticity until that day. Léonie was very proud to capture the attention of all fifteen women who were working around the wash-house when she came to dip her linen in the fresh water of the big stone basin.

'This time, it's really happening!' she announced, as she untied the sheet which she had stuffed with her employer's hankies, shirts and underpants. 'Yes,' she continued, girding herself in an oil-cloth apron, 'he's gone to fetch it from Brive, he'll come back tonight with . . .'

'Pity us,' commented her neighbour, 'that's all we need!'

'Doctor Fraysse would never have entertained such an idea!' added another gossip. And all the housewives agreed.

No one disputed the young doctor's professional ability, nor his kindness, but many distrusted the new-fangled ideas which he expressed, and practised on the sick.

One of his latest fancies was to send some of them to a colleague in Brive who owned a mysterious and worrying machine. It seemed the patient was made to enter a sort of box – part metal, part glazed – which filled almost the whole of a small, dark room; the machine lit up suddenly with a glare which hurt the eyes, but it was said that it allowed you to see what illness the patient was suffering from. One of the fascinations of this mechanism was that it was absolutely painless. As for its usefulness, Doctor Delpy said it was marvellous. He maintained that it had already enabled him to save several people, and to reduce some complex fractures. All the same, old Doctor Fraysse had never felt the need for this cupboard-thing to treat people, and he had done it more cheaply!

Another of Doctor Delpy's ideas was that children should not spend too long in the cowsheds; that they should not rake out the dung, nor play with the animals, nor drink unboiled milk. To listen to him you would think they caught chills from goats, chest infections from cows and worms from dogs!

All that was easy for him to say, but who was going to look after the flocks if you started listening to rubbish like that? The children's work was to take the animals to the grazing, to watch them, to clean out the litter – exactly as their parents had done before them, and they weren't dead yet!

Doctor Delpy had other fads of that kind; he maintained that the brandy given to children when they had an attack of worms could poison them, even kill them! As if half a glass of liquor mixed with a good spoonful of fresh soot could harm anyone, if it was taken on the first day of the new moon! A good plum brandy was certainly less dangerous than the doctor's latest eccentricity – the acquisition of an automobile, which, according to Léonie Malcroix, would make its debut in St Libéral that very evening.

A motor vehicle had already passed through the village. Its arrival had created panic at first, to the great satisfaction of the madman driving it, one of the company engineers. The monstrous machine, in which four people were imprisoned, had climbed the main street, and none of the bystanders would be quick to forget the infernal noise, the clouds of dust it raised, the confusion and fear aroused as it passed, among humans as well as animals.

Luckily, the monster had simply dashed through. It had been seen taking the road to Ayen at mind-boggling speed, vanishing as quickly as it had appeared. It had not been seen again, and no sensible person wished for its return.

Only a few thoughtless young people were happy about the doctor's purchase, looking forward to, if not sitting in the vehicle, at least the opportunity to touch it, to look at it, to admire it. Pierre-Edouard was one of these scatter-brains who approved, and professed themselves proud to belong to a village which was going to have a car.

Nevertheless, almost all the villagers, whether for or against, happened to find themselves in small groups in the main square that evening when an urchin, sent out as a scout, arrived at the gallop and warned them that he had heard the machine breasting the last rise. Instinctively all the gawpers moved away from the road, left the verges empty, ranged themselves against the houses or around the trees; some cautious ones even climbed onto the steps of the Mairie, while others sheltered under the church porch.

And suddenly, the noise was there. Every eye was on the turning from which the engine would emerge. First of all came a dog; maddened and trembling, it shot into the square in a crazy zigzag race, stopped for an instant and then, with rounded back and tail between its legs, plunged into an alley. Then the automobile appeared.

Magnificent! Red coachwork with silver edges, long copper bonnet, enormous lamps and gold velvet up-holstery, it throbbed with a final deep-throated roar which seemed to propel it into the centre of the square, where it stopped, surrounded by fumes and smoke, but silent at last.

Doctor Delpy took off his goggles, pushed back his helmet with ear-flaps, so that it hung around his neck, unbuttoned his heavy coat and jumped down to the ground. They were astonished to see him so dashing, so alert, not at all disturbed by his experience. He took out his pocket-watch, did a quick calculation, and smiled.

'Fifty-two minutes from Brive, you can't do better than that! And of course I lost a lot of time because of the construction work!' he threw out as an aside.

He added more, but the words were lost in the general hubbub. Already he was surrounded by enthusiasts, who questioned him excitedly, silencing the grumblers and old fogeys who beat a retreat, still moaning and prophesying dire calamities.

The triumphant doctor replied graciously to the multitude of questions, gave all the technical details, and expounded on the exceptional performance of his Renault. He even invited the mayor and Doctor Fraysse to take a seat, and gave them a lap of honour. The manoeuverability of the machine, its responsiveness, the security provided by its brakes – it was all delightful.

As the inquisitive villagers slipped away one by one to their various tasks, they were succeeded later in the evening by the railway company workers. They glanced at the vehicle without interest. For them an automobile was not a rare beast; they had seen others, and better ones too! One of them was so disrespectful as to press the fat bulb of the horn, which emitted a piteous cry.

'It's time to put it away; these fellows are so cheeky, they're capable of starting it!' remarked Doctor Delpy, emptying his aperitif glass.

He bade goodbye to the major and Doctor Fraysse, who were sitting with him on the terrace of the inn, turned the motor with a firm hand and set off.

'Well, it really is fantastic, progress,' commented Antoine Gigoux. 'Just think, St Libéral with a car! Who would have believed that ten years ago!'

'You'll have to get used to it; there'll soon be another one,' predicted Doctor Fraysse.

'Are you going to buy one?'

'You must be joking! At my age! Besides, what use would it be to me? No, but I bet you an aperitif that our squire will want to keep up with the times. Just wait till he comes back from holiday and you'll see . . .'

And sure enough, one evening six weeks later Jean Duroux entered the village at the wheel of a Panhard and Levassor sparkling with chrome. But only a few boys rushed to admire it. The adults did not react; they were accustomed to cars.

All summer the Vialhes worked non-stop to keep up their productivity, and it was a good growing season. The first sales of vegetables were already beginning to repay them for their perseverance.

Jean-Edouard and his son maintained an inhuman work-rate for several months. Caught between haymaking, reaping, picking the plums and delivering them to Objat, hoeing and collecting the various crops, the two men lived only to work. They rarely slept more than a few hours at night, only occasionally allowed themselves a quarter of an hour siesta, and they even broke the Sabbath – greatly scandalising Father Feix – unable to rest until they had done their all to make each square metre produce its maximum.

Exhausted and dazed, they often went whole days without speaking to each other; the only words they addressed to the women, when they came to help, were to demand food or drink, or to indicate the pressing tasks to be accomplished.

At last September came, and with it harvest time. They could slacken their pace then, and take a breather. Of course the potato-digging would take many more days, but they were encouraged by the certainty that their crops were no longer in danger; that the money was there under the faded potato-haulms, in the dry bean-pods, in the abundant rows of vegetables.

Until that moment they had feared the worst, worried about everything – drought and hail, floods, disease, parasites, all the natural disasters they could do nothing to prevent. Now, since the heavens had spared them, since they had only to bend down to collect the reward of their sweated labour, they could at last allow themselves a few moments respite, a more human life style, and a more balanced rhythm of work. They could also resume contact with the life of the village, and pause to chat with neighbours once more.

Jean-Edouard's ideas had excited great jealousy, but now admiration and esteem grew, as many saw the considerable amount of work accomplished by the Vialhes. A few neighbours even came to help them occasionally during the course of the summer; just like that, spontaneously, for an hour or two, to show that they were happy and proud to be on good terms with the most courageous and astute farmer in the commune, with the one who had first understood that the railway could bring prosperity.

Some even took the opportunity to try to get Jean-Edouard to disclose his plans; that was a waste of time! He certainly had an idea, but he would not reveal it. However, it was obvious that as soon as the next growing season began many farmers would launch into the cultivation of vegetables and attempt to dispose of their produce at the company canteens. But they all knew that if there were too many practising this system there would be a slump. Well, how could they prevent over-production?

'Miladiou, you can tell *me*, can't you?' said Jeantout, when he came one evening to hoe with Jean-Edouard.

'If I tell you, it'll be all over the place!'

'But I won't say a word! Besides, it's not me that's going to compete with you; I haven't got enough land, as well you know!'

'I'm not stopping anyone having ideas, doing the same as me . . .'

'You want to make me think you're going to plant the same crops? Do you take me for a fool? Next year Pierre-Edouard will be in the army; you couldn't grow that much all by yourself!'

'We'll see . . .'

'That's right, and when we see, it'll be too late to copy you and queer your pitch!'

'Possibly . . .'

'You're a bloody swine!' commented Jeantout. But his tone was so admiring that this could not be taken as an insult.

Eventually Jean-Edouard overheard two or three comments at the inn and learned that his daughter was spending time with Octave Flaviens; he was so tired by the last months of work, so drained, that even he was surprised at his own reaction.

Most of the village already knew. The two young people had been seen making eyes at each other in all the corners best-known for their supposed seclusion. Their latest nest was one of the caves which opened on to the old mine cutting, probably where he had once sheltered from the storm with Gaston and Jeanout, that half-collapsed tunnel where lovers took refuge, all naively believing the sanctuary was known only to them. 'But,' as Gaston said, 'if I could find as many gold napoléons as virgins had been deflowered in that hole, I'd be as rich as Rockefeller!'

Contrary to the general expectation, Jean-Edouard did not explode into one of his customary rages, but his suppressed anger was no less terrible. He returned home, went about his business without a word, and waited for dinner-time.

When the whole family was seated at the table, he served the soup as usual and began to eat. It was only after he had mixed some wine with his bouillon, drunk it to the last drop and wiped his moustache on the back of his arm, that his enormous hand came down on Louise's shoulder and transfixed her, whilst the other hand, the open palm shining and lined with callouses, smashed against her cheek.

'That'll teach you to run around! And that,' he added, striking once more, 'is to remind you that we don't like sluts! And now, get your things together. Tomorrow I'm taking you to Tulle, to your cousins. They'll make you work, that will keep you busy! You can come back when I've sent that little upstart of a spear-carrier packing, and believe me, that won't take long . . .'

Louise rushed from the table and took refuge in the bedroom. The door slammed behind her, and they heard the sound of the key hastily turned.

'What's going on?' stammered Marguerite, surprised by the speed of events and disturbed by her husband's icy calm.

'What's going on is that you don't look after your daughter properly — she's been running after that miserable little surveyor for months!'

'And you think that . . .' murmured Marguerite, completely devastated.

'I don't know anything at the moment, but I'll find out tonight.'

'And if by any chance she were . . .'

'We'll deal with that.'

'No,' Marguerite tried to reassure herself, 'I don't believe there's any harm done . . . I would have noticed, I know about these things . . .'

'What's she done?' asked old Léonie. She had become completely deaf, and did not understand what the scene was about.

Jean-Edouard did not bother to reply, but looked at his second daughter.

'What are you laughing at?'

'I knew about it, I did!' crowed Berthe.

She did not have time to dodge the awful blow which threw her against her brother.

'That's to teach you to connive with her,' growled her father. 'And so you know what to expect as well, in case you were by any chance thinking of copying your sister some day. And you, did you know too?' he shouted at his son.

'If you think I've had time to bother about that . . .' replied Pierre-Edouard, without lowering his eyes.

'I asked whether you knew!'

'Yes, and so what?' For the first time in his life, Pierre-Edouard openly defied his father. For a moment Jean-Edouard was powerless, then he recovered and clenched his fists fiercely.

'My God! So you don't care if she disgraces herself with that squirt? You don't care if everyone laughs at us? Well, answer me, in God's name!'

'No one laughs in front of me,' stated Pierre-Edouard quietly, 'and I don't see what disgrace there would be if Louise married Octave . . .'

Jean-Edouard was nonplussed, stunned by the calm way his son had just expressed such a stupid, incredible hypothesis that it left him speechless.

'But . . . but you're raving!' he mumbled at last. 'There's no question of that happening; have you gone mad or something?'

He poured himself a glass of wine, which he emptied in one go, then pushed back his plate and got up.

'Good God! Just wait while I have a word with that little beast,' he snarled as he marched towards the door. 'Marry her! I swear you *must* have gone mad!'

He went out into the night.

Jean-Edouard threaded his way between the drinkers, managed to make a space for himself at the bar, and ordered a plum brandy. The inn was packed, full of shouting workers and merry-makers pressed around the tables where players were laying down their cards.

At the billiard table Octave Flaviens and Doctor Fraysse were quietly playing a game, oblivious to the uproar around them.

Jean-Edouard leant towards the barmaid. 'Go and tell the doctor I would like to see him, and I'm waiting for him outside.' He paid for his drink, emptied his glass in one gulp and went out.

All that crowd confused him, and made the scheme he had in mind useless. In his plan, he entered an almost deserted inn, caught the fellow by the ear, sent him out with a kick up his backside and gave him ten minutes to pack his bag; all this punctuated by a few slaps around the face, not to mention a cuff or two round the head, and the matter was sorted out!

But the thirty or so drinkers gathered in the saloon put that out of the question. He was not going to make a spectacle of himself, become a laughing stock in front of strangers! Besides, a good number of them were capable of taking the lad's side, just for a laugh.

'What's the matter?' asked the doctor as he joined him.

'I'd like you to tell that little brat with you to come and see me.'

The doctor took a long puff on his cigar, and its glowing

end lit up his worried face. 'People have been telling you things . . .'

'You're damn right they have!'

'You're not going to make a fool of yourself?'

'I'll do what I have to do! Would you please tell that fellow to come here, I have a few words to say to him . . .'

'Okay, but I'm coming out with him. I don't trust you and your words . . .'

He went back into the inn, leaving Jean-Edouard even more furious at the certain knowledge that everyone knew about his daughter's misconduct. The proof was that the doctor had immediately understood.

'You want to see me?'

The young man's confident voice surprised him; it was not that of a guilty man caught in the act.

'Yes, and I've a good mind to smash your face to teach you to respect my daughter!' he shouted, advancing on Octave.

'Let him speak!' ordered the doctor, stepping between them.

'First of all,' retorted Octave, 'I would ask you not use "tu" to me, we are not related in any way. Secondly, if you touch me, I shall be forced to lay a charge, and I have a witness. Finally, I would like to take advantage of this opportunity to assure you that I have never shown any disrespect towards your daughter.'

'Good God, don't take that tone with me! You've been seen together, and I know where too!'

'And so what? Talking isn't forbidden, nor dishonourable!'

'That's what you say, and I know how it ends up! Well listen carefully – either you get out of here, and right now, or I'll lay charges myself! My daughter's a minor, I have the law on my side. You'll see how we get rid of hangers-on!'

'You're being absolutely stupid,' the doctor intervened. 'Anyone would think you wanted to make yourself a laughing stock!'

'You go back to your flowers and leave me in peace; I know what I'm doing!'

'No, you don't know anything! There's no law preventing two young people from talking to each other, and you have no rights over Monsieur Flaviens!'

'Except the right to thrash him if I see him around Louise, is that clear?'

'Listen,' said Octave, 'I don't know what I've done to you, and it doesn't matter now. But I would like to give you a warning too: I'll wait as long as I have to, until she comes of age if necessary, but I shall marry Louise.'

'Well, you could wait for ever for that, you little squirt!' yelled Jean-Edouard. He was about to rush at the younger man, then he controlled himself and strode away.

*

Marguerite was waiting for him, sitting by the fireside. He noticed her eyes reddened with tears and the damp handkerchief held tightly in her hands.

'Well?' she asked feebly.

'Oh, the filthy beast!' he growled. 'Where are the children?'

'Pierre's gone off to sleep in the barn. He left his bed for Berthe – she couldn't get into the bedroom, Louise had locked the door. She's only just opened it.'

He approached the corner of the room where the bed was tucked away, and bent over Berthe. 'Are you asleep?'

'Leave her,' interrupted his wife.

'Yes, it doesn't matter if she does hear; she'll learn from it,' he said, coming back to the settle.

'Well?' asked Marguerite again.

'How should I know!' he growled, angrily poking the smouldering logs.

'You want to take her to Tulle?'

'Yes, at least there she won't see him any more.'

'Our cousins will have a good laugh . . .'

'We don't have to tell them the whole story. I'll say that she asked to go away somewhere . . .'

'And why should she do that?'

'Because she can't step into the street any more without being whistled at by all the ruffians from the railway company! Because every evening they come around the house making a racket, that's why!'

Marguerite, unconvinced, shook her head and began to cry silently. She was sure that their relatives would not be deceived; that they would laugh at her expense, only too happy at this turn of events.

These cousins were fruit and vegetable merchants, grander and richer than the Vialhes; they behaved in a crushingly superior manner whenever they met, which was only once or twice a year. They kept on good terms despite that, but Marguerite was convinced that her cousin had no love for her; that she was jealous that Marguerite had three fine children while she herself was childless.

'Stop blubbering!' he ordered. 'It's decided.'

'And what about him, what did he say?'

'Don't talk to me about that worm – I think I'd have knocked him out cold if the doctor hadn't been there!'

'He knows? Him as well?' she moaned.

'You bet! Him and everyone else! That little slut has dragged us into an ugly situation. Oh, the little baggage! If ever old man Bouyssoux hears about it! And he certainly will . . . But I'll go and see him, as soon as possible. The best thing would be to bring the wedding forward a bit. But not too much, we don't want people to start talking. I think Easter would be a good time, what do you think?'

'Yes, that would be fine. I haven't finished the trousseau, but after all . . .'

'What a good thing we found out before that little turd touched her! Think back, could she be . . .'

'Don't say that! No, no, she can't have . . . It's not possible, she wouldn't have done that to us, in any case!'

'Then she really would have been in trouble! Good,' he said, getting up. 'Tulle tomorrow, old Bouyssoux the day after, and the wedding in six months. And while we're waiting, let's go to bed.'

'Don't hit her again,' begged Marguerite, 'your cousins will see the marks . . .'

He shrugged, and went into the bedroom. He marched towards his daughter's bed, carrying the oil-lamp at arm's length, and noticed with satisfaction that she had obeyed him: her bundle was ready.

'I know you're not asleep. Well listen. All this, I'm doing it for your own good, in six months you'll thank me for it. And now go to sleep, we'll have to take the six o'clock train to La Rivière. I'll explain to you tomorrow what we're going to tell our relatives.'

Pierre-Edouard watched the moving rays of the oil-lamp until they showed that his parents were in their bedroom, then he slipped out of the stable and set off down the main street.

Despite the late hour there were still many drinkers in the bar of the inn, but none paid any attention to his arrival. A glance around showed him that Octave Flaviens was not there; without hesitating he climbed the stairway which led to the bedrooms, walked to the door of number seven and knocked.

'What is it?' grunted Octave.

'I've come on behalf of Louise,' whispered Pierre-Edouard.

He heard bare feet slapping on the tiles, then the lock grated and a hand half opened the door.

'Oh, it's you!' murmured Octave, raising his lamp to face-level. 'Come in. You must excuse me, I was already in bed.'

He was rigged out in a shirt which stopped at mid-thigh and revealed lank, hairy legs; he looked a bit ridiculous, and Pierre-Edouard wondered how his sister could be in love with a man like that. Without his well-cut clothes, which set him off to advantage, he looked weak and puny, almost pitiful. 'He's as thin as a green woodpecker,' thought Pierre-Edouard. 'One blow from Father would smash off his head.'

'Well?' asked Octave, sitting down on the edge of the unmade bed. He felt around on the bedside table, picked up his box of cigars and held it out. 'Do you smoke?'

Pierre-Edouard helped himself, and contemplated the man for whom his sister had risked so much; he felt a surge of pity at his weakness and dishevelment. He felt so strong in contrast to Octave, so powerful that he almost felt the need to protect him, to comfort and help him as he would a younger brother.

'Well?' asked Octave again.

'My father is taking her to Tulle tomorrow morning, to our cousins. They live in Rue de la Barrière, you can't miss it. They're fruit-merchants, it's written on the house.'

'What went on at your place?'

'It wasn't too bad.'

'Did he hit her?'

'Not much, just a cuff or two. Nothing really . . .'

'You think that's nothing?' broke in Octave. 'Two blows! And . . . after that, she didn't run away!'

'Run away? And where would you want her to go? Besides, if she'd done that I wouldn't give much for her chances when father found her!'

'Don't say that! And what else did she say to you then?'

'Well, not much; she spoke to me out of the window, and it was difficult, because our mother might have heard. Just . . . she'll expect to see you in Tulle, that's all . . .'

'Of course,' murmured Octave, rolling his cigar between his fingers. 'Tell me, do you really think your father would be opposed to our marriage?'

'I rather think so, yes.'

'But why?'

'He has other plans, I believe . . .' Pierre-Edouard evaded. 'But then, perhaps you'd better know,' he expanded suddenly. 'He wants her to get married at Easter, I heard just now; I was listening at the door.'

'Get married? But this is barbarous! We're not in the Middle Ages! She has a right to some say in the matter, after all!'

'Huh! It's the custom,' explained Pierre-Edouard, shrugging his shoulders. 'Right, now it's time I went back.'

'She didn't say anything else?'

'Yes, she sends you a kiss . . .' admitted Pierre-Edouard, very embarrassed to relay such a message.

'Will you see her again before she leaves?'

'Yes, but she'll be with Father, so . . .'

'Too bad. Thank you for coming,' said Octave, holding out his hand. 'I'd like to say that I think we'll get on very well, when we're brothers-in-law.'

Pierre-Edouard shook the hand that was offered but kept quiet. Brothers-in-law? That certainly wasn't the road he saw them going!

9

DESPITE Marguerite's fears, the relatives in Tulle did not seem to suspect the real reasons which forced Jean-Edouard to entrust his daughter to them. In fact, they were overwhelmed with work, hardly had time to ask questions, and were also undoubtedly delighted to take on an extra employee at little cost to themselves.

And Louise played the part to perfection, according to her father's instructions. She was lively and smiling and deceived everyone with amazing ease; she declared she was delighted to get away from the unpleasant atmosphere in St Libéral for a while, and glad to work with her cousins.

Jean-Edouard was not entirely taken in, but he was somewhat reassured. He convinced himself that his daughter would eventually be beaten at her own game: her false cheerfulness would soon be followed by the eclipse of this silly love-affair. As night fell he reached St Libéral in high good humour, happy to have resolved so satisfactorily – and with all necessary speed – the problem which he had only taken in hand twenty-four hours earlier.

To close the matter finally, he went into the inn even before going home; he ordered an absinthe and asked to see the young assistant surveyor. It was very satisfying to hear from the landlady that Octave had left that same morning: from now on he would be staying at the hotel in La-Rivière-de-Mansac.

'He was a proper gentleman,' sighed the landlady, 'I'm sorry he's gone. Aren't you?' she asked, with an ironic smile which annoyed him.

'He'll be closer to his work,' he retorted. 'That'll be better for him. And for everyone . . .'

Old Bouyssoux made him wait on the doorstep before

inviting him in. Standing at the foot of the steps, they first discussed the weather, the crops, the flocks, the year in general, the condition of the vines, and the start of the hunting season.

Bouyssoux complained of his aches and pains, and envied the youth and health of his visitor; twelve years older, he abused the privilege of age quite shamelessly. What's more, he knew all about the reasons behind this approach, and took great pleasure in testing Jean-Edouard's patience.

'Now, come on in,' he said at last. 'You're in luck, I'm all alone; we won't be interrupted. My wife and son are picking potatoes. I can't bend any more, my back . . .'

They sat down at the table and the old man filled their glasses.

'It's like this,' said Jean-Edouard. 'I've come back to see what you think of the idea I mentioned to you last spring . . .'

The old man slowly rolled a cigarette and stuck it under his grey moustache.

'Well,' he said, 'it's okay with me, but it's my son . . .'

'How do you mean, your son?'

'Well . . . there's been talk in the village; living out here, we don't know exactly what's going on.'

'I've sorted that matter out.'

'That's what I heard,' agreed the old man, happy to demonstrate that news reached him very quickly in spite of the three kilometres which separated him from the village. 'Yes, that's what I heard . . . But you have to understand my Léonard. He's a serious fellow, and very proper. He wouldn't like to take on a brat that didn't belong to him . . .'

'My God!' Jean-Edouard pounded his fist on the table in fury. 'That's not how the Vialhes behave! And you know it!'

'Well I know that your daughter hasn't been very wise . . . You got her out of that, it's true, and that's good. The other little suitor has gone off to rub up against someone else, that's good too . . . But how are you going to prove to me that a third thief hasn't already taken his place, eh?'

'I forbid you to talk like that!' shouted Jean-Edouard, leaping up. 'If you're going to take it like that, you can tell your son to find another girl! I'll keep my daughter, she won't be losing much!'

'Don't sound off like that! What I've been saying, it's just to make sure . . . And when were you thinking of for this marriage?'

Jean-Edouard pretended to reflect on it; he emptied his glass, it was his turn to roll a cigarette. Bouyssoux waited. He passed the time by calculating how many months ahead Vialhe would risk setting it; he had come to an understanding with his son on a date beyond which, if there were a birth, it would be impossible to withdraw without dishonour.

'I talked to my wife,' he said at last. 'We thought it would be fine if we had it – well, let's say at Easter. Is that all right with you?'

'In God's name, why couldn't you have said that earlier! If it's at Easter, you must be sure of your daughter! Well, why did you let me go on talking, eh?'

'Just to see what sort of stories are being spread about us, and to prove to you that the Vialhes have always been respectable.'

'Okay,' grumbled the old one, cross at being lectured. 'And as a dowry?'

Once more, Jean-Edouard pretended to reflect.

'As dowry, first of all she has a full trousseau,' he said as he lit his cigarette with exasperating slowness. 'And then I'll give her . . . Now, let's say . . . eight thousand francs.'

'Phew!' exclaimed the old man, surprised at the size of the sum. 'So it's true you're making all that money with the railway company!' He nodded, but continued very quickly: 'Eight thousand francs, that's good, but for land?'

'No land.'

'How's that, no land? We'll see about that!'

'Nothing, not a single square metre. The land – that's not to be divided, that's to be kept; you won't see any of the Vialhes' plots given to anyone outside the family in a hurry! The trousseau, eight thousand francs, the girl;

nothing more. And, for your part, how do you propose to set up the young people?'

'Well, I . . . The boy will get everything, one day, he's an only child . . .'

'One day, yes, but what about now?'

'Bah, we'll manage something . . .'

'No, no,' insisted Jean-Edouard, now that he was confident of success. 'It must be arranged beforehand, and in front of a solicitor. I'd like my son-in-law to have land in his own name, and animals of his own and some implements too!'

'Oh, oh! How you do go on! I'm not going to move out into the barn! *You* give them some land!'

'Never. It's staying in the Vialhe name. Come on, let's see what you're going to put in the basket for them . . .'

They argued for another two hours and finally agreed. Everything was arranged down to the smallest detail, and it was even accepted that Louise would spend two months in Tulle; time for her to forget, and to prove to everyone that there was no reason for hurrying.

When she returned, Léonard could come and court her. He would call on his intended for almost three months, which was perfectly proper and would silence all the malicious tongues. Then would come the wedding, and Jean-Edouard would do everything to make it one of the finest in the area.

Jean-Edouard took the situation in hand with such speed and energy that the laughter changed to respect; those who, three days earlier, had been telling jokes behind his back were the first to admit that he managed his family with as much intelligence and astuteness as he cared for his farm.

The admiration reached its peak in the weeks that followed, as he was seen each day coming down from the plateau with carts full of superb potatoes. Incredible rumours circulated about the weight of the crop sold to the railway company, and the amount of money this represented.

He let them talk, convinced that it was better to be envied than pitied. But, contrary to what his neighbours thought, he did not dispose of all his potatoes to the steward. He sorted them and kept several tons of the poorer ones; this reserve stock was part of his plan of action for the year to come.

At the end of October, with all the crops in, he ploughed his fields and sowed them with cereals. People were slightly amazed, but pleased to see him give up his vegetable production, and grateful to him for giving his fellow farmers the chance to try their luck in his place.

'And after all,' said a few jealous souls, 'he's made enough this year! Besides, when his son goes, he's going to be virtually on his own, what else could he do?'

But those who knew him well recognised that he was planning a new project. It was quickly executed, and once more took everyone by surprise. Of course everyone had been asking questions since the beginning of November; that was when Jean-Edouard, his son, the carpenter and two labourers began erecting a huge lean-to shed against the barn wall. At first the neighbours thought that Vialhe was putting up a tobacco drying-shed, but his fields, covered in oats, wheat and barley, destroyed this hypothesis. It was Jeantout who was the first to understand.

'You old devil, I see what you're up to,' he said, after examining the building. 'How many are you going to put in it? Go on, you can say it, nobody can compete with you!'

'You guessed it then, this time?'

'By Our Lady . . . oh, I should have thought of it earlier, I knew you wouldn't rest on your laurels. It doesn't matter, the idea is fantastic. But with that amount of space you're going to keep a bloody horde of them!'

'Forty here, thirty there,' explained Jean-Edouard, indicating with his head. 'And over there I'll have room for six sows and the boar.'

'Got to think it out and be brave enough to do it,' commented Jeantout.

'Well, yes! This year vegetables, next year pigs.'

'And the company will buy them from you?'

'You bet! You don't think I'm going into this blind, do you?'

No, Jeantout did not think that. He was sure his neighbour had worked it all out in advance.

'And when are you going to begin?'

'Now. For a start I'm going to buy forty young porkers at the next fair in Brive, plus six breeding sows and a male, and after that I'll rotate my stock.'

'But that's going to take a lot of feeding!'

'That's been thought of,' said Jean-Edouard, walking to a shed. 'See here,' he said as he opened the door.

Jeantout looked at the huge pile of turnips and beets, and whistled in admiration.

'Yes, with all that, you've got something to start with. But after that, what will they eat, in the summer?'

'What rubbish you talk; my cereal crops, of course! And then – listen, and I'll tell you what's going to happen. You're all going to grow spuds next year and a whole heap of vegetables. The railway company won't be able to take it all, there'll be too much of everything . . .'

'And then what?' asked a worried Jeantout.

'Then you'll be quite happy to sell me your surplus for the same price the catering manager would give you. Believe me, my pigs aren't going to die of hunger. The steward has promised me all the left-overs from his kitchens, as well.'

'You're a cheeky devil,' muttered Jeantout enviously. 'My God, you'll earn hundreds and thousands again, and we get damn all . . .'

'I'm not stealing from anyone,' said Jean-Edouard drily.

'Well no, but . . .'

'But what?'

'Nothing . . . So you think it's not worth planting spuds? There'll be too many?'

'Listen,' Jean-Edouard lowered his voice, 'you do what you want, but if I were you, I'd lay off the potatoes and the rest. There's only one thing I'd grow . . .'

'What? Well, tell me, dammit!'

'Yes, and then you'll talk about it, and everyone will copy you, and then you'll come whining to me again!'

'Are you mad? Go on, say it, what is it?'

'Salad stuff.'

'Salad? You're making fun of me!' cried Jeantout, who was quite plainly disappointed in his friend.

'All right, do what you like, but don't come and complain afterwards! This year, I could have sold twenty times more than I'd grown. You have no idea how much salad they eat in the summer, no idea. I couldn't supply enough, not by a long way, even though I had a bloody great square of it planted!'

'Basically, it's not so stupid, but I'd have to be sure I could get rid of it . . .'

'If that's the only problem, I'll speak to the catering manager.'

'You'd do that?'

'Why not?'

'Oh well, then . . .' muttered Jeantout in an embarrassed way. 'Listen,' he said suddenly, 'I have to tell you, there are plenty of us who've had it up to our eyes with the mayor and his son. He's too old and his lad is too bloody stupid. So, next time, it's you we're counting on, you know that?'

Jean-Edouard hid his satisfaction with a shrug.

'We'll see . . . What's definite is that with the railway we'll need a mayor who stirs himself to bring a bit of life into this community . . . I've got some ideas about that too, believe me . . . We'll talk about it another time. But for the moment, you mustn't say anything, it's too early, the elections are too far away. But don't worry, I'll do the right thing when the time comes . . . As I'm sure I can trust you to do,' said Jeantout, contemplating the new pig-unit.

For the first three days Louise thought she would go mad, and she had to call on her reserves of energy and willpower so as not to break down. To avoid thinking too much, she threw herself completely into the work, and astonished her relatives with her strength, courage and ability.

The apple and walnut season was at its height. She very

quickly learned to sort the apples according to size and quality and to line them up in their boxes; as soon as they were closed and labelled they were sent off to Paris, Lyons and even London. She did not balk at bleaching the nuts, and burnt her hands mixing the fruit in baths of chlorinated water to remove marks of dirt or mildew.

In the beginning the dozen employees who worked for the wholesaler regarded the new arrival with a jaundiced eye; her relationship with the bosses made her suspect, and conversations stopped when she approached. In less than two days, Louise had won over all her working companions. Without quite understanding why she was there, without recognising her as one of them, the workers still appreciated her company, approved of her good manners, and laughed at her jokes. None of them guessed that she was always on the point of bursting into tears and that her shouts of laughter masked sobs.

Her cousins were kind to her and, having no reason to distrust her, left her completely free to wander the town as she pleased during the infrequent breaks from work. Of course it went without saying that she was not allowed out after nightfall; this was an unnecessary instruction, as she had no desire to go out then.

At last the long-awaited Sunday arrived. Even though she had not been able to arrange anything, nor to speak to Octave, she felt certain that this day would not pass without him appearing. She did not know where or how he would give a sign of life, but she was sure he would succeed in getting news to her.

During busy periods her cousins worked on Sunday mornings. Nevertheless, because they knew the Vialhes' religious convictions, they promised her that she could take her day of rest; besides, her aunt would also take an hour off to go and hear Mass, and it would be a pleasure to accompany her to the Cathedral.

She got up early, mad with impatience, dressed and did her hair with great care. She had not brought many things in the bundle she had put together in such haste on the night of the row, but she did possess a black skirt finely edged with lace, new stockings and an attractive pale blue blouse; she cleaned her sabots and polished their pale leather straps.

When she was ready she mooched about the house, aimlessly waiting for the time of the church service. She didn't dare go into the depot, where her cousins were working with four or five women who had volunteered in order to earn a few extra sous; so she pushed open the door and went out into the street.

It looked such a beautiful day, a wave of bitterness rose in her heart. In weather like this it would be a joy to go and mind the animals in the warm hours of the afternoon, to sit down at the foot of a chestnut tree and, in feverish anticipation, to watch the path by which Octave would arrive. Why hadn't they listened to the doctor and been more circumspect! She almost began to cry, and realised that only the presence of witnesses would strengthen her self-control. She went into the depot, kissed her cousins, greeted the workers, made a joke and even began sorting apples.

'Leave that,' said her aunt, 'you'll get yourself all dirty. We're about to go now anyway.'

'All right, I'll wait for you outside.'

She was proud of having overcome that crisis of despair, and went out singing.

*

Louise was greatly impressed by the ceremony of the High Mass. Used to the little church of Saint-Libéral, she was amazed by the immense nave, the iridescent cloth of the celebrant's chasuble; by the red-and-white surplices of the six choirboys, the richness of the chandeliers and the candlesticks resplendent with enormous candles. She started at the first thunderous chord of the great organ, and her bewilderment made her aunt smile beside her.

It was as she turned round furtively to see whence this flood of music gushed that she saw him. He was there, just behind her. She mastered the impulse to hold out her hand, controlled herself in time, but felt herself turn pale and forced herself to stare at the back of the priest bending over the altar.

She was deliriously happy to know that he was there, but, wondering how she could meet and talk to him, she did not really follow the remainder of the service; if she complied with the movements, the genuflexions, the signs of the cross and responses, it was purely out of habit.

So, for her sake, he had come to take part in the Mass. She felt overwhelmed with gratitude, for on this point they were completely divided. She had been terribly upset when Octave had declared that he did not believe in God or the Devil; she could not understand how he, who was so intelligent, so good, could call himself an atheist.

'Take note, Louise, that I am not forcing anyone to agree with my point of view. I am in favour of liberty. You're free to believe whatever you like, so don't bother about my ideas.'

This tolerance had lessened her sorrow, but she secretly promised herself that she would reform his opinions. In any case he had assured her that, to please her, he would in principle accept a religious marriage, and he had no objection to the baptism of their children.

'I was baptised and it didn't kill me, so do what seems best to you for our little ones. But, as for me, I don't see what I'd do at a Mass!'

And yet he was there. She sensed him behind her back and noted from the sound of his chair that he was rising and kneeling at the correct moments.

'Are you coming?' asked her aunt, touching her arm. She jumped, realised that Mass was over, and panicked at the idea of having to leave again without having spoken to him.

'If you would permit it,' she whispered, 'I'd like to look around the cathedral . . .'

'Of course; you'll get back alone all right. See you soon.'

She was amazed to have found an alibi so easily, and remained seated in her chair for a few moments without daring to move. At last she turned round. Octave was still there, standing, impeccably dressed, apparently deeply immersed in an act of prayer. He lowered his head imperceptibly to greet her, then whispered: 'You go out first, I'll join you . . .'

She obeyed like a sleep-walker; emerged on to the courtyard and made an effort to admire the stained glass window at the entrance.

'Come,' he said, as he rejoined her, 'let's walk on the embankment.'

'And what if we're seen together?'

'We're not in Saint-Libéral. Here two people in love are not forbidden to be together. Come on, let's walk, you're not in any danger.'

She smiled at him and held out her hand.

Father Feix knocked his clogs against the steps to remove the sticky earth, and pushed the door of the presbytery open. Despite the damp cold of this late November morning, he had just spent two hours digging a large bed in his garden, and he was aching all over.

He went up to the fire, which was almost out, and stretched out his swollen fingers in their worn mittens to the embers. He moved the logs closer, worked the bellows, made the flames spring up and lifted his cassock to try to warm his legs. Bu he knew really that nothing would rid his body of these recurring attacks of pins and needles which ceaselessly and coldly reminded him that he was old, worn out, miserable.

Of course Doctor Fraysse gave him some pills from time to time, recommended infusions or herbal teas, but neither of them was convinced that these treatments had any effect.

Father Feix felt that his time was up and that his years – perhaps even months – were numbered. He did not rebel against it, did not complain, continued his ministry as best he could; but sometimes, when weariness overcame him, he began to wish secretly that death would release him. What good did it do to try and manage a church in the heart of a community which no longer recognised it!

Everything was changing too fast, evolving in a

direction which he felt was wrong. The village had become a sink of debauchery where the railway-workers crowded in and got drunk. There was dancing on Saturday nights until three o'clock in the morning, the licensees were making fortunes, and, although the village had at first cold-shouldered the strangers, more than half the inhabitants were now doing business with them. Already the young people were daring to patronise the inn and they danced too, girls and boys, until all hours . . .

And what could one do about that, since everyone seemed to enjoy this immorality? What good did it do to dwell on what he felt in his heart, to repeat it to the few old ladies who still came to Mass? It was not these poor simple souls who needed to be convinced, but the others, those who no longer came to the services.

He left the fire's gentle warmth and went to the entrance to pick up the paper the postman had just slipped under his door. The sight of an envelope on top of *The Cross of Corrèze* intrigued and even worried him. It was years since he had received a letter.

He picked it up, examined it, went to sit down by the fire, ripped it open nervously and read it. He was vexed with himself for the rest of his life for his first, fleeting reaction, and he never forgave himself for having, for at least ten seconds, greatly failed in Christian charity. But the fact is that a wave of self-satisfaction surged over him when he realised how events had proved him right. He recovered himself quickly, begged God's forgiveness for the base thoughts which had just been guiding his spirit, and re-read the letter. The page trembled at his finger-ends.

He slipped the paper into his pocket and rose, went out and walked over to the church. There, kneeling at the foot of Saint Sacrement, he prayed for a whole hour, despite the intense cold which took hold of him as the minutes passed.

One o'clock was chiming as he rose again. He had eaten nothing for lunch, but did not even consider that as he headed bravely towards the house of Doctor Fraysse.

10

DOCTOR Fraysse and his wife were drinking their coffee when their maidservant showed Father Feix in. The doctor, astonished at this visit, almost upset his cup, and remained dumbfounded for several seconds.

'What's happened?' he asked, getting up. 'This is the first time you've ever come to my house. Something must have . . .'

'That's right,' admitted the priest. 'Excuse me for disturbing you, but I must speak to you. And it's not about pruning roses,' he added with a sad smile.

'Well, let's go into my study.'

'No, no,' said his wife. 'You stay here by the fire, you'll be more comfortable.' She went out and shut the door.

'This is what brought me,' said the priest, holding out the letter.

'Please sit down,' invited the doctor, as he put on his pince-nez. He read, sighed and then made a face.

'Ah, that unpleasant episode,' he murmured. 'The little fools, I warned them . . .'

'Yes; it's because Louise told me you knew that I've come to see you. I don't know what to do, and yet they're counting on me,' he said sadly.

'Don't get in a state, let's just think about it. Young Louise and her Octave have been seeing each other every Sunday for almost two months. Between ourselves, that big ninny Jean-Edouard should have known that the matter wouldn't be so easily dealt with. Well. . . !

'To summarise, next Monday Louise is supposed to return to her family, and everyone knows that poor simpleton Léonard Bouyssoux is going to be there the same evening to begin courting her. Today is Saturday, and Louise tells us that this evening she will leave her relatives' home to join her lover, God knows where! And all in order to get married without delay. Between you and me, she's not telling us why they're in such a hurry . . .'

'You think that . . .'

Doctor Fraysse paused, and smiled.

'*Caro autem infirma*, as your Gospels say, I believe . . . Yes, the flesh is weak. But in their case, and from what I've seen of them, I hesitate to give an opinion. Anyway, that's not the question.'

'Perhaps there's time to send a telegram to warn the relatives,' suggested Father Feix timidly.

'Oh, no!' interrupted the doctor. 'The young people have confided in you, you wouldn't betray them?'

'And if it's for Louise's good?'

'Don't make me laugh! You know Léonard. Can you see that imbecile with Louise?'

'After all, it is her parent's choice, and . . .'

'And nothing!' the doctor cut him off. 'Look here, I promised not to get mixed up in this affair, but I see that you may force me to!'

'Well, I don't know what to do.'

'Jean-Edouard must be told everything, and made to understand that basically young Flaviens is a good match. It's true, after all; he may become an engineer in the end! Or almost . . .'

'Jean-Edouard is capable of dong something stupid! You must remember that the wedding is planned for Low Sunday. Also, the girl's a minor, she can do nothing without his consent . . .'

'I know. She can do nothing, except . . . There it is, we have only to tell him that she's pregnant . . .'

'Oh, no!' protested the priest. 'That's impossible, I refuse to tell a lie!'

'Bloody hell!' raged the doctor. 'Who's talking about lying? She's spelt it out – "For we are going to get married as soon as possible." '

' "We are going to", and not "We have to". It's a nice point!'

'Bravo! I didn't know you were such a Jesuit! In fact

you're quite ready to punish her for *not* having sinned, as you call it! Here is a girl who, as far as we know, is a virgin, an unwritten page, and who, because of that, risks finding herself in the arms of an idiot she doesn't want! And your blessing is enough to make his taking her legal, and blessed by God. Dammit!'

'I beg you, don't swear; you know perfectly well that I don't know what to do.'

'Excuse me,' said the doctor, getting up. He walked to the side table, uncorked a bottle of plum brandy and filled two glasses: 'Here, this might give us inspiration.'

'No, no, thank you, not just now . . . I haven't had time to eat, and I fear that alcohol on an empty stomach . . .'

'You should have told me!' cried the doctor. He strode to the door, opened it and called to the maid: 'Adèle! A plate of something for the Father's lunch, and at the double!'

It was after Father Feix's lunch, after coffee and brandy, that they decided to go together to tell Jean-Edouard. It was understood that the doctor would assume responsibility for any lies which might be necessary in the course of what would be a very difficult interview.

They found Jean-Edouard in the new piggery; if he was intrigued by their visit, he gave no indication of it.

He had bought about forty weaners at the last market, and was lavishing great care on them. He leant his fork against the wall and advanced towards his visitors.

'Well, Father, you've come to bless my new pigsty? What an excellent idea. I expect it was Marguerite who asked for this . . .'

Every year, Father Feix went round the barns to bless the flocks. It was an old custom which his parishioners considered very important, almost as important as Rogation Day, the ceremony in which he blessed the fields, begged mercy from the Lord, and asked for fair weather and good crops as a reward for man's work.

'Listen, Jean-Edouard, if you wish, I'll come back another day for the blessing, but I'm pleased that you asked me,' said the priest in confusion.

'Well, so what brings you both here?' asked Jean-Edouard with a frown.

The priest felt wretched at having to announce the news, and he turned to the doctor to beg for help.

'Good God,' grumbled the doctor, 'it's not a tragedy, after all, it's not the end of the world! All right,' he gulped, and decided to take it on himself. 'Louise has written to me; she's left her cousins' house, she's going to marry Octave Flaviens, and you will no doubt be a grandfather within a short time. That's what we've come to tell you. Okay, it's not very amusing, but it isn't a catastrophe! At the end of the day what matters is that your daughter should be happy!'

Both he and the priest were astonished at Jean-Edouard's reaction. They had expected shouts, threats, even a brandished shotgun; they saw only pallor and silence. Such a heavy silence, so oppressive, that the priest felt he ought to break it.

'I understand how you feel, you know. You see, I could exult and say: "I told you the railway would bring misfortune!" But no, believe me, I'm as hurt as you. Louise is my daughter too; I baptised her, I taught her the catechism, and I was looking forward to marrying her. But there it is, it's the will of God which has thwarted your plans; it must be accepted whatever it brings. . .'

Jean-Edouard looked at them, but did not seem to see them. He took up his fork, arranged the pig's bedding-straw, then put down the fork again and patted his pockets in search of his tobacco; his fingers were trembling so much as he shaped the cigarette that the paper split. He added another paper and rolled it.

'Well, so that's it,' he said at last. 'Okay, fine . . .' He lit his cigarette and breathed in a lungful. 'Okay,' he repeated. 'She marries her spear-carrier. But since it is you she's written to' – he looked at the doctor – 'tell her that the Vialhe family no longer recognises her as one of them. She's chosen, and that's that.'

'Don't be a fool!' cried the doctor. 'I understand that you're disappointed, but that's not a good enough reason for disowning your daughter! Good God, do I have repeat it? It's not a tragedy! Well, don't overdramatise it, don't insult the future!'

'I said it was over, and I'm not going back on it.'

'Listen,' it was the priest's turn to try, 'no one is asking you to give her a party right now. But she is your daughter, and her children will be your grandchildren! You have no right to . . .'

'I said that's that; don't offend my ears with your rights! The kids she has will be. . . what was it, just now? Oh yes, Flaviens. They will never be Vialhes, I don't want to know them. Let that be fully understood; that she should never venture to set foot in the house. The door will be closed, you tell her that.'

He took up his fork again and foraged in the litter.

'Oh, yes!' he continued, stopping his work, 'she'll need authorisation. I'll get it to you – you, the go-between!' he shouted in the direction of the doctor. 'You're surprised I thought of it? Well, let me tell you, one disgrace is enough. I don't want anyone to be able to say that there are bastards from a Vialhe girl, here or anywhere else. There never have been, and that little slut is not going to start!'

'I'm sure your feelings will change later on,' ventured Father Feix, 'but still, I'd like you to reassure me that you won't go for your son-in . . . well, the husband of your daughter. You're bound to see him again, his work here isn't finished.'

'No, I shan't see him. And even if he were standing between you two, I still wouldn't see him! He can come in peace, the village doesn't belong to me. But if by any mischance either he or she set foot on my property, my house or my land . . .'

'Good, all right,' interrupted the doctor. 'Well, I think time will heal all. Now we'll leave you, but believe me, it gave us no pleasure to come . . .'

Jean-Edouard watched them disappear, crushed the cigarette between his fingers, and cried.

He had dry eyes when he went into the house half an hour

later, but Marguerite immediately knew from his expression that something had happened.

'Where are the children?' he asked.

'Berthe is bringing in the sheep, Pierre-Edouard's bedding down the cows.'

'Call them immediately. Now, by God!' he shouted, as she hesitated.

As soon as they arrived, he announced the news to them, and they knew that it was pointless to say anything whatsoever.

'And you,' he said, looking at Berthe, 'get it into your head that I'll have my eye on you. You're not going the same way as her. If I see you so much as look at a man, I'll split your skull! Now get back to work, I've still got things to do . . .'

By nightfall he had sorted everything out. His first visit was to old Bouyssoux. With him two or three sentences were sufficient to bury all their plans. Plus one last sentence, a warning: 'And if you want to laugh, wait until I've left, and gone some distance too. I'll smash the face of anyone who laughs, even old men . . .'

He strode away and returned to the village. Once there he went into the Mairie. Ten minutes later he had resigned from the council and as president of the syndicate.

As he passed by the doctor's house he delivered the paper which permitted his daughter to be legally married as a minor; everything was within the law, including the mayor's stamp as witness to his signature.

It was dark when he returned to the house. His mother, wife and two children were waiting to dine with him. He took his place and served the soup.

'The day after tomorrow is the market at Objat,' he said, stirring his bouillon. 'We'll buy those six young sows and the male we need. Since I have no need to go to Tulle,' he said, looking at Marguerite, 'we might as well make the most of it.'

There was a lot of talk throughout the village, and even beyond, but no one dared to reveal to any member of the

Vialhe family that they were aware of the misfortunes which had befallen them. Of course some people were vastly amused and considered that this event was exactly what was needed to take Jean-Edouard down a peg or two; and if by any chance he were in the mood to climb on his high horse again, they would always be able to ask casually after his daughter and the baby!

But those who laughed and rejoiced did so discreetly. They knew that Jean-Edouard would be merciless.

Besides there were many who, even if they envied and didn't much like him, admired his attitude, not only towards his daughter (that was his personal problem), but also in resigning and withdrawing from all public life; that proved he was aware of the dishonour, and had chosen the right solution. Others in his situation might have tried to cling to power, but who could respect the opinion of a town councillor (canvassing to be mayor, too) and a president of the syndicate who was not even capable of looking after his own daughter?

The conduct of his wife was also beyond reproach. In one instant Marguerite had aged ten years, and it was no secret that this affair tormented her day and night. It was enough to see her pass down the main street, upright and dignified, with no attempt to conceal her tear-filled eyes. None of the gossips dared let slip the slightest allusion to it in front of her either.

As for old Léonie, she was so deaf that one could not be sure that she knew what was going on; in her conversations there was no sign of awareness. That left Grandfather, but he had not left his bed for months now and had become incoherent; he did not need to be worried by what had happened to his grand-daughter.

Only Pierre-Edouard and Berthe showed chinks in the armour of their perfectly correct behaviour. The young man was pitied most of all, for everyone knew that he adored his sister and suffered from her absence and her banishment; it was felt he was within an ace of defying his father and openly taking Louise's side. Some hoped secretly that he would do that, just so that they could enjoy the confrontation. They felt sorry for Berthe too, for it was obvious that her father forbade her any excursions. For the whole month of December the behaviour of the Vialhes was secretly observed, then the gossips grew weary of it and busied themselves with the end-of-year celebrations.

Pierre-Edouard lived sadly during his last days of liberty. He had received his call-up papers, and knew that he must join his regiment on 7 January.

It was not leaving for the army which embittered him, but going away without seeing Louise again, and without the smallest sign of life from her. Even Octave Flaviens stayed out of sight; you would think he had left the railway and the area.

And now he was being sent into exile, to the back of beyond, without even knowing whether his sister was married or not. His posting had arrived the week before Christmas, and he had been quite happy to get it. It unlocked the doors of his house, allowed him to escape the oppressive and unhealthy atmosphere where every word might be misinterpreted by his father, or the slightest gesture taken as a sign of rebellion.

Nevertheless, despite being glad to sally forth, he had been vexed by his assignment. He had naively believed that, like most of the young men in the area, he would be sent to Tulle, to Limoges, to Périgueux, possibly to Bordeaux – and why not even to Brive! – in some infantry regiment or other. He was way off the mark, and had looked at the piece of paper uncomprehendingly for several seconds, the time it took him to search his memory for the location of Besançon – where the devil was it?

'Where are they sending you?' his father asked.

'Fifth artillery regiment in Besancon . . .'

'And where's that?'

'In Doubs, a long way off. Up there, dammit!'

'Oh well! We won't be seeing much of you . . .'

His father had said nothing more, but Pierre-Edouard knew that he was angry. He had hoped that his son would be in a garrison close by, and would return frequently to give him a hand.

Since then Pierre-Edouard had made the best of a bad job; he was going to see something of the country, and then, the artillery was an important branch of the service. So he would have set off with a light heart, if it had not been for Louise . . .

Her absence was deeply felt on Christmas Day, a dreadful day, sad enough to bring tears; neither he nor Berthe knew what to do, what to say. Finally he took his gun and climbed to the peaks, but those places reminded him too much of his sister – their adventure in the snow, Léon's thrushes, the wolves . . .

And now, this afternoon of New Year's Eve, he was killing time as best he could by splitting wood with huge blows of the axe. He brought down the heavy chopper on a billet of chestnut wood which exploded, then prepared another log.

'Keeping warm?'

He lifted his head and saw Léon, who had just spoken to him from the roadway.

'Yeah . . .'

He had not seen Léon for several weeks, and felt embarrassed to have to start a conversation, which he had no doubt would inevitably touch on Louise.

'Got time to come out?' asked Léon, having made sure that there was no one else about.

'Well, look here. . . .' muttered Pierre-Edouard, pointing to the pile of wood.

'Don't muck about. Put that down and come on. I've got news of your sister.'

Pierre-Edouard stuck his axe in the chopping-block and slipped on his jacket. 'Wait for me; I'll fetch my gun, we'll make the rounds.'

He bounded towards the house, returned with his 12-bore (with central percussion, a present from his grandfather on his sixteenth birthday) and caught up with his friend, who was already climbing up through the wood towards the plateau.

'Have you seen her? How is she?'

'At first sight, like someone in love . . .'

'Don't play the fool or I'll tan your hide!'

'Keep your hair on! Dammit, it's very good to be in love! Yes, I met her, and him too. They came to see me this week at Tulle market.'

'My God! The market was on Tuesday, now it's Thursday – you could have told me earlier!'

'Hey, I've got work to do too! If you want to know, I was in Limoges yesterday.'

For the last two years Léon had been his own master, and was doing very well in his particular line of business. He was exempt from military service as the family bread-winner, and despite his youth had plunged into cattle-dealing. He still rented his farm, but the solicitor had entrusted him with several hectares of excellent pasture land as well, and he made the maximum profit from this.

'Well, what did she say to you?'

'They're getting married on the second of January, at Aubazine. The day after tomorrow, that is. And they'd really like you to be there.'

Pierre-Edouard felt a sudden wave of joy. His sister was getting married, she wanted him there too; it was reason-able, normal, that was how one should live, not under a burden of sorrow and bitterness.

'I'll be there,' he said. 'You bet I'll be there! How is she?'

'I told you, like someone in love.'

'And . . . Does it show much?'

'That she's in love? Yes, of course! If she weren't your sister . . .'

'Stop fooling! Does it show much that . . . well, that she's expecting a baby?'

'Are you joking or what?' Léon guffawed. 'Your sister, a baby? And where would she put it? Flat as my palm she is, a fine girl and as pretty as a picture! Ha! She tricked you all!'

'Don't say that!' cried Pierre-Edouard, catching his arm. 'I tell you, Father said so. I don't know where he got it from, but it was he who told me. Besides, why do you think he let her get married, eh?'

'Listen,' said Léon, smiling, 'as far as I know, you and girls, you haven't got very far, you need a bit of help to learn a thing or two . . . But I know what I'm talking about when it comes to these things, if you don't mind me saying so. Your sister wanted Octave, so she went off with him, that's all. But that doesn't mean to say that it's gone any further. Besides, I've listened to them, they're still saying "vous" to each other, can you imagine it? Hardly credible, is it? And, believe me, she's looking after her reputation; in that way, she's a Vialhe! . . . He's rented a room for her with an old lady who's half blind, so she didn't check your sister's age, and he lodges in the Station Hotel when he goes to Tulle! Yes sir! At the Hôtel de la Gare! She told me so and I believe her, because I've got an eye for it, and I can tell the difference between an innocent girl and a woman . . .'

'Well!' Pierre-Edouard was flabbergasted. 'That's how it is . . . And, I thought . . .'

He was suddenly very proud of his sister; very proud that she knew how to control her life, without mistakes, sticking to her idea of marriage, to her idea of honour. She was going to be able to get married in white, and no one could deny her that right.

'What time is the wedding?' he asked.

'Eleven o'clock.'

'Thank you for everything. Now I must go back.'

'Look,' Léon stopped him, 'she's invited me, but it's really not my business; I don't want to go.'

'That was good of her, too,' murmured Pierre-Edouard. 'Yes, you must accept, you must come. Then there'll be at least one inhabitant of Saint-Libéral who can one day tell them how it all really happened. No one will ever believe me.'

'If you imagine that people would rather believe a cattle-dealer. . . ! Well, all right, I'll come. That'll double the crowd, eh? And we can make the journey together.'

11

'TOMORROW we'll go back for some more wood – we'd better make the most of you while we've got you. When I'm alone . . .' Jean-Edouard announced on the evening of 1 January.

The day had been just as bleak and gloomy as Christmas Day; to keep busy, Jean-Edouard and his son had spent most of the afternoon cutting firewood.

'No,' said Pierre-Edouard, 'I shan't be here tomorrow.'

'What?' growled his father.

'I'm going to Brive,' said Pierre-Edouard. 'I have something to do.'

He had not breathed a word to anyone about what Léon had told him; not even to Berthe, who would not have known how to hold her tongue.

'Miladiou! I don't like your manners,' grumbled Jean-Edouard. 'No, you're in the wrong place! You're not a soldier yet! Tomorrow we're going to get wood, whether you like it or not!'

'Then you'll have to go on your own.'

'And what are you up to in Brive?' questioned his father, forcing himself to control his temper.

'We're having a dinner, all the fellows in my class,' said Pierre-Edouard, without batting an eyelid. He knew that his father would soon find out that he was lying, but he didn't care; he'd be a long way off when the deception was revealed.

'A dinner! A dinner!' muttered Jean-Edouard. 'And that's going to take all day? Hah, you lead a fine life, you young ones! All right then, you'll come with me,' he said, looking at Berthe. 'You haven't got a dinner, have you?'

The girl shook her head, lowered her eyes and kept quiet; she knew that her only defence was to remain mute.

It was still dark when Pierre-Edouard climbed into Léon's dog-cart. Léon touched the horse, and it started off at a gentle trot. They took the road which descended towards Perpezac and Brignac and soon arrived at the railway workings.

'They're getting on fast now,' Pierre-Edouard remarked.

'Yes, another three kilometres and they'll have reached us. But it seems it wasn't all easy going among the rocks over Ferrière way; that's what held them up. But that's all right for your father – the longer it takes the more profit he makes!'

'They say you're not losing by it either,' said Pierre-Edouard drily.

'Huh! I sell them a few surplus cows from time to time, some sausages perhaps, but I'm not making a lot of money out of that, believe me.'

'Your horse goes well,' observed Pierre-Edouard, after several minutes' silence.

'Yes, we'll soon be in Brive. I won't be long there, I must just pop in to the abattoir to check on two carcasses. Don't worry, we won't miss the train . . .' He fell silent, spat out his cigarette, then continued. 'You know, it gives me a funny feeling to be going to your sister's wedding.'

'Me too; I can hardly believe it. Time passes quickly, doesn't it? You remember the wolves?'

'You're asking me do I remember? You made me throw away my thrushes; I lost more than five francs!'

They got off the train at Aubazine station at 9.20. There Léon, who really seemed to know everyone, borrowed a horse-cab. The cab had no hood and they had to muffle up, for it was bitterly cold.

'Go on!' cried Léon, shaking the reins, 'be brave, old girl! Talk about an old nag!' he observed, as the animal slowed down for a breather on the long hill which led to the village. 'We'd be quicker on foot! It's going to take us almost an hour to cover these four kilometres. Still, we are sitting down!'

'Yes, but we're freezing. Push the old crock on so that we get there!'

'Don't be funny; if I push her, she'll kick the bucket! I know her well, I sold her to him . . .'

'You managed to sell an old hack like that!'

'Easy,' claimed Léon. 'Give her to me for an hour and I'll make her ten years younger.'

'Oh yes?'

'Of course! Two litres of oats in four litres of dry white wine, a good grooming with sugar to make her coat shiny, a dab of polish on her hooves, two drops of vinegar under her eyelids to make her eyes sparkle, a good layer of lime on her teeth, and to finish off, a quarter of a peeled onion stuck up her backside – that way a horse'll prance around like a three-year-old stallion!'

'You're a dreadful scoundrel!' exclaimed Pierre-Edouard. 'But next day, don't you ever have any trouble?'

'Well, no. For proof, you saw how the buyer greeted me. Besides, he can't complain, the beast isn't dead yet! And then, to tell the truth, the day after the sale I'm not there . . .'

Freezing rain mixed with snow was falling when they finally arrived in Aubazine. A heavy pall of fog sprawled down from the Pauliac mountain and darkened the whole village.

Léon went straight to the inn, gave the horse and cart over to the stable boy, and rushed into the dining-room, where a huge fire was crackling.

'Two mulled wines, and in big bowls!' he ordered, sitting down by the fireside.

Their drinks were just being served when Louise and Octave came into the room. Pierre-Edouard stood a few seconds without moving, then he went to his sister and hugged her.

'You know,' he said, 'you showed us a thing or two, and it's not over yet. Oh, I can tell you, you really did it!'

'Don't say it, I know . . .'

'Who told you?'

'Doctor Fraysse. He wrote to Octave,' she explained, controlling her tears, 'and if he talks to you about it, you can tell Father that I shan't be coming back. Never.'

'Come, come,' interrupted Octave, 'we'll see about that later on. Today is a special day! Here,' he said, turning to a tall fellow who had just come in, 'I'd like to introduce my witness. And you, Louise, have you asked Monsieur Dupeuch if he agrees?'

'Me?' said Léon with feeling. 'Witness? But why not Pierre-Edouard instead?'

'He's still under twenty-one,' explained Octave.

'So you'll accept, Léon,' insisted Louise. 'It would please me, and it will always remind me of our adventures in Saint-Libéral, you remember?'

'Yes,' muttered Léon, his throat tightening. It was the first time anyone had ever spoken to him with such spontaneous kindness.

'Fine,' he said at last. 'If you want me to, but . . . Thank you for thinking of me.'

The formalities at the Mairie were extremely brief, and they realised that the mayor had been forewarned by his colleague in St Libéral; he was carrying out his duties because he could not really do otherwise, but his attitude showed just how much he too disapproved of this marriage.

The church was hardly more welcoming, and the young vicar responsible for the ceremony sped through the blessing in a trice. Then he reminded them in a few words of the mutual duties of husband and wife, and could not prevent himself from glancing slyly and inquisitively at Louise's extraordinarily flat stomach when he talked about the Christian education of children. At the end he offered a short prayer at the altar of the Blessed Virgin, had the registers signed, and disappeared into the darkness of the nave.

At the meal the atmosphere was no more cheerful. It was obvious that Louise, despite the happiness which shone from her eyes, could not forget all she had endured and sacrificed to achieve this pitiful, almost clandestine, ceremony on a dark and freezing day.

As for Octave, he was attentive to his wife's every movement, but he too was deeply hurt at not being able to offer his young wife a big, jolly family festival, a feast spiced with song, laughter and discussion, a dance enlivened by some cheerful lasses and fellows — all the things that go to make a happy wedding.

During the meal, Louise informed her brother that they had found lodgings in Terrasson, and were going to live over there for as long as Octave was needed on the railway. Afterwards they would leave for Orléans, her husband's home town.

'And I'm going to work too,' she said. 'Octave didn't want me to, but I really don't see why I should stay idle, just waiting for him to come home. Later, when a baby is expected, we'll see.'

'She had to say it,' thought Pierre-Edouard. 'She doesn't want any suspicion that the child came before the husband!' He glanced at Léon, and smiled at his dumbshow which neatly declared: 'You see, I told you so!'

'But what will you do?' he asked.

'Some sewing for one of Doctor Fraysse's colleagues. It was he who recommended me.'

'He's a good man,' agreed Pierre-Edouard. Then he announced his imminent departure on army service, and the conversation dragged a little; Octave and his friend talked of their own service, evoking memories of interest only to themselves.

With the dessert Léon insisted on treating them to champagne. Everyone scolded him for such extravagance, but he persisted, opened the bottle and filled the glasses himself. With a mock clumsy gesture — which fooled no one — he managed to break Louise's glass, so that the sparkling wine spilt on to her white bodice.

'There,' he said, 'that brings good luck. Here's to the young couple!'

A little later, when it was already beginning to get dark, it was he who gave the signal to leave.

'Yes, you'll have to excuse us! We mustn't miss the train, and with that old nag to get us there . . .'

Louise and Octave accompanied them to the stable.

'So that's it,' said Pierre-Edouard, after kissing his sister. 'Good luck, and . . .'

He shook his brother-in-law's hand, and climbed into the cart.

'See you soon!' called Louise.

He nodded yes, and forced his mouth into the ghost of a smile. He was convinced that months, probably even years, would pass before that wish came true.

During his last two days at home Pierre-Edouard barely opened his mouth, but no one paid any attention to that: less and less was said in the Vialhe house. He could not forget that spoiled wedding, where everything rang false, when everyone was forced to appear pleased; he could not forgive his father for being the indirect author of that travesty of a ceremony which reeked of sadness.

Then it was the day of his departure.

'Come back as soon as you can,' his father advised. 'You know that there's no lack of work here!'

'And be careful,' added his mother.

He went to kiss his grandfather, but could not be certain that the old man recognised him; then he brushed his lips on the faded cheek of his grandmother, who innocently asked him where he was going. Finally he kissed his parents and his sister, picked up his modest suitcase of pressed cardboard, and opened the door.

'I wanted to tell you,' he called before leaving, 'on Saturday I was at Louise and Octave's wedding. They are very happy and they're not expecting a baby yet! Léon can tell you all about it, he was a witness . . .'

He slammed the door violently behind him, and strode away.

For several years Father Feix had hardly managed to sleep

more than four hours a night. So, instead of lying awake and chilled, tossing in his bed, he preferred to delay his time of going to bed as long as possible. He sat down by the fireside, where he could at least gather a little warmth for his legs and hands, which were always frozen.

Once installed on the settle, he first took up his breviary. Then he embarked on *The Cross of Corrèze*, which he read and re-read from first to last line. Towards one o'clock he recited his rosary five times, to which he added the litany of the Most Blessed Name of Jesus and of the Virgin Mary. Then, since sleep still evaded him, he meditated while drinking a large bowl of lime-blossom tea.

All this brought him to two o'clock when, sleepy or no, he went to lie down; he never failed to thank the Lord on waking if he had managed to doze until six.

So he was quickly at the door when there was a knock towards eleven o'clock, that night of 18 January. He opened it, and recognised Jean-Edouard.

'It's my father, he's just going . . .'

'Wait for me so that you can light my way; I'll be right with you.'

He threw his heavy cloak around his shoulders, fetched his holy oils and joined his visitor. They were soon at the Vialhes'.

Unconscious, emaciated, hardly recognisable, old Edouard was in agony, his nostrils already pinched; only a tenuous breath, barely perceptible, showed that he was still alive. Nevertheless, Father Feix estimated that he had time to administer Extreme Unction in full, and while reciting the prayers he anointed the gaunt body six times, touching the eyes, ears, nostrils, mouth, hands and feet of the dying man. Around the bed, Jean-Edouard, Marguerite and Berthe murmured the responses. As for old Léonie, crouched by the fire in the living-room, she was crying silently, staring at the flames which danced at her feet without seeing them.

When he had finished the last orison, the priest moved away from the bed.

'Listen, my child,' he said to Berthe, 'you go and look

after your grandmother; he doesn't need you any more. Go on, I'm going to stay here.' He knelt at the foot of the bed and began his vigil.

The old man passed away at three o'clock – without a sound, without a gasp, in a silence hardly disturbed by the sputtering of the two candles placed on the bedside table. The priest gave the final blessing, and then made way for Marguerite and her daughter as soon as they came in to lay out the corpse.

'Do you want me to walk back with you?' suggested Jean-Edouard, who had followed him into the living-room.

'No, stay here,' advised the priest.

He approached old Léonie, shook both her hands, then walked towards the door.

'You would be doing a good deed if you informed Louise. Do you want me to do it?' he asked.

'Don't bother with that,' cut in Jean-Edouard, 'I know what I have to do.'

The priest went out, and already behind him he heard the plaintive wailing of the three women; it was only a discreet quavering at the moment, on the surface of their lips. But soon, when the village awoke, when day dawned, they would howl like animals, wail with open mouths, as if to empty out their pain, their sorrow, and so that everyone in St Libéral would know that death had struck at the Vialhes'.

The burial attracted a huge crowd. Since the morning of the death Jeantout, delegated by Jean-Edouard, had toured the countryside to announce the news at every farm; even the most remote received a visit.

And the people came, for the Vialhes were known by everyone, and because the deceased had always been a good man, esteemed and respected. Relatives who had not been seen for years wanted to be part of the obsequies; even the ones from Tulle came, and God knows, Jean-Edouard had good reason to refuse to receive *them*! Nevertheless he welcomed them, greeting them as if nothing had happened, as if it were not from their house that his daughter had run away.

Naturally, when the whole family came out of the house to walk behind the hearse, everyone noticed Louise's absence. Pierre-Edouard was not there either, but that was different.

And yet, when they found themselves in the cemetery after the Mass, by the open grave where four men were slowly lowering the coffin, everyone saw the modest wreath placed among the rest. It was the smallest, no doubt the cheapest; a few artificial flowers interwoven with a purple ribbon, and on it, for what it was worth, the letters in silver:

> To our late lamented Grandfather.
> Octave and Louise, his grandchildren.

The death of his grandfather made Pierre-Edouard very sad. He had always had a great affection for him, and often remembered the old man's joy on the day he got his certificate. He did not remember the same emotion being shown when Louise and Berthe achieved the diploma in their turn, nor that they received a napoléon of twenty francs, as he had. He had never wanted to spend that napoléon; he kept it carefully like a good luck charm.

He learned of the demise of his grandfather by telegram, brought to him by the post orderly during a drill session.

'What is it?' demanded the sergeant, having ordered 'at ease'.

'Nothing, Sergeant,' he stammered, embarrassed to have to announce news which concerned only himself in front of all his comrades.

'As you like! But if it's your girlfriend making a date, make her wait – you're nowhere near in the mood to give her a smacker!'

The quip roused several perfunctory laughs, and he forced himself to smile as well.

He did not ask permission to go to the funeral; he had been enrolled for too short a time to hope that they would grant him leave. All his class were confined to quarters for months to come, and would not even have the right to go into town until after their basic training and vaccinations. And finally, he had no desire to return to St Libéral in such circumstances, no desire to immerse himself in civilian life again for forty-eight hours. He had struggled enough getting used to his new state, and knew that any absence, however brief, would only make things more difficult.

Taken in hand on arrival by an old NCO with enormous moustaches and legs like barrel-hoops, Pierre-Edouard and his friends had been forced to submit to all his bullying without saying a word.

'From now on,' the artillery sergeant had bellowed, having lined them up as best he could on the parade-ground, 'From now on, you're no longer "Gentlemen", but lowly gunners, crewmen, riflemen! You've been chosen to serve in the best division in the world, and it's a great honour for a load of no-hopers like you. But to be an artilleryman's an achievement, and I'll make you achieve it; *I* shall, you swine. And if anyone's not happy, he can always ask to be transferred to the foot-sloggers, those despicable infantrymen, only good for cannon-fodder! Now, everyone to the stables! For now you're going to collect horse-dung for me. You're going to learn that before touching a gun you have to know how to look after the ones that pull them, look after the horses and ride them! And when your backsides are as leathery as old drumskins, then perhaps we'll let you have a look at a seventy-five!'

Since then there had been nothing but fatigue duties in barracks, room and equipment inspections, parade sessions and musket-drill, on top of cleaning the stables, grooming the horses and polishing the harness.

Pierre-Edouard, accustomed to work in the fields, was not overburdened by the work rate required here; it was far less than he had to bear when hoeing on the plateau! On the other hand, he had difficulty in getting used to military discipline, which allowed the stupidest idiot, just because he was a brigadier, to use any means to break the spirit of the strong-willed.

So he adopted the habit of silence, sank into the mass of recruits, and did nothing – either good or bad – which might draw attention to himself.

*

When Father Feix's old housekeeper came, as she did every morning, into the main room of the presbytery, and saw the old priest on the settle in front of the cold hearth, she thought he had fallen asleep there on returning from Mass. In fact, as Doctor Delpy confirmed shortly afterwards, he had been dead for more than five hours. Dead, alone by the fireside, where he sat each evening.

His passing shook the parish; the parish he had served for almost half a century, in which he was the most respected figure, even by those who disliked him, criticised or complained about him, for everyone in the community was obliged to him in some way. He had baptised and taught the catechism to all those under forty, married half of the couples; with very few exceptions, every household had received him at least once to administer the last rites to someone who lay dying, or to conduct a burial.

Thus his death saddened the whole community – and worried them, for they wondered who would replace him as head of the parish. In any case, whoever the new priest was, it would take him years to get to know his parishioners; their old secrets, their quarrels and ancestral feuds, the subjects never to be mentioned to someone or other – in short, everything which had made Father Feix part of every family, who had the right to give his opinion even if his advice was not followed. They even went so far as to forget his outbursts against the Republic, and his grim opposition to the railway line.

So, despite the spring workload in this month of April, there was a crowd on the day of the burial. Few of the men actually went into church, and if no one was surprised at the attendance of the squire, the solicitor and Jean-Edouard, there was a lot of talk amongst those waiting in the square, at the inn or in the bistros, when the mayor and Doctor Fraysse entered.

As luck would have it, a dozen navvies from the railway were already installed at the bar of the inn when the wheelwright, Fernand Fronty, walked in, followed by several friends, to empty a jar while awaiting for the coffin to emerge. 'My God!' shouted one of the drinkers brazenly, 'you're making a great fuss over a priest. It's only one old crow less!'

'Take that back!' ordered the wheelwright, marching right up to him.

Fernand Fronty had never set foot in the church since his first and probably last communion twenty-five years earlier, and everyone knew of his profound indifference to all things religious; he had barely greeted Father Feix when he passed him in the street. Yet his reaction surprised no one. The priest was what he was, but he was theirs, and those lousy foreigners had no right to say anything about him. When they insulted him, they insulted the whole community.

'Take it back!' repeated Fronty, grabbing the drinker by the shirt.

Sober, the man would certainly have complied after one glance at the wheelwright's breadth of shoulder. But he did not notice the huge arms, shaped by twenty years of daily exercise with the plane, axe and sledge-hammer, nor the fist, as big as a ham, which held him by the collar.

'Damn the crows!' he yelled. 'They're all . . .'

No one ever found out what they were, for the wheelwright's backhander propelled him unconscious into the middle of the room. His companions hesitated for a second, and then very wisely put their noses into their glasses; it was really too early in the day to organise a good fight. Besides, they were still clear-headed enough to make an accurate assessment of Fernand's strength.

'Miladiou!' he commented, taking his place at the bar, 'I'm not going to let that worm insult our priest! All right?' he asked pointedly, smiling threateningly at the other workers.

They nodded hastily in agreement, and cleared off as soon as their companion was fit to walk.

*

Jean-Edouard retreated into isolation, but that did not mean that he neglected his farm; quite the opposite. His daughter had brought him dishonour and forced him to abandon his political ambitions, therefore he had nothing to lose and no one to plan for.

So, to demonstrate that he was still a force to be reckoned with, he anticipated Jeantout in salad cultivation. God knows why, as he had no need to do it to earn money. His pig-rearing was going well. He supplied the railway company and also sold his surplus at the main markets of the area, in groups of ten or fifteen bacon pigs, fattened on the scraps from the canteen.

He planted out half a hectare of lettuce simply for the pleasure of it; he gave over the field called The Gardens to this, for it had the best aspect and gave the earliest crops. A further advantage was that he gave responsibility for the crop to Berthe. While she was busy with that, she would not think of acting like her sister!

Jeantout was angry at this spiteful act, but he said nothing. He knew only too well that his neighbour was just looking for an excuse to explode in fury.

Jean-Edouard was not content with earning a lot; he wanted his money to bear fruit as well. To achieve this he didn't mind falling out with the mayor and the squire when he did them out of two hectares of good land on the plateau. It had been put up for sale by the solicitor, who now also wanted to buy a car. These fields bordered on the property of Antoine Gigoux and Jean Duroux, and it suited the two men very well to come to a secret understanding, hold down the price, and divide the land.

Jean-Edouard got wind of the affair, went to Monsieur Lardy and put a bag of napoléons on the table; twenty minutes later he was the owner of the two hectares. In the same way he snapped up a hectare of meadowland set in the valley, not far from the mill, under the very nose of Léon Dupeuch. He heard mention of it one morning at St Libéral market; the business had almost been done, and because he had already signed the private contract Léon had committed the error of talking far too much.

Jean-Edouard immediately went to Perpezac and found the seller – an old spinster who drove a hard bargain, but was so grasping that she was very happy to renege on her signature and follow this generous new buyer all the way to the lawyer's office. Jean-Edouard placed his pieces of gold on the table without a qualm, pocketed the deeds to the property, and returned to tell Léon.

'God damn it!' growled Léon, 'that's not the way an honest man behaves! I could take you to court!'

'You won't do that, you'd lose money by it. And as for honesty, that's not something a cattle-dealer can talk about!'

'Okay,' said Léon, 'you've conned me, but don't worry; I'll short-change you, one day ... And I'll find other pastureland easily, whereas you'll have to look a lot further before you find Louise again ...'

Ten years earlier Jean-Edouard would have knocked him cold. But he was suddenly aware of his age, and realised that Léon was perfectly capable of beating *him* up.

'You'll be sorry you said that!'

'Oh yes,' jeered Léon, 'I'll be sorry, like Louise is sorry about Léonard, that old decaying bit of rubbish you found! You know what they say? Since then he's made do with his goats! Oh, he was lovely, the future Vialhe son-in-law!'

And he burst into insolent laughter.

When he announced his latest purchase to Marguerite, Jean-Edouard said nothing of his visit to Léon. Neither of them had talked about Louise since she left, and that worm Léon was not going to break their silence on the subject with his spiteful words.

He had expected that Marguerite would try to make him relent, but to his great astonishment she had never said anything which could be interpreted as a plea for mercy. He knew that she adored Louise, but she had been so delighted with the planned marriage, so proud of the advantageous match awaiting her daughter, that she could not forgive her the destruction of the project, nor the shame she herself had since suffered.

She was not about to forget that her daughter had deceived her in four ways. First she had compromised herself with a stranger; secondly, she had pretended to accept her parents' decision; then she had led them to believe that she had got herself into trouble; and lastly she had used that miserable lie to marry a good-for-nothing, a poor man without land. No, she would not plead for her daughter, never. To allow her to return one day would be to accept that she was right to behave like a tramp; well, Louise had done wrong, and if God was good, the future would give proof of it!

'That makes ours one of the finest farms,' she murmured, musing on the new purchase, 'but it will give us more work, and already . . .'

He shrugged his shoulders – work didn't frighten him, and in eighteen months Pierre-Edouard would be back; what luck that the 1905 law had reduced army service to two years! It wasn't like in his time; he'd had to do five years, enough to drive you mad!

PART THREE

The Confrontation

12

THE inauguration of the line took place on Saturday 31 July 1909; from now on it would join Saint-Libéral-sur-Diamond to La-Rivière-de-Mansac.

Once more the work had been delayed, halted less than a kilometre from the village as the result of a substantial landslide caused by the very wet spring. On a stormy night in May the rush of water had carried away twenty metres of the line, both rails and sleepers, and gouged a huge gully in the road. It had to be filled in and the repair strengthened and reinforced with stonework. Eventually the building work could be restarted, and the line linked up to the brand-new station at St Libéral.

The arrival of the first train was the excuse for celebrations to which the whole community was invited, and everyone agreed that the town council had arranged matters well.

With the help of the squire, who was still a general councillor, Antoine Gigoux had managed to get the district prefect and their Parliamentary deputy to attend; the latter had the honour of cutting the tricoloured ribbon which barred the track. The united brass bands of Brignac, Perpezac and St Libéral played the Marseillaise, and the train arrived just as the final chords rang out.

The convoy entered, beribboned, whistling, at full steam, covered in flowers and flags and crammed with workers and urchins; puffing into St Libéral, it halted at the little station amidst cheers, applause and cries of joy.

After the photos, in which everyone wanted to be included, there were kisses, congratulations and slaps on the back; then many settled into the carriages for a short but exciting journey in reverse, and a triumphant return.

A gigantic banquet had been planned, at which the

workers and the villagers were to sit side by side, fraternise, and reconcile their differences. In the evening they all danced in the square; a great deal of drinking went on too . . .

At midnight a superb firework display came shooting from the engine, thanks to the generosity of the squire. The sparks rose high in the sky and announced the news: St Libéral was connected to the rest of the world!

No member of the Vialhe family joined in the festivities. Nobody cared whether they did or not. Who still remembered that it was partly Jean-Edouard's perseverence and his mediation which had brought the train this far?

Pierre-Edouard distinguished himself in the tests which marked the end of the corporals' training course – his captain, on the strength of his school certificate and his general air of intelligence, had officially entered him in the list of candidates for his first stripes.

Pierre-Edouard obeyed orders and acquitted himself well. The 75 gun, 1897 model, soon had no secrets from him, and on the day of the test he managed to fire at a fine rate of fifteen shots a minute – and better still, to place all the shells within the prescribed circle. (Admittedly, he had promised his gun-crew of six the greatest binge of their lives if they helped, proving their goodwill by their speed.) When he was questioned on the theoretical working of the Schneider 75, he was able to explain the functioning of the hydraulic brakes and the melignite shells, both time- and percussion-fused.

That evening he joined a happy band of successful examination candidates who strolled through Besançon bawling out 'The Artillery-man of Metz' and various coarse jokes. They visited several bars then, still singing and reeling more and more dangerously, they set off for Ma Fifine's brothel, determined to finish the evening by proving to the women that artillerymen were the best and fastest shots! Unluckily they came across a police patrol in the town; the officer in charge was a surly fellow, narrow-minded and possibly envious of them, who dispatched them summarily to sleep it off at the police station.

During his first six months serving the flag, Pierre-Edouard had heard very little news of St Libéral. It was true that he himself did not know what to write in the few letters he occasionally sent to his family. What could he say that would interest his parents? That he had some very good friends, among them a workman from Paris, a farrier from Orléans, a farmer from Brie and another from the Chartres area? That would not matter to them, he thought. Or should he write to them about the only man from the Corrèze apart from himself in the regiment? This was a Sergeant-Major, the worst sort of non-commissioned career officer, an evil drunkard, like an old diseased boar, who delivered his orders and insults in patois after a drink or two! A disgrace to the whole of the Corrèze! No, that really was not something to describe to his parents!

As for asking for news of the village and the farm, he knew the main facts; the death of Father Feix, the arrival of the train, the flourishing market for pig-rearing and the purchase of more land.

This acquisition really cheered him up; he remembered the location of the plots perfectly. But he thought with longing of all the days that separated him from the moment when he could at last harness his plough there, goad the animals, and mark his first furrow in this new Vialhe land.

What he would really have liked to ask for in his letters was news of Louise, but it was unthinkable to risk it. He was sure that his father had not forgiven him for attending his sister's wedding. To beg for news of the outlaw would be considered a grave insult.

He had indeed tried to write to her directly by addressing his letter to Octave Flaviens, care of the railway company. But he had received no reply, and he presumed that the message had got lost. Or possibly (but he refused to believe it) that his sister had decided to sever all ties . . .

Almost a year had passed before he could at last return to the village to spend his regulation leave. He arrived on

Christmas Eve by the evening train, very conscious of the impression he made on his fellow-travellers, with his beautiful artillery uniform enhanced by the two broad red stripes of a corporal.

'You must be the Vialhe boy?' asked an old peasant who climbed on at Perpezac station.

'Certainly am, Monsieur Mathou,' he agreed, without taking his eyes off the passing countryside. His heart was full as he followed in the train the route which he had taken so often on foot and knew in every detail.

'Well, so you're a soldier! I was just saying to myself that it's been some time since we saw you!'

'Yes, indeed!' he said. 'It's been a while.'

'Bah! It goes quickly nowadays, not like in my time! Well, there you are, on leave I suppose? You'll find some changes in the village. And your father, how's he?'

'Fine, I think,' he said in astonishment.

'We hardly see him. It's true he's had some problems . . .'

'What problems?' he asked anxiously. The last letter, dated a month ago, had given no cause for concern.

'Oh, didn't you know? Ah, the poor chap! He lost forty pigs in a week, and I've heard say they were damned fine animals, worth more than two hundred livres each! A touch of swine-fever and it was all over. It seems he only managed to save a dozen, and they don't look too bright!'

'Well,' thought Pierre-Edouard, 'he must be in a fine old mood . . .' But still he was relieved; for a moment he had feared that one of the family was ill.

It was almost dark when the train stopped at St Libéral station. Pierre-Edouard jumped down to the ground, gazing around, trying to make out what had changed in his world.

Apart from the station, which was completely new and had been only foundations when he left, he noticed the additions made at the inn; a big extension — bedrooms probably — had been attached to the main building. The bakery had been enlarged as well. The grocery had been repainted. The butcher's shop, previously quite small, now

166

opened onto the main street, with a large window in which hung strings of sausages and enormous hams. He walked down the street and noticed an unfamiliar motorcar in front of the solicitor's house. So he had bought one, too!

He met several people who hesitated for a moment before returning his greeting. And suddenly, there, at the end of the street, already engulfed in darkness but still discernible, he saw his home. He hastened his step.

'But you should have let us know!' repeated his mother for the twentieth time.

He had told her repeatedly that leave was always in danger of being revoked, but she stuck to her point and rather held it against him for arriving unexpectedly like this.

'You see, we hadn't got anything planned for Christmas Eve, but with you here it'll be different!'

'I hope so,' he agreed as he bent to the hearth to rearrange the logs. 'Father's not here?'

'He had to go to Objat to fetch some medicine for the pigs. I'd better tell you that . . .'

'I know,' he interrupted, 'Old Mathou talked to me about it. And Grandma, where's she?'

'Oh, poor thing, leave her. She's already in bed.'

'And Berthe?'

'In the cowshed.'

'I'll go there.'

He went out, the dog frisking with delight around his legs. He pushed the door to the cowshed with his foot, entered and savoured the rich smell of the animals. Berthe was milking the old cow, Grey. She jumped, then put down her bucket and rushed to hug him.

'There, there!' he said, as he stroked her hair. Then he held her away from him and looked at her.

'You're not very plump,' he ascertained, 'but you've grown very pretty all the same. Well, anything new here?'

'Nothing,' she said, shrugging.

'And Louise,' he murmured, 'have you any news of her?'

'The last I heard she was in Terrasson, but I don't know any more. You know, I can't go out . . .'

'So they're still the same, the parents?'

'What do you think? Look out, here's Father.'

He heard a horse's hooves and was amazed. 'He's bought a horse and cart?'

'Yes, last summer.'

'And he didn't even write to tell me that,' he muttered, a little annoyed.

He went out and walked towards his father, who was just getting down from the trap. Jean-Edouard turned round and examined the silhouette marching towards him; it was now completely dark.

'Oh, it's you!' he said at last. 'You should have let us know! But you've arrived just in time; you can help me inject the pigs.'

By Boxing Day, Pierre-Edouard knew that he could no longer get along with his father. He was saddened by this, for he had really hoped to establish a good relationship with him, one man to another. But it was impossible. And yet he was not questioning his father's authority as head of the family and master of the land in any way – if only his father would not take advantage of him, but accept that he was now more than twelve years old!

Indirectly, it was Louise who was again responsible for the row. On the morning of the 26th, Pierre-Edouard went to visit old Doctor Fraysse, and found out the address of the doctor at whose house she was working. He was so pleased with this information that he decided to go to Terrasson straight away; he returned home and changed.

'Where are you going like that?' called out his father.

'To town.'

'That's it – to town? Let me tell you you're not in the barracks here! There's plenty of work to be done. And if you want to spend your days in town you'd better put up in a hotel!'

'Listen, I've a right to enjoy my leave!'

'That's right, and I only have the right to work while I wait for you! You haven't even been to see the land!'

'I will, there's plenty of time. But now I'm going into town!'

'Which one?' questioned Jean-Edouard, who felt vaguely that his son's activities must have something to do with Louise. And he suddenly remembered that, a year earlier, Pierre-Edouard had told him he was going to Brive for a dinner with his school class. A dinner? Oh yes! Except it was a wedding!

'Which town?' he asked again.

'That's none of your business,' said Pierre-Edouard, marching towards the door.

'Miladiou!' grumbled his father, 'go on talking to me like that and you won't need to set foot here again!'

'Ah, well!' called back Pierre-Edouard, shrugging, 'then all you'll have to do is chuck Berthe out, and you'll be happy at last!'

Jean-Edouard sprang at him, grasped him by the arm and almost hit him.

'All right,' he said as he released him, 'go where you like. After all, I've been working alone for twelve months, and I've not been doing too badly!'

He passed in front of his son and set off towards the piggery.

Pierre-Edouard took three and a half hours to reach Terrasson. Twenty kilometres on foot held no fears for him, and at least these were accomplished without a full pack on his back, without a gun, without cartridge pouches, and with shoes which were not killing him. After having a snack at the first bistro he came to, he found the doctor's house with no difficulty and rang the bell.

He shuffled from one foot to the other, hardly knowing what to say to the old lady who, in three words, had just destroyed his happiness. Louise had been gone for a month. The railway construction yard was being closed, and Octave had returned to Orléans.

'But she is all right, as far as you know?' he asked at last.

'Yes, but . . . Are you a relative?'

'Her brother.'

'I should have guessed,' exclaimed the old lady, 'she looks like you. Yes, she's very well, and has no problems at all with her pregnancy.'

'Ah! she's expecting . . .'

'Yes, in January.'

He calculated immediately that the baby would arrive a full year after the wedding. Who would dare to gossip now!

'And you haven't got her address?'

'Yes, of course I have!'

This news lifted his spirits again; he had not come in vain.

He looked forward to the end of his leave with relief – not that he felt the slightest enthusiasm for the idea of returning to life in the barracks, but the atmosphere in his family was growing daily more oppressive.

And this despite having devoted all his time to the work on the farm, apart from his escapade to Terrasson. He found that he enjoyed returning to this work, but his father was so despotic that Pierre-Edouard could not accept all his strictures with good grace.

His father ruled and supervised everything, ordered the family by voice and gesture, as if he feared for his position as patriarch – which he now was in fact, since the death of the old man – and the slightest complaint unleashed a thunderbolt of recrimination. Pierre-Edouard noticed in amazement that his mother supported her husband totally, rather than trying to moderate his severity.

It was true that his parents needed to present an impenetrable defence to the attacks from without. Pierre-Edouard soon became aware of village opinion; as far as his parents were concerned they were consumed by envy, by jealousy, sometimes even by hate. Previously Jean-Edouard had been admired; now he was criticised remorselessly. He was not forgiven for his success, his money, his purchase of land, his ruthlessness in trampling on anyone who got in his way.

Added to this, many were angered at having to admit

that, once he had left the buying syndicate, it had survived only six months before sinking without trace. Last but not least amongst their complaints, since his resignation the town council had staggered from one crisis to the next; no one could ignore the accumulation of mistakes, the energy wasted in disagreements, which increased the electors' dissatisfaction. Some even predicted that Antoine Gigoux, ageing fast, would not stay until the end of his term of office; that he was preparing to resign in favour of his son. Now, many of the electors did not want to hear any mention of that candidate. They knew he was supported and encouraged behind the scenes by the young teacher, who was the new secretary at the Mairie, and they foresaw that they would be landed with a town council which many considered too left-wing. The opposition had rested their hopes on Jean-Edouard and he had betrayed them, as if he wanted the whole world to be punished because his daughter had run away.

Certainly no one could overlook the offence; what she had done was unforgiveable. But all in all, was that any good reason to make everyone suffer for it? Many who had admired him a year earlier for his noble attitude as an honest man ill-used by circumstance, now felt that he had made too much of what was essentially a private matter.

A few days in St Libéral were enough for Pierre-Edouard to gauge the resentment many neighbours felt towards his father, and, by association, all the members of the family. Even Léon reproached him curtly with his father's dishonesty, and he had a lot of difficulty in convincing Léon that he didn't know anything about the meadow business.

The discovery of all the bitterness surrounding the name of Viahle, added to the heavy, tense atmosphere of mourning which he found at home, spoiled his leave. He was almost happy to climb into the train one morning to return to Besançon. Only the knowledge that Berthe was utterly miserable prevented him from humming to himself as the train moved off.

He had not heard her speak more than three or four times during the whole of his visit. Mute and obstinate, the young girl submitted to all the work and trials imposed by her parents. She did not complain but retreated into complete silence. She seemed to be awaiting some miracle which would at last allow her to live.

The railway workers finally left the village at the beginning of February 1910. Their departure created a void in the life of St Libéral. They had been there for two and a half years; everyone had grown accustomed to their presence and, above all, to the trade they brought. Not everyone had known how to squeeze the maximum from this mass of consumers, as Jean-Edouard had done, but everyone had profited in one way or another from this lucky windfall. Its disappearance affected the economy of the community, and very soon they came to speak nostalgically of the good times when the railway yard had been open. This feeling, tinged with regret, was not solely due to the loss of substantial profits.

In two and a half years a tide of fellow-feeling had flowed between the strangers and the indigenous population; many were saddened to know that those long winter evenings of story-telling in the inn were gone forever. They used to gather in groups in the bar and listen open-mouthed to the fabulous tales recounted by some of the old navvies, who had toured the whole of France and North Africa. One of them, an old foreman in his sixties, had even been gangmaster on the cutting of the Panama Canal in 1886; thanks to him, life in the Americas was depicted in snippets during the course of the evenings. Since then a few privileged listeners had continued to narrate to others the old man's marvellous adventures. True or false, they also formed part of the good times when the railway yard was open.

With the departure of the workers, the peace and silence which had been forgotten for more than two years returned. St Libéral re-discovered its life, its customs, its humdrum daily round, hardly disturbed by the train passing through twice a day. And it was during this re-adjustment to the intimacy of village life that the new priest arrived.

Since the death of Father Feix the community had lacked a priest; Masses and various ceremonies had been provided by a curate from Objat. He was a likeable man, he could not be faulted, except that he was a stranger. He was accepted as such and tolerated simply because the Bishop had assured the parish that they would shortly have their own priest.

Months passed without an appointment being announced, despite the respectful enquiries from some of the faithful. It was necessary for the squire and the solicitor to take the matter in hand, and visit the bishop's palace to plead the community's cause.

Father Paul Verlhac arrived a month later, by the evening train. He was young and full of energy and had fought his first campaign as a soldier of Christ as curate at Tulle and then at Uzerche. His nomination to St Libéral raised him to the rank of priest, and he was very proud of this title. But he foresaw that he would need a lot of tact, patience and humility to become the really good shepherd he wished to be. So he began his ministry with great discretion.

They were grateful to him for his circumspection. A few spiteful tongues maintained that he was hiding his cards, some even whispered that he had a troubled past – that his departure from Uzerche was the result of some unpleasantness (there was talk of women, and also of notorious drunkenness) – but the majority of parishioners accepted the young priest, who bravely undertook the responsibilities of his new role and began to get to know the flock slowly and cautiously, like a farmer cultivating a new plot.

Pierre-Edouard agreed to join the training detachment for non-commissioned officers mainly to fill his increasingly boring days. A military career held no attraction for him, but the theoretical and practical courses required for the training were less dull than the everyday drudgery imposed on the troopers. In the end he was quite pleased to be forced into intellectual tasks.

He quickly absorbed the basics of trigonometry and

geography necessary to a good artilleryman, and turned with pleasure to the field exercises and various manoeuvres. These excursions allowed him to escape from the barracks for a while, and to explore a landscape and agricultural system which had nothing in common with the Corrèze.

Having no news of his parents, he conducted a correspondence with Louise instead, and was deeply moved to learn that she had chosen him as godfather to her son. Little Félix was now four months old, and would be baptised as soon as Pierre-Edouard was allowed leave to visit Orléans.

Louise recovered slowly from a difficult confinement; she had undergone a caesarian section which almost cost her her life. She seemed to be very happy and very much in love, but he wondered whether it was not rather forced, for she never mentioned her parents, Berthe or their neighbours. To read her letters you would think that nothing had happened before she ran away; that she had absolutely no interest in any part of what had been her life for eighteen years; that the only things that mattered from now on were her husband and her son.

He was a little saddened by this rejection. How could she pretend to have forgotten her childhood, her farm, everything? He remained bound to his land, body and soul; he missed it, as he missed the work, the animals, the plough, the long days of toil.

However, he knew that he had to reckon with his father's character; as the date of his discharge approached, he worried more and more about his future, and dreaded the resumption of their stormy relationship.

13

THE electors of St Libéral did not pay much attention to the voting for the Legislative Assembly in May 1910; they were absorbed in the spring farmwork, and a little sleepy and indifferent in their newfound peace and old re-adopted customs. Perhaps they would have reacted differently if Jean Duroux had stood as a candidate, but he was busy with the preparations for his elder daughter's wedding and had other things to worry about: he let it be known that his mandate as general councillor was sufficient; he had abandoned any other political ambitions.

So the men voted without great feeling or conviction; they knew that electoral gifts would not reach the area for a long time. They were all benefiting from the railway line, and expected nothing more.

But if the elections were quiet and quickly forgotten, another important event enlivened the summer. It brought further disruption to the lives of all the farmers, and there were many who considered it more significant than the opening of the railway.

The news emerged one morning at St Libéral market and had spread around the whole region before sunset: Teyssandier of Brignac had just bought a steam-driven threshing machine and was going into big business!

Everyone knew Teyssandier; he already visited all the most important farms of the canton each summer, set up his thresher and team, and dealt with the sheaves to the slow rhythm of two pairs of oxen who walked tirelessly around the mill. But his machinery was so archaic (he had inherited it from his father, who had acquired it in the '70s), so cobbled together, so temperamental in its functioning, he only agreed to get it going beside the big cornstacks, where size justified moving the engine into place and laboriously starting it up.

Many of the small farmers could not make use of that machine, and had to thresh their whole harvest with a flail. Those were exhausting days which left them all, women as well, with sore shoulders and arms, burning hands, and ears filled with the penetrating drumming of the ash staves hitting the straw-covered floor. So they were glad to learn that henceforth, thanks to this modern machine with its greatly improved output, Teyssandier would call at most of their smallholdings. And if they were really too small to justify the journey, there was nothing to stop the farmers from bringing their wheat sheaves to the machines.

So it was with impatience to see this marvel at work that they completed the harvest. Only a few moaners and a few old women maintained that all these machines would be the death of good workmanship, the ruin of the labourer, and would one day put the small farmer out of business. Moreover these old-timers stated quite positively, and quite mistakenly, that a threshing machine, however modern, could never produce such fine grain as that threshed by hand and cleaned on the wind, any more than a mowing-machine was capable of reaping a meadow as clean as a well-sharpened scythe wielded by a good workman!

No one listened to those old crabs; it was they who had put up the fiercest opposition to the train, who swore at the cars and insulted the passengers, who held that fertiliser was a concoction of the devil. And it was they who cried it was a lie, or a demonic invention, when they were assured that normal men, neither the excommunicated nor the damned, could climb into an aeroplane and rise into the air like crows. However, although not a single person in the village had been involved in such a miracle, many believed in it. The newspapers had talked about it for a long time, and besides, the squire had seen one of these flying engines during a journey to Paris, and he was no liar.

So the whiners and the grumblers were left to their old-fashioned ideas, and the threshing-machine was welcomed.

Teyssandier's acquisition forced Jean-Edouard out of his isolation, and the haughty silence he had affected towards his neighbours. But it was with anger in his heart that he undertook the necessary steps which allowed him to re-establish good relations with those he needed as friends.

He should have been the first to rejoice about the new machine; his harvest was one of the largest in the community, only exceeded by that of the squire. A thresher worthy of the name therefore had a job to do at his place, and he undertook to feed it as it deserved. But if he was secretly delighted at this purchase by the contractor, his happiness was spoiled by one problem which he could not solve alone; the manpower necessary for the efficient working of the machine . . .

He had to find at least a dozen strong men at whatever cost, who would be ready to help at the right moment. And those to whom he should have turned were the neighbours he no longer spoke to, and who might perhaps turn him down with a shrug of the shoulders. But he needed twelve men.

God knows he had counted and re-counted the jobs! The result was always twelve approaches, twelve visits during which he would be asking for favours. He needed one man to throw the sheaves from the rick to the thresher. Two other hands there, one to untie them, the other to feed the machine, then a fourth to watch over the sacks as they filled and tie them up when full. After that; three fellows to lift the hundred-kilo sacks up into the loft. Finally a minimum of three men to hump the threshed straw to the barn, where the two last ones would stack it. He himself would spell each of them in turn.

There was no way out of it; he had to call for help, say to Jeantout, for example: 'I need you, I'll come and give you a hand in return. . .' He had to invite all those people to come and work for him, to drink his wine, to eat at his table; he was obliged to open his house to them.

He imagined for a short while that he could do without their services, prove to everyone once again that he was clever and strong enough to succeed alone, without anyone's help. But he realised what a ridiculous spectacle he would make of himself, trying to thresh his whole harvest with a flail; it really was impossible. Perhaps he might have risked it if he had been twenty years younger and had Pierre-Edouard to help. . . But now; no, it was unthinkable.

He was so afraid of being refused that he could not get over the welcome he received. Even Jeantout, who had good reason to bear a grudge against him, did not refuse to come and help. But if no one made any reference to his past attitude and behaviour, he was sensitive enough to divine that no one had forgotten it. He had expected they would try to teach him a lesson by rejecting his request, but quickly understood that he had under-estimated his neighbours. No one prevaricated, everyone agreed directly, without any discussion, without even doing him the honour of making him beg, without giving him the opportunity to justify all the improprieties in his behaviour, which had mounted one upon another since Louise's flight.

It was not by refusing to come to his aid that his colleagues made their point; it was by agreeing. From now on he would stand indebted to them, would owe them a favour and feel himself at a disadvantage with them, until he had discharged the debt of work. And his worst fears would be realised if no one ever did ask for his help. Then, in everyone's eyes he would be shown up as a person to be ignored, a person so untrustworthy that he could not even be taken on to work . . .

On the surface he showed no visible sign of this humiliation; only Marguerite and Berthe felt how deeply he was distressed. It was Berthe above all who felt the repercussions of her father's mortification. She seemed to have resigned herself to the persecution which was her daily lot. She knew that whatever she did, her father would always find some reason to vent his anger on her. Nor was her mother any gentler with her and, although she did not add to her husband's constant bad temper, she at least made it clearly understood that she agreed with him on every point. The girl's only defence was to enclose herself in total silence, to suppress any sign of rebellion or tiredness, to dull the mind slowly into a state close to autism.

Even the arrival of the threshing-machine left her indifferent. It was nevertheless an exceptional event.

They learned that Teyssandier – who really knew the country well – was to begin his campaign of threshing in the hamlets scattered in the hills; in Fage, Peuch and Abeille Peak. He knew that up there the sun beat down fiercely, and the harvest was ripe well before that in the plain. Then he would turn to the Heath and the farm of old Bouyssoux, and finally he would reach St Libéral. Fate decreed that the first farm he came to on this route would be the Vialhes'.

Jean-Edouard was not the only one to have to call on his neighbours for help; Marguerite also had to appeal to several acquaintances to prepare the meals for the hard day's work. Teyssandier, his helper and a young labourer were added to the twelve men recruited by her husband, and it would not do to be stingy with the food for these fifteen fellows – sixteen, counting Jean-Edouard!

So, helped by Berthe and three neighbours, Marguerite installed herself in the kitchen twenty-four hours before the day of the threshing. She knew that the whole family, and she especially, would be judged by the manner in which they fed their guests. If one single person considered that she had stinted the quantity or the quality, everyone would say that the Vialhes had lost their sense of hospitality and their good manners, as well as their daughter. It would be whispered that they had grown mean, more disposed to get work on account than to feed those who, out of the goodness of their hearts, had come to their aid.

So, even if it meant they all died of indigestion, she would prove to them that the Viahle household was just as prosperous and well-run as ever, despite the unhappiness it had suffered. In short, she was upholding her rank.

She therefore sacrificed numerous chickens, prepared an enormous pot-au-feu, a brawn and some calves' feet. To these first provisions she would add, in due course, clear soup with noodles, two sorts of pâté, ham, pickled pork, tomato salad, cucumbers and lettuce, kidney beans, salsify in a glaze, cheeses; then would come a variety of fruit and jam tarts, and finally *merveilles*, those lightly fried cakes which she cooked to perfection.

Would any worker dare to say that he was still hungry? Anyway, she would be watching closely to make sure no one toyed with their food, refused a dish, turned their nose up at a chicken leg or a slice of cherry tart, and if they all fell under the table exhausted, so much the better!

Apart from the cooking she dressed the dishes, polished the plates and cutlery, laid the table; even her mother-in-law had to bestir herself and join in the work.

Old Léonie was now isolated by total deafness and did not understand the reasons for this great to-do, and so she murmured vague queries as she began to shell an enormous heap of kidney beans. Completely cut off from the world, several times during the day she ventured a question, but in vain – no one took the trouble to answer her any longer, except with a shrug. What good was it trying to communicate with the poor woman, when even a gun-shot would not make her blink? It was equally useless to put the answer down on paper; she could neither read nor write.

Despite this she persisted in talking, ceaselessly asking questions on a subject which tormented her like a thorn beneath a nail. She had seen Pierre-Edouard in uniform during his leave, and had deduced that he was completing his military service. But where was Louise? Why had she been away for so long?

Old Léonie tipped a handful of beans into the stew-pan and looked at her daughter-in-law. An idea came to her.

'All this, would it by any chance be for Louise's wedding?'

For the first time, and because it all seemed quite reasonable, she openly expressed the fruit of her silent thoughts. She had been there at that meal during which Jean-Edouard had slapped the girl. She had not seen her since then, and had patiently formulated an explanation for that scene. Her grand-daughter had certainly been at fault and had been sent away; that was quite proper. She had to get married quietly, probably at Rocamadour, that was where all the girls in a hurry went. But now, after such a long time, she could return and no one would take exception to it. So it would be for her, her husband and child that they were preparing the feast . . .

Nevertheless, in her role as grandmother she would have to appear shocked, to tell Louise that it was wrong to have eaten her Easter eggs during Lent. That was not how it was done in respectable families, she would tell her, and then it would not be mentioned again.

'Well, that's good, isn't it? She's coming back?' she repeated.

Marguerite blushed and glanced at her daughter, and at the three neighbours who were silently plucking the chickens.

'Isn't that so? Answer me!'

Marguerite shook her head violently, but her furious look did not stop her mother-in-law, who suddenly saw the light:

'Well then, if it isn't that . . . What is it? Where can she be, Louise, eh? I'd have known if she were dead, wouldn't I? Poor little thing!'

Her daughter-in-law hesitated, certain that her neighbours were eagerly watching her reaction — then she confirmed it. And her nod of agreement was a challenge to the whole community, to all the gossip, all the speculation. Who would now dare to speak of Louise again? It was high time that this whole affair was finally forgotten; high time for an end to the questions about whether she and Jean-Edouard would one day forgive Louise. Now the matter was closed. The neighbours would pass on the news, and everyone would know that the Vialhes had cut themselves off from their daughter.

She ignored her mother-in-law, who now began to cry

silently, without stopping her work of shelling the beans. Marguerite grasped a chicken and pushed it towards Berthe.

'Go on, stop dreaming! Hurry up, time's getting on!'

Instinctively the neighbours quickened the pace of their work as well, as if humbled by such resolve, such hardness of heart.

Marguerite reported the scene to Jean-Edouard; on reflection she was not sure whether she had acted wisely, but he agreed with her completely.

Curiously enough he felt comforted, relieved of a burden he had been carrying for a long time. From now on, as Marguerite had said, there would be no further misunderstandings; everyone would know once and for all where they stood. He felt stronger, more secure, certain that the weaklings would no longer pity him, the cowards no longer make excuses for him and commiserate with him, the jokers no longer smile at his expense.

Once again he would show them, all of them, what it was to be a Vialhe! He discovered that he no longer felt worried at the idea of collecting the thresher and the steam-engine from the Heath.

Teyssandier had decided that each hirer should go and fetch the equipment from its last work-place. So Jean-Edouard would go to old Bouyssoux; when the work was finished, someone else would come and take delivery of the engine from him.

That evening, when there were still two good hours of daylight left, he connected up his two pairs of cows, called to them and made his way to Jeantout's place. He had asked him, and Gaston as well, to accompany him with their own cows; four pairs of animals would not be too many to pull that heavy equipment. It seemed that the steam-engine was a formidable weight, and six cows had sometimes been needed to get it up the steeper slopes.

Dinner was in full swing when he arrived at the Bouyssoux farm; the atmosphere was jolly, laughter rang out and pitchers of wine were doing the rounds, as the men called for them and held out their glasses.

Jean-Edouard had not spoken a word to Bouyssoux since he had broken off the marriage. Each man sedulously avoided the other, and even took care that they did not have to greet each other at the market in St Libéral. Today, however, they would have to speak . . .

'Good evening, everyone!' called out Jean-Edouard, as he approached the table under the shade of a large umbrella pine.

All the men fell silent, and even the tipsy heads cleared in a flash as they understood that the slightest remark could precipitate a scene. Everyone knew that old Bouyssoux considered Jean-Edouard, and all the Vialhes, his enemies; his slanders were circulating round the whole region. One of his least malicious lies was that Jean-Edouard and his whore of a daughter were responsible for his son not getting married. (His Léonard had not, in fact, been able to find a good match anywhere.)

'Well, did it do a good job?' asked Jean-Edouard. Sober, Bouyssoux would not have fallen for this trick, but his mind was dulled by fatigue, noise and dust, and he was drunk on the strong wine which he had been taking since daybreak. He jumped feet first into the trap.

'Did a good job?' he exclaimed. 'And how! I told them, everyone,' he shouted, with a sweep of the arm towards the workers, ' "Yes, sir," I told them: "Have a good look, you won't see another harvest like this one at the Heath in a hurry!" We were threshing all day! And that machine, it can deal with any amount!'

Jean-Edouard nodded, and turned towards Teyssandier.

'Good, we can take it? I wouldn't like to be too late getting back; we need to be able to set it up this evening and start as early as possible tomorrow morning. Because at my place,' he said, addressing Bouyssoux, 'it will be working for two full days! Well, yes!' he added, as if apologising. 'I sowed more than thirty plots of oats, so it will take more than one little day to swallow all that, even if it's a very greedy machine . . . Let's go. Jeantout and Gaston are going to manage the thresher; I'll take charge of the steam-engine . . .'

Already he was backing his animals up in order to harness them to the steam-engine.

'My God!' cried the old man with a false laugh. 'You don't think you're going to pull that boiler with your two pairs of animals! I bet it won't move a single metre!'

Jean-Edouard smiled.

'You'll lose again, Bouyssoux. Everybody knows that your draught animals are hardly as strong as the sick goats which give your son so much pleasure . . . And everybody knows that mine are as strong as oxen! But then of course, our place isn't like yours, we don't ration their food . . .'

He called the four animals by name, gently touched their horns with his goad, and set off without even turning round. The animals braced themselves, joined forces and dragged the heavy machine after them.

A murmur of admiration ran through the crowd of helpers. Say what you like, Jean-Edouard, he was really something!

From five o'clock in the morning Teyssandier and his two aides were busy about the steam-engine; they filled it with water, stoked and lit the boiler, greased the belt-pulleys and stretched the drive belts.

The neighbours arrived in small groups and wandered around it at a distance, frightened of the machine, nodding their heads as its mysteries were revealed.

The thresher impressed them more than the steam-engine, which after all was rather like the locomotive that passed through the village twice a day. The thresher, on the other hand, was nothing like the antique model which Teyssandier had brought out for so many years.

It was enormous, magnificent, with orange paintwork and the name of the genius who manufactured it spread out in huge letters: MERLIN-VIERSON. It was worrying, too: full of pulleys, gears, belts which crossed over, valves and grids, slide-valves and trapdoors.

It was said to be capable of threshing ten quintals in an hour; but if they were not mistaken, that meant this new-fangled quintal of a hundred kilos, not the measure used in the country, which reckoned a quintal as the sum of five times ten kilos. This colloquial unit of measurement created a lot of trouble between the generations. The young people, instructed by the teacher, said that a quintal weighed a hundred kilos, and that its name did not come from the old French word 'quinte', as the ignoramuses thought, but from Arabic 'quintar'. What a fuss and complication! For their elders, a quintal would always be fifty kilos. So, whatever some people said, it was actually *twenty* 'quintals' that the thresher dealt with in an hour, and that really was a lot!

At about a quarter past six Marguerite called everyone and offered the first refreshment of the day. The men were a little intimidated, for it was a long time since any of them had entered the Vialhes' house; nevertheless they did justice to the soup, to the pâté, the ham and the soft cheese; but they talked little, not daring to restart a dialogue which had been broken off so long ago by the master of the house. A feeling of unease hung over them, and it was with relief that they left the table to gather around the threshing machine.

The engine had got up steam and was humming like a bread oven; its tall chimney spat out thick black wreaths of smoke, and terrifying jets of steam forced open the valves.

Teyssandier explained the work to each man, and advised them to beware of the belts and pulleys, which he warned were capable of slicing off a head or an arm.

Everyone took his place, a little tense, alarmed at the thought of serving such a monstrous machine, and full of admiration for its owner who dared to go right up to it. The piercing whistle, so unbearably shrill, surprised them all. They recoiled.

Teyssandier manipulated the valve, and the engine emitted a great cry from the boiler, which was ready for work. And this wave of sound broke over the village, echoed on the surrounding hills, announced as far as Yssandon and Perpezac, and even further, that a day's work was beginning at the Vialhes'. With a slight movement he released the great lever which freed the gigantic driving-wheel.

At first there was nothing but a low murmur followed by a long hissing of the belts as they stretched, and a clicking of the cogs as they engaged. Then he increased the pressure.

Suddenly the noise enveloped them, its intensity throwing them into a panic. They recoiled a step or two further. The speed and uproar grew, the machine changed its rhythm and began to whirr regularly, and already all the dust and chaff which had collected in its innermost workings shot out in all directions, stinging their eyes and throats.

'Right!' shouted Teyssandier as he climbed on to the machine. 'It wants some wheat!'

Jean-Edouard was the first to get a grip on himself; he nimbly scaled the rick, grasped a sheaf and threw it on to the deck of the thresher. It was immediately untied by the labourer and the wheat stalks spread out in front of Teyssandier, who pushed them slowly but deftly towards the metal beater drums, which were vibrating like humming tops. They swallowed them with a greedy crunching, and all the men listened to the progress of the corn and the straw as it passed through the entrails of the thresher.

And everyone wanted to admire the first blond grains, taking them in their cupped hands as soon as they dropped, shining and clean, out of the drum. Jeantout drew out a big fistful, examined it and passed it to Jean-Edouard, who leaned down from the top of the mill, wanting to see it too. He admired the grain, smiled, then spat on his hands and signalled for another sheaf.

Then all the men took up their positions, for they were all in a hurry now to be part of this revolution of steam-threshing.

They worked until midday, and the heap of grain in the Vialhe granary grew higher. Marguerite came round many times to pour the men frequent large glasses of chilled wine, which they all swallowed eagerly, for the heat was intense and the dust awful.

They had gradually grown accustomed to the noise, and when Teyssandier stopped the engine's transmission the silence could almost be felt. The thresher ran on, still whirring round for a short while, then its note changed, grew softer, murmured and finally stopped.

Now they looked at each other, grey with dirt and streaming with sweat; they were astonished, and laughed, at being able to speak without having to yell. Reeling with exhaustion, they all went to the well and doused themselves with big buckets of fresh water. So there was already good-natured banter as they sat down around the table.

Immediately – even though they had been dreading this reunion, and each had solemnly vowed to remain silent to avoid the dangers of hazardous conversation, even though Jean-Edouard himself had been prepared for silence – they all began to talk.

There was so much to say about the machine! And so much to laugh about, when comparing its results with threshing by flail! Such shouts of laughter at the way Jean-Edouard had snubbed old Bouyssoux the previous evening! However, that was a thorny subject which threatened to get out of hand. . . But everyone agreed with Jean-Edouard; he had done a bloody good job, putting that old sod in his place, that's how you should speak to that savage at the Heath!

As the dishes and glasses flowed by, they renewed the bonds of friendship and esteem. Jean-Edouard did not forget for one second that he was under an obligation to his neighbours from now on, that he owed them, all of them, the good turn they had done him; but he did not feel inferior to them any more. Quite the opposite, in fact.

He realised that all these men were at heart very proud to have been chosen as workmates. He was honest enough to admit that he too had always felt flattered when someone came to beg a favour. Was that not proof that you could rely on him, that his level-headedness, his strength and knowledge were recognised? He looked at his companions, understood that he had chosen them for their good qualities; by his approach he had paid tribute to them, and they were grateful to him for it.

He had been mistaken in believing he could detect a malicious plan when they had accepted so promptly. Jeantout, Gaston and the others were not there to teach him a lesson, at least not in the way he had expected. They were there because they were happy to meet again, as before, in his home. Happy to prove that mutual help and good neighbourliness were the right thing at all times. Yes, that was the real lesson, and it was no shame to learn it.

14

A heavy, cold and clammy drizzle soaked the town and transformed the rays of the gas lamps into the dim glow of candle-ends.

Pierre-Edouard had lost his way in an area far from the one he was looking for. Angry with himself, and angry with this unknown and unprepossessing town, he decided to ask the way yet again.

An old strawberry seller, who was sorting his unsold wares before covering his cart, assured him that he was on the right road; another two hundred paces and he would see the Cloister of St Aignan on his right. The alley which he had been trying to locate for more than two hours lay just behind it; he could not mistake it or overshoot, it ended in the River Loire.

He slowed down and searched through the mist for signs of a bar. He had need of a glass of something to give him courage, so as not to turn right round and set off at a run for the station.

He had looked forward to his reunion with Louise all summer, but now it was turning into a nightmare. God knows how he had counted the days that remained until little Félix's christening! Instead of that celebration, planned for the last Sunday in October, a telegram had arrived the previous day; it was now fingered into fragments at the bottom of his pocket. Four words had made his heart pound and now caught at his throat, slowed his steps, killed all his courage; 'Octave dead, come . . . Louise.'

He pushed open the door of an estaminet, ordered a Calvados, and emptied it in one gulp.

'Hi there, soldier,' chaffed a drinker, 'I heard you like that better than facing the guns!'

He did not reply, but his expression was enough to stifle any further remarks. He held out his glass to be refilled, swallowed it down with one flick of his wrist, paid and went out.

The bedroom smelt of gas lamps, unchanged baby, medicine, death. At first he did not recognise Louise. He had left a girl, fresh, plump and pretty, and now a tired woman, aged and thin, was clasped in his arms.

What to do, what to say? Nothing except to stammer: 'Come, come,' as he stroked the head resting on his shoulder.

He gently pushed his sister away and greeted the old lady seated beside the bed. Obviously Octave's mother. Then he looked at the dead man.

A shock, and then suddenly a glimpse into the past. Octave in his bedroom in the inn, back there in St Libéral ... He relived the scene and remembered the slight young man, so slim, frail and defenceless, with his nightshirt flapping at his thighs, revealing his skinny legs; the hands too delicate, too white, which fingered the little cigar.

In death Octave looked more emaciated, pale and pitiful, but he was recognisable, and the fingers entwined with a rosary were indeed those which had offered him the box of cigars. Yes, truly Octave had changed less than Louise ...

He made the sign of the cross, collected his thoughts for a few moments, and then returned to his sister.

'How did it happen?'

She shrugged her shoulders and wiped her eyes. 'Galloping consumption ...'

'And why didn't you tell me anything about it?'

'What good would it have done ... Besides we didn't know, we thought it was asthma ... And when the doctor told us, two months ago, it was already too late. There it is ...'

He should have raged at her, told her that she had really been blind and stupid not to suspect it earlier! That the emaciation and pallor of her husband were obvious signs;

that he himself had been filled with compassion at the sight of Octave, quite pitiful in his nightshirt two years ago. But he remained silent.

'You have at least told our parents?'

'No.'

'You must,' he insisted. 'I'll do it, if you like.'

She shrugged her shoulders.

'And Félix?'

'He's sleeping, over there.'

'I'd like to see him.'

He had been prepared for the sight of a sickly baby, rather puny, like his father; he was surprised at the strength and size of the child – an enormous infant with plump cheeks and chubby hands all dotted with dimples.

'My goodness!' he gasped. 'Don't get angry with me if I tell you that's a real Vialhe you've got there!'

'I know. And at his birth he was just as difficult and uncooperative as a Vialhe . . . That's not meant for you!' she apologised hastily.

He pretended not to have heard.

'Our parents are going to be proud of him, you'll see. They'll be mad about him!'

'Certainly not!'

'Why's that? You don't think they'll leave the door closed to you now? We'll see about that!'

'Open or closed, it makes no difference. I won't be returning.'

'But you're mad! So what *do* you propose to do?'

'I'll manage . . .'

'But him!' he pointed with his forefinger towards the baby. 'You've got to bring him up, feed him, look after him!'

'Exactly! He's mine, all that's left to me, and I'm keeping him,' she said forcefully.

And suddenly he recognised her again; stubborn, sure of herself, strong and resolute. Once again, she intended to lead her life as she thought fit.

'You must understand,' she explained in a firm voice, 'if I come back to the village, everyone will insinuate – even tell me outright – that Octave's death was a punishment from Heaven. And besides, our parents would want to take charge of the little one, and I won't have that!'

'But,' he repeated, 'what are you going to live on?'

'I told you, I'll manage,' she replied sharply.

'My God,' he grumbled, 'you're worse than a mule! Well, I'll tell the parents, we'll see . . .'

'Tell them if you like, I don't think it's worth discussing any further. By the way, the baby has been christened . . .'

'But I thought that . . .' he said in disappointment.

'Yes, I know, don't worry. In the register, you are the godfather. It was Octave who wanted the ceremony brought forward . . .' He looked at her and saw her eyes fill with tears. 'Yes,' she continued, 'he knew it would make me happy to know he was baptised before . . . before he went away, you know . . . And yet he didn't really believe in it . . . It was just to make me happy. So he was baptised a month ago. He's called Félix Octave Pierre . . .'

'You were right,' he murmured, 'it was best to do it.' He cleared his throat, and continued with a sigh: 'Your husband – I have to say it, your husband was a gentleman.'

Pierre-Edouard wrote to his parents as soon as he returned to Besançon. His sister had made him promise that he would reveal neither her address nor her plans; he kept his word and limited himself to reporting the tragedy in a few short words. Then he mentioned his nephew and, as he wanted them to know whose side he was on, he did not hesitate to tell them that he was very proud to be little Félix's godfather, and very proud to have known Octave Flaviens as well.

He waited almost a month for the reply, and understood when he read it just how right Louise had been. Of course his parents regretted Octave's death, but should it not be seen as a sign from Heaven, a cruel but just punishment for Louise's improper behaviour? Naturally, if she asked, she and her son could return to the farm; there was plenty of room and work for them. They would not turn her away, and no one would mention the past, for everyone in the family and the village would realise that she had paid the price for her transgression.

But if she wished to return to the fold, it would have to be done discreetly, modestly, in all humility. As for the child, they would look after it, of course . . . Finally, Pierre-Edouard himself should understand, once and for all, that he was free to feel as he liked about his sister – on condition that he kept his feelings to himself and never tried to preach to his parents again.

Having said that, they were looking forward to showing the community what two strong, industrious men could make of land which only needed to be broken in.

He crumpled the letter and threw it away in fury; it did not even merit a reply. Besides, what would he say? Every line, every word, clearly showed that his father – supported by his mother – remained obdurate as head of the family, and intended to continue as such.

But Pierre-Edouard's doubts grew stronger; would it be possible for him to bear his father's tyranny without reacting? It was only two and a half months until his release. Since he had become a non-commissioned officer, he knew how intoxicating power and command could be, although he had never abused his modest authority; he knew it would be almost impossible to return to the humiliation of passive obedience.

Once more Marguerite acted adroitly; so cleverly that Jean-Edouard had to congratulate her. Thanks to her the Vialhe family rapidly regained the prestige they had lost when Louise ran away.

Since the threshing, proper relations had been re-established with all their neighbours. Gradually all Jean-Edouard's meanness and spite were forgotten, but their memory was not swept away completely, and everyone knew that the slightest thing could break the bridges of friendship once more. The proof of this lay in Jean-Edouard's continued refusal to take charge of the buying syndicate, and insistence that he would not take on the role of mayor; many had hoped he would stand at the next elections.

One single step taken by Marguerite was sufficient to rekindle the esteem and sympathy of the majority of the community. Two years earlier they had been objects of pity, because of their unhappiness. Then, as the months passed, this had turned to dislike when they seemed to want to make the whole village feel the burden of their misery. But now the neighbours were sorry for them with good reason; pitying and forgiving, for this time it was a serious matter . . .

Despite being new to the parish, Father Verlhac had begun to discover the character of his flock; he also knew many secrets and gradually, with tact and patience, learned the family histories.

As far as the Vialhes were concerned, public rumour had alerted him to their unhappiness from the moment he had arrived in the village. He knew of Louise's love affair and of her parents' attitude to it; although he personally disapproved of their harshness, he had not yet found the right opportunity or excuse to broach the subject with Marguerite or Jean-Edouard. So he thought that Heaven had come to his aid when he saw Marguerite waiting for him as the church emptied after Angelus; she asked to speak to him.

'Is it urgent?' he asked, for he had decided that he wanted plenty of time for an interview in which he hoped to persuade the Vialhes to forgive their daughter.

Marguerite nodded, and he noticed her downcast expression, her sombre appearance.

'It's about saying Masses for someone who has died . . .'

He thought a moment, and remembered that Grand-father Vialhe had been dead less than two years. 'For your late lamented father-in-law, no doubt? I didn't know him, but I've heard well of him. It's good of you to be concerned about his salvation.'

'No, Father, it's not for my father-in-law, it's for our poor son-in-law . . .' murmured Marguerite. For the first time in her life she used the word 'son-in-law' to describe Octave.

Father Verlhac was out of his depth; he had not yet

194

sufficient understanding of human cunning to comprehend all the clever, calculating hypocrisy in Marguerite's request. Old Father Feix would never have swallowed a bait like that; he knew his faithful flock too well, and would have immediately seen through this stratagem. Besides, Marguerite would never have tried that game with him.

But Father Verlhac was young, more inclined to see good than bad. He never entertained the slightest suspicion, so it was in good faith that he became the tool of his parishioner in her carefully prepared plan.

'Your son-in-law has died?' he exclaimed. And he was really very sad.

Marguerite assented with a sorrowful sniff, gave a few details, recalled with great discretion and humility the reasons for their silly quarrel, which had taken place so long ago, lamented the sad fate of her daughter and little Félix, then offered the young priest the fee for twenty-four masses, one a month for two years.

'It's simply that we've suffered so much unhappiness already, Father, that – well, we don't want to talk about it, you know what people are like . . . I know some will say that we're pleased about this tragedy . . . So if you just announce on Sunday that you're saying Masses for our poor son-in-law, that will be enough. The neighbours will know that we don't want to be visited, we don't want to talk about all our misfortunes, and that'll be that.'

'Of course,' agreed the priest, 'I understand. Take heart, my dear woman; I shall pray for you, and for him . . .'

Thus the whole community learned of the loss the Vialhes had suffered. Everyone was genuinely sorry for them. How could you hold a grudge against people like that, who were victims of one tragedy after another! Besides, everyone greatly appreciated their discretion and their gesture. With these twenty-four Masses they showed Christian forgiveness towards the young assistant surveyor, including him in the parish and the family at the same time; for each month during those two years Father Verlhac would announce, as was the custom: 'Mass for the soul of Octave Flaviens, son-in-law to the Vialhes.' In addition, each Sunday for a year he included the deceased in all the Masses, when he remembered the dead of the parish.

Thanks to this posthumous reconciliation one could at last talk about Louise quite safely. She was no longer a fallen woman, a runaway, but a poor and pitiable widow. Her loss ennobled her, and surrounded her parents with an aura of respectability.

The wedding of Jean Duroux's elder daughter was an unforgettable event. It was remembered for years and impressed everyone just as much as the festivity and rejoicing organised when the railway line was opened.

It was gorgeous. Even the weather co-operated for one day, although it had been frightful since the beginning of the month; the squire led his daughter to the Mairie beneath a pale October sun.

Only the chief attendants – twelve bridesmaids and their escorts –and the closest relatives could fit into the little hall, where Antoine Gigoux welcomed the husband and wife-to-be, and fought to control a paralysing bout of stage-fright.

The remaining friends – at least twenty more ladies and gentlemen, so well dressed it was difficult to tell who was the richest – gathered on the steps of the Mairie and clapped each time the fiancés said 'I do'.

The inhabitants of St Libéral, intimidated by such splendour, squeezed into the main square and held their breath. They were overwhelmed. Jean Duroux had hired the whole of the inn for the chauffeurs and valets, and they had revealed (in confidence, of course) the lofty station of the guests. There were more than a dozen counts present, three dukes, several lords – among them a Scotsman in his ceremonial kilt, who so transfixed the spectators that they did not dare to laugh – not forgetting two former government ministers, three deputies and two prefects. And to watch over the security of these important persons, all the gendarmes of the Ayen force were on parade, in their best uniforms.

The wedding party crossed the square and proceeded towards the church. They were received by Father Verlhac, also very intimidated by the archbishop who was present, a cousin of the young groom. He was to undertake the blessing of the rings, receive their vows and deliver the address.

For more than three weeks Father Verlhac had not known which way to turn. First of all he had to clean the church from top to bottom, take out and beat the old carpets, scour the chandeliers, the censor, the little hand-bell; wax the pews and chairs, dust down the statues, scrape off the rivulets of wax which surrounded the Virgin's feet, hunt the spiders' webs hiding in the copper lights.

He also had to repair the best altar cloths and orna-ments, wash, iron and starch the eight red chasubles for the choirboys, and their surplices, heavy with lace.

Finally, to avoid any mistakes, he had rehearsed the high nuptial Mass with the choir, a complex ceremonial to be performed before a congregation more used to cathedrals than to the simplicity and poverty of his church.

The crowd entered and Father Verlhac immediately noticed a ripple pass through the congregation, a sort of embarrassment, a hesitation in taking their seats. He panicked and turned to the archbishop, silently begging for help. The prelate reassured him with a smile, and leaned towards him.

'It's nothing, my son. They are accustomed to an usher showing them to their seats, according to their rank and relationship to the couple. Here there is no one to guide them and they don't know where to sit! It's much better this way; it's very good for them to be reminded from time to time that they are all equal before God. Let them be, they'll get settled eventually!'

Father Verlhac forced a timid smile, and turned to examine the altar for the last time. He heard the scraping of chairs and a gentle hubbub, then all fell silent. The congregation was finally seated.

'You see,' whispered the prelate, 'God takes care of

these matters so well! The old man, there, on the right, in the morning coat, he's a former government minister, a Freemason of course, who voted with both hands for those villainous anti-clerical laws. You know who is beside him? One of my cousins, a knight of Saint Sepulchre, who was received and blessed by our Holy Father the Pope less than a month ago! Amusing, isn't it?'

The ceremony was perfect, and if Father Verlhac was distracted for a moment no one noticed it; he promised himself a severe penance when he caught himself, his heart full of joy and amazement, estimating the value of the collection. Truly, the baskets of coins and notes were a disturbing sight for such a poor priest as he! Never had he imagined such alms; enough to help him forget all his money worries for a long time – and God knew how serious those worries were.

A peal of bells sounded as the newly-married couple stepped out of the church; the square was dark with people and all the village boys were there. Generously the young groom threw them a handful of sweets, among which twinkled the occasional ten-franc coin. A few punches were exchanged as these heavenly gifts were collected up, but that did not disturb the general good humour.

Perspiring with happiness, Jean Duroux was savouring his triumph. Helped by his daughter he had at last made his dreams come true. His son-in-law, a well-bred fellow of thirty-five, was from the true nobility – from the Napoleonic Empire admittedly, but with a real coat-of-arms, won with great honour by his ancestors, who had made history for France by distinguishing themselves at the battles of Marengo, Jena or Austerlitz! His son-in-law even boasted of his great-grand-uncle the cardinal, who, he maintained, had been advisor and friend to his Holiness Pope Pius IX!

Despite that, he was a straightforward person, and not proud, as the villagers quickly concluded. He willingly shook them by the hand and inquired about the progress of the farmwork, the health of their animals and relatives, without any haughtiness. He loved hunting too, and he won the respect of all the men when they learned from Célestin that he was in the habit of letting off both barrels at partridges, and that his gun was even more beautiful and more expensive than the squire's.

Added to all these qualities, he had a solid fortune judiciously invested in the Land Banks of France (in bonds of 500 francs which earned 3% per annum), in the Orléans Railway Company (also at 3%), in sugar refineries in Egypt (at 4%) without forgetting the Consolidated Russian Loan (of 1901, at 4%) and his stocks in the Electricity Company of Moscow (at 5%); so Jean Duroux's great happiness was easily understood. One could also very well understand why he had not hesitated to augment his daughter's 300,000-franc dowry with one of his properties in Brest and two of the tenant farms belonging to the château estate.

The whole wedding party lined up in front of the church, set their smiles and posed patiently for the photographers. That done, the guests climbed into the gleaming automobiles which would take them to the château, but Jean Duroux, with his daughter and son-in-law, joined a group of men in their Sunday best who were waiting in front of the inn.

They were almost all there; Gaston, Jeantout, Léon and a great many other farmers, besides the smith, the butcher, the baker, the miller, the postman, the village policeman and the station-master, the carpenters and the masons and, strutting amongst them, the gendarmes from Ayen, their shiny uniforms bursting with pride.

The only ones missing were the solicitor, the two doctors, the mayor and the priest, but everyone knew that they were invited to the wedding breakfast, and were probably already in the château, mixing with high society. All the men gathered in the square were very proud to know that the others were up there, as representatives of the community.

Jean-Edouard was not there. He had excused himself, and everyone agreed that his recent sad loss was good reason for his absence.

Jean Duroux invited them to go in. He had very honourably and thoughtfully decided to offer a drink to all those who wished to share his joy; so, while the bells pealed, they all joked and squeezed into the saloon of the inn. There the squire treated them to champagne, to everyone's amazement, for there were many who admitted that they had never drunk it before.

As for Léon, the sparkling wine transported him back ten years; to that first night of the century, when his sister had been born. What a lot had happened since then! And how he had come up in the world!

He was in a fair way to becoming one of the more important stock-dealers in the area. He did not have what you would call really close friends, and some people did not trust him completely, but at least he was respected: for his money, to be sure, but also for his acknowledged skills and his perfect eye for judging an animal.

Everyone clinked glasses, wished the couple every joy, congratulated the happy father of the bride, and in a welter of compliments and good wishes, accompanied their hosts to the huge red Renault, which set off to the cheers of the crowd.

At the château the celebrations went on for three days, and in the evenings everyone in the village could hear the strains of the orchestra the squire had hired. And everyone approved of the marvellous fireworks which were the crowning glory of the wedding night – that sumptuous wedding which figured long and large in the history of St Libéral.

15

1911 began with rain. One would have thought all the water in the sky had been chucked down during the previous year, and that after the floods – even Paris had been up to its belly in water – the sun would appear. But the rain was still there, persistent, penetrating and glacial.

However, Pierre-Edouard and his friends faced it cheerfully. What did spouts of water matter now? They were free at last, released from military service, to return to the civilian life which had been interrupted two years ago.

The exhilaration of freedom, girls, good wine – what joy! And the Devil take the barracks, the uniform and the fatigue details; damn all those cowardly NCOs and officers who had wasted twenty-four months of their youth; they wished they might never see them again, with their stripes, their hellish rules and their bloody guns!

Pierre-Edouard and his companions dispersed throughout Besançon, still quite amazed that they could lark about without the risk of being apprehended by a patrol of the Military Police. They were still careful, however, for they were under military jurisdiction until their demobilisation papers had been stamped by the police in the capitals of their respective cantons. They plunged into the nearest bar to change into their old civilian clothes – they would put their uniforms on again for the train journey.

Pierre-Edouard realised that he had grown appreciably. His jacket was tight across his shoulders, but he was delighted to put it on. Thanks to it he could push behind him First-Sergeant Vialhe of the 2nd Battery, 3rd Unit, 5th Artillery Regiment of Besançon, and at last became Pierre-Edouard Vialhe again, of Saint-Libéral-sur-Diamond! That was worth a round of drinks, or even several! As the highest in rank, he ordered the first . . .

Night was coming on as the band of happy revellers – some of them staggering dangerously – made their way tunefully towards the station. There, after weighty slaps on the back, a last exchange of addresses and promises to meet up again one day, the little group separated, dispersing on to the various platforms to wait for trains to Paris, Strasbourg or Nancy.

As for Pierre-Edouard, he had to cut short the protestations of friendship and jump nimbly into the Lyon train as it ground out of the station.

The day after his return, Pierre-Edouard set about re-discovering his world, and it was with delight that he strode across the fields, the meadows and the woods of the farm. Everything was in good order, well-kept, and the thirty-one walnut trees on the big field had grown luxuriantly, a perfect line of white trunks.

As for the animals, they were superb, shining with health – only the horse was not up to standard; he found its coat dull and eyes sad, and made a note to speak to his father about it. But in his happiness he quickly forgot the animal and gaily set about renewing old friendships with people in the village, the neighbours, Léon, anyone who called out to him and offered a drink to celebrate his return.

He immediately noticed that their attitude to his parents had changed. The village no longer criticised them, but sympathised with them, and the feeling was genuine. He guessed that this was connected with Octave's death and was astounded, but he said nothing, although he was determined to get to the truth of the matter.

He could not believe the extent to which his parents had managed to draw a veil over Louise's flight, nor that Octave's death had led them to absolve the fault. For, if that were the case, what was the meaning of that letter which had made him so furious?

When he returned home he observed more clearly what was going on. Back in the family he was aware of a strange feeling; a sort of false bonhomie that was overdone and did not ring true. At first sight the atmosphere did indeed seem to be less tense; his father appeared less imperious and his mother less worried. But that only highlighted Berthe's downtrodden expression, and his grandmother's total bewilderment; everyone was ill-at-ease.

He guessed that the whole business of Louise was poisoning their relationships, and was inwardly revolted by the idea of spending his whole life on guard, of biting his tongue so as not to show his parents the grief that would no doubt afford them a certain mean satisfaction.

He decided to lance the abcess immediately. He was of an age to feel he should not have to pretend and deceive if he wanted to write to his sister, send a postal-order to his godson, or pin his photo above his bed. False alibis, secret meetings, news via intermediaries and accomplices – that was schoolboy stuff; he was a man, and intended to make that fact known. He started to open the wound during the evening meal.

'Have you any news of Louise?'

His father started, surprised by the attack, then he reddened and his breathing quickened.

'Miladiou!' he scolded after a pause. 'What gives you the right to ask questions like that? Louise does as she pleases, it's not our business! Anyway we don't know anything, and we don't need to know!'

His voice rose; he got up.

'After all, she didn't even tell us . . . well, about the death of that man, did she? Nothing! It was you who told us! So why are you starting to interfere now, you fool! Do you think we give a damn! She doesn't want to come back and live as an honest woman? All right! Let her manage as best she can! She doesn't even want to write? All the better, we don't have to answer! And I warn you, I don't want to hear any more talk about this! Do you understand?'

Pierre-Edouard rummaged in his pocket, took out his wallet, pulled a photo from it and threw it on the table.

'I shall talk about it if I wish to,' he maintained calmly. 'Louise is my sister and' – he pointed to the snapshot –

'he is my godson. And one day he'll come back here, with Louise, whether you like it or not!'

'But, but . . .' stammered his mother, peering at the photo, 'we wrote to you to tell her that she could come back whenever she wanted! Just think, we are having twenty-four Masses said for . . . well, for him, you know.'

'Oh, so that's it!' Pierre-Edouard suddenly understood why the neighbours had changed their opinions. 'That's it . . . So you're making good use of him? Outside you pretend and here . . . Here, no one is allowed to talk about it! Bloody hell!'

'What do you mean, make use of him!' shouted his father. 'We're to blame for having Masses said?'

'No, I don't give a damn about the Masses.'

'Well, what *are* you complaining about?'

'Me? I'm not complaining. I merely think that Louise was absolutely right about what she could expect if she came back.'

'And now she has the right to judge us!' exclaimed Jean-Edouard, banging on the table. 'No, you tell me, who made off with the first fellow who came along? The good-for-nothing. Who was it who disgraced us for two years? Just so, two years for the whole community to laugh at us, eh?'

'And now, is there no disgrace any more?' Pierre-Edouard asked quietly. 'Now she's a widow, is there no more shame? Is that it? Octave had to die so that it could be forgotten, so that people would respect you and pity you? Hah! Would you like me to go to the neighbours and tell them what the Vialhes' daughter is doing, would you like me to go and explain to them, just to amuse them a little? You'll see if they don't laugh to your face, you and your Masses!'

'What is she doing?' Jean-Edouard was suddenly very worried. He expected the worst.

'Charring, in God's name! The Vialhes' eldest daughter is a charlady! Their land is the best in the whole commune, and she's a charlady! She washes floors to earn a pittance! But she still prefers that, she knows only too well what to expect if she comes back. She doesn't want any of your "I told you so! If you'd listened! It served you right, what happened! It's God's punishment . . ." Damn it, she was right to stay where she is!'

'Where is she?' demanded Jean-Edouard.

'I'm not going to tell you. Don't worry, it's a long way away, no one here will find out!'

'Tell me where she is!' commanded his father, marching towards him.

Pierre-Edouard rose, and suddenly noticed that he was taller, sturdier, stronger than his father. He shook his head.

'I'm not going to tell you; not you, nor anyone else. And if you want to hit me, do it, but remember that I'll go out that door and I won't come back for a long time . . .'

They stood looking at each other, sizing each other up.

'Very well, keep it to yourself.' Jean-Edouard finally turned away. 'But listen here, I won't say it again; don't ever dare to lecture me again. Never, do you understand? I wrote as much to you before! Tonight you didn't take any notice of that, but I think you've drunk too much to celebrate your return, so we'll overlook it for once. But that's the last time. Next time you'll feel the back of my hand . . .'

Pierre-Edouard shook his head, doubting whether such a threat would be carried out. He had just discovered that his father was no longer invulnerable; that he could be resisted, that he was almost an old man and whatever he did, he would soon have to let go the reins which had grown too heavy for him. The reins which he, Pierre-Edouard, would take up.

Jean-Edouard was not about to give up his place, and it took his son only two days to understand that.

First of all, although Jean-Edouard was still wary of taking part in community affairs, everything demonstrated that he had regained his status; he alone was spoken of as the next mayor. Then Pierre-Edouard had to admit in all honesty that he managed his farm and livestock with skill, knowledge and great experience. Finally, despite appearing to give way during their stormy discussion, absolutely nothing had changed in his attitude or conduct.

It was obvious that he lost his temper less readily and less violently than before, but his looks and silences were enough to maintain his authority; it was enough to see Berthe walking with her head down and back bowed to understand that he set great store by obedience; that an order was not to be repeated twice, and that the only way to live in peace while he held sway was to fit in with his wishes.

Pierre-Edouard could no longer do that. Everything urged him to react, to give his opinion, even to criticise, and each time there was a confrontation.

The first serious quarrel came when Pierre-Edouard, ferreting about in the barn, noticed the reaper, and saw immediately that it had been misused and poorly maintained. Several points on the bar were broken, the pinions were dry and unevenly worn down; finally, to compound this negligence, his father had not folded back the blade after the last cut of the season, and there it was, jammed in a mass of rust. There were even two sections missing, broken off by some stone.

'Bloody hell!' exclaimed Pierre-Edouard, as he entered the stable where his father was feeding the cows. 'Have you seen the state of the reaper?'

'What about the reaper? It's January, and it's a long time till we'll need it!'

'And a good thing too! It's little better than a wreck! It was practically new when I left, and now it's just a heap of iron.'

'Come right out with it, then – I don't know how to look after it!'

'Too right! It wouldn't have cost you much to stick some oil in the gears! And to change the broken points and to bloody well take off the blade! Now it's rusted away and it's your fault!'

'You're beginning to annoy me,' observed his father

drily. 'So you're not happ ? Well, go and clean the machine and leave me in pea e! Go and scrape it off, that way you'll be earning your supper at least! You've done damn-all for two years, it's high time you put something into the business!'

Pierre-Edouard controlled himself, shrugged his shoulders, and went back to the reaper. He spent the whole day on it, got it moving with plenty of oil, changed the parts, tightened the nuts, greased the gear-wheels. But it did not calm his temper in the slightest.

He was still in a black mood next morning, when he came out into the yard and saw his father harnessing the horse to the cart; he remembered the poor impression the beast had made on him.

'Are you going far with him?'

Jean-Edouard felt like telling him to mind his own business, but he deigned to reply.

'To the miller; he still owes me three sacks from the last grinding.'

'To the mill! With that horse! Have you had a good look at him?'

Jean-Edouard sensed a dispute in the offing. He had indeed noticed that the horse was limping, but he was sure it was no more than a shoe loosely nailed, nothing to prevent his journey.

'I know,' he said, 'he's limping a bit, it's nothing.'

'But – bloody hell! You can see he's suffering damnably!' Pierre-Edouard burst out. 'I swear he is! How long has he been lame, to have got such a dull coat and sad eye? And you want him to do ten kilometres, in this rain and on the stony roads!'

'Exactly, and he won't die of it!' maintained his father, tightening the girth.

He was slightly embarrassed. He specialised in cows, ewes and pigs; he did not know much about horses, found them difficult to understand, with their delicate temperaments and digestion. But it was not for his son to teach him about an animal which he'd already kept for two years! So he interrupted when Pierre-Edouard tried to examine the sore limb.

'Let go that paw and shut up!' he rasped.

'It's not a paw,' said Pierre-Edouard automatically. Horses held no mysteries for him. Each battery of 75s used a minimum of sixty horses; sixty beasts to be cared for constantly, groomed, watched for the slightest sign of a wound, infection or weakness.

'What you're holding on to isn't a paw? Well what is it then?'

'A hoof,' replied Pierre-Edouard distractedly, busy feeling the sole.

He took out his knife, scraped away the mud and earth and touched the heel. The animal started and tried to break free.

'Stop mucking about and let me get going,' said his father, shaking him.

'Dammit, shut up!' shouted Pierre-Edouard, completely forgetting who he was talking to.

'Are you speaking to me?' growled his father, and dispatched a violent blow to his ribs.

'Yes, you! Your horse has a sore – probably infected, because it's oozing magnificently. A fine cock-up, and he's been lame for a good long time. And you couldn't be bothered to pay attention to it! Look at his action, your mount! He's been suffering for weeks, it hits you in the eye, doesn't it? But if it amuses you to kill him, go on then, take him on a tour of the countryside, gallop him to the mill so that everyone will see that you don't know a thing about horses!'

'And you, you worm, you think you know about them?'

'More than you, but that's not difficult! You can hardly tell a horse from a donkey . . .'

'Good God! I don't expect to meet asses like you! And now get out of the way so that I can get going, clear the decks! By Heaven, will you leave that animal alone!' he yelled as he lunged towards his son, who was already unharnessing the horse.

'Listen,' said Pierre-Edouard, as he unbuckled the

straps, 'I'll take care of him for you, it's not difficult. I'll use copper sulphate, the same as for foot rot with the ewes.'

He took another blow to the stomach, shook himself but continued to unharness the mount. It was then that he felt a cuff to the ear, not a heavy blow, one which he would have ignored a few years earlier. But this was one too many; it came too late.

He turned briskly, placed his hand on his father's shoulder and held him at arm's length.

'I warned you the other night. One thump and I'm out the door. Is that what you want? Well, we're in agreement.'

He slapped the horse's rump and it set off limping towards the stable.

'You can see that he is lame in the right hind leg,' he said, sticking his hands in his pockets. He gazed at his father for a long time, then turned and marched towards the house.

An hour later he was on the road to Brive. He was lucky to be overtaken by Maître Lardy's car, just before Perpezac; the solicitor recognised him, stopped, and drove him into the town. On the way Pierre-Edouard had no inhibitions about explaining that he had quarrelled with his father and left home.

That evening the solicitor related the story to his wife; the dining-room door was open, and the maid heard it all. The next day, before the midday bell had sounded, the whole village knew that Pierre-Edouard, the Vialhes' eldest son, had got into a fight with his father, packed up and taken to the roads.

Some of them were convinced that the quarrel had erupted over a natural son he had fathered on a barmaid in Besançon. Others were sure that he had left for North Africa. Actually, nobody knew where he was going, not even Pierre-Edouard himself.

Strangely enough he left, if not happy, at least content. Content and liberated. He had long foreseen that his relationship with his father would be problematical. He had prepared himself to accept what came, but he was unaware that even he had limits of endurance . . .

Two days had been sufficient to demonstrate the gulf which separated him from his father. So, what was the good of perservering? He had no more illusions; he would never be able to submit to his father's fist. Their complete disagreement on the subject of Louise was only one among many; even without her the rift would have opened up.

Although he was relieved to escape the foul atmosphere in the house, at the same time his heart was heavy at leaving his land, his farm, St Libéral – everything which had been his life, the things he had dreamed of during those two years in the barracks.

Of course he knew that one day he would return as master; that the farm, the fields, and the animals would be his. But he had naively believed that the time was approaching, almost upon him, when his father would stand down; that had suddenly faded into the distant future. He would have to wait patiently for several years before being able to stamp his ways without hindrance on the Vialhe lands, which were his of right.

That did not mean that he had the slightest wish for his father to die; that thought did not even occur to him. He had simply become a man, with the intentions and impulses of a man. Emerging from boyhood, he rose against an old man of fifty-one who did not understand that he was fairly of an age to accept a share in the decisions and the activities. Jean-Edouard could not yet prepare himself for his role as grandfather, and begin to fade discreetly out of the picture.

Indeed, everything showed that his father continued to insist on being recognised as the sole decision-maker. Well, what good would it do to stay? It would be better to leave, try his luck elsewhere, discover new horizons and wait . . .

Meanwhile, he had to live. He had about a hundred francs in savings, plus the napoléon from his grandfather, which he hoped he would not have to use. One hundred francs was not a fortune, but at least he was assured of several months of peace. That was if he kept himself to one meal a day — and there were plenty of cheap cafés which offered one for twelve sous — if he was content with a hunk of bread and a glass of water in the evenings, and spent the night in the stable, and most of all, if he economised on tobacco — at eight sous a packet, you could earn a living by re-using cigarette butts!

Anyway, he had hopes that he would not have to wait long before finding work. Naturally there was no question of him staying in the area; he did not want to run the slightest risk of accidentally coming nose to nose with his father at some market or round a corner in Brive or Tulle. Besides, he foresaw that his first jobs would not perhaps be exalted, and he declined to sully the family reputation. No one had any need to know that the Vialhes' eldest son was reduced to working for others, when his father owned one of the finest farms in the community. It would become known if he stayed in the region. Sooner or later some pedlar would recognise him and prattle about it.

On the other hand, if no one knew where he was, he had a good chance that they would make up some mysterious but honourable situation for him. Hadn't he heard in the village that Louise had inherited a pension of 1,000 francs from her husband; that her parents-in-law were in no want, which explained why she preferred to bring up her son close to them?

He had not denied it. Why tell all those gossips that Octave's illness had eaten up all the household money; that instead of well-to-do parents-in-law, Louise had a mother-in-law who only survived thanks to her modest work as a seamstress? What good would it do to tell them that Louise had left Orléans and was now working in a château, a huge edifice, isolated in a fishing and shooting region somewhere on the other side of Chateauroux, in a country of mist and rain, a sad corner in the depths of a huge dark forest.

Of course she was not a charlady, as he had told his parents in that burst of anger; she did not scrub the floor nor empty the night-soil buckets. Better than that! She was the sewing-maid, and had no complaints about her work, nor her employers, and she was lucky to be able to keep her son with her. But she was a long way from a pension of 1,000 francs and rich parents-in-law!

As for him, if he were clever enough to get himself forgotten, they would doubtless soon be saying that he had found a good position. Perhaps they'd even be a little jealous of him.

He did not hesitate for long. Perhaps he subconsciously knew where he would go when he decided to leave the house. The idea must have been already there, as a possible escape route if agreement with his father could not be effected. Now he had to act on it.

He bought ten-sous' worth of bread and some sausage, and took the road for Paris. If it did not rain too much, if it didn't snow, he could reach his goal within about twelve days. It would have taken him two fewer in summer, but the January nights were too long and came on too early to allow him a daily walk of twelve hours. Not that he was scared of the dark, but he did not want to run the risk of finding himself on a strange path, without a farm in sight to shelter him, at eight o'clock in the evening. It really was too cold to sleep out under the stars.

Just as Louise's story had enlivened the village, so did Pierre-Edouard's, but it too faded quickly and was forgotten; it was discussed for several days and then dismissed from conversation and memory.

Few sought to analyse the compulsion which had propelled Pierre-Edouard so quickly into the outside world. He was not the first to want to fly the nest for a while; that type of quarrel between father and son was relatively common, and of no consequence.

It was after all quite normal for a young man to let off steam, make the most of his newly-attained adulthood and try to stand on equal terms with his elders. It was also quite normal for the latter not to let their toes be trodden on, to give reminders that they were still the boss.

In standing up to his father Pierre-Edouard had been

surveying the terrain, to see whether his young strength was sufficient to supplant that of the head of the family; it was proof that he had character and was a son worthy of his father. He would return in a while, only too happy to find his home again – including the paternal scolding – his work, his place at table and somewhere to rest. They would pretend to believe it if he said he had discovered America. They would even accept his explanation for returning to the cradle without smiling – the father's health just before the harvest always gave cause for worry, and excuses for the young prodigals – and no one would speak about the little adventure again.

So nobody criticised Jean-Edouard's attitude; on the contrary. Besides, he exhibited absolutely no sign of being discouraged or resentful. He even assured Gaston that he had got quite used to his son's absence during the last two years, and was perfectly capable of doing without him.

'Well,' said Gaston, 'you'll see him back in a little while! These young people, they're all the same, they lose their tempers at the slightest thing. We'll see him again within six months, I'll be bound.'

'No doubt,' agreed Jean-Edouard, but he didn't believe a word of it. He knew that his son had not left on impulse; his decision had been a considered one. The break was definite; he would not return until he was sure of having control of everything.

Although he hid it carefully, that made him furious. Had not he himself been forced to wait more than forty years to be the boss? Had not he too suffered the questions, the advice, sometimes even the orders, of his own father, right to the end? So what right had that boy to call him to account, try to teach him his job?

Truly the cuff he'd received had been well earned! And if by any chance he was of a mind to return shortly, tail down and pockets empty, he would not enter the house until he had apologised. Just as Louise would have to apologise if she one day reappeared.

But this comforting scene was only a dream. Neither of them would ever give him the satisfaction of humbly begging his forgiveness. They were too stubborn for that, too proud. Too Vialhe, perhaps . . .

His bad mood was exacerbated by Marguerite's attitude. She had supported him in the conflict with Louise, and on that matter she always saw things from his point of view. Now she did not conceal that she was not entirely on his side in the latest battle. Of course, she said, Pierre-Edouard had behaved badly and spoken rudely; but hadn't he himself shown a lack of patience and understanding as well? And what was to become of them now, without the strong arms of their son?

Yes, indeed, that was a big worry. Until now he had waited patiently for that good pair of hands, waited and worked as best he could, without accomplishing all that was necessary to get the maximum yield. He could no longer farm alone. It was too hard, and he was no longer twenty years old . . .

Only a fellow like Pierre-Edouard could have helped him to manage all the work of the farm for optimum output. And because he was counting on his return, he had sown a hectare more of seed than the previous year, set aside and prepared a fine area for cultivating tobacco, maize, peas; even spread phosphates on the meadows to increase their yield, as a result of which he had acquired three extra cows.

And now he found himself alone again, defenceless, with all that work waiting for him, which he could never satisfactorily complete.

He gave himself until April to come to a decision. By that time, if Pierre-Edouard had not returned, he resolved to take on a labourer. It was the only solution. He discussed it with Marguerite, who agreed enthusiastically.

'We'll put him up in the corner of the stable. With lodging and food, what will that cost, a farmhand?'

'Not too much,' he was sure. 'We'll see. It'll depend on his work . . . But with two packets of tobacco a week, some old clothes occasionally, we might get away with four francs a week. And that's paying too much, definitely. Just think, a few years ago, any workman would be happy to get supper, a pile of straw and a few sous a month!'

Pierre-Edouard reached Meaux eleven days after leaving Brive. He had been lucky on the way, and taken advantage first of a weaver's cart, then a wine-merchant's dray. These conveyances were slow, especially the one loaded with barrels, but they still allowed him to gain a day.

Passing Chateauroux he should have made a detour to go and see Louise, but the journey of almost fifty kilometres deterred him. Besides he would have had to leave the main road, plunge into the forest of Niherne, cross part of the Lancosme woods, then venture into the Brenne, that region of lakes and marshes, where he feared he might get lost, or at the very least find himself alone and without shelter at nightfall. He decided it was more sensible to forgo this excursion and continue on the main road.

He arrived at Meaux during the course of the afternoon, reckoned that he could reach his destination before evening, and quickened his pace. Once he had reached Villeroy he had no doubt that he would easily find Moureau Farm – a farm of 180 hectares belonging to the parents of his regimental friend, Jules Ponthier, about which he had heard stories for the last two years. A farm so beautiful and so large that it made his fifteen hectares of land seem quite pathetic!

Happy to be so close to his destination, he stepped out, covering the last fifteen kilometres in less than three hours. Night was falling as he passed through Villeroy and was shown the right direction; he set off down the track which led to Moureau Farm. From the distance he admired the huge buildings surrounded by ploughed fields which stretched to the horizon. There had to be work here.

As soon as he crossed the threshold of the huge covered gateway which opened on to the farm yard, he was frozen to a statue by three enormous long-haired dogs who launched themselves at him with menacing expressions and impressive howls. He had not reckoned with this and waited patiently, certain that someone would be disturbed by the chorus of barking.

'What is it?' shouted a woman, coming out of the cowshed at last.

She approached, and quietened the dogs.

'I'd like to see Jules Ponthier.'

'Which one, the father or the son?'

'The son.'

'Don't move, I'll call him.'

Jules emerged and walked to meet him.

'Well, brigadier, you've got bloody good guards!' shouted Pierre-Edouard.

'It's you! What a surprise! What are you doing here? Now, if you'd told me!'

They clapped each other on the shoulder and greeted each other.

'But what are you doing here?' asked Jules again. 'I thought you'd gone home!'

'Oh . . . No, you see . . . I went home and I left again. But it would take too long to explain it to you. Now, I'm looking for work. There you have it. I hope you have something I can do,' said Pierre-Edouard, sitting down on one of the big stones which marked the entrance way.

'Bloody hell,' muttered Jules, 'there's a turn-up! I'm not boss yet, you know . . . And at this time of year . . . To tell the truth we've got enough gangers . . . You have to understand the ploughing is over. And we have plenty of carters as well . . .'

'Are you mucking me about? You're not going to tell me that you can't find me a job?'

'Well, I'd like to take you on, but . . . Hell, you must see, I'm not the boss yet,' repeated Jules.

'So there's nothing for me to do but set off again? That's it, is it? I've covered more than five hundred kilometres for nothing? With friends like you . . .'

'All right,' sighed Jules, 'come on, I'll try anyway. But don't blame me if it doesn't work out, okay?'

They stepped into the hall, where Pierre-Edouard was aware of a long table, piled with about thirty plates and as many glasses at one end. Then he recognised the woman who had received him at the gate, stirring up the fire beneath a kitchen range; she must be Jules' mother. Finally he saw his comrade's father, seated in the inglenook; a man of about sixty, tall, with a harsh face, grey moustache and tufted eyebrows.

'Who is it?' grumbled the old man.

'Pierre-Edouard Vialhe; you remember, I talked about him, a friend from the regiment.'

'Oh, yes. So what does he want?'

'Well . . . He's looking for work, and he thought that —'

'Work? At this time of year? Where's this friend of yours from? Paris? Doesn't he know that no workers are taken on in the country in the winter?'

'Yes, I do know,' said Pierre-Edouard, 'but I thought . . . I can do whatever you like, hard work has never frightened me.'

'Dammit, I tell you there's nothing! There's no shortage of fellows looking for supper and a roof over their head at the moment! But in this house we don't feed people for nothing!'

'Listen,' pleaded Jules, 'we could put him with the team digging the drainage ditches. One man more wouldn't be in the way, and you know that swine of a Polack is drunk after lunch, and all the fellows take advantage of that.'

'I know, but even if it's only for the morning, the Polack works like two men, and when it comes to the hoeing, there's no better team-leader.'

'But I'm sure Pierre-Edouard would be very useful here,' insisted Jules. 'You know, he's capital with horses. When it comes to ploughing, he'll hold the plough better than most, I'm sure of it.'

'You know how to plough?' asked the old man.

'Of course,' interrupted Jules. 'He's got land too.'

'So why did you leave it?'

'Our holding is too small,' lied Pierre-Edouard, who was certain that if he gave the real reason for leaving, this man would turn against him — he was too like his own father! 'There wasn't enough for us all. But I know how to plough, to sow, to milk, everything . . .'

'All right, we can only try him,' decided the mother,

coming over. She gave him a long look, sizing him up. 'You'd better not turn your nose up at the supper, you . . . Fine, we'll take you, but only because Jules keeps on about it! We'll take you on to clear out the ditches. In the spring, if you're still here, we'll see what you can do . . .'

Pierre-Edouard glanced towards the old man. He had dissociated himself from the conversation. Obviously what happened next did not concern him.

'Well, that's settled,' continued the woman. 'You begin tomorrow. We'll put you up, we'll feed you and you will have — well, let's say twenty sous a day! And that, I must say, is good pay, considering that we don't need you! After all, we're not going to throw out a friend of Jules, are we?'

Pierre-Edouard agreed in silence, still in a state of shock at his reception, and most of all at the derisory sum which would reward his daily labour of ten or twelve hours. Twenty sous a day, thirty francs a month — and that only if they paid on Sundays, when no work was done, so that was extremely unlikely — twenty sous a day was the price of half-a-dozen eggs!

PART FOUR

Exile

16

THE municipal election campaign split the community into wildly opposing factions. It re-awakened old disputes, grudges and jealousies. It was grim, sometimes even violent, and left many with lasting scars of bitterness, defeat and frustration.

As soon as it was established that Antoine Gigoux was withdrawing from the contest and promoting his son in his place, a delegation rushed to Jean-Edouard, to beg him to throw himself into the fray. He prevaricated, referred to his personal difficulties, his busy work programme – of course he was now employing a labourer, but if he wasn't watching him all the time . . . He made them go on asking for a long time before he eventually agreed to enter the lists and lead the team who could and should soon settle into the Mairie, if all went well. Certainly they had to bear in mind that the electors had the right to split their votes, were free to cross out such and such a person and replace him with a candidate of their choice, but despite that Jean-Edouard had high hopes of retaining a comfortable majority of supporters on his ticket.

But he knew it would be hard work to oust the opposing party. The Gigoux lad might be worse than useless; he still had the advantage of his father's solid reputation, and was supported by the schoolmaster's enthusiasm, eloquence, electoral and political skills. And he had several loud-mouths, like the wheelwright, on his side, and allies among the shopkeepers – including the Chanlat couple, who did not stint the free drinks in their pub for anyone who was lukewarm or undecided.

'No matter, we should be able to make them squirm!' maintained Jean-Edouard. 'I'm going to re-open some old files . . . First of all, the dormitories and canteens for the railway navvies. We know very well who built them all; it was Gigoux's brother-in-law ... Then there's the organisation of the market. Before I resigned, I asked for an extra train to run on market days to carry the animals. Nobody listened to me, no wonder the market is going downhill. And then the syndicate, have you seen what's become of it? It just happens that since it closed the miller has started to sell seed, soon he'll start on fertilisers ... Well, after all, everyone knows he's Madame Gigoux's cousin! As for the local taxes, there again it's high time to stick our noses in, and it'll smell, all right ... I tell you we must take matters in hand before it's too late! By the way, I hope the priest will support us?'

'Well, by God!' asserted the baker, 'you don't think he could be for Gigoux? Then we'd have to inform the bishop that his priest is red!'

No one took this up, not grasping the implications. Besides, they all knew that the Gigoux lad and his friends were far from being red, hardly even pink, just faintly socialist ...

'Yes,' concluded Jean-Edouard, 'the priest will be for us, definitely. We must win.'

But two days after this call to arms, the news broke. A real bombshell! Jean Duroux was standing as candidate and throwing all his weight into the contest – as an honest, popular man, the squire, and a general councillor.

This blow beneath the belt disconcerted the fighters already in the ring; it demoralised young Gigoux's friends as much as it did Jean-Edouard's. They very nearly threw in the towel when they discovered that Doctor Fraysse was supporting the squire and almost all the names on his list; it was a good list on the whole, including some decent people, shopkeepers and farmers who were irreproachable.

However, one particular name made Jean-Edouard start and fly into a rage; he calmed down very quickly. Now he knew where to direct his attack, and it would be vicious. Jean Duroux had made a big mistake when he accepted Léon Dupeuch in his team, an error which could cost him the mayoralty. St Libéral was not about to elect a cattle-dealer like Léon; that good-for-nothing, that swindler, that scum of the markets, that ill-bred son of a suicide!

It was Léon they should attack, and without mercy; destroy him in such a way that the mud flying from that fight would stick to all those who had welcomed him into their group as well, starting with the squire . . .

It was not out of political ambition that Léon had decided to throw himself into the race for the town council. Politics did not interest him, and he rarely even followed the contests at second-hand when he happened on a newspaper from time to time. As for the administration of the town, he took it as it came, and was quite prepared to see young Gigoux – fool though he was – succeed his father.

But Jean-Edouard's candidature had touched him like a whiplash, reawakened all the anger he had suppressed when he had been so dishonestly cheated out of the meadow by the mill. Since then he had hated Jean-Edouard, considering him a lucky devil, a tyrant, a brute and false to the core, all at the same time. Much as he liked Pierre-Edouard, the mere sight of his father turned his stomach.

After all, he knew every detail of the real reasons which had impelled Pierre-Edouard to leave. Not only was he aware of all the background to the story but, to make matters worse, he knew where and how his friend was living since his exile.

He had been very surprised, but also deeply touched by this proof of trust, when he had received a long letter from Pierre-Edouard two months earlier. This letter was not a long list of complaints – though it said plenty about his father's attitude – but was written solely to ask for news, and not just any news; only about the land, the buildings, the animals . . . Pierre-Edouard wanted to watch over his estate from afar through a third party; he was relying on Léon . . .

The latter was in a quandary as to how to reply, since he hardly knew how to write his name; but, very conscious of the honour his friend had done him, he had dictated a long letter to his young sister, little Mathilde. At eleven, she was writing so well that she could perhaps become a school-teacher one day, said the good nuns at Allassac, to whom he had entrusted her education.

Pierre-Edouard had not shown any further sign of life, but Léon knew that other letters would arrive during the following months; for instance, there was no doubt that Pierre-Edouard would be worrying about the haymaking and the harvest at the moment.

So he was inspired by two grudges — one over the meadow, the other in support of his friend — when he decided to make old Vialhe bite the dust. He immediately saw that young Gigoux would not be up to Jean-Edouard's weight; the latter had regained all his prestige and pride. He was a good speaker, a good administrator, an excellent farmer. Only someone like Jean Duroux could beat him. So he would have to convince the squire . . .

That was much easier than Léon had anticipated. Deep down Jean Duroux was only waiting for one thing; to be asked, to be assured that the community needed him. Léon pleaded on behalf of his fellow citizens, and was just as convincing as he could be in the marketplace.

He deliberately skated over young Gigoux's candidature, and got busy illustrating all the dangers which lay behind the election of Jean-Edouard: an honest man, he had no doubt, despite his trade in provisions with the steward of the railway company . . . And then wasn't it a bit worrying that this mayor-to-be, called on to represent and serve all the citizens of the community, was opinionated and stubborn, narrow-minded even, to the point where he had maliciously ejected not only his unhappy daughter, but also his son and heir? If he were to act with such obstinacy once he was elected, some fine injustices would result . . .

'Yes,' agreed Jean Duroux, 'and I haven't forgotten the rude way he stole that land on the plateau right under my nose. Do you remember? The piece belonging to the solicitor; I was to have shared it with Gigoux. He behaved quite improperly that time!'

'Who do you think you're telling! He did exactly the same to me over the meadow by the mill. Oh, I don't bear any grudges, but it just shows you!'

'That's right, it all comes back to me now. Yes, definitely, I believe I shall have to stand as a candidate. But who will support me?'

'Everyone in the village, for certain! But I thought that these people would suit your views,' said Léon, taking a list from his pocket.

Jean Duroux studied it and nodded his head. 'Yes, very good. But you're not on it. Why not?'

'No wish to, really. Besides, I don't know about that sort of thing.'

'Now don't make a fuss; I'll put you in for a position, see, in third place. With you in charge, I'm sure the market in St Libéral will quickly become the biggest in the whole area!'

With every passing day the electoral campaign intensified; public meetings, combative debates, home visits followed one another at a frantic pace.

Direct attacks and poster campaigns were countered with false innuendoes, dark predictions and lies. All the dirty linen was brought out; the outgoing party was openly blamed for the poor management of town business and alleged bribes they had taken. But there was also talk about those who had grown so rich so quickly as a result of the railway line . . . In the end they even attacked the sumptuous wedding the squire had provided for his daughter; a scandalous waste of money at a time when the working classes and peasants had such difficulty in making a living! More than three hundred thousand francs for that chit of a girl, whilst a worker hardly earned eight francs a day! And the wedding itself had cost hundreds and thousands!

Sometimes, usually at the end of an evening, after the generous rounds paid for by the candidates, threats were uttered, fists were clenched, blows were even struck . . .

Two days from the ballot none could say for certain who would win. Then Léon revealed his trump card.

225

Until then he had wisely restricted himself to quiet but effective persuasion; and he was allowed to talk because he spoke gently, without malice or insults. He politely demolished his enemies' arguments without ever getting worked up; softly, just as he would demonstrate to a farmer that his cow was too thin or too worn out. Better still, he knew that all discussions needed to be punctuated from time to time with a good joke, which lightened the mood and encouraged agreement and sympathy to his view. So people were glad to listen to him, and even his fiercest critics were disconcerted by his calm, his self control, his good humour.

So everyone took him seriously when he made an announcement during a small informal meeting: he had it on very good authority that his colleagues, the stock-dealers, would no longer set foot in the village unless they had the promise of an extra train on market days.

'But,' called out one of his audience, 'that's exactly what old Vialhe wants! Good God, he's been saying it often and long enough!'

'Yes,' conceded Léon, 'but Duroux says the same . . .' He stopped, smiled, and looked around at the small group in a friendly way.

'Between ourselves, lads, do you know what it takes to get an extra train twice a month? Eh? You have to make representations to the Railway Company . . . And who will the company listen to? Gigoux? He's much too timid; I don't see him arguing with those gentlemen . . . Vialhe? You know him, he'll play the bully-boy and get thrown out! Then there's our squire. He's a general councillor and he knows everyone, did you see the guests at the wedding? He knows how to talk to people like that, he's accustomed to it . . . Believe me, there's no one but him will be able to get that train for the animals. That's what all my colleagues said to me, just the day before yesterday at Tulle market. They're counting on the squire becoming mayor, because if he doesn't they won't get their train, and you — well, you can say goodbye to the market at St Libéral . . .'

Léon paid for the drinks and left the bar, certain that he

had sown the seeds of doubt and fear. Shortly afterwards he entered the inn, espied a group of drinkers, and repeated his confidential news to them.

Father Verlhac was well aware that a false step could reduce his status to nothing, so he confined himself to prudent neutrality. He let it be known that electoral prejudice was not part of his pastoral role; he was vicar to all of them and intended to remain so. It was therefore no use relying on his endorsement.

Despite this, he was secretly hoping for the defeat of Gigoux's son. Not that he was a bad fellow, far from it; but he was poorly advised by the secretary at the Mairie – who happened to be the teacher, a blatant sectarian and anticlerical, with whom the priest could never agree.

The teacher behaved absolutely correctly as regards the children, and (as far as the priest knew) never tried to turn them against the catechism. Despite this praiseworthy impartiality, his secular and materialistic teaching was so divorced from Christian and Roman faith that the two men could never have anything in common. They were not enemies; they avoided each other.

When he thought of Jean-Edouard the priest experienced a sort of vague embarrassment; he could not make out his true character, and wavered between classifying him amongst his good, reliable parishioners, or in the opportunist category.

To this was added the indefinable impression that he had been used by the Vialhes. There was something suspicious going on in that family, and the more he thought of the Masses paid for by Marguerite the more his unease grew. What sort of people were they, who had services read for their late son-in-law – and attended them without fail – whilst their door remained firmly closed to their own daughter? And they had turned their eldest son out so quickly that he, the parish priest, had not even had time to meet him! Really there were too many mysteries or sordid tales for one to have complete confidence in Jean-Edouard Vialhe . . .

That left the squire, and the priest admitted to himself that this was his preferred candidate. Jean Duroux fulfilled all the necessary conditions for a good mayor. He was honest, stable yet liberal, and enjoyed an excellent reputation throughout the country. He was even counted among the men admired by the bishop; one would wish to support him – though very discreetly, of course.

The priest asked no more than to help him a little, and not only through prayer, but his position forbade him from proclaiming aloud where votes should be cast. It was useless even to make delicate allusions, to try to influence his female parishioners. The ballot did not concern them, and they had only one desire: for it all to be over and peace to return finally!

Despite all this, and because he could not bear to be inactive, he decided to lend a hand – and he knew how to do it without getting his fingers dirty.

Father Verlhac waited until the day before the ballot. Then, at about half past eleven, he watched out for the squire to arrive, sure that the latter would not fail to appear in the village at the aperitif time.

As soon as he caught sight of the squire, shaking hands, greeting each elector, raising his hat even to the women working in the communal wash-house, he strode out of the presbytery towards him. He knew that he was immediately the focus of attention for everyone in the square and main street.

'Sir,' he cried as he approached, 'I apologise for disturbing you in the midst of your work, but never fear, it's not the candidate I wish to see, everyone knows that I don't concern myself with politics. My request is purely personal . . .'

Jean Duroux, only too happy to be seen in conversation with the priest, hurried to fall into step, and they entered the presbytery together. The door closed behind them.

'Well, it's this,' began the priest, after inviting his visitor to be seated. 'You will be aware that the bishop is to honour us with his presence in three months' time. He is coming to confirm fourteen of our children.'

'I know,' said Jean Duroux, who did not see where this was leading at all.

'Sir, I have a very serious problem to put to you. You know custom has it that when His Lordship comes into the area, he should be received with all due respect?'

'I know, I know,' interrupted Jean Duroux, looking at the pendulum clock.

'For several years my brothers in neighbouring parishes had an understanding, they undertook this heavy burden. Knowing the age, poor health, and indeed poverty, of my late-lamented predecessor, they invited His Lordship to them for the midday meal. But this year, the awe-inspiring privilege falls to me again . . .'

'And what's the problem?'

'The problem?' repeated the priest, indicating the room with a wave of his arm. 'Do you believe that I can receive him here with dignity? I have nothing, sir; just two bench seats, three plates, four glasses, two of them chipped, a cracked dish, two miserable pots, a few twisted knives and forks . . . Oh! I'm not complaining, it's quite enough for me. But for His Lordship the Bishop . . .'

'But what the devil are you getting at?' asked Jean Duroux. 'Do you want me to send you over some china and a few good bottles? Listen, you can count on me,' he said, getting up to leave.

'No, no, sir, it's simpler than that. You know everyone understands your feelings for us – I mean for the Church – and that's why I have turned to you. I know that you are personally acquainted with the bishop. I know that he respects you a great deal, he told me so when he appointed me here . . . So I thought, excuse my boldness, I wondered, whether it would be at all possible for you to invite His Lordship to dine with you on that day . . . He would surely understand the situation, and would be delighted.'

'Good Heavens!' cried Jean Duroux, as he too understood, 'that's a brilliant idea! But of course he must be my guest! I'll write to him this very afternoon! He can't refuse, can he?'

'I believe not,' said the priest, fetching out a bottle of

pale yellow wine. He filled two glasses, one of which really was chipped; he held out the other to the squire.

'I don't think he will refuse,' he continued, 'and I believe, in the utmost confidence of course, that he would hope to be received by the mayor of St Libéral . . .'

'I'm counting on it,' confirmed Jean Duroux. He emptied his glass and turned towards the door.

'I'm sure,' he paused a moment, 'you would have no objections if I were to announce this good news to a few friends?'

'One hides nothing from true friends . . .'

'Between ourselves,' murmured the squire, returning a few paces, 'you have no fear that His Lordship would disapprove of this . . . this scheme?'

'Personally, I see no scheme! Only the jealous may perceive it as a political move, but everyone knows that I don't go in for politics . . .'

'You're a stout fellow, Father. I know several bishops who lag far behind you in diplomacy!'

'I have no ambitions in those circles, and believe me, if I could have received the bishop here . . . But it really is impossible, isn't it? Everyone will understand that, even the agnostics!'

It was very soon understood that Father Verlhac had been in some embarrassment (and all the witnesses were in agreement on this point), and had passed on a message from the bishop; it was a favourable response to an invitation from the château which had been expressed some two months earlier . . .

All this was seen for what it was, but nevertheless it proved that Jean Duroux really was somebody. The reds might well shout that the squirearchy were past it, that true republicans did not like the nobility, let alone bishops and priests and their silly flocks; it was no use, many of the undecided opted for Jean Duroux. He had once again proved that his arm was strong and influential. After all, who else in the village could boast of having a bishop to dine?

The day of the election was quiet. Passions had calmed. Already many considered that the die was cast. Here and there, in the bars or the inn, they were taking bets on how many votes this man or that would get.

The hours dragged on towards the counting of the votes. That took a long time, for almost all the papers contained crossings-out, split votes or names which appeared on no list at all. There were also several spoiled papers. One raised a few worried laughs through clenched teeth: 'I vote for my donkey, he's cleverer than the lot of you!'

At about nine o'clock the results were at last announced. More than two-thirds of the candidates on the squire's ticket were elected in the first round; Jean Duroux collected almost eighty per cent of the votes. Léon, too, had a very good score.

The applause rang out, the men congratulated each other, the losers were silent and the remainder of the results were declared. They applauded heartily when they learned that Jean-Edouard, Jeantout and Gaston had also gained an absolute majority. As for the others, including Gigoux, there was nothing to stop them continuing as candidates; there remained two seats to be decided.

The inn was invaded to toast the outcome at the expense of the newly-elected councillors. Jean Duroux perched himself on a table and improvised his first speech as mayor. It was impeccable, moderate, assured them that he was delighted to welcome into his team men of the calibre of Jean-Edouard, Gaston and Jeantout; thanks to them it would be possible to get down to work immediately, for they already had a good knowledge of council administration.

Jean-Edouard, squeezed in at the back of the saloon, was boiling with rage. He had lost thirty-four votes compared to the previous elections; his total did not allow him to hope for the position of deputy mayor. And what really made him raging mad was to see, over there, in the front row, that swine Léon, who had been given twenty-nine votes more than him by this electoral dunghill!

There was one consolation in the midst of this débâcle:

that imbecile young Gigoux had suffered a real rebuff, and if by any chance he was elected at the second ballot it would still not be on his vote!

Despite his defeat and his urge to tell all those idiots around him what he thought of them, he clinked glasses, feigned happiness and good humour, even accepted congratulations from old friends. He too paid for a round of drinks, and was among the last to leave the saloon.

Once alone, he was at last free to express his torment. 'So,' he reflected, 'you can put it all down to the family; one reckless daughter and one disrespectful son . . .'

Marguerite was waiting for him by the fireside; she rose as he entered, saw his face, and thought he had been defeated.

'Well?' she asked timidly.

'It's Duroux and his nest of fleas!'

'And you?'

He shrugged his shoulders. 'Elected, but with thirty-four votes fewer than last time! Just think, that muck-heap Léon got more than me!'

'You're elected? Well don't complain! You know, you've come from so far behind that I was afraid they'd beat you. They're so jealous of us, they bear such a grudge against us!'

He looked at her, nodded, and finally smiled.

'You're right, perhaps they do bear a grudge; perhaps they're jealous of us. Well, they haven't seen the last of it! I'll show them, I'm not finished yet! I promise you, they're not about to see a Vialhe give in!'

Pierre-Edouard leant on his hoe, turned and smiled. Once more the Polack was beaten; the quickest worker with the hoe had met his match. He was still more than twelve paces behind in thinning the beets.

The young man rolled himself a cigarette and surveyed the vast field where eighteen men were working, bent towards the ground. Some of them were more than thirty metres behind him.

They were walking along bent double, aching all over;

some of them were even working on their knees to be closer to the ground, to assuage the pain which ravaged their backs and stabbed at their kidneys. They had bound up their knees with rags and plaited straw, and resembled grotesque misshapen dwarves. They hobbled between the rows, their tools in front of them, hopping on their straw-covered stumps to which the heavy clay clung in damp clods.

And all of them repeated the same movements a thousand times, combining thorough weeding with an effective thinning of the young beet-plants, which were growing so densely that their roots could not develop properly.

This operation, rendered necessary by direct sowing, had been a great surprise to Pierre-Edouard when the master had sent them into this vast field a fortnight ago. He was sorry to have to chop into the young plants; in his heart it seemed such a waste to cut away so many like weeds, leaving only one plant every twenty-five to thirty centimetres.

Down in St Libéral they did things differently. First of all a single row was sown, taking great care not to squander the precious seeds, those tiny grains from which four or five red and green shoots would soon sprout. When the plants reached fifteen centimetres in height, and their roots were already swelling, they were delicately and lovingly drawn out and replanted behind the blade of the plough, in that strip of fresh soil which opened up behind the slow steps of the cows.

But down there at home, on the plateau, you considered yourself fortunate if you had planted out three hundred square metres of beet, three plots . . .

Here, of course, in this country, where everything was of monstrous proportions, it was impossible to farm like that. The field in which the men had been breaking their backs for two weeks was forty-eight hectares, four hundred and eighty plots. It was crazy!

There was no way out; he had to get used to the sight of these immeasurable sweeps of land, to this plain, to ploughing furrows that sometimes stretched for half a kilometre. At first Pierre-Edouard had felt he could never grow accustomed to such excess. Everything was too big, too vast; even the farm buildings overwhelmed him with their bulk.

From the first evening there had been one amazement after another: first of all that gigantic table, around which the twenty-two farm workers gathered at a quarter to seven. They waited standing up until the master and mistress had taken their places, one at each end of the table; only then did they sit down.

Jules signalled to him with a wave of the hand to find a space between a stripling who stank of horse manure and an old man of at least fifty-five, whose dry and wizened hand trembled as he retrieved the foul quid of tobacco from his cheek, where it had deformed his face like an abcess.

At the end of the table, the master cut thick slices of bread from a grey loaf and passed them around. Then a serving-maid appeared, a dim-looking girl with sunken breasts and bony hips, who placed a cauldron of broth in front of the lady of the house. Just as the master had distributed the bread, so the mistress shared out the soup, a mixture of bacon fat, cabbage, potatoes and bread.

Pierre-Edouard observed that no one touched his plate; he took care not to plunge his spoon into his own. He was mesmerised by the ceremony, as well as by the silence, and waited in absolute stillness until all had received their rations.

The master was served last, and he then tapped on his plate with the blade of his knife; that was the signal, the men could eat at last. There was little conversation during this astonishing meal; just a few murmurs here and there, a few grunts, a few belches and the slurping of soup as it was swallowed with famished greed. 'Hey you, Polack!' shouted the proprietor suddenly. 'Tomorrow you'll have this young fellow to dig the ditches with your team. It seems he knows how to work ... How far did you get today?'

'Seventy-two paces,' announced the man, in a strong accent.

'My God! You've done nothing! That's twelve fewer than yesterday. Do you think the soup's for free here?'

'It's all full of stones there . . .'

'Tell me, are you trying to teach me about my own land? Go on like that and you can do without your booze in the morning!'

Pierre-Edouard learned later that the Pole was paid only ten sous a day in money: to make it up, he had the right to a litre bottle of brandy every morning and two litres on Sundays. The master profited by it, and would have gladly paid all his workers in this sort of money. The alcohol cost him nothing. It was an appalling vitriol, 72% proof, which only the Pole had the power to swallow without flinching.

'No more booze, no more work; I'll be off!' grumbled the foreman.

His boss shrugged, and turned towards the head carter.

'And that manure, how many cartsful?'

'Nineteen.'

'Couldn't you manage twenty, eh? Well, it'll do . . .'

He wiped his plate with a crust of bread, gulped down the morsel, wiped his moustaches and snapped shut his clasp-knife. The blade clicked, the meal was over.

Since then Pierre-Edouard had grown accustomed to this ritual. Nobody ate before the master, and nobody ate after him either. But that evening he was still astonished at such strictness as he followed the men to the dormitory.

He entered a building attached to the stables: a single room, dark, with a low ceiling and walls black with grime. Here and there, in an unbelievable muddle, the men had established their corners, their lairs. It was an incredible accumulation of old packing-cases, upturned to serve as tables, cobbled together as cupboards, set up around mean wooden bedsteads with shapeless torn mattresses.

Pierre-Edouard was about to cut and run, to return to

235

the open road and march south until he reached exhaustion point. However, he controlled himself; he was dead beat. He decided to spend the night under shelter and make off at daylight.

'Hey, mate! There's an empty corner over there by the partition,' one of the men showed him. 'Don't worry if you hear a ringing in your ears in the night; the stallion's just the other side, and he likes to lash out at the planks! Where are you from?'

'From the Corrèze. Limousin, you know?'

'No work down there?'

'Not much,' he explained, holding out his tobacco pouch.

The man seemed astonished at such generosity; he hesitated, and then rolled himself a cigarette.

'What's your name? Me, I'm Moïse Coutôt. I'm from near Lagery, in Champagne, not very far away.'

'I'm Pierre-Edouard Vialhe.'

'Do you know about farming?'

'Yes.'

'You'll see, the Pole's a real pig. Towards midday he gets in a foul mood with the drink. He sobers up just in time for supper.'

'And the owners?'

'Oh, them! Huh – like all masters, want work, always work, but to get any money out of them . . . Well, they're masters, that's all. They treat you like dirt, but there are worse. You'll see, it's not bad here.'

'Good . . . And Jules?'

'Do you know him already?'

'You bet, I did two years' army service with him! And he told me that things were good here.'

'Oh, I see! Jules, he's one of us – works just the same, has to do his share like everyone else. You know, with this mistress it's no good thinking you'll get any supper if you haven't earned it. You have to admit she's quite something, that woman!'

'But she doesn't give the orders, does she?'

'God dammit, no! But she has the money, and the land

belongs to her too; make no mistake, the master only came here as a son-in-law, a while back. Well, that's what I've been told.'

Pierre-Edouard shrugged; he couldn't care less about all these trivialities. At dawn, he'd be on his way.

He had stayed. In the morning, when he was already making up his bundle, Moïse came towards him.

'Come on, hurry up and get your breakfast, the others are already there.'

How could he explain that he was going to leave, hit the road again? The other man would immediately understand that he was giving in, like a baby; perhaps he would even think that he was frightened of work, that really he was only one of those fireside boasters who drifted around looking for bread, but not for work.

And Jules would think the same; Jules, who had done everything to get him taken on. Besides if he fled, left, where would he go? To Saint-Libéral? His pride would not let him.

No, it was impossible to leave immediately. At the end of the month, that would do all right, but not this morning. Anyway, he owed them for supper and the night's shelter, and never let it be said that a Vialhe stole his bed and board! He threw down his bundle and followed his companion.

And then, gradually, he had grown accustomed to the life, accustomed to seeing nothing unusual in the twenty-seven enormous Percheron horses, the fifty-two dairy cows, hundred sows and twenty-eight ewes the farm accommodated.

They had cleaned out the ditches until winter's end, and he had shown them straight away that he knew how to handle the tools. Then, one morning in spring, he found himself with the handles of a plough in his palms once more.

He had never ploughed with horses, and the Dombalse plough which he had to guide was much wider and heavier than the little plough of his youth, the one he'd used to turn over the Vialhe earth so long ago.

'You're sure you know how to plough?' asked the master ploughman when he arrived at the gate of the field.

'Yes,' Pierre-Edouard assured him.

He knew he was being watched, weighed up by the men around him – eleven ploughmen all in a line, each behind his implement, whip furled under the arm, waiting for the master ploughman, Octave, to start. It was for him to open carefully the first furrow, a perfectly straight furrow of the correct depth which would serve as a guide to the rest.

Octave spat out a long jet of tarry saliva, stained black from the quid of tobacco which he chewed all day, and turned to look back towards the farm which lowered in the distance through the morning mist. He surveyed the track which led to it, making sure that the farmer was not coming towards them with long silent steps.

'Well, if that's the case, since you know how to plough, you begin!'

It was a trick he played on the young ones. Their confusion, even panic, and the mess they made of the few metres he let them cover, gave him a good laugh, to start with; and then he could sound off and bawl out the novice; that gave him a chance to reinforce his authority, and make them understand that nobody could take his place as master ploughman.

Pierre-Edouard spotted the catch at once, saw the sly looks of his work-mates and their stifled laughter. One glance at his plough made him shake his head. 'You must take me for an idiot!'

Behind his back, one of his neighbours had surreptitiously loosened the anchor screw. The way it was set, the plough would only have scratched the surface and zig-zagged all over the place.

He adjusted the machinery and checked that no other joker had tampered with the harness or the horses. Only then did he grasp the handles, raise the rear wheel of the Dombasle, urge on the horses, and guide them, lining up the ploughshare.

'Go on,' he cried. 'On, my beauties!'

He braced himself against the plough and began his first

furrow. He knew immediately that he could steer it right to the end of the field, as straight as a ruler and perfectly regular.

It was a pleasure to work land like this. The soil was fine, aerated, just damp enough; it sang as it slipped past the mould-board. He had fought his first battles with the soil of the plateau – good earth, but heavy, compacted, difficult to separate from the sub-soil; sometimes it stuck to the metal blade, often fell unevenly, exhausting man and beast.

But here, what a delight, what joy! Even the stones were no trouble; they grated briefly on the metal and then disappeared.

'Stop!' he heard from behind.

'Go and get stuffed!' he shouted over his shoulder.

'In God's name, stop, I tell you! The master's coming, I'll get into trouble!'

And now Octave was running beside him. 'Give me the handles and go to the end of the line, he can't see us yet! You must know,' Octave squirmed, 'this is my place; if he finds you here, he'll think we spend all our time fooling around!'

Pierre-Edouard looked round and saw that the men, one by one, were setting their ploughs to the field. He ran to the driverless team and pushed it into plough-land.

Everything was as it should be when the master arrived. From that day forward Pierre-Edouard was respected: not only could he plough like the boss, he was a good fellow too. It was better not to think what might have happened if the farmer had caught him opening the first furrow! Octave could have lost his job; he was paid a considerable salary, a hundred sous a day, and not for playing the fool or wasting time. That's why he made the others work strongly and steadily for ten hours a day.

Pierre-Edouard threw away his cigarette and smiled at the Pole, who had at last caught up with him.

'Little squirt! Think it's funny to get ahead of me?' shouted the man, as he wiped the sweat streaming from his face. 'I've a good mind to smash your face. What's the master going to say when he finds out I'm not the ace any more, eh?'

'He won't see anything, and the work's done anyway!'

'Yes, but what about me, what does that make me to all those lazy sods?' asked the Pole, gesturing in the direction of the men toiling away behind him.

'It makes you a good Pole! Besides, they don't care, they don't even understand what you say to them! So, keep talking!'

For the last two weeks the farmer had been taking on day-labourers for the thinning. They had arrived in little groups, jabbering away in some lingo or other. Only Pierre-Edouard managed to understand their speech. That was no sign of great talent: the Limousin dialect had common roots with Catalan, Piedmontese, Italian and Spanish; those languages from the lands full of sunshine, but full of misery too, whence the poor fellows set out, travelling from farm to farm, according to the season and work available, hiring out their strength for a bowl of soup and a few pence. They were only happy when they heard the chink of coins. As for their supper, it was served in the barn; there was no question of opening the house to those foreigners!

'You, tell them to work faster,' ordered the Pole.

He took a flat bottle from his back pocket, reviewed the level of the liquid remaining in it, then plunged the neck into his toothless mouth. 'Tell them, go on, damn you!' he repeated, after having his drink. 'Do you want a sip?' He offered the bottle.

'You're mad! Keep your poison.'

'Well tell them, go on!'

'No, I don't care if they do nothing! I'm not paid to make them work, and you're not either. Does that bother you?'

'The master will bawl us out tonight, and how!'

'Then let him bawl! Anyway, he always bawls at us, that ass, it's his little weakness! You know something, I don't understand that fellow. He's richer than anyone should ever be allowed to be, he has land as far as the eye can see, he has cows, ewes, everything, and he spends his time bawling at everyone! To listen to him, you'd think nothing was ever right and he's surrounded by a team of shirkers. Even poor Jules gets told off! What an idiot that Jules is! If I were him . . . And Madame, she's just the same. When she serves the soup, you always have the impression that she's disembowelling some poor animal with each ladleful! My God, they're real beasts, those people! And to cap it all they make out they're "gentry" – huh, never pleasant, never a smile, nothing. Beasts, I tell you! You know, Polack, down our way, we're not rich like here, although we work just as hard. We're not rich, no, but we still know how to laugh! Listen, for instance, once in the village . . .'

'There's the master!' whispered the Pole.

'So what? We can still talk, can't we?' grumbled Pierre-Edouard. But he held his tongue and went back to his work in silence.

17

THE new town council kept its promises. It took Jean Duroux less than a month to arrange for the railway company to lay on an extra train, just as the stock-dealers demanded.

At a stroke, the market took on an unprecedented importance, and the financial rewards were enjoyed by all the electors. This success was partly due to the judicious manipulation of the railway system, but it was equally Léon's creation, for he had taken great trouble to attract as many of his colleagues as possible to the village.

He also lured in several wholesalers from Brive, Objat and Tulle who specialised in veal, for he guaranteed that the farmers of St Libéral produced the best white veal in all Corrèze. At the same time he spread the message to the breeders, as he toured the regional markets, that they would benefit by coming to sell at St Libéral, where, according to him, good beasts fetched the highest prices in the département.

Soon everyone for forty kilometres around knew that St Libéral market was by far the best! Twice a month hundreds of calves were lined up in the market-place. These Limousin calves were lovingly reared in the darkest corner of the stable, fed exclusively on milk, to which the best breeders secretly added raw eggs. They were groomed and coaxed and fussed over to extremes, to produce the fine red-blond coat called 'leveret's fur' which was the guarantee of tender, melting flesh of palest pink, almost white.

St Libéral market had established a solid reputation within less than two years: it reached its peak when machinery as well as animals began to be displayed. There were also three special fairs each year, one of them with prizes, where not only cash but rosettes were also awarded; magnificent blue, red or green badges that were the pride and joy of the winners, and brought great honour to the stables where they were displayed.

The prize-fair was established on the feast of Saint Eutrope, the patron of the parish, and the council decided to supplement it with an agricultural show, which would attract a considerable crowd of exhibitors, stall-holders and the curious. Even the gypsies, the basket-makers, the tumblers, the showmen with bears and monkeys, set up their caravans close to the village. They would probably have camped there all winter if the village policeman had not forced them to take to the road again once the fête was over, for there was a local bye-law expressly forbidding this.

The Deputy himself deigned to appear during the course of the day. It was eight months until the elections for the legislative assembly, scheduled for late April 1914, and it seemed sensible to him to support and praise such a dynamic council, such a united team, a living example of democracy and fraternal republican unity.

All these achievements intensified Jean-Edouard's hatred for Léon – that good-for-nothing, the illiterate whom Jean Duroux had dared to choose as his deputy! Léon had succeeded in no time at all in executing all Jean-Edouard's plans for the town; if only the electors had placed him at least second, or failing that third! – first was asking too much, in competition with the squire. Then it would have been he, Jean-Edouard, who received the credit for all this.

Instead it was Léon who, having pillaged his ideas and projects, reaped the benefits. Léon who, confident of his popularity, was now directing the syndicate which Jean-Edouard had revived and which, thanks to him and him alone, improved its business turnover each year.

Nobody could dispute that. This success was his, and, if it didn't outdo the squire's achievements at least it equalled them, proved that its architect was not the stubborn narrow-minded diehard some jealous people liked to call him.

Besides these humiliations, Jean-Edouard had family problems. First of all there was his mother's health. The poor woman was going on seventy-nine, and had become worse than a child. She never stopped talking, quite incoherently, all day long; she soiled her bed and could not feed herself any more; for long periods she became obsessed by an idée fixe which she repeated obstinately until the family was exhausted. She wanted to see Louise, and would go on about it for days and nights. She would call for her at the top of her voice, sometimes at two o'clock in the morning, and attack Berthe when she tried to calm her down. It was impossible ever to leave her alone in the house; the poor woman was capable of setting fire to it.

So she took up all Berthe's time every day. Luckily the girl cared for her without a murmur — indeed, without a word; you could easily have believed that Berthe had lost her power of speech.

Another worry for Jean-Edouard was Marguerite, who was in the middle of the change of life; her character was affected by it, and her moods changed like April winds. Sometimes she was happy and full of go, then she fell quickly into the darkest despair and reproached him for driving Louise away, accusing him of being wicked and cruel to prevent her knowing her grandson.

From here she would go on to defend Pierre-Edouard, to justify his actions, to approve of his departure; it was sickening. Sickening and tiring. And he had to bear all this under the bovine gaze of Abel, the labourer he had employed for the last two years.

Not a bad old man, Abel; he was nearly sixty, and a relatively good worker when watched, but he had no ideas or initiative; he was stupid to the point of waiting an hour by a broken plough-stilt without knowing whether he should change it or not. Abel was such an idiot that he talked to all and sundry about Grandmother's madness, Marguerite's scenes, and the master's bursts of anger . . .

And how could he remain calm when everything

conspired to infuriate him? Especially the postcards, always addressed to Berthe, which that worm Pierre-Edouard sent twice a year, one for New Year and the other for her Saint's day.

Jean-Edouard regarded these messages as deliberate provocation. The words were nearly always the same. 'I hope you are well; Louise and Félix are well, I am very well.' They sounded like a challenge to him, an insult which he had to suffer passively, for the writer never put his address. The cards were posted at Meaux – what was he doing at Meaux, the fool, when there was so much work at the farm! – and even the pictures and captions seemed deliberately chosen to defy him.

Jean-Edouard saw red when he deciphered the golden, flowing letters on shiny paper to read 'I'm far away but I am thinking of you . . .' Set in the centre of a heart or a bunch of flowers, they must have leapt to the eye of the postmaster and the postman, those two gossips.

'The little toad!' he muttered. 'The day he comes back I'll show him I'm thinking of him too! He'll get such a thrashing!'

But he was all the more furious, for he knew in his heart of hearts that his son would never take that from him again. And then, would he ever come back?

He doubted it sometimes, and felt a dark mood of discouragement. He saw old age approaching, and the terrible tiredness which accompanied it; fatigue often undermined his strength and effectiveness already. And that fool Abel would not be able to manage the farm if he were unlucky enough to fall ill . . .

Now that he was considered worthy to be called a ploughman, Pierre-Edouard did not regret having stayed on Moureau Farm. He had eventually got used to his employers' taciturn natures, to their severity, their miserliness and their total lack of humour. He had even managed a good laugh when he thought of the sleep they must have lost when they were forced to raise all their workers' salaries.

They hadn't had any choice in the matter: in June 1912, just after the haymaking and a week before the corn harvest, more than two-thirds of the men, including himself, had packed their bags and threatened to leave the Ponthiers to manage their eighty hectares alone.

By this time day-labourers were no longer touring the farms; either they had been taken on for the season, or they had followed the example of others and fled to the towns, for work which they heard could pay eight or ten francs a day.

The farmers were trapped; with what they held most dear under attack – their harvest, and with it their money – they gave in, and old Ma Ponthier, whey-faced with anger and humiliation, opened her purse and laid out the coins. Since then, as a ploughman Pierre-Edouard had earned two francs seventy a day in summer and two-twenty in winter. That was very different from the twenty sous he had received in the beginning!

Naturally the mistress had immediately tried to cut down on their food; the gruel grew thinner, the slices of bread less heavy. But, she was warned, probably by the farmgirl, that eighteen men were about to leave – this time without notice – and she felt obliged to thicken her stew, to make it more substantial, so that the food was at least nourishing, if nothing special.

Pierre-Edouard always wondered whether the slut had spoken out because she enjoyed telling tales, or for fear of seeing her customers depart. She would climb into the hayloft for fifteen sous, and enjoyed the attentions of three-quarters of the workmen; she easily earned twenty-five francs a month, a nice little nest-egg.

Pierre-Edouard had always refused to touch that sack of bones. There were plenty of pretty girls elsewhere, and for free! All one had to do was go and seek them out . . .

With the help of Moïse, who had worked in the area for more than ten years, Pierre-Edouard explored the country for thirty kilometres around; he spent his Saturday evenings and Sundays at the little dances at Yverny, at Puisieux, Nantouillet and Villeroy. Once he and Moïse even dared to go as far as Sevran. But there were too many townies over that way, too many factory-workers, too many smoothies – the dancers would not deign to look at two miserable peasants like them.

Another time they pushed on as far as Coulommiers, where the young bucks of the area very quickly objected to their success with the girls, to their way of doing the polka or schottische, and most of all to Moïse's remarks. He inexplicably but implacably hated the people of the Brie region, quite unreasonably holding them responsible for all the miseries of the dog's life he led; Pierre-Edouard had even heard him insult a Percheron mare with the words 'Bloody bitch of a bastard from Brie!'

'All cunning devils,' he announced, 'not one better than the other, and proud as priests with it! By God, they're not like the fellows round our way! Anyway we've got wine, whereas they can only make cheese!'

Pierre-Eduard took care not to ask Moïse from Champagne why he had left his own area to live in enemy territory. But that evening, when attacked by a dozen men from Coulommiers, he had been forced to take sides – and to hit out hard to get away.

'I told you they were all hooligans and sons of pigs! You saw the dirty fellows! Twenty to one! Hooligans, cheats! And their girls, no better than rotten beets, at least that's what they smell like!' bellowed Moïse, as soon as they had shaken off their pursuers.

He had a nose like a tomato and was snorting like a worm-ridden horse. Pierre-Edouard agreed with his companion for once; any inclination to impartiality was overridden by a rapidly swelling left eye. They climbed on their bicycle and set off for the farm. For Moïse actually owned an old bike, a strong machine on to which he had fixed a luggage-carrier, where Pierre-Edouard perched when they set off on their adventures. On the return journeys, Pierre always steered, because Moïse could not hold his wine, still less spirits, but always mixed them anyway. So he would climb on the back with great difficulty, his clogs trailing on the ground, and grasp instinctively for the driver's belt. Despite this grip he often fell off heavily, and each time he simply curled up and continued his sleep on the ground. Pierre-Edouard had to kick him in the ribs and help him up, otherwise he would certainly have ended these nights in a ditch.

During his first year at the farm, Pierre-Edouard went out with Jules as well. But since Jules had started hanging around a girl from Yverny – a big lusty wench, plump as a brood-mare, whose father farmed a hundred and fifty-eight hectares – he couldn't be relied on any more.

Besides, Pierre-Edouard had never really rediscovered the friend he had known in Besançon; one of the boys, always among the first to have a laugh, pay for a round, or pass under Fifine's red light, always yelling the same overworked joke which he considered witty: 'We gunners have had enough of breach-loaders; we want to unload our breeches!'

Yes, that Jules had been left behind in some bar in Besançon; he had nothing in common with the Ponthiers' son. He worked like the other labourers, and never carried tales to his father about the two or three shirkers among them, but now that he was back under the thumb of his parents the spark had simply gone out of him.

Besides that, he had never understood why Pierre-Edouard had come to work on the farm, accepting such killing work for such a miserable wage.

'But, for God's sake, why do you stay here?' he often exclaimed. 'If it were me, with a school certificate; well. . . !'

'Well, what?'

'I would be . . . in Paris, you'd see! You could get a job in government! Or I'd have re-enlisted; you could have been a company sergeant, or even a warrant officer!'

'Are you sick or something? And what would I do in the government or the army?'

'Well, nothing, that's the point! And at least you'd be earning a penny or two, and doing damn all for it!'

'Money, money, you make me tired with your money! What I want is my land.'

'Your land? Perhaps it's all disappeared since you left, perhaps your father's sold up . . .'

'Don't worry, that won't happen. I'm keeping an eye on it . . .'

Thanks to Léon, he had three long letters a year packed with information, stories and every particular about the life of St Libéral, the farm, the state of the land, the crops and the yield. Léon even gave him news of the livestock: 'Your father has sold the bay mare, she was old, at least eighteen; I believe he got 215 francs for her, that's good, I wouldn't have taken her at that price, it was Fleyssac of Objat who bought her.' Or again: 'The plums are fine, your father must have picked at least two tons from what I can see from the roadway . . .' Then: 'Berthe is all right, but she's not happy, she needs to go out and enjoy herself a bit, but . . .'

Pierre-Edouard had been pleasantly surprised when he read the first letter. After he had sent his, he began to have doubts, and reproached himself at the thought of Léon struggling to read it and suffering torments to write a reply, if he even attempted it. But in place of the laborious essay he had expected, he received a polished epistle, without spelling mistakes, in good French; the handwriting was a little childish, to be sure, but well joined-up, perfectly readable, with capital letters and punctuation where required. He supposed that Léon had set himself to writing late in life, just as he had learned his arithmetic, for the sake of his profession.

As a result of this he felt close to St Libéral, to his land and his animals, despite the distance which separated him from the village. If necessary he could leave at a moment's notice, return home and set to work immediately. He knew exactly which crops had been sown on which fields, the precise number of cows, ewes and pigs. But he was waiting, in the certain knowledge that it was still too early to return and live on equal terms with his father.

Pierre-Edouard accepted his lot patiently, thanks to this correspondence. Besides, he recognised that he was experiencing and learning about a completely different form of agriculture from that of his youth, however awful the work, the weariness and discouragement.

The Ponthiers were hard, grasping people, but the farmer knew how to cultivate the land, how to care for and enrich it. He rotated the crops wisely and manured the land generously; as for spreading fertiliser, it had nothing in common with the methods which had brought Jean-Edouard Vialhe such renown. At St Libéral his father had used phosphates almost exclusively, and in very small quantities, since they were expensive. Sometimes he added guano from Peru, but very sparingly and carefully.

Here, old Ponthier spread not only phosphates, but also potash and sulphate of ammonia in ample measures. In addition he used selected wheat seed each year, usually 'Good Farmer' or 'Reliable Early', which he had sent direct from Vilmorin (in St Libéral everyone sowed seed taken from the previous year's crop); so his seedlings were beautifully uniform, rarely affected by diseases such as rust or blight, and delivered the finest, highest yields Pierre-Edouard had ever seen. He, who had been so proud when his father had harvested a dozen bushels from a hectare – an enormous quantity for the Corrèze – was speechless when he realised that his master was harvesting twenty-three! Enough to make the farmers of St Libéral cry with shame!

As for the buxom cows of Normandy, they were much fatter and better built than the few milkers of St Libéral, and easily produced eight to ten litres more milk each day. They did have mangers full of beets, clover, barley and molasses, however.

Even the pigs raised by his father did not compare favourably with the ones here. The black-spotted Limousin breed demanded little special feeding; they happily accepted potatoes, cooked beets, mouldy corn, chestnuts and even acorns, and produced finer meat than this Craon race, fattened on full-cream milk and barley flour by the mistress. But what a difference in shape, in growth and in weight! Here the porkers bordered on 200 kilos at barely fifteen months, whereas at St Libéral they hadn't reached 150 kilos at that age. And what did the butchers demand? Animals with some weight on them, of course! Pierre-Edouard was dreaming of a Craon-Limousin crossbreed with the flavour of the one and the yield of the other, hoping that he would be able to realise this idea some day.

Then there were the three huge reversible ploughs, called Double Brabants, which the farmer purchased for the 1912 ploughing season; they were mechanical marvels, so easy to manipulate that a sturdy lad of twelve could drive them. Pierre-Edouard had not yet had the honour; only Octave and the two oldest ploughmen were privileged to use them. The other ploughmen had to be content with the old Dombalse and to hold on tight to the handles, whilst that lucky devil Octave and his two colleagues walked along, practically with their hands in their pockets, beside their new machines.

And those were not the only implements which fascinated him. Besides the mechanical reaper, which he already knew about, he discovered the huge rake which turned the swathes of hay in no time, spread it out carefully to dry in the sun, and did the work of ten men. As for the reaping and binding machine, he had seen one at work on a neighbouring farm, and his employer intended to purchase one for the 1914 harvest. He had boasted of it – even telling them the price, 885 francs – and announced that, thanks to this machine, they would never be able to blackmail him again on the eve of the harvest!

'On that day, you wretches, I won't need to stop you going through the door – I'll even help you on your way! Because from then on, you can wait for a pay rise forever!'

This malicious comment did not stop Pierre-Edouard from dreaming of the day when he, too, would reap the corn with a fine machine like that, but on his own land.

While he was waiting he did not waste a crumb of all he observed. He developed his knowledge, he stored it away, he refined it. One day he would make use of it.

Léonie Vialhe passed away peacefully, at the age of

seventy-nine, on Tuesday 28 April 1914. Her death was welcomed as a release by Marguerite and Berthe, for she had required constant care and had sunk to a near-vegetable state in recent years. Although Jean-Edouard was also deeply relieved, he was nevertheless affected by losing the last tie with his youth. From now on he was the oldest in the family, whether he would or no; he had become the patriarch, who would, quite logically, be the next to go . . .

While still alive his mother had provided a measure of security, a constant which, quite illogically, had given him confidence, a defence against his own old age. His fifty-four years seemed nothing compared to the seventy-nine of his mother; once she had gone, he suddenly found that they weighed more heavily. And the fact that twenty-five years separated him from his mother was no comfort. It passed so quickly, a quarter of a century, and was so quickly filled! Twenty-five years ago, that's when he had married Marguerite, as if it were yesterday . . . And since the past years had flown by so fast, should he not expect to see the years to come gather pace?

It took him more than two weeks to overcome this lowness of spirit. He reasoned with himself. Of course he was no longer young, but he was still strong, despite the pains which ravaged his kidneys and back during the heavy work, despite the constant tiredness, despite his whitening hair and moustache.

Spring burst forth all around him, and swept away the dark thoughts.

Winter was really over, you could see the grass growing. Jean-Edouard decided to put his cows out to pasture. They had been confined to the cowshed since November and, although they had been fed as much as they could eat, they needed sunshine and fresh grass now. They had already been mooing for several days, stretching their muzzles towards the door and refusing their hay. It needed all his attention, and Marguerite and Abel to help him, when he untied them each morning and evening to let them drink, lest they slip away and make for the fields.

So on the 16 May he decided to let them loose in the least exposed meadow, the one with the earliest growth, Combes-Nègres. He untied the ten animals, drove them into the courtyard and opened the gate.

What a rush, what speed! The cows charged forward frantically, lowing with pleasure, running happily between jumps, spinning round and kicking out their legs. They left the village and at last stopped to sniff each other slowly and carefully to get to know each other again, to test their strength by clashing horns briefly, until the dog snapped at their heels and put a stop to that.

But when they reached Combes-Nègres there was a serious settling of accounts, for Jolie, a fat, ten-year-old Limousin, was challenged by an impetuous heifer – a fine beast, heavy and well-built, who had claimed the bull's attentions a month earlier.

Jean-Edouard saw the battle commence; sent off the dog, and ran to separate the combatants himself as well. Nothing worked; neither old Miro's fangs, nor his volleys of blows and shouts. The two adversaries were firmly entangled, head to head and bellowing; they arched their backs and put all their energy into the struggle, pushing each other to and fro to regain lost ground.

Suddenly the heifer lost her footing, for she was less experienced in fighting; she turned her side towards her rivals' horns as she slipped round. Jolie butted her violently under the belly and propelled her to the edge of the ravine. Her hooves gave way beneath her weight and she fell down about three metres. From above Jean-Edouard clearly heard the crack as she fractured her right tibia.

He tumbled down the scree towards the beast, and swore as he saw the huge swelling stretching the skin on her thigh. He climbed back on to the path, drove the other cows into the meadow, and left for the village at a run.

'And you say he won't be back until this evening?' Jean-Edouard fumed.

'Well, yes, Monsieur Vialhe. But if you like I can help you!'

'Little squirt,' he grumbled to the butcher's young assistant, 'I could cut you in two with a blunt knife, and you want to slaughter an animal! So where is he, your master?'

'At Brive. He's at a wedding today, and I'm keeping the shop.'

'Huh, it's well-equipped with you there!' shouted Jean-Edouard as he left.

He would have to go as far as the post office to contact the butcher in Ayen. Thanks to the telephone (a recent installation and Jean Duroux's great pride) he could call the post office in Ayen and request the operator to alert the butcher. But would he feel like coming, and if so, when?

The injured beast needed to be slaughtered immediately. Each passing minute reduced his chances of getting any money for her; if the pain and shock were to make her feverish, only the knacker would be happy. She needed to be slaughtered now.

Jean-Edouard had killed a great number of pigs in his life; he didn't like it, but he did it expertly. Executing a cow was a different matter: you couldn't play around, you needed to know the right technique. Was there anyone in the village capable of undertaking such an operation, apart from that idiot of a butcher who wasn't there? Who could stun it, bleed it, skin it and divide the carcass, and all at the bottom of a ravine? Nobody, except Léon. That was almost a part of his job, and since he dealt with cattle there was a fair chance he had already had to do it. But to be forced to call on him for help!

Jean-Edouard's soul revolted as he set out at a run and slipped down the alley which led to Léon's place. He reached the house, knocked and examined the building. It was quite new, large and well built. There was no sign of the hovel in which the cattle-dealer had spent his youth. That fellow had certainly made his fortune quickly! 'And with our money . . .' he thought, as he banged on the solid oak door.

'Don't exhaust yourself, I'm here,' announced Léon, coming out of the stable. 'What brings you here?'

'An accident. I have a heifer who's just broken her thigh-bone.'

'So what? I only buy them in good condition.'

'I know that, dammit! But she needs to be slaughtered, and the butcher's gone off for the day!'

'That's a nuisance, but I don't see what I can do about it.'

'Oh, for goodness sake, don't play the fool! You must help me. You know how to slaughter. Come on, get your gear and come quickly. We can't let the animal suffer! I told Abel to get the neighbours; there'll be several of us, we'll help you.'

'It's not my job, and I don't see why I should do anything for you, except perhaps thank you for taking the meadow by the mill.'

'Good God! You don't want to bring up that old business again, do you?'

'Why not?'

Jean-Edouard was beside himself with fury, but realised just in time that one word out of place would lead to the total loss of his heifer.

'Well, all right, I went a bit too far there, I admit. Let's forget it.'

'Damn it all! You're quick to forgive yourself!' Léon mocked him, slowly rolling a cigarette. 'Hey,' he shouted towards the stable, where one of his workmen was grooming a horse, 'a rope, the big pulley and the set of knives too, ask my mother for them. He'll follow us,' he explained. 'Well, where is this animal?'

She had not moved. Around her stood Abel, Jeantout, and Gaston; Marguerite was there too, sitting by her head, soothing her with words and caresses and crying silently.

'Well, what do we do?' asked Jean-Edouard.

'Not so fast, not so fast,' recommended Léon, feeling the animal with expert hands. 'Not good, that leg, she'll lose several kilos. And she isn't plump. Not thin, but lacking a bit . . . You can see for yourself, you won't get much for her . . . And then some of the tenderloin will be missing. What do you want for her?'

'Heavens, how do I know! I thought that . . .'

'Yes, yes,' interrupted Léon. 'That I was going to slaughter her and you'd toss me a coin and perhaps a bit of sirloin, and sell the rest to the butcher! That won't work. Here's what we'll do: I'll buy her, I'll slaughter her and sort it out from there. Any other ideas and it's good evening to you! Well, what's your price?'

'That's not how it's usually done!' countered Jean-Edouard, and felt encouraged by murmurs of agreement from his neighbours.

'I don't care what's usual! It's not my usual job to slaughter animals, and if you don't like it, Monsieur Vialhe, I'm off!' Leon assured him with a smile. He had him hooked and wasn't about to let him off the line. He had waited for a chance like this for a long time.

'All right,' sighed Jean-Edouard at last, 'Four hundred and fifty francs, that's what I want.'

'Oh, fine, you should have said straight away you were dragging me up here for a good laugh!' exclaimed Léon, as he scrambled back up the slope. 'Take good care of yourselves, all of you!'

'Name your price!' yelled Jean-Edouard.

Léon stopped halfway up, shrugged his shoulders and assumed a disgusted expression.

'What do you want me to say. . . ? You can see she's not fat, and I shouldn't be surprised if she weren't feverish already.' He went back to the animal and lifted one eyelid.

'Hullo! Look at that eye, it looks feverish, I'm telling you! But the longer we leave it . . . So, just to help you out, I'll give you . . . Let's see, what does she weigh, not heavy, is she? Let's say eighteen pistoles!' He instinctively employed an old form of coinage peculiar to cattle-dealers. 'Sixty crowns, if you prefer . . .'

'Good God!' Jean-Edouard was choking and his hands began to tremble. 'A hundred and eighty francs, for that animal! Do you want me to knock your block off! Swindler! It wasn't enough to run against me in the elections! You have to steal from me as well!'

'Come, come, Monsieur Vialhe, at your age, it doesn't

do you any good to get in a temper! I told you I wouldn't forget the meadow by the mill ... You see, today, the tables are turned. It's my decision. Come on, shake on a hundred and eighty francs! I've got other things to do. It's agreed, eighteen pistoles?'

'Dammit, she's worth four hundred and fifty!' insisted Jean-Edouard.

'Perhaps she was a short while ago, before she fell, but now ... I'm beginning to wonder whether even eighteen pistoles ... I'm giving it away ... I'm sure if we wait a bit she'll go down to fifteen, or twelve ...'

Jean-Edouard looked at his neighbours, who had moved away in embarrassment. They didn't want to take sides. Of course Léon was openly taking advantage of the situation, but they all remembered the meadow by the mill ... That time it was Jean-Edouard who had behaved badly. So ...

'Give me the money,' he said at last.

He counted the francs and put them in his pocket.

'Leave that,' he ordered Marguerite, and drew her away, helping her to climb the embankment. Before they reached the path they were startled by the dull thud of the poleaxe splitting the skull.

18

PIERRE-EDOUARD tore open the little blue envelope with trembling hands. The postman had walked out to meet him as he was coming back from the wheat field; he had been using a scythe to cut a pathway for old Ponthier's new binder.

'Here,' he said giving him a coin, 'I can't offer you a drink, my flagon's empty.'

'Don't apologise, lad.' The postman wiped his forehead. 'I know how it is. It's not good, is it?'

'What?'

'The telegram.'

'No.'

'It's very rarely good news . . .'

Pierre said goodbye and hurried across the fields towards the farm. Just before reaching it he read the message again: '*Félix very ill, come. Louise.*'

He looked at the date, 15 July. The plea had been sent that very morning, and perhaps since then . . . He went straight to the dormitory, stuffed his few belongings into an old bag, and strode towards the owner's house.

'What do you want? And where are you going with your bag?' called his boss from the barn where he was working.

'I'm leaving,' he announced as he approached.

'What do you mean, leaving? In the middle of the harvest! I believe you haven't sobered up yet from yesterday! Or are you trying to repeat the trick you played two years ago? If that's the case, you can go!'

Pierre-Edouard shrugged. 'I have to go, my sister has sent for me . . .'

'Oh yes? Just like that, she clicks her fingers and you go? And the harvest, have you thought of that?'

'Shut your mouth,' growled Pierre-Edouard, advancing

a step towards him, 'you can stuff your harvest! I'm off, and you owe me a fortnight's pay!'

'Listen, you little bastard, if that's how you want it – we'll pay you, oh yes, but I advise you not to come back. Never! If you try, I swear I'll set the dogs on you!'

'Don't worry, there's no danger of that! I've had enough of working for you and killing myself in your bloody fields! You won't see me back here in a hurry! Come on, give me my money and I'm off.'

'Go and see the mistress, and go to the devil!'

'Comes to the same thing!' shouted Pierre-Edouard as he walked away.

The farmer's wife counted out his money exactly and pushed the coins towards him. 'When I think we took you on to please Jules!' Her voice grated between clenched teeth. 'And you leave right in the middle of harvesting; that's not the way decent people behave!'

'Don't talk to me about decent behaviour; seek the beam in your own eye!' He put his money in his wallet and left. Coming out of the yard he spotted his workmates in the distance, building up a huge stack of barley; he waved to them and took to the road.

'If you want work, it's no use going to the château; you need the farm, son, over there, behind the trees,' the gardener warned him, looking him up and down.

'No, it's not that, I've come to see my sister. Louise, Louise Flaviens; she works here, at the castle,' explained Pierre-Edouard.

He had been travelling all night, changed trains three times, and to complete the journey he had hired the services of a good man who owned a tilbury.

'Oh well, yes, I wondered . . . You do look like her, that's true. I expect you know that your nephew's almost done for?'

'Do you know anything about it? That's why I've come,' asked Pierre-Edouard.

'The doctor came by this morning – he comes every day, but he don't tell me nothing.'

'But you would know if, well, if . . .'

'If the little fellow had gone? Of course, my wife would have told me!'

Pierre breathed easier. 'Where's my sister's room?'

'Up there, in the attics.' The man waved his arm towards the roof. 'You go through the servants' entrance, turn right as soon as you get into the courtyard, the door at the bottom of the first tower. Climb up there and you'll find the servants' quarters.'

Pierre-Edouard thanked him and strode towards the Château de la Cannepetière; doves fluttered around one side of the enormous building, whilst more of them were resting in the centre of a formal garden, with beautiful banks of rose bushes and avenues of chestnut trees where peacocks called.

He heard the cough long before reaching the top storey: a harsh and terrible cough, which seemed to use up all the breath and rose to wheezy rasp, as painful as the death-rattle of a cock strangled at the highest pitch of its final cry. He ran up the last few steps, and darted towards the room where he could now hear a panting gasp between hollow gurgles. He entered without knocking.

'Yes, yes, honestly, he's getting better,' Louise explained a little while later, 'but yesterday morning I thought that . . . So I sent for you. It's silly, I'm ashamed of myself.'

'You did the right thing,' he said as he stroked the child's damp forehead.

He smiled at him, spoke to him softly, awkwardly; he was moved to discover in Félix, not the baby he had known, but a little man with a turned-up nose, bright eyes and curly blond hair. And he talked, wanted to know everything, his eyes following Pierre-Edouard everywhere, so happy to meet him at last.

'But what is the matter with him? Tell me, what have you got?' he asked the child.

'Whooping-cough,' the little invalid spoke feebly. 'It's there, it's burning,' he explained, touching his chest and throat.

'Yes, but it's getting better, the doctor just said so. You'll soon be well,' Louise comforted him, 'and now you've seen your godfather.'

The child smiled, but was immediately overwhelmed by a long fit of coughing; it was exhausting and terrifying, and left him panting and out of breath.

'Good God, what a dreadful infection!' said Pierre-Edouard. 'What are you giving him for it?'

'The doctor left some medicine, some syrup; and I make him an infusion – do you remember the one Granny gave us to get rid of colds, with mallow, poppies, hollyhocks and honey?'

He went one better: 'And she used to make mustard plasters!'

'I've made them for him.'

'And they sting,' murmured the child.

'Yes, but it helps you get better too,' Pierre-Edouard assured him. 'The more it stings, the more it cures! And how are you?' he asked his sister.

She had changed during the intervening three years; she had put on weight and looked happy again. She did seem tired, worn out by the disturbed nights and the bedside vigil; despite that, she appeared in better form than at their last meeting.

They talked for a long time. He passed on to her all the details of home life faithfully transmitted to him by Léon; named the neighbours and relatives who had come to Grandmother's funeral – he spoke of it all so minutely that you would have thought he had arrived straight from St Libéral. Finally, he told her about his departure from Moureau Farm.

'It's my fault,' she reproached herself. 'I made you lose your job.'

'It's no great loss! Now I've left, I'm wondering how I could have stayed there so long. Three and a half years, just think!'

'Why don't you go back home now? Perhaps father . . .'

'No, he hasn't changed; Léon told me. And for that matter, why don't you go back yourself?'

'Oh, me . . . that's different. You know, I don't miss it any more. I'm settled here – my employers are kind, and I have good accommodation, good food, good wages. Just think, I get thirty francs a month now; that's good, you know! The best part is that I can keep the little one with me. And then . . .' She faltered and blushed as her brother gazed at her questioningly. 'Yes, I was going to write to you about it, and then Félix fell ill. I'm going to get married again.'

'Well, what a surprise!' he whistled.

He had never imagined that his sister would have been able to cut herself off from the memory of Octave, that she would want to start her life anew. A wave of anger flooded through him. My God! She had created the whole mess, upset the entire family, quarrelled with her parents, only to jump into the arms of another man four years after the first one had disappeared! Perhaps his father was right when he maintained that she was too quick and easy!

'Do you mind very much?' she asked sadly.

He pulled himself together, reproaching himself for his first reaction. Basically his burst of anger was just as stupid and unjust as his parents' reaction had been so long ago. Just as she had done five years earlier, Louise was doing the opposite of what others wanted and expected, without asking his opinion, without realising that she was free to make different plans. For he had firmly placed her among the widows who wore mourning and sadness all their lives, who accepted their fate passively and discreetly. He had never imagined that she could one day fall in love with someone other than Octave, and be happy with his usurper.

'Yes, I can see you hold it against me,' she continued. 'Oh, I know, you helped me so much with Octave.'

'No, I don't mind, but you gave me a shock. I would never have thought . . .' He fell silent. What had he thought? That his sister was the sort who would submit to her fate? That was poor judgement of her character!

'You know,' she reminded him, 'I'm only twenty-three. Do you think it's fun to be alone all the time? Of course, I have Félix. But after all, is it wrong to want to live with a man? Is it wrong to want to keep house for him, to cook his meals, to wait for him, to love him, to sleep at his side, to grow old with him? Do you think it's wrong?'

'No, no!' he assured her quite sincerely, 'there's nothing wrong in that! You're quite right. I simply wasn't expecting it, that's all. Anyway, it's none of my business. You know, what matters is that you should be happy. And him too,' he said, pointing to the child.

She smiled. 'He will be, don't worry. Jean liked him straight away. And then, you know, life is strange – Jean lost his wife three years ago, she died in childbirth and their little girl didn't survive either. So, when we met . . . You see, we can share our sorrow, that's what it is. I know that for him it won't be the same as with his first wife, and for me it's like that too; it will never be the same as it was with Octave. But we can't change what's happened, life's like that . . .'

'I understand. What does he do?'

'He's a forester. He earns a good living. And the baron is going to let us have a cottage, in the middle of the forest. It'll be good there, it even has a garden.'

'And is he young?'

'Thirty-two, that's not so old. You know, I've talked to him a lot about you. I'm sure you'll get on very well.'

'Why not . . . And when are you getting married?'

'We had chosen the 25th, before the boy was ill. Well, since he's getting better we won't postpone it.'

'The 25th of which month?'

'Of this one.'

'Good heavens, so soon!'

'Why wait longer? We've known each other for two years.'

'And you never told me . . .'

'It's not easy in letters. I was going to write, I swear it, just before the boy's illness. You believe me, don't you? I wouldn't have got married again without telling you beforehand!'

'I believe you. But you know, on the way here, I didn't think you'd be announcing your wedding for next week.'

'Yes. This way, if things turn out badly, at least we'll be married.'

'What could turn out badly?'

'The situation. Jean says we might be going to have a war. Well, you'd know more about that, eh?'

'Huh! I don't think it'll come to that, it's just a political matter, that's all.'

'Jean thinks it'll happen; he reads the paper every day. It seems that it's been very bad since the assassination of that poor prince, or king, I don't remember which . . .'

'Go on! I read the paper too, sometimes. Well, all right, there's been this assassination, down there, devil knows where; so what does it matter to us? Besides, in the train I read in someone else's paper that the President has just set out for Russia. Do you think he would go trundling off so far away if it was as serious as Jean says? Go on, I know why he told you that; because he's in a hurry to get you to the registry office!'

Despite his great age, Doctor Fraysse had not changed his habits at all. He pushed open the door of the inn, as he did every evening, to compete with Antoine Gigoux at billiards. They chose and prepared their cues, began to play, and took up the conversation where they'd left off the night before.

'So you're still ready to take on the Prussians?' joked the former mayor.

'My dear Gigoux, I'll tell you once more, it's not for old men like me to decide; I can't attack anything much these days, sad to say. But your mockery and scepticism won't stop the war. I'll take a bet with you on that!'

'But of course it'll be stopped! Jaurès is right, we must create a great international peace movement. That's what all sensible people are hoping for!'

'I'll tell you something; your Jaurès is a fine one. I won't go so far as those who think that he's sold out to the Germans, but I do say he's a lying swine!'

'You have no right to say that! Nobody has ever done as much as he has in the cause of peace.'

264

'Eternal peace, yes; the peace of the graveyard! When I think he was against the three-year military service, and for disarmament! In the name of God, Gigoux, open your eyes a little! You don't see that the Austrians and the Germans are just dying to start a war! Go and talk about peace to Franz-Josef or the Kaiser! Really, you are stupid; it would be laughable if it weren't so sad!'

'You're nothing but a warmonger! It's a good thing everyone's not like you!'

'Warmonger, me? I would remind you that I've spent my whole life looking after people. Are you telling me I've been trying to finish them off for the fun of it!'

'Well no, I didn't mean to say that!' Antoine Gigoux apologised.

'I know. But your blindness worries me.'

'My what?'

'You see nothing, my poor Gigoux. You and a few others, including our dear teacher, dream of world peace. I do, too. But I know that some dreams never come true. We're going to have war, I can feel it; there's no other way out. And believe me, it doesn't make me happy. I know what it's like, you see; I was there in '70. It's abominable, war . . . And that's what I tell all the young people in the village, the ones who really want to fight. The poor things, if they only knew what it was like!'

'So you see why we must campaign for peace!'

'Of course, of course,' sighed the doctor, 'but go and explain that to the mad dogs who are growling at your heels! They won't even give you time to speak, and once you've been bitten you'll have rabies too, and goodbye to your lovely dreams of universal peace! Look, there's our squire and his town council come to drink to some new decision they've made. Don't make that face, my old friend; after all, your son was only beaten by twelve votes. Anyway, that's all in the past.'

'Have you heard the news?' asked Jean Duroux coming up to them. 'Austria has just mobilised eight divisions. This time I fear the worst . . .'

'And why is it the worst?' called out Léon. 'We're going

to smash their faces, for sure. We've been talking about it long enough!'

'Especially you,' spat Jean-Edouard. 'It's all very well for you to talk; everyone knows you're excused military service!'

'Come, come, my friends,' Jean Duroux intervened. 'We haven't come to that yet! I have complete confidence in our government; I'm sure that every effort will be made to avoid conflict.'

'May God hear you,' murmured the old doctor, and his serious tone made an impression on everyone.

Pierre-Edouard grasped the fat bundle of rye, swiftly bound it up, placed the sheaf behind him and gathered a fresh armful. Beside him eleven other men were busy with the binding; they were walking at the heels of a dozen men with scythes who swung their long blades in almost perfect harmony to lay low the tall stalks.

Pierre-Edouard could not get over his good fortune. First of all he had had no trouble in finding a job at the farm belonging to the château, thanks to Louise of course, and at an incredible salary – two francs ninety a day, twenty centimes more than at the Ponthiers' for the same work. Secondly, little Félix was much better; he was cheerful again, and the colour had come back into his cheeks. Lastly, he had been able to witness his sister's marriage the previous day.

The quiet ceremony was celebrated first at the town hall and then in the church at Mézières-en-Brenne twelve kilometres away. Today Louise, Jean and Félix had moved into their little forest cottage, a real love nest, perched in the middle of the woods more than six kilometres from the château.

He had not been able to help them settle in; the weather augured ill, the air felt stormy, the harvest must be got in. It was a Sunday, but this was a serious matter. The farm manager had offered a bonus of a franc to those who would work, and they had all come.

In the three and a half years on Moureau Farm, Pierre-

Edouard had got used to vast spaces, to great plains interspersed occasionally by a few pretty woods. So he was like a fish out of water, astonished by this new landscape which had been his home for the last ten days.

Here were no huge stretches of good rich soil; there were fields, big ones, but poor and sandy, full of puddles, divided by a maze of deep ditches and surrounded by woods or by moors of heather and bracken. A poor region, where even the rye seemed to have difficulty in growing — he had noticed that as he grasped it. Watery land, too; he could not get over the number of pools and marshes.

And amidst it all a profusion of game, which had to be respected despite its depradations; these losses did not seem to bother the farm manager. For instance in this field of rye, which was not all that marvellous anyway, Pierre-Edouard reckoned that the toll taken by fallow and roe-deer or wild boar was more than forty sheaves; they had wallowed in it like pigs, which made the reapers' work all the more difficult.

'But the baron has twelve hundred hectares, a thousand of them forested; he values them more than the soil,' explained his new brother-in-law. 'And then he doesn't need it to live off. Besides, hunting is his great love. I'll show you his pack of hounds, it's really something . . .'

And Pierre-Edouard was speechless when he saw the seventy-five English crossbred hounds sheltering in the kennels. Then he began to laugh quietly, at the thought of the three or four dogs which were Jean Duroux's pride and joy back home in the village.

He had to force himself not to give Jean a chilly reception when Louise introduced them. He could not stop thinking of Octave, his quiet air, his gentle voice. But he was quickly convinced his sister had not been mistaken in her choice.

'Well, so you're Pierre-Edouard! Christ Almighty! Louise talks of nothing but you. Thanks to her I've known you for two years; I'm glad to shake you by the hand. It seems you muddled through together, down there in the Corrèze!'

Yes, he had been won over by this tall, well-built fellow, a handsome man who watched and waited on Louise and was full of affection for Félix. Jean maintained that sooner or later he would come with his wife to the Corrèze, to explore the area she had talked about so much. And Louise approved of this plan. He joked readily, too:

'You haven't got any trees down there in the Corrèze, have you? It's too poor.'

'No trees! We have the most beautiful chestnut trees in the world!' protested Pierre-Edouard and his sister.

'Go on! A few twisted saplings, some miserable aspens, a few broom brushes. No, I couldn't earn a living down there. I need trees; you've seen the oak plantations we have here?'

These really were beautiful and well maintained; it was Jean who looked after them, and he was more than a little proud of them.

'Of course, compared to the forest at Tronçais, it's pathetic,' he added, suddenly becoming serious. 'But if I'd stayed there, where I worked for five years, I'd never have got to know your sister, that's my consolation.'

He had found consolation, for that and his other losses, and so had Louise: what more could one ask?

Pierre-Edouard dexterously bound another sheaf and looked up at the sky; the storm was receding. He felt completely happy, content to be there doing work he enjoyed, amongst companions who seemed to have accepted him, despite the fact that he didn't understand half of what they were saying – they had such dreadful accents! Happy to be able to say: 'I'm all right here. There's Louise, Félix and Jean; the pay is good and I like the country, and if I want to, I can stay, and that's what I'm going to do! Tomorrow I'll write to Léon.'

He gathered another sheaf and began to whistle. Life was beautiful.

PART FIVE

The Red Furrows

19

JEAN-EDOUARD was struck by the silence when he stepped out into the main street; such a heavy silence, so deep, that he was quite frightened by it. It made him want to talk, to say something, anything, just to reassure himself that it was possible to disturb the abnormal peace, the unbearable, unnatural calm which oppressed the whole region. Even the animals seemed beaten into a sort of stupor; nothing moved, all animation suspended.

'It's not possible, God help us!' he murmured. 'It's as if the whole village has died since they left . . .'

They had left in a state of happy madness, a sort of collective hysteria, after several days of sheer lunacy!

First of all there was a dramatic scene on 1 August, with the teacher as principal actor, standing out in the centre of the square: the teacher waving his newspaper, running from side to side towards onlookers attracted by his cries. The teacher, a man normally so calm, was crying, really crying, huge tears which shone on his cheeks. The poor man held out the paper and stammered between hiccups and pathetic sobs:

'They've killed him, like an animal! They've murdered the only man who could have saved us, all is lost! They've killed Jaurès!'

And then the same day, towards five-thirty in the afternoon, when everyone was still in a state of shock from the morning's news, the postmaster rushed out of his office waving a telegram and shouting:

'Mobilisation order! Extremely urgent! First mobilisation day, Sunday August the second.'

So there was a state of alarm, a frenzy. The men ran to and fro, as if there were a fire, finding out the news. The cries, of joy, of hate! And all those words!

'We must leave immediately!'

'And the harvest, you idiots, what's to become of it?'

'Shut up!'

'Call the train, quick, quick. They're expecting us!'

And by evening the first departure, the first farewells. Then on Sunday all the young people streamed away, the lifeblood of the village. On the next and following days the older men left; obedient to the instructions on the coloured pages of their military handbooks, they went to present themselves to their units on the second, third or seventh mobilisation days.

Then there was silence in the village; emptiness, paralysis. And still there were others who had not yet joined up; there were still several fathers of families, and the older men, between forty and fifty-one, who would be called up in the following days. But they were not making any noise, they were making ready.

Jean-Edouard walked up the main street towards the Mairie.

'I was expecting you,' said Jean Duroux, shaking his hand. 'Well, how many of us are left at the final count?'

'From the council? Four – no, five with Dupeuch; you, Gaston, Jeantout, myself and then Léon. We can't count André and Jacques, they're leaving the day after to-morrow.'

'We shall have to get ourselves organised. Just think! No postman, no policeman, no butcher nor baker, no one left. Even Doctor Delpy, our priest and the teacher have gone . . .'

'Yes, and almost all the farmers in the community. What are we going to do? We're already behind with the harvest, with this weather. Have you seen how much there is still to bring in and thresh?'

'I've seen . . . but, you know, everyone agrees that it won't be for very long, a month or two perhaps. No more.'

'And everyone is wrong!' maintained Doctor Fraysse, coming into the room. 'Believe me, I see it as a long drawn out affair, this war. A year, maybe more. No, I'm not a defeatist!' he insisted, catching Jean Duroux's disapproving look. 'I'm simply telling you that it will be terrible and long. I know them, the Prussos! I saw them in '70. They only attack when they're sure of themselves. Oh, they won't win this time! President Poincaré is no Napoleon, luckily! But they won't be on their knees in two months, as you're saying. And that's what brings me here. You can inform everyone who's still here that I'm starting work again.'

'But you can't . . .' The squire was worried. 'Well, I don't have to tell you that it's hard work.'

'I know, I'm seventy-nine, and so what? You'll just have to find me a horse and cart. But I think Léon could provide that.'

'You can take my team, for free,' interrupted Jean-Edouard. 'It's just as good as anything that old swindler might sell you. Strutting about pretending to be a gentleman, when everyone else of his age is serving the flag!'

'He has a family to support,' argued Jean Duroux, 'and we should be glad that a few men like him are staying here. We're going to need them.'

'And the old folk,' the doctor agreed. 'You're going to have to work with all the former members of the council, like Antoine Gigoux. And with the women too.'

'Yes, we're going to organise all that. But I'm still convinced that it will all be over soon.'

Saint-Libéral came to life again, soberly, at a gentler pace. There really were too many hands missing for the bubbling activity of pre-war years to revive; the incessant toing and froing as from a hive in the honey-making season, the powerful rhythm of men at work.

Jean-Edouard demonstrated his remarkable flair for organisation, and it was partly thanks to him that the community emerged from its paralysis. He very quickly established teams of all the able-bodied men, women and children, who went out into the fields to finish the harvest, to bring in the sheaves and store the produce under cover.

It was amazing to see the stiff old men, sometimes leaning on young boys, but remembering and repeating the swing of the scythe by instinct. The women doing men's work; harnessing the animals, leading the teams, handling scythe and sickle, grinding the flour, cutting the meat, lighting the fire at the forge; they took over as heads of families with a hitherto unsuspected authority and power!

Jean-Edouard worked without respite; he was everywhere at once, and many were grateful to him for the loan of his mechanical reaper to cut the last patches of corn. He went round the farms where he knew there were no menfolk, always followed by Abel, whose grin grew more and more vacuous, and by Berthe – who, everyone agreed, had grown into a beautiful girl. He did not pause until the last sheaf was safely in, and proved once more that however dreadful the tragedies which beset him, he was not defeated by them, but rather made stronger and more determined. It was as if he had been waiting for just such a test to show his true mettle.

Inspired and intoxicated with fanatical energy, he was avenging all the wrongs he had suffered for the last five years; the slights, the family set-backs, the mayor's chain which had been denied him. They had thought him weakened and discouraged, but he came to the top stronger than ever; became again the man who had fought like a lion for the railway, the syndicate, the market, for all that was dear to his heart and that he believed he should do.

Jean-Edouard fulfilled his role wonderfully, admittedly helped by Jeantout and Gaston, and the squire also rose to the occasion. He gave his time unstintingly, and drew up a list of the worst affected families, where there were no men, the father long dead and the son away, where only women and children remained. He made sure that help went to them first, and sometimes even gave money from his own pocket to the most needy.

And then to him, as the elected mayor of the community, fell the most terrible task of all, the one which left him a changed man. What a shock when he opened the telegram announcing the first death from among the villagers, the first martyr, whose death was to drive all the mothers and wives mad with fear, though they crossed themselves every day! This death was going to destroy the unity of a family which he, Jean Duroux, had to visit without delay; it was he who must plunge them into black despair!

For a fleeting moment he was tempted to delegate the burden to a third party, to one of his assistants, or to the old doctor. But he pulled himself together immediately, wished that Father Verlhac could have accompanied him, and went out.

With hesitant step and hunched shoulders he made his way towards the inn. The first death was that of André Chanlat, the son of Jacques and Léonie, the innkeepers. He fell on the twenty-fourth day of the war. He was thirty-one and had two children.

Berthe stuffed her things into the big sack of coarse blue cloth she normally used to carry the dirty linen to the wash-house, and set it down against the door. Then she put on her Sunday clogs and smoothed her dress, all the while keeping an eye on the town square which was black with people.

Almost all the villagers were there for the funeral service, conducted by the old priest from Yssandon, in memory of André Chanlat. His death had caused general confusion and consternation. Despite the absence of body or coffin, which made the ceremony seem vaguely unreal, the mayor and town council had decided to honour the sacrifice made by this young father.

Berthe looked at the clock and then half opened the door. Presently she heard the whistle of the train; it always whistled as it started round the last bend just before the village, then it slowed down and came up beside the main street at walking pace.

She grasped her bundle, went out without a backward glance, ran towards the track and hid in the ditch. The funeral procession filed slowly past. She stood up suddenly, jumped into a compartment and threw herself down in it.

She had calculated that few people would be curious

enough to turn round to watch the train pass. If she had judged it right, they should all be giving their attention to Jean Duroux and the funeral oration which he was delivering at that very moment – a very beautiful speech, no doubt, very sad. As for other travellers, it was highly unlikely that anyone would get on at St Libéral station. Who could possibly need to go to La Rivière or Brive, since the war had started? And if anyone did get into her compartment, what could they say? She had a right to take the train, hadn't she?

The carriages crossed the square, slid into the station and stopped with a metallic squeak. She held her breath and forced herself to count to three hundred. If she did not hurry, the train would leave again when she reached that number; it never stopped more than five minutes.

It set off sooner than she expected, almost without a sound, without a cheery whistle, as if the driver were in a hurry to get away from a place marked by death, as he could tell from the black flag hanging above the door to the inn.

Berthe breathed more easily. She had succeeded. She had overcome all the difficulties and completed the first stage – by far the hardest part – of a plan she had been hatching for years, an idea which had sustained her, allowed her to survive without going mad when she had to submit to her father's inflexible will, her mother's sternness, her grand-mother's senility.

At last she could begin to live, to laugh, without fearing her father's anger or her mother's scoldings. God knows Louise and Pierre-Edouard had had good reason to leave! And how she had counted the days which separated her from freedom!

It would have been a terrible mistake to have fled earlier, an irretrievable error which would have condemned her to continue that joyless, aimless, and loveless existence. She knew her father too well; she dared not leave him whilst he had any hold over her. That identity card, which he had used and abused, had been in his hand only the day before yesterday; she had been about to escape from him and he hadn't even realised it! For yesterday, 25 August 1914, Berthe had attained her majority.

She was twenty-one, yes, but cautious as a wild-cat, with a strong intelligence refined by years of observation, of silence, of rebellion hidden under a false passivity.

She knew that her father would not hesitate to use any means to force her to return home, if she gave him half a chance; to send a couple of policemen to the station at Brive, for instance, to welcome her as she alighted from the train. Not to stop her – he no longer had the right to do that – but to keep her there for an hour or two, to give him time to get there himself. Convinced of his rights, his duty even, he would place a hand on her shoulder and take her back to the house, whether she would or no . . .

But she was cleverer than him, more cunning; she had been contemplating her departure for such a long time that she had studied every detail, each minute possibility that, if neglected, might bring her plans to naught.

The note she had slipped under her parents' bedcovers would not be found for hours. For the moment, everything depended on her parents not noticing her absence for a while. And even if they returned early to the house, there was no immediate evidence that she had fled. They would probably think she was in the cowshed, or the vegetable plot.

Later, of course, at suppertime . . . But by then it would be much too late; nothing could be done to try to catch her. Yes, every passing minute told her that she had won.

When the train arrived at La Rivière-de-Mansac, she jumped down onto the platform, barely pausing, for she saw the other line of carriages, the ones which would take her away forever. She knew that she had five minutes to spare to buy a ticket. It was relatively easy to travel without paying between St Libéral and La Rivière, but that was not advisable on the main line. Confident, with the easy tread of a seasoned traveller who knows exactly where she's going and is surprised at nothing, she moved towards the ticket-office.

If her father set out to look for her, it would be at Brive.

But he, who believed he saw and knew it all, hadn't thought of everything. He had not taken account of the women who gossiped around the village wash-house, where Mother Bouchard, the cobbler's wife, explained that her husband always had to leave the day before for Thenon market, where he had a thriving clientele, because there was no proper connection in the morning. He always caught the 18.16 for Périgueux . . .

Jean-Edouard and Marguerite noticed Berthe's absence far sooner than she had expected, and she would doubtless have swiftly devised an alternative plan if she had realised that her departure would be discovered even before the train set her down at La Rivière-de-Mansac.

It was Marguerite who had the first suspicions. She too had put on her Sunday clogs, to go to the funeral. She took them off as soon as she got home and slid them into their usual place under the stairs, then frowned when she noticed that her daughter's good clogs had disappeared.

'Well she must be mad, poor Berthe!' she cried to Jean-Edouard, who was changing into his work-clothes in their bedroom. 'Call her! What's got into her, putting on her best shoes to clean out the cowshed! I'll teach her how much they cost, I will!'

Five minutes later they were forced to face the facts: Berthe was not in the cowshed, nor in the garden; nor was she minding the animals, for Abel had led them up on to the stubble fields on the plateau.

A strange presentiment led Marguerite to open the wardrobe, and she stood dumbstruck for a moment; most of Berthe's things had gone. All that was left were a few old rags, some skirts and aprons worn threadbare.

'Jean!' she cried feebly. 'Look, she's taken everything, all her things; she's done it to us, her as well . . .'

'Bloody hell!' he swore. Then he controlled himself: 'What in God's name are you trying to say? Who could she have gone with? There are only old men left around here! Well, she won't have left alone, she's not capable of it. Besides, where's she supposed to have gone to, eh?'

'I don't know, do something, we have to find her . . .'

'My God, yes, I'm going to find her! What's that girl thinking of? That she decides what happens here, like the others did! Just you wait, she'll get a good hiding . . . Come on, come with me, we must ask everyone. Somebody must have seen her . . .'

'But then everyone will know! What will they think of us?' protested Marguerite.

'I don't care! We need all the neighbours to help us. Come on, hurry up, we'll question them.'

It was Jeantout's mother who very soon told them. She had been unable to walk for years, and her only pleasure was to watch the main street; she had seen the girl climb into the moving train.

Jean-Edouard ran to the post-office to telephone the police station at Ayen, and explained the situation in a few words.

'And it's most important that you tell your colleagues at Brive to keep her there until I arrive!' he said to the sergeant at the other end, whom he had known for years. 'What's that? What's it got to do with her age, anyway? She's my daughter, isn't she? She's . . .'

Suddenly he realised, and his voice fell; his energetic shout dwindled to a barely audible whisper. 'She was twenty-one the day before yesterday,' he finally admitted. 'Oh, I see . . . Right.'

Some of the villagers who saw him returning from the post-office thought that he had just learned of the death of his son.

Berthe arrived in Paris the following morning. She was deafened and exhausted by a night on the train, and came staggering out of the Gare d'Austerlitz almost on the point of giving up. Despite her strength of character, her desire to change her life – to *live* – she was ready to climb back onto the train and return to St Libéral's peace and quiet.

She knew no large towns except Brive, so she was frightened, almost petrified, by the noise, the crowds, the crush of cabs and taxis, the terrifying roar of the overhead railway which passed just above her, the continuous rumbling of military convoys. Through her confusion she suddenly became aware of the incredible madness which had impelled her to flee, which was now forcing her to act independently. She remained paralysed by fear for a long time, frozen to the spot in the middle of the pavement.

Then she gradually came to her senses, collected her thoughts, and began to resolve the problems she was faced with one by one.

First of all, she was glad that she had not left without some money. The 832 francs which she had hidden under her skirts really belonged to her. It was made up of small coins her grandparents had given her long ago, which she had carefully kept for years, and the savings which old Léonie had patiently accumulated, stored in her chest between two piles of linen.

'These savings,' her mother had told her as they returned from the burial service, 'will be yours, for your dowry. For the time being I'll look after them, you don't need them just now. But never fear, they'll come to you on your wedding day.'

She had taken the hoard from her parents' wardrobe just before leaving. The nest-egg was somewhat diminished by the cost of the journey — 25 francs 75 — but it was still significant, and made the future less bleak. This money would guarantee her bed and board for several months.

She urgently needed to find work, however. Convinced that a town as huge as Paris would provide opportunities for every sort of job, she tossed her bag over her shoulder and set off down the Boulevard de l'Hôpital.

At St Libéral there was little talk about her flight, and few sympathised with her parents. What was the departure of one girl, compared to the slaughter which stained the countryside red and laid the young men to rest in the stubble!

Already the village was coming to terms with another death — a lad of twenty-three, killed three days after the Chanlats' son — and six wounded, two of them in a serious condition. So what did it matter that little Berthe had run away to live her own life? It was simply proof that her father was as hard as ever, just as strict, and that he had not learned his lesson from what had happened with Louise and Pierre-Edouard!

And if she had left to join up with a boyfriend (some of the women were convinced of this), one could only hope that the lass would make the most of it and enjoy her man! Make the most of it while he was alive and strong, fit to make her happy night and day, to show her how beautiful life had been before . . . Before men had gone mad and begun to massacre each other indiscriminately, killing kids of twenty as well as fathers of families.

The Vialhes' closest neighbours, friends such as Jeantout, Gaston, the mayor and the old doctor, even took the trouble to show Jean-Edouard that Berthe's departure was of no consequence and held no dishonour. They all reminded him that she was an adult and free to lead her life as she wished, even if it was a trial to her parents to accept this at first.

'Of course it's all right,' said Jean-Edouard ironically, one evening when the squire was trying to reason with him. 'I've lost my third and last child, and I'm supposed to be singing!'

'I didn't say that! You haven't lost anything at all. Your children are still alive! Talking of which, have you had any news of Pierre-Edouard?'

'Yes, at least he's written to us. He's at the front, I don't know where. You know how it is, they're not even allowed to say where they are. And you, your son-in-law?'

'He's okay; he can't say where he is either, somewhere up there, like all the rest . . . So you mustn't torment yourself about Berthe. She's in no danger, her . . . By the way, did you know that Léon had signed up?'

'I don't believe it, that little twerp? For what? The supply corps, I bet! I thought he was exempt from service?'

'Only as head of a family. He's realised that his sisters can manage on their own now. One has got a job in Brive, and Mathilde is nearly fifteen. No, he's not in the supply corps, he's in the infantry. He left yesterday to join the 126th at Brive . . .'

Jean-Edouard nodded, but with an unhappy expression; it did not please him to have to admit that Léon had done the right thing.

'But then, if he's gone as well,' he said suddenly, 'there are no young men left at all in the community! Only the old ones like us!'

'Well yes, nothing but old men . . .'

'What will become of us? Just think of the grape-picking, the ploughing, the sowing, everything! How are we going to get all that work done?'

'With the women, my friend, with the women. You'll have to get used to the idea: if this war continues, and I'm afraid that it will, it's the women who are going to take the place of the men. Everywhere. In the fields and on all the farms . . .'

'That's never been done before!' protested Jean-Edouard. 'My God, there have been other wars and that's not been done! Can you see women doing the ploughing? Perhaps the harvest and the easy jobs, but not the ploughing! Go on! This war won't last because the other side needs the men, just as we do, to work the land, to produce food. When there's no corn, then they'll have to stop their bloody war, or they'll die of starvation! That's what'll happen, and your idea of women doing the ploughing, that's not going to happen tomorrow, that's never been done!'

Jean Duroux shrugged his shoulders. 'And a girl who jumps into a train the day after she's twenty-one, have you seen that before, in the past? Don't get in a state, I'm not saying that to annoy you, you know me. But believe me, our world, the real world we lived in until last month, doesn't exist any more. I'm afraid it's dead and gone forever.'

Berthe wandered about for five days, feeding on crusts and sleeping each night in a different room. Each evening found her with less energy and less courage than the previous day.

The capital was in a frenzy, preparing for a siege or even for street-fighting, and she wandered the streets without knowing where she was going, along the most miserable thoroughfares of the poor areas and the prosperous avenues of the 7th district. She even had to reject amorous admirers, attracted by the fresh complexion and graceful, slender figure of the little girl from the country. But no one offered her any honest work.

Paris was at fever-pitch and in a torment. Day after day the front gave way, collapsing on all sides. Already hundreds of thousands of Parisians were fleeing to the provinces in the south and west, leaving others to worry about stopping the barbarian hordes who, they were convinced, burned everything in their path, cut off children's hands, massacred old men and violated women and girls.

The most fantastic rumours spread like flies from a decaying carcass: it was said that the governor of Paris had just been assassinated by a spy, that Joffre had committed suicide, that the government was about to flee to Bordeaux, that von Kluck was at Montdidier and making straight for Compiègne, Senlis and Paris, that more than five hundred thousand Parisians had already left town . . .

Truth and falsehood were closely interwoven in stories which played on the popular imagination, creating an overcharged atmosphere, close to delirium. They changed hourly, and exacerbated the cowardice and defeatism of some and the anger, energy and patriotism of others.

How could she find work in the midst of such madness! Berthe was discouraged and worn down by the lonely days of walking, but on the sixth morning she set out again on her search. In vain she offered her services at several laundries, grocery stores, butchers' and even bars. In vain she asked the caretakers of fine-looking flats if any of the tenants were in need of a maid, a cleaner, a cook?

By chance she started down the rue Saint-Jacques; a crowd blocked her way in front of the Val-de-Grâce church. A long convoy of lorries was just arriving – on some of them you could still see the names of the grand stores underneath the red crosses, for they had been delivery vans only a month earlier – and the wounded were being carried out of them by the dozen: pale bodies, drained of blood, which groaned, dressed in red trousers on which the blood had made dark patches, their blue-grey greatcoats smeared with mud and torn by purple holes made by shrapnel or a bullet, their heads sticky with sweat, grime and powder, their limbs dislocated, smashed, sometimes missing.

Berthe was seized by an impulse; it inspired her, propelled her forwards. Here there was work for her, work which she did not find repugnant, which she knew how to do. Had she not cared for her grandmother all those years?

'Let me through,' she commanded as she cleared herself a way through a crowd of onlookers.

She reached the front and strode towards the ambulances. An old policeman wanted to push her back. She drew herself up and eyed him scornfully: 'I work here, can't you see I'm a nurse!'

The man muttered a vague apology, and watched her move towards the stretchers.

20

PIERRE-EDOUARD groaned, kicked out fiercely at a great gangling fellow who had just stepped on his stomach, and tried to get back to sleep. The straw in the wagon stank of sweat and horse manure and urine.

He turned over and stuck his elbow in the chest of his neighbour, who protested softly. The train had been on the move for hours, jolting and grinding along. Added to this were the snorts and whinnies of the horses on the other side of the wagon, who sometimes delivered great kicks to the boarding separating them, just to stretch their legs.

Pierre-Edouard, unable to sleep again, got up and walked to the wide-open doorway. Here sweet fresh air came into the wagon and made the atmosphere almost fit to breathe. Dead tired, he leaned out, his face to the wind, examining the night. It was inky black and revealed nothing about which direction the convoy was heading. Anyway, what did it matter . . .

He wanted to smoke, and started to take out his pipe and tobacco pouch, then remembered the ban. Of course, with all that straw . . . He made do with sucking the stem of the short pipe between his teeth. He had changed over to a pipe since the beginning of the war; it was the only way to smoke without the worry that he would reveal his position to the enemy lines. And even when extinguished it gave some relief from the desire to smoke, and to a certain extent it helped with the awful pain in his head and ears caused by the hellish noise of a battery of 75mm guns in full action.

He went back to his sleeping place on tiptoe, but stepped on a body.

'For God's sake! Try to be more careful!'

'Don't swear at me, Jules,' he retorted peaceably, as he snuggled down in the straw.

Jules! What a face he had made, poor Jules, on meeting him back in the barracks! Yet it was logical that it should happen like that. Weren't they both from the same regiment, the same squad, the same battery? One little point made Pierre-Edouard happy: he had worked for almost four years under the authority of Jules' father – and what authority! – only to find Jules, no longer son of the boss but a simple bombardier, under *his* orders. The orders of a farm worker on twenty sous a day!

Pierre-Edouard nursed no grievance against his colleague; he knew he wasn't responsible for his brute of a father nor his bitch of a mother. And anyway, it was all so far away, so childish even, that the memory of life before the war was softened, like those of childhood! He had not believed the war would really happen, had thought it impossible, yet all of a sudden he had been tossed into the middle of a battle, into the slaughter, down there in Alsace. Now the train which had left Alsace the previous evening was taking them to an unknown destination.

Alsace! How happy they were to tread the soil, what ecstasy to be among the first liberators of the area! They were greeted with kisses, hugs and tears of joy; all the people vowed they owed them an eternal debt of gratitude! That had not lasted long.

The 5th Artillery Regiment, under Colonel Nivelle, had been incorporated into the 7th Army Corps of General Dubail's 1st Army, then assigned to the Army of Alsace under General Pau. On the extreme right wing, they had pushed towards Thann from the morning of 7 August. It was a baptism of fire for Pierre-Edouard and all the others, an unforgettable initiation into a murderous folly which spurred them on to kill, to go on killing, faster and faster, speeding up the firing rate, pushing it to the furthest limits of endurance for both guns and men. It transformed them from peaceable chaps, hardly capable of killing a hen, into a species of happy barbarians who shouted for joy when their shrapnel burst among the cavalry or infantry or, best of all, in the middle of the enemy gun-emplacement. That

77 Battery loomed over them, surrounded them with its missiles, launched its red and black scrolls into the sky; as the ammunition spun away and exploded, it tossed pieces of shredded corpse all around.

Then there was the constant and exhausting repositioning, the parts to be put on to the guns, the line of fire to be adjusted, the horses to be brought back under control when they took fright and kicked, the guns and ammunition wagons to be hitched on in haste as they bent low under enemy fire: advance, retreat, turnabout. Mulhouse was liberated, then re-taken, bombarded, destroyed. Then the advance towards those places with difficult names – Buetwiller, Guewenheim, Burbach, Munster.

Finally, on the evening of 22 August, when they had reoccupied Mulhouse, came the incredible news – denied by the officers but discussed and spread about by the soldiers and warrant-officers – that the British Army was in retreat, forcing the French to give way in turn, to withdraw, to let the enemy retake the land so dearly bought . . .

'We don't even know where we're going!' thought Pierre-Edouard in a sort of stupor. He searched for somewhere to lay his head, felt around for his kitbag but did not find it, and so rested against Jules' back and fell asleep.

The 5th Artillery Regiment disembarked next day in Amiens. On 25 August, Colonel Nivelle informed his men that the 7th Army Corps was now under the command of General Maunoury of the 6th Army, and they would be in charge of the northern defence of Paris . . .

Pierre-Edouard had to make an effort not to fall asleep; despite the jolting gait of his mount and the clanking of the whole artillery convoy, it was difficult to stay upright in the saddle which had been torturing his buttocks for the last four hours.

On the previous evening, 3 September, the 7th Army Corps had begun its march to the south east; they left the defensive positions they had occupied between Mesnil and

Dammartin just as the northern horizon pulsated with the ominous red light of Senlis and Creil in flames.

The long artillery convoy entered a sleeping village – or was it deserted? Pierre-Edouard looked without interest at the tumble-down cottages, then suddenly woke up.

'Well, well, well!' he murmured, gazing into the shadows. 'There's no mistake, we're in Nantouillet!'

He urged on his horse and caught up with Jules, who was with the ammunition chest thirty metres ahead.

'Hey, Jules, have you seen where we are?'

'Yes, at Nantouillet. We're just passing old Lachaud's café . . .'

'Bloody hell, if I'd known . . .' whispered Pierre-Edouard. 'Just think, we're heading straight for Monthyon!'

'Yes, and the farm's over there, just to the right,' said Jules, indicating the plain with outstretched arm. 'My God, I wonder whether . . .'

'No, no,' Pierre-Edouard reassured him, 'they haven't got this far yet. You can see, everything is peaceful here.'

'Maybe, but they're banging away hard enough over by Meaux . . . Hey, why are we stopping? They're not going to make us camp here in the open!'

'Dismount, dismount,' was whispered along the line.

'I think we're going to finish the night here,' said Pierre-Edouard. 'Really, we could have pushed on as far as your place; it would have done me good to see your father's face, after he ordered me never to set foot in his house again! All right, I'm only joking. Basically he's a good fellow, your father, I've nothing against him.'

The morning of the 4th was heavy and oppressive. The 6th Army took up its position, reinforced its defences, closed off the routes which led straight to the capital. On the left wing they linked up with the English army of Marshal French, which was hidden between Lagny and Signy to block the Marne valley.

There were agonising hours of waiting before the great push which was to overrun and decimate von Kluck's 1st

Army, which had been threatening Paris on the east side. They knew from continuous aerial observation that his 2nd, 3rd and 4th Corps were boldly deployed between Betz and Meaux.

Two groups from the 5th Artillery Regiment set out at about four in the afternoon and advanced to Plessis. Pierre-Edouard and Jules saw Moureau Farm on their right, less than two kilometres away: the fields, the massive buildings, the huge corn stacks which they themselves had constructed, only six weeks earlier.

'It's too bloody, too bloody . . .' said Jules, examining each plot of his own ground on the horizon.

'Don't worry, we'll be back,' Pierre-Edouard comforted him, for he too was affected by the sight of familiar ground.

All the villages and hamlets he could make out over there in the distance, Neufmontier, Peuchard, Saint-Souplets . . . All those places he had visited with Jules, or with Moïse, his bicycle and his famous binges; where he had danced, flirted with the girls, lived – without appreciating just how lucky he was to live, to dance, drink, have fun, work; a gift from heaven, a present fit for a king.

In the evening they camped at Cuizy, which was swamped by a flood of light infantry, Algerians, cavalry; a solid mass of armed men.

The order to attack reached them on the night of 5 September, at 2.55 a.m., accompanied by an unequivocal message:

'No more looking to the rear! A troop which can no longer advance should hold its ground, at whatever cost, and die in position rather than retreat. No weakness will be tolerated.'
JOFFRE

Since the death of the Chanlat boy, Jean Duroux and his friends in the council no longer dared to finish their discussion at the inn. The establishment had a gloomy atmosphere and a large photo – draped with black crêpe – of the deceased in his hussar uniform, hung in the middle of the main wall; it interrupted the drinkers accusingly, cut short any desire to tarry there, to imbibe and debate as if nothing had happened.

Besides, how could they let the Chanlat couple and their children overhear the normal run of their conversations: the war, the news of a son, a nephew, a brother . . . Gaston alone, who only had two unmarried daughters, was not affected by it. But the others – Duroux, Jeantout, Jean-Edouard, even Antoine Gigoux – just lived for the next letter, the one that told them all was well. And they comforted each other, passed on vague snippets of information which a soldier occasionally managed to slip into his missive. The censor was thorough.

As for the papers, full of news which they endlessly dissected – they began to realise that these were controlled, muzzled and one-sided; the articles, so idiotically soothing, even euphoric, were nothing but a collection of lies and rubbish. Who could still believe what some of the scribes triumphantly maintained – that German weapons were no good, that their shells did not explode, that the Boche (the name was just emerging) did not know how to fight, that they were as timid as rabbits, that they were so hungry there were thousands of them queuing up for a mess-tin of soup! That good soup which the fine Frenchmen offered them without bitterness . . .

'Yes, but who to believe, what to believe?' asked Jean Duroux that evening, as he emerged from the Mairie with his councillors. Old habits die hard, and all four turned instinctively towards the inn; then suddenly stopped, embarrassed, as if caught in the wrong, as if people would think they had forgotten.

'Go on, don't be as stupid as the Boche!' called out Doctor Fraysse from his garden. He was delicately pruning the withered blooms from a huge climbing rose; he slipped the secateurs into the front pocket of his gardening apron and came towards them. 'I've been watching you for more than two weeks, you are silly! Do you want the Chanlats to close the inn? Don't you think the village is sad enough without that?'

'Not at all!' retorted the mayor. 'But if you think it's jolly . . .'

'Who's talking about jollity! For the time being all we can do is try to make a living, to keep going. The Chanlats need you, need all of us, to be there, to talk and play billiards. And I made Gigoux promise that he would come and play billiards with me, starting this evening. Come on, the Chanlats have enough troubles as it is, without you treating them as if they had an infectious disease as well!'

'It's not like that!' protested Jean Duroux. 'It's out of respect for them, they're in mourning.'

'I know what I'm talking about!' The old doctor was carried away. 'I understand human beings better than you! I tell you they need us. *Need*, have you got it? To live! To live, by God! So as not to die of sorrow! And if they're left all alone, that's what will happen! Come on, we'll all go together, like in the good old days. While we're on that subject, Duroux, is there any news?'

Jean Duroux regularly telephoned his daughter in Paris, where she had bravely remained. Her information was therefore more recent, but no more trustworthy, than that which arrived in letters to the village.

'Not much,' replied the mayor. 'Here's what the head-lines of the Paris papers said this morning: "Seventh September. Yesterday a counter- attack started along the whole front, a brilliant success for our troops." You have to admit that it's pretty vague – and besides, we don't even know where the front is exactly!'

Pierre-Edouard spurred on his mount, jumped the swollen corpse of a horse which had opened like a rotting fruit, and made sure that the gun and ammunition chest were following. He shouted encouragement but could not hear his own voice, such was the pandemonium.

All around them shells were falling like a shower of hail, across devastated fields and charred haystacks. Their fiery explosions mixed with the smoking trails of the cannon-balls, and throbbed like clouds of wasps whose nest is disturbed by a ploughshare.

And everywhere bodies, countless bodies; poor disfigured corpses biting the earth with bared teeth, their arms stretched wide, or gently laid out, backs on the golden stubble, as if to follow the sweet passage of the clouds with fly-filled eyes – pitiful remains which the wheels of the gun-carriages mutilated a second time as they charged over them at full gallop.

Five batteries of guns, among them Pierre-Edouard's, were forcing their way towards Puisieux, which lay under a dark cloud of enemy dust, where they were killing each other in a pitiless hand-to-hand battle. Huge waves of spiked helmets were hurling themselves constantly at this objective, in vast grey squadrons. Puisieux could only be saved by fire from the twenty 75mm guns charging to its relief.

Twenty cannon and their ammunition chests, almost three hundred horses driven at full speed in a mad charge, rushing into the heat of the battle, to a cauldron of molten metal, a dead heap of ruins which had to be defended.

The convoy plunges into the conflict, into the thick reeking fog of burnt powder, stones, earth and shattered bodies. Orders stream out, precise, according to the regulations; instructions seem superfluous, ridiculous, for already the men are busy, unhitching the horses, unloading the ammunition, preparing the weapons. But the orders serve their purpose; they reassure, they prove to everyone that the battery team is complete, that every man is at his post, aware of his role, ready to fulfil it to the best of his ability, just as they did during exercises, a long time ago, on the firing range.

Fast, faster, for every second counts, for it depends on you to get the barrel ready for firing, ready to belch out, to stem the flood which rises, advances, swells, which is going to annihilate you; for those men who are running towards you, yelling, are going to overwhelm you, massacre you. They are so close that all the scientific theory – the positioning, the drift, the correction of the trajectory – is reduced to nothing. There is only one order which flies along the line of barrels:

'Set to zero! To zero, for God's sake, light the fuses and fire at will! Watch the recoil!'

And suddenly the salvo, resounding, rolling out, swelling, speeding away.

'Watch out, it's slipping!' shouted Pierre-Edouard. 'Christ, hold on to that cannon, it's running back!' The spade was thrust into the ground, a hole was dug and the gun carriage steadied.

Firing began again, methodically.

Pierre-Edouard whirled round and looked at the bugler who was shaking him. The man had his mouth open, he must be bellowing an order.

'What?' he yelled.

'Stop firing!'

Finally he understood the order from afar, a faint murmur smothered by the surrounding noise. Then with a tired wave he signalled to his men to hold their fire; turned towards them, reeling with fatigue, and leant against the left wheel of the red-hot cannon. Like many of his comrades his nose was bleeding, and a thousand bells were ringing in his skull.

In front of him, across the ravaged fields and shattered undergrowth, stretched the bodies of men, as far as the eye could see; cut off in mid-charge, at point-black range, little patches of grey, crouching low, insignificant. Above them, an occasional tracer rocket left a trail of fire.

'What we've done to them! Just look what they've taken, the buggers!' exclaimed the second loader, leaning against the other wheel.

Pierre-Edouard smiled faintly and kicked at some clods of earth; then he wiped his nose and blew into his empty pipe. In front of him the loader was lighting a cigarette.

'Lend me a fill of tobacco.'

The man stretched his arm across the gun. A dry crack halted his movement. His cap flew up like a butterfly taking wing. Numbly Pierre-Edouard watched his companion slide gently across the wheel. The bullet had punched a hole in the top of his skull. The smoke from the cigarette he had just lit drifted gently from his half-open lips.

'My God, now I've seen it all!' he cried, as he knelt beside his colleague.

He thought he really had seen all there was to see since the previous day; every impossibility, every monstrosity. Seen everything, even taxis crammed full of armed men making their way towards Nanteuil: a fleet of taxis, hundreds of vehicles going up to the forward line, a staggering spectacle, crazy, which made him and his friends shout for joy.

Joy, yes. They had needed that so badly after the carnage, the bombardment, the corpses; after the explosion of one of the guns, struck by an 150mm shell, a monster fired by a cannon so far away that they could do nothing about it, it was out of range, far beyond the five kilometres reached by the 75mms.

Seen everything, even farms burned down, like that of Jules' future father-in-law, close to Yverny. Its blackened walls were still smoking and between them, amongst the rubble and hay cinders, they could make out the charred skeletons of the tethered cows. Even huge stacks of corn which crackled into flame like torches dipped in resin; even whole waves of men laid low with one blow, wiped out by grapeshot and shells.

Days as long as centuries, with the capture of Neufmontier, Monthyon, Saint-Souplets and Villeroy as well, so close to Moureau Farm. It had been bombarded too, the roofs damaged, but it was still standing, at least it had been three hours earlier ... How could you know what might happen in three hours, when a man could die in less time than it took to exhale the smoke of his last cigarette ...

He felt someone shaking him; he closed the dead man's eyes and straightened up.

'Got to go,' said a bombardier.

'Where to?'

'I don't know.'

'You never know anything!' he shouted intemperately, and then immediately regretted giving way to anger.

How could he have known six months earlier, when he was dancing with the girls in the inn, that he would be back in Puisieux on 7 September, twenty feet from the ruins of the inn, not to laugh and drink and tease the girls, but to kill men at point blank range? Men of his own age, who surely must have wanted to drink and laugh and make love, as he had done?

Ever since that impulse had driven Berthe towards the ambulances, she had lived surrounded by the smell of death, of infected wounds and blood. But nothing repelled or disgusted her. Not that she was insensitive to the suffering of others, far from it; it was just because, for the first time in her life, she felt she was something more than the obedient daughter who had docilely submitted to paternal authority and had been obliged to supress her own wishes and ideas. At last she had a feeling of being alive, even if it was amongst cries and pus and gangrene. She had the confidence that she was doing a job no one had forced on her, which she had chosen to do – and scores of women and girls from every background and area had chosen, like her, of their own accord, to wash, dress, bandage and feed these men.

For the first fortnight she did not dare go out of the Val-de-Grâce Church. She was so afraid that she would not have the strength to go back in again that she preferred to live there, in that world of suffering, nibbling a sandwich at intervals, sleeping a few hours in the dormitory, but always available, ready at any time of day or night to run to the side of a wounded or dying man.

Years of looking after the old woman had accustomed her to the most disagreeable tasks. Nothing offended her, and she quickly got to know her companions. The volunteer nurses were always full of good will, although the sights and smells and the atrocious wounds sometimes made them feel sick or faint. They appreciated her strength of character, her calmness, her kindness and spontaneity.

Then she made friends with a young hat-designer who came there each evening after work, and who suggested to her quite straightforwardedly that Berthe should share her room, in rue Servandoni. She accepted, but could not rest until she too had started making hats for ladies to pay her rent. It took her more than a year to perfect her skills, and then she put them to use with great taste and foresight; she kept one step ahead of the fashions, and presented the elegant ladies with exactly what they wanted when they wanted it.

She rapidly became more Parisian than a native of Saint-Germain, and was soon recognised as an exceptional stylist. None of this prevented her from continuing her work as a nurse every morning. It never occurred to her to give that up; she had chosen it, and nobody was going to stop her seeing it through.

Despite Jean-Edouard's predictions, the women did begin ploughing. They had to, for everything indicated that the war would be long; the men would not be back for the sowing. So if they were to find anything to harvest, the ground would have to be cultivated . . .

Everyone set to, children and old folk – even the squire's wife was to be seen behind the harrow, guiding it and shaking it out in the freshly sown fields, although she had never touched a farm implement in her life before.

When the time came for school to start again in the autumn, a new problem arose. The teacher's wife alone could not provide education for eighty-seven children. The solicitor's wife volunteered her services, as if nothing had happened; as if the fiancés of her two daughters had not been killed one after the other, one boy from Saint-Robert lost on the Marne, the other, from Allassac, fallen in Lorraine.

Thanks to her, the school was well organised, and in October the playground rang with the laughter and shouts of children. They no longer played longtag, prisoner's base or hopscotch; it was the capture of Château-Thierry or the taxis at the Marne. Since three further deaths had plunged the village into mourning, eight of the schoolchildren were now fatherless.

*

The squire's son-in-law, a lieutenant in the 5th Dragoons, was seriously wounded on 25 October. They learned later that he had taken part in the battle of Yser and had fallen at Dixmude, hit in the stomach by an exploding 105.

As soon as he heard the news, Jean Duroux rushed to see Jean-Edouard. He found him picking nuts, saw him suddenly go pale, and remembered that five times already he had been the unhappiest of messengers, the one each family feared to see coming.

'No, no,' he stammered, 'it's not for you, it's not Pierre-Edouard . . .'

'Who is it, then?' asked Jean-Edouard in an expressionless voice.

'My son-in-law. Wounded. My daughter's just telephoned; I'm leaving for Paris straight away, for a long time possibly. So you'll have to take my place at the Mairie, there's only you . . .'

'And Jeantout, and Gaston? Or why not old Gigoux, he's used to it all . . .'

'Don't argue, I don't have the time. You'll have to take my place. I'm going to tell the others, I know they'll agree with me. Now go and put your wife's mind at rest, she's crying up there at the window. She must be thinking that I've come – the same as you did.'

'Yes,' murmured Jean-Edouard, 'and from now on I'll have to make these visits . . . By God, it will be heavy, your sash of office!'

Jean-Edouard devoted all his energy to this new task. He attempted to pull the village out of the economic quagmire into which it had sunk since the departure of the men. The markets had lapsed since the beginning of the war and he tried to get them going again, but it was no use. Too many of the stock-dealers were at the front, and those left behind (the old men and the cowards) soon learned that their best interests lay in quietly touring the farms and picking off their prey one by one. The women were easier to dupe if you could discuss it with them alone, inside the barn. Gathered together in the market place they would surely have been as cunning as the men, but isolated, often ignorant of dealing, confused by and unprepared for the high inflation and worried by rumours of requisitioning, they were easy prey.

In order to limit the exploitation of innocent people, Jean-Edouard decided to fix a list to the door of the Mairie each week, giving the current price for each commodity. Besides that he organised, together with Jeantout and Gaston, deliveries of beasts to the markets at Brive or Objat, which were still continuing. They gathered together the stock to be sold and haggled over the price, hoof by hoof, as keenly as if they were their own property.

He tried to keep the syndicate going too, but in vain, for the deliveries of fertilisers grew gradually worse. Besides, who could afford fertiliser? Its price had doubled since the beginning of the war.

Then it came — what he had most feared, and it made him ill for days — a brief telegram announcing the death of Edouard Duffraisse, one of the carpenter's sons. Within a fortnight he had to make three further visits, and each time he left a home full of tears.

The village counted nine dead by the end of the year.

21

Spurting out of the thick pall of smoke that lay over the ground, two green rockets streaked across the sky.

'Lengthen the range!' ordered Pierre-Edouard, eyes glued to his binoculars. 'Faster, for God's sake!' he commanded, as he ran to one of the guns of his battery, where shrapnel was just being cleared out of the mouth of the loading-chamber. He adjusted the barrel and the level and corrected the angle of fire.

'Prepare for ranging fire!' he shouted, as he examined again the battle lines on hill 196 between Beauséjour and Mesnil. The 122nd and 142nd Infantry had been trying to capture it since morning, at the cost of terrible slaughter.

He located the explosion of the first shells, too short . . . 'Lengthen it, in the name of God! We're still hitting our own men!'

Further away, he hoped beyond the French lines, the fat red blossoms of shells glowed.

'Good, keep that trajectory, but watch the air-hole! In twelves! Faster!'

He did not even hear the 210mm shell, was hardly aware of the fantastic sound of the explosion. He felt himself thrown into the air, saw a huge expanse of sky, and then was buried under a big red wave.

For the third time since the beginning of the month, Jean-Edouard inscribed a birth in a fine round hand, a new citizen of the commune of St Libéral.

'Jean Marie Léon Mouly, born 14 March 1915 at 12.40pm — better put one o'clock' suggested Doctor Fraysse, bending over his shoulder to read. 'A fine boy,' he commented, 'another one. It's crazy the number of births I'm expecting this month. And that's nothing compared to next month; that will beat all the records! Really, I'd never have thought that the announcement of a war would act as such an effective aphrodisiac,' he said, smiling: Jean-Edouard looked at him questioningly. 'Yes, I didn't think it would turn all the poor fellows on like that, and their wives too.'

'Well, they made the most of it before leaving, and that's understandable, because since then . . .'

'Anyway,' said the doctor, more seriously, 'however many births we have, they'll never fill the gaps left during the last eight months . . . You know, I'm almost sorry not to have died earlier, then I would have avoided seeing this catastrophe.'

'Come, come, don't say that. Besides, we need you.'

'Not much. Since the war started, no one's ill any more! It doesn't occur to people to think about their little aches and pains. Even the old folks are hanging on, they want to see victory! By the way, you know the village is going to have to help Marty's widow; she still hasn't received her pension.'

'I know, I've been dealing with it, I wrote to the préfecture, but everything's in such a muddle! If the squire were here, he'd have got them moving, but me . . .'

'Poor Duroux, I don't think we'll see him for a while.'

The squire had returned once to the village, a lightning visit to sort out some business, but had left for Paris again immediately; his son-in-law was still in a critical condition.

Jean-Edouard closed the Register of Births, then sorted through his desk and held out a pamphlet to the doctor:

'Look, instead of paying out war widows' pensions, this is what they dream up, the fools! All this writing just to remind me about daylight saving and to put the clocks forward an hour! What use is that rubbish!'

'It's a good idea in the towns,' the doctor admitted. 'It reduces electricity consumption. But here, you're right, it's ridiculous. They should know that we don't have electricity!'

'It's like their posters for war loans; I don't know where

to put them all! Here, look at this: "For France, invest your gold! Gold fights for Victory!" They're not satisfied with just taking all our young men; they want to beggar us as well! I tell you, it'll all end badly . . .'

'But you've contributed, like everyone else!'

'Of course, but against my better judgement . . . Do you know what a seventy-five millimetre shell costs? Go on, have a guess! . . . Fifty-two francs!'

'Where did you get that from?'

'I went to see André Lachaud in the hospital. He was next to a boy who'd been working in munitions.'

André Lachaud was the first man from the village to be seriously wounded – he had fallen on 18 August, and would soon be returning home. For him the war was over, but so was fishing: he had lost both arms.

'Yes,' repeated Jean-Edouard, 'fifty-two francs for a shell! I don't earn that much every day, that's for sure. That's the price of a young calf! And it seems they fire off thousands of these a day! They ought to come and calve the cows, they wouldn't be able to do it!'

'It would be good to speak to these people face to face . . . By the way, have you any news of Pierre-Edouard?'

'Yes, yes, he's okay. He writes from time to time, just a few lines to reassure his mother. Nothing, really . . . She writes the replies; I've nothing to say to him.'

'You're not going to tell me that you still bear a grudge against him?'

'I told you, I've nothing to say to him. If you must know, he never asks about the farm, or the animals and the crops. He doesn't care! So we're not about to come to any understanding. And then, I don't know whether he'll ever want to come back here . . . He must have found a good job up there near Paris. It doesn't surprise me, he's got his school certificate, so . . . The farm's not good enough for him now.'

'And Louise? And Berthe?' insisted the old doctor, who was the only person who dared ask these questions.

'Nothing,' admitted Jean-Edouard with a shrug. 'Come on, don't let's talk about that any more. That's all in the past now.'

Pierre-Edouard tried to struggle, but his arms were too heavy, too weighed down to make the slightest movement. He attempted to speak, but felt as if he were blowing into a huge bowl of milk; very creamy, thick, sweet, warm milk. So he gave up and waited. But his brain was working.

His first thought was that one of the guns in the battery had exploded; that had become quite a common occurrence. The staff at headquarters had done their best to hush up the business, but all the artillerymen knew that almost two hundred 75mm cannon had blown up since the end of December . . . more than sixty a month, along the whole front. And it wasn't the sort of accident you could conceal for long, because at least six men were blown to pieces with each explosion. Naturally there was talk of sabotage, in order to keep up morale; but it wasn't that, it was just poor workmanship and the terrific firing rate demanded of the guns. They heated up, and then shattered suddenly like the glass shade of a paraffin lamp. That's what must have happened.

Pierre-Edouard felt someone moving him, pawing at him, whispering very far above him.

'It's the adjutant, get his dressing pack . . .'

Adjutant? Well that wasn't him. He was battery sergeant-major. At least . . . No, he *was* adjutant, had been for a week, to replace the last one who had been cut in two by a fragment of a 150mm shell as big as a fist and sharp as a razor (after the adjutant, it had gone through one horse and stuck in the neck of the next!).

He felt someone cleaning his face, then his eyes, and a finger was inserted into his mouth to clear that big lump of milky curds which was bothering him. He struggled and retched.

'Don't choke me, dammit!' he spat out. He opened his eyes, and saw his comrades through a vague pink blur. Even Jules was there.

'You great oaf, Jules! What are you up to here?' he stammered out.

'Blimey, you had a close shave,' explained Jules,

crouching down besides him. A 210. Seven dead, and we thought you were done for too . . .'

'What have I bought?'

'At least a month behind the lines!' joked the orderly, sponging away the blood still trickling down.

'Don't muck me about! What happened to me?'

'A fine hole in your head, you can see the bone; another on your forehead, a third on the cheek. It's still pouring blood, but it shouldn't be too serious.'

'And why am I seeing red everywhere?' he asked anxiously.

'It's nothing, blood and mud. We'll clean that up.'

'Hey, if my gob's blown to pieces, I'll frighten off the girls.'

'Don't you believe it! They love that, the girls do. The more bashed up you are, the keener they are. It excites them . . .'

He tried to raise himself, managed to kneel, then darkness swallowed him.

He spent a month in a hospital behind the lines. As soon as he was able, he wrote a long letter to Léon, reproaching him for sending no news since the beginning of the war. Then he wrote a note to his mother, brief as usual; he did not feel there was any point in mentioning his wounds to her.

Having done that he filled his free time with interminable games of cards and tried, like all his companions, to seduce some of the young nurses. But they were much less sociable than front-line gossip maintained, and only one or two allowed liberties without alerting the whole building: out of charity, almost, they allowed a touch on the bodice or a pat on the behind. He was not upset. He tried his luck, not really to gain anything, rather in line with the tradition that all wounded men (as far as they were able) were representatives of the men on the front when it came to girls.

The doctors' fears of a skull fracture proved unfounded. His wounds healed quickly; even the gash across his cheek didn't leave too bad a scar; just a furrow, a ridge, a souvenir.

He went back to the front and found his regiment; the battery was pouring a constant bombardment on the localities of Gussainville, Maizeroy and Les Eparges, twenty kilometres south-east of Verdun.

Three days later, Jules had to be evacuated; he had a fragment of shrapnel in the stomach and another in the chest. If all went well, if no infection set in, he would be back on his feet in a couple of months . . .

Pierre-Edouard accompanied him to the ambulance. 'Jammy devil,' he said, forcing a smile, 'you'll be home for the harvest, what a stroke of luck! Give my regards to your old folks, and the Polack. And tell him to drink a few to our health. We'll be needing it.'

After this war, which was supposed to last a month, had lasted a year, headquarters at last decided to allow home leave. Pierre-Edouard received his in September 1915. Six days, what could you do in six days? He could not decide, and very nearly set out for St Libéral. He'd had no reply from Léon, and was worried about the farm and the livestock. Of course his mother sent him some news, but it was brief, incomplete and vague. The poor woman filled her letters with exhaustive suggestions, advice, and tirades against Berthe and Louise, those runaways; complaints about how busy his father was, getting behind with the work; how expensive everything was; about the cursed war which would not finish.

Afraid to go back to the same sad atmosphere as before – it would probably be worse, since Berthe's departure – he decided to spend his leave in Paris. Then the return would be less painful than if he had to wrench himself away from the land he missed more and more – the Corrèze, the only land which mattered to him.

He arrived in Paris on 3 September, found a room in a hotel close to the Gare de l'Est, immediately ran a bath and washed himself. He scrubbed his skin almost raw, as if to erase the memory of the rats and lice, all the vermin crawling about at the front. When at last he was clean, he lay down and slept for fifteen straight hours.

The next day, rested but confused by the bustle, even gaiety, which animated the capital, he strolled along the boulevards, from café to café, with a dreadful feeling of being out of place in this crowd of thoughtless, happy people, the women sporting blue, white and red ribbons or dressed up as nurses, the plump and shiny young men. You could see straight away that the war, the killing war, did not concern them; they were profiting from the other war, the one that brought in good returns, and they were proud of it.

His amazement, and his bitterness, reached its climax when his gaze fell on the window of a chocolate shop in the Boulevard de la Madeleine, called the 'Marquise de Sévigné'. He thought he was dreaming. There before him, for the delectation of the customers, lay a 75mm shell. In the name of God, a shell, in aluminium foil banded with copper, painted in the colours of France, filled with decorative chocolates. Price: 15 francs for the small one, 20 francs for the large one! And there was more; a little ammunition box made of cardboard, with a gun in relief on it, filled with twenty-four tiny chocolate shells. Price: 8 francs 50 . . .

'Well, that's the limit!' he murmured. He could not come to terms with such insensitivity. Shells stuffed with chocolates! And why not a bottle of perfume in the shape of a grenade or a gas mask?

'Bloody civilians, eh?' spoke out a staff-sergeant from beside him; he too had been drawn by the window display.

'You can say that again! The bastards, they deserve a faceful of real shells!' he exclaimed, in relief at sharing his indignation. 'You're from the 120th line regiment?' he asked, after examining his neighbour's badges.

'Well, yes.'

'Were you at Mesnils, at the beginning of March?'

'Rather!'

'We were too.'

'Oh, you artillerymen,' said the other, 'you're set up behind the lines! Just right for shooting at our backs. Can't even be bothered to adjust your guns, idle sods, just like at headquarters . . . All right, I was only joking,' he apologised as he saw Pierre-Edouard stroking the scar on his cheek. 'All the same, it's true, you know; sometimes, you shoot like shit. You could be more careful, eh?'

'We do our best, but . . . Come on, let's go and drink to the health of the united gunners and infantry!'

'And after that we'll go and look for some women. It would give me very great pleasure to have a go at one of these bloody civilian women!'

They set off for Montmartre chatting like two old friends.

As he walked away from the hospital where he had just closed his son-in-law's eyes after eleven months of suffering, Jean Duroux was struck down by a heart attack.

He fell in rue de Bellechasse, a few metres from his apartment. He was fifty-five. They buried him in the family mausoleum in the cemetery of Montparnasse.

The news of his death reached St Libéral two days later. The whole community was affected by this latest bereavement, which was announced in the village square by the policeman's wife. Jean-Edouard, who was mayor from now on, consulted Doctor Fraysse, his friends and some of the old men before deciding not to organise a funeral service.

The custom had been abandoned since the beginning of the year, and only the first three deaths in the war had earned this honour. How could they continue the tradition, when it had to be repeated every month? It was impossible; it was digging a knife into the wound and accentuating the atmosphere of sadness and suffering which prevailed in the village. In thirteen months of war the community had lost eleven men, killed randomly at the front.

Thus no ceremony marked the death of Jean Duroux; his was just one death among many. Besides, the old curate from Yssandon did not want to be bothered by that sort of service; he was in charge of several parishes and really did not have the time to run from one village to the next every time a man fell at the front. The squire's departure grieved everyone, but there was already so much distress, so many tears, that little was said about it. Each person was enclosed in his private sorrow, his personal worry.

When the first soldiers came home on leave and the wounded were invalided out of the army, the people of Saint-Libéral found out about the real war, the one which the newspapers had been carefully hiding. Though the men from the front talked little; they seemed like strangers to everyone, not quite right in the head, as if drunk. Nevertheless, they said enough to increase the general malaise.

Everything got worse. Prices went mad, and whatever one did money was slow to come in. Everyone did their best, but for lack of manpower some plots had to be left fallow; all those, for example, which had been cultivated without machinery before the war, and there were many of them. They were the fields on steep slopes where the plough could not be used, but which had yielded the best and earliest crops before 1914, the spring vegetables which had brought renown and wealth to the region. And these plots were not the only ones which had to be abandoned; others, although suitable for ploughing, were also covered with weeds. There had been no time to turn the soil just when it needed doing.

Of course the men on leave lent a hand, but what could they do in a few days, poor fellows? And besides, they were already so tired, so worn out, they needed their rest!

Léon came back on 10 September, but was hardly seen by anyone. He slept like a log at first, like the others, and then strode alone across all his land, trailed around the markets at Brive and Tulle, and left again without bothering to set foot in the Mairie. Jean-Edouard did not forgive this slight.

A week after returning from his leave Pierre-Edouard received a long letter from Léon, several pages of neat writing. Thanks to this he got to know the farm again; but he was upset to learn that his father had left the Malides field fallow, and all the market-garden plots, due to lack of manpower and time.

Having said that, the animals were all right, they were in fine form. According to Léon they were fetching incredible prices; he had seen two-year-old heifers, just in calf, sold for 625 francs each at Brive market! A year earlier they had been worth 200 francs less. As for calves, he had seen them starting at 150 francs, even not particularly good ones! That was crazy, but hadn't everything gone crazy since the war started?

In the postscript he learned that his friend had been at the front for more than a year, and could therefore send no further news. If it was important for Pierre-Edouard, he could always write to Léon's sister Mathilde, who would inform him just as well. Perhaps he should know that it was she who had been writing the letters from the very beginning . . .

'What a cheat!' thought Pierre-Edouard, laughing to himself. 'And I'm an ass, thinking that he had learned to write! I was amazed at the beautiful letters, as if written by a professional. What a damned swindler that Léon is!' But he did not hold it against him, and resolved from then on to correspond with little Mathilde, the kid Léon had seen born.

Two days later a brief note from Louise left him speechless, on the verge of tears. Jean, the quiet forester who so loved his trees, was dead, somewhere in a corner of Champagne.

Across the whole front the second winter began, and there was no guarantee that it would be the last.

1916, 1917; terrifying years, months of ceaselessly repeated nightmares, days and nights of horror. Ghastly slaughter from the mustard gas which seeped into their cold guts and froze them rigid in an endless winter, sinister waves of gas sinking down into the stinking, muddy trenches, heralding a spring without hope. Like false storm clouds, it spread a greenish layer over the heavy dusting of flies on the battlefield as it sweltered in a heatwave which ripened no harvest; a stealthy mist which merged almost invisibly with the drizzle of autumn and the fog of November. Vile gas, corroding everything, spreading its deadly putrefaction everywhere.

Pierre-Edouard suffered it all; knew despair, exhaustion and that overwhelming depression which paralyses the spirit, binding him in a strait-jacket of numbed fatalism, leaving only the most basic urges alive: to eat, sleep, survive; forget the past and obliterate the idea of any future, existing only in the present.

He even forsook the memories and ideas which he had once liked to evoke: his fields, his land, Saint-Libéral. All that was too far away, too emotional, untouchable; in another world, an inaccessible universe. If he continued to send news occasionally to his mother, he never wrote to Léon's sister, for the idea of worrying about his land, his animals or his crops seemed ridiculous, childish. Such things had no significance in the face of death; death which had made Louise a widow for the second time and continued, all around him, to cut down his comrades.

The months rolled by, punctuated by the lunatic battles. Eix and Douaumont in February; the forest of Caillette and Thiaumond in April. Then the Somme, in June, with engagements at Monacu farm and at Cléry; finally, at the end of the month the biggest, the longest, artillery bombardment ever undertaken by the French, lasting six days without a break. There was shelling on an unprecedented scale to prepare for a formidable charge on 1 July. At 7.30 am assault troops were thrown forward on a forty-five kilometre front towards Bapaume and Péronne.

And then nothing; they were bogged down in another winter, long months when the unusually cold weather froze the two armies into the hardened mud of their trenches. In February 1917 the temperature fell to minus 20°, paralysing the men, the horses, the whole war.

It was a short respite, broken by the squalid butchery of the Chemin des Dames and on the Craonne plateau. After that, neither Pierre-Edouard nor his colleagues were proud to have had a colonel called Nivelle at the beginning of the war.

In October, while the rumours of mutinies and executions drifted to and fro, Pierre-Edouard was granted leave again. He was so in need of rest, of silence, of peace, that he set off for Saint-Libéral without a second thought.

22

FEW people recognised him. There was no trace left of the young man who had taken to the road one morning in January 1911. Then they had thought that he would soon return, quiet and repentant. He had not reappeared until today, almost seven years later, formed, sculpted and hardened; a mature man with none of the youthful traits they remembered.

He arrived on the morning train and was immediately struck by the silence in the village; by the emptiness of the main square, the lack of movement, the absence of men. He passed several women, some in mourning, who returned his greeting shyly, self-consciously, as you respond to a stranger who is friendly for some unknown reason.

Coming to his own home, he was surprised by the state of the yard; its untidiness, the dirt in little piles everywhere, the tools left scattered about. Before, everything had always been put away, the yard clean, swept by his grandfather and grandmother, who made a point of showing passers-by and neighbours a well-kept farm. Now it was obvious that nobody had time to rake up the cow-pats, to lift the dung-pile onto a cart, to put each implement in its place.

The house was empty. There nothing had changed; he put down his bag and went back out, to the stables, where he found a wizened old man, with the thick lips of a simpleton, who would not look him in the eye. He recognised the labourer Léon had mentioned.

'Are you Abel?'

The man stepped back, sheltering behind his pitchfork, and only just managed to swallow his saliva.

'Answer me, then! I'm not going to hit you, you're too thin. Well, where are my parents?'

'You're not the Vialhes' boy, from back then?' stammered the old man.

'Of course. Where are my parents?'

'You're older than I'd have expected. Hey, if you come back, I'm going to lose my job, aren't I?'

'You're even stupider than I was told! Where are my parents?'

'On the plateau, the Peuch field; they're ploughing. Say, is it true you were at the war? Is it finished then, since you've come back?'

Pierre-Edouard muttered something rude and went out. Soon afterwards he strode up the track which climbed to the high fields, and felt himself reborn.

A curious relationship was established between himself and his father. It wasn't good, it wasn't bad – it was neutral.

Jean-Edouard still considered his son a rebel and had not forgiven him for leaving, but he could not keep his vow to take him in hand again; too many years had passed, too many things had happened. But since he was also secretly delighted that Pierre had returned safe and sound – and, though he'd never admit it, very proud of the warrant officer's stripes, the chevrons for war service, the Croix de Guerre with two stars shining on it – he considered it prudent to confine himself to gruff enquiries, to avoid any outburst, of either bitterness or pleasure.

In fact, although he did not want to accept it, his son disconcerted him, even amazed him, as a man can astonish and surprise you, when you think you know him well and he suddenly reveals a totally unknown side to his character and takes your breath away.

For his part Pierre-Edouard was far too weary, too tired to want to start any discussion at all, let alone the slightest argument. It seemed childish to cross swords with his father. So he too adopted a manner bordering on indifference.

Although he was prepared for it, the death of several of his friends in the village affected him deeply. Jacques

Bessat and Edmond Vergne, dead; dead also André Duplat, the Delpy brothers, Edouard and Jacques, Serge Traversat, François Laval, and many more; it was enough to make you cry.

He was not feeling affectionate towards his mother, either. He found her just as whining and tearful as in her letters, complaining all the time that Berthe had gone and she had no news of her, that Louise never wrote; moaning about the mountains of work, the rise in the cost of living and all those lovely gold coins which his father had been forced to exchange for paper money.

'What are you moaning about?' he cried on the first evening, during supper. 'Berthe's not at the front, so she's not in any danger, is she? You've lost your gold? That's just too bad – better than losing your arms, or your legs, or anything else! As for Louise, let's talk about that! There you are crying into your soup about silly things, and what about her! She's been widowed for the second time! Yes, she remarried, she was perfectly entitled to. Her husband died two years ago in Champagne. And now she's alone! And there you are, happy as a draft-dodger, and *you're* complaining? My God!'

Jean-Edouard was present at this little scene, but he did not open his mouth to silence his son; instead his anger was turned viciously on Abel, that malign idiot, who had the cheek to snigger and dribble into the soup he was slurping at the end of the table.

Pierre-Edouard carefully avoided showing himself around the village. There were too many women in mourning whom he might offend, too many worried wives and mothers who would want reassurance and information; he did not have the courage to talk to them.

So he turned his steps towards the woods, the peaks and the plateau. There, in the silence and sweetness of autumn, he forgot the hails of bullets; he regained his strength, recovered his soul, learned to enjoy days without alarms, gun barrages and disembowelled comrades.

On the third day of his leave, his wanderings took him as

far as the White Peak, where Léon had dragged him with Louise seventeen years earlier, to check the snares for thrushes – the thrushes which they'd had to throw to the wolves! He smiled and gazed down on the plateau where, far away, his father and mother were ploughing the Peuch field. Neither of them had wanted to accept his offer of help.

'We'll manage by ourselves, we're used to it. Have a rest, go on,' his father had said.

He hadn't pressed it. Besides he did not feel that basic urge to work, that keenness which had propelled him to labour happily behind the plough before the war . . .

Fifty metres below him, at the base of the peak, he noticed seven or eight cows clambering among the remains of broken-down blackberry bushes, amid the scrub and broom where the blackbirds were singing. They were beautiful Limousins, whose rounded shapes owed nothing to the poor pasture over which they ranged so erratically. A dog jumped around, brought them together, tried to herd them towards a meadow still covered in clover. But the cows were skittish, and galloped into the bushes, where they delighted in scratching themselves to get rid of the flies.

'That piece of clover used to belong to the squire,' thought Pierre-Edouard. Then he was entertained by the appearance of a small figure, which ran through the broom bushes hurling insults at the cows. He got up, tumbled down the slope, cut off the animals and turned them towards the meadow.

'Thank you, Pierre!'

The voice was breathless but light; he turned. For a moment he stood stock still, astonished, in front of the girl who was smiling at him. From up there, he had taken her for a boy.

She looked good enough to eat; a brunette, rather small but well formed, with bright deep brown eyes, a little nose, slightly tilted, cheeks rosy from the fresh air and a very sweet smile framed by vivid red lips. He noticed her breasts, modest, but filling her bodice nicely, admired the slim waist, liked the soft curve of her hips beneath the heavy skirt and blue apron.

'You know me?' he asked eventually.

'Oh, yes!'

'Well, I don't know you. Are you from the village?'

'Of course.'

'That's it,' he said, after staring hard at her, 'I know! You're Gaston's youngest daughter, little Françoise.'

She gave a clear little laugh which made her eyes sparkle with a mischievous gleam. 'Françoise is twenty-five! Do you think I'm that old?'

'So whose daughter are you?' he asked, using the formal 'vous' as she had done, without realising that he was now addressing her as an adult.

'I am Léon's sister.'

'My goodness! Is it really you, Mathilde?'

He looked her over anew and nodded his head. Mathilde! He had not seen her since he had left to do his army service, and remembered her as a chubby-faced urchin, almost a baby.

'You really didn't recognise me?' she wanted to know.

'Good heavens, no! How could I? So it was you who wrote the letters! But where were you seven years ago, when I came back from conscription?'

'With the nuns, at Allassac. Léon wanted me to be educated,' she said with a smile.

'And with good reason! Tell me, you used to say "tu" to me, have you forgotten?' He used 'tu' again himself.

She blushed a little. 'No, I haven't forgotten, but then I didn't know . . .'

He drew nearer and put his hand on her shoulder. 'So it's you, Mathilde,' he repeated. 'So . . . You know, you're really very pretty now,' he added earnestly, 'yes, very pretty. And I'm very glad to get to know the person who has been writing me such beautiful letters at last. Talking of which, where's Léon? How is he?'

'Fine. He was home on leave in August. He's a corporal,' she added proudly, 'and he's got a medal, too!'

315

'That doesn't surprise me. And where is he?'

'When he was here he told me that he was close to Rheims. It's very dangerous up there, isn't it?' she asked with sudden anguish.

He recalled that Léon had been like a father to her; the head of the family, a sort of god who had brought her up, returned from each market with a trinket for her, who adored her. He pulled her gently towards him and stroked her hair.

'Dangerous, up there? Don't you believe it! It's one of the least exposed sectors, almost the quietest on the front.' Neither voice nor eyes betrayed his lie. 'Up there, they have champagne instead of plonk! You don't realise how lucky Léon is!'

'But the newspapers say . . .'

'The papers say all sorts of things, as usual. Go on, don't you worry about him. He's got his wits about him, he'll have found a good corner!'

'He's not a shirker!' she protested, with an offended look.

'Not at all! The proof is, he's got a medal.'

'That's true.' She was suddenly calmer, and examined his face intently. 'And you, where you are, is it very dangerous?' she asked, placing her hands on his shoulders.

'No, it's quiet there too . . .' he murmured, moved by her closeness.

His eyes darted towards her bodice and he became obsessed with a thought which seared through him, quickening his breath and heartbeat. He tried to chase away the seventeen-year-old memory, of that evening when his mother and grandmother had talked of Mathilde and of the birthmark she bore on her breast – but which one? the left or the right? – a mark like a little crescent moon. He forced himself to blot out the disturbing picture.

As a child he had imagined that sign, a little brown sickle on the smooth body of a baby, but today . . . Today it was right before his eyes, there, a few centimetres away, the sweet furrow which separated the tiny round breasts, one of which – but *which* one, for God's sake! – was decorated with a beauty spot . . .

She increased his agitation without even realising it.

'All the same' – she gently stroked her finger across his cheek –'you've been wounded. Forgive me, you didn't have that mark before. You can tell it's recent.'

He turned his head a little and grazed the back of her hand with his lips. Her skin was sweet, fresh as spring water. He pulled himself together and moved away a little.

'You know, you're more dangerous than a battery of four-twenties!' he joked, in a tone which he hoped sounded relaxed. 'It's lucky that you're Léon's sister! Hey, look at your cows, they've run away!'

'Huh, they won't go far. Besides, they never leave our land.'

'How do you mean, your land? These fields belong to the château!'

She shook her head. 'No, since she was widowed the squire's daughter has let them to us.'

'Well, I *am* surprised. But now I think about it, where's the rest of Léon's herd? He's got more than seven cows, hasn't he?'

'Yes, and he's got two farmhands, old fellows, and then there's my mother and me; we manage. Tell me, you're not going back straight away?'

'You mean this morning? Oh, I can help you look after the animals if you like,' he assured her with a smile, 'but what will people say if they see us together?'

'There's nobody about, and besides, everyone knows I'm sensible!'

'Sensible?' he asked, with mock solemnity. 'Well what are you doing here then, right next to me?'

'I'm not in any danger with you. I know you, you see . . . I wrote the letters, but I read yours as well. Because Léon doesn't read very well, either . . .'

'Oh, I understand! Just wait till I see him again, your lout of a brother, I'll give him what for!' he grumbled in embarrassment, remembering that he had shared news of some of his conquests with her brother. He was sure he had even named names, and described some of their attributes.

She saw that he was upset, and guessed why intuitively. 'Oh, I bet you're thinking of all those girls!' she cried gaily, 'but that's all old stuff. And at that time I was so young! Besides, you know, that doesn't worry me, I still trust you. I'm not a silly little girl, so there's no danger!'

He felt a fool, awkward and clumsy. He was much more upset than he liked to admit, disturbed by this little slip of a woman with dark eyes who in a few minutes, with a few words, had aroused feelings he'd never experienced before, of unexpected sweetness. It bore no relationship to what had pushed him into the arms of Justine, the petite Parisienne he had bedded during his last leave, or that hot little number, Françoise.

'That's right,' he murmured at last, as he stroked her eyelids gently with the tip of his finger, 'you're right, there's no danger.'

Then he kissed her lightly on the cheek, and took her hand. 'Come on, let's go and look after your cows, that'll do me good.'

Going back was terrible, worse than anything he had feared. He knew full well that each end of leave was torture to the spirit, a terrible tearing apart which some did not survive. Those were the unhappy ones who sprang forward like madmen at the height of a bombardment, to meet the burning blow which would release them from this uncontrollable nightmare, this cancer which undermined them from within.

The train was barely a hundred metres out of St Libéral before Pierre-Edouard succumbed to the deepest despair. The evening before, when he had realised that Mathilde was even more upset than he was at saying goodbye, only her vulnerability had strengthened him, forced him to pretend to be unconcerned and cheerful although he was a million miles from such feelings.

He had almost succeeded in making a joke, had been rolling his eyes at her, when she had lain down, warm and tender, under the trees on the White Peak and pulled him to her, against her, on to her, in an embrace full of ardour, a total surrender. At that moment he could have done anything, got everything – and spoiled everything, easily, which would have made his self-reproach even more violent.

For although Mathilde was still the virginal girl whom he had loved at first sight a few days earlier, yet he knew that now, for her as well as for him, the waiting would be longer and more terrible. Wasn't life hard enough without adding the pangs of separation, just for the fun of it?

At the front, he had noticed how vulnerable those married and engaged comrades were to the absence of the wife, the fiancée, the children, the girl-friend, to that emptiness. It was they who frantically awaited the arrival of the post orderly, who read and re-read the letters from which flower-petals, curls of hair, ribbons or photos sometimes slipped; they who were gnawed by anxiety and pain when deprived of news, sometimes to the point of despair.

Until today he had not known this form of torment, and neither had Mathilde – for although she worried about her brother, she did not await Léon's return in the same way as she awaited his own.

And it was for that he blamed himself; for dragging her into this madness. With her he had forgotten about the war, had pretended to believe that the future belonged to them. Instead, he should have done his best to prevent the kindling of that flame in her, the passion which from the first moment had impelled them irresistibly towards each other.

But it was too late to step back, to erase from his mind the memories which revolved round her, the centre of his universe. He did not even want to; all his being strove wildly to remember. And already, there floated before his eyes the slight silhouette of a girl, her face, her hands. And her laugh rang out.

When the school-leavers of 1918 were called up it was a

fresh blow to Saint Libéral, and the crop planting was further restricted.

Gradually the fields which had been abandoned for several years returned to the wild; grew shrubs, ash, oak and hornbeam. Elsewhere bracken, broom and ferns took over the places once cleared by men, encroached on the fallow plots, and invaded the meadows no longer trimmed by scythes.

Production fell appreciably in the community, as it did in the country as a whole. Paradoxically, money flowed as never before, because of galloping inflation fuelled by shortages. The beginning of the war had harmed the economy, but its continuation inspired a new dynamism. Everything was saleable, because everything was in short supply.

From 1916 onwards, this situation had encouraged Jean-Edouard to sow wheat on every available field – at least, on those he had time to cultivate. Like everything else, the price of wheat had reached giddy heights, despite being taxed (in theory anyway) at 33 francs on every 100 kilos. From 25 francs for 100 kilos in 1914, it climbed to the fabulous sum of 50 francs after the 1917 harvest, and they said it would reach 75 francs before the end of 1918.

For men of Jean-Edouard's generation, accustomed to counting in sous and centimes rather than in millions of francs, this flood of money felt like a crisis. Besides, however large the sums written on them, these new banknotes were not, in their eyes, worth anything like the gold coins of which successive subscriptions to the war effort had relieved them.

Of course Jean-Edouard had not donated all his gold; he had preserved a precious store of twenty-franc gold napoléons. Nevertheless, his conviction that paper money was worthless inspired him to search for more land. But who would sell land in the middle of a war! He alerted the solicitor as to his needs, and waited.

He had to be patient until May 1918. About the 15th of the month, the elder daughter of the late lamented Jean Duroux informed Monsieur Lardy that she wished to sell the two smallholdings which formed her dowry, as quickly as possible; there were fourteen hectares, of which four and a half were good land situated on the plateau. Many years later, they learned that the unhappy widow had sold all her assets before marrying an American officer and following him to his country.

As soon as he received the letter, Monsieur Lardy went to tell Jean-Edouard.

'You say she's selling her two smallholdings?' asked Jean-Edouard, as he distractedly rearranged the papers and circulars piled on his desk.

'Both of them, yes. So, as you told me you were looking for land . . .'

'Yes, but not fourteen hectares! What would I do with it? I haven't time to plant the land I've got already!'

'Pierre-Edouard will come back soon. This war can't last much longer.'

'Oh, Pierre-Edouard, if I have to depend on him! And anyway, I haven't enough cash to buy fourteen hectares.'

'Well, it's a bargain. I don't understand why she's selling. It's really bad timing, if she'd come to me I would have told her so. But she wants it done quickly, so . . .'

'How much?'

'Roughly 1,900 francs a hectare. A gift, isn't it?'

Jean-Edouard fiddled with his pen-holder and made a face. 'It's enough, I tell you. When I think I paid 1,250 francs for the lot you sold me before the war!'

'No jokes, please; you know very well that everything has doubled or tripled in price since then, except land. That's how it is: who wants to buy in times like these!'

Jean made a quick decision. 'Fine, I'll take the fields on the plateau. You say there are forty-five chains? That'll do. But I can't manage the rest.'

'You're making a mistake. It's a bargain, I assure you.'

'Maybe, but I haven't enough money.'

'Go on . . . I understand that you don't want to break into your reserves, but in that case, why not borrow? You couldn't make a better investment.'

'No,' Jean-Edouard interrupted him drily, 'the Vialhes don't eat borrowed bread. When we buy, it's with our own money. I'm not about to get involved in borrowing, that's the way to ruin a family. I prefer to have less, but use my own money. I don't want to owe anything to anyone.'

'Pity, I think it's silly not to take it. Well, that's your business. Good, I'll make note of your offer and see who might be interested in the remainder. In any case, I have to warn you in all honesty that the land you're interested in will go to the highest bidder.'

'Of course,' agreed Jean-Edouard with a smile. 'If you can find anyone else who wants it.'

The 150mm shell fell less than fifty metres from the battery; a second missile came within twenty metres. 'They've picked us out, the next ones will be for us and we'll get it in the neck . . .' mused Pierre-Edouard as he crouched behind a rough shelter.

It was always the same: all went reasonably well whilst they could fire from concealed positions, but if by any chance an aeroplane or observer on the ground picked out the source of the shots from the smoke, then all hell was let loose. Then the enemy held the trumps. In the push towards Compiègne they had infiltrated the Matz valley and were now encamped on the Lataule plateau. From up there, they could see everything . . .

'Now they've had time to adjust their range,' thought Pierre-Edouard, 'it won't be long before it's raining down thick and fast.'

He touched the little photo Mathilde had sent him, which lay in the pocket next to his heart. That was his last movement, his last thought, before an enormous sun exploded in front of him. It was 2.30 p.m.

That same day, 9 June, and at the same hour, Monsieur Lardy arrived at the Mairie to inform Jean-Edouard of the results of his negotiations. Since his first visit three weeks earlier everything had changed, and in a way that he could not have foreseen; the situation had taken an incredible turn. In thirty-five years at his job the solicitor had never experienced such a change of direction. Nor had he ever discussed matters with such a young negotiator. He was still amazed – and admiring – at the way little Mathilde had managed the business! He reflected yet again how much the war had changed things by giving women the opportunity to take responsibilities.

'Well?' asked Jean-Edouard.

'She's not giving in, and as far as I can tell she's prepared to raise her bid as well . . .'

'Hell and damnation, the little worm! That little slut! She's worse than her brother! You told her that I would go to 2,150 francs a hectare?'

'Naturally, but she immediately announced that she would offer 2,200.'

'But she's mad! And where's she getting her money from, for goodness sake?'

'It's not hers, you know that, it's her brother's. And he's got plenty; the war hasn't stopped his herds from growing . . .'

'What a swine! My God, that thief!'

Jean-Edouard had been in a temper for a whole week. At first, when the solicitor told him that Mathilde had announced her intention to buy, he had thought it was a hoax.

'You're joking? Anyway, she can't do anything, she's under twenty-one.'

'Indeed, but she's become emancipated since Léon left.'

'So what?'

'So she has a perfect right to act in her brother's name, and that's what she's doing.'

He was struck dumb, amazed that a girl no taller than three goats' tails had the audacity to carry thróugh such an operation, alone.

'Bloody hell!' he argued obstinately, 'I don't know much about the law, but surely she can't sign anything! It would have to be Léon who did that! Since he isn't here, and the sale is urgent, well . . . Look, if you want, I'll sign right away, and pay!'

'It's not as simple as that. Besides, the signature is not a problem. When he left, Léon gave power of attorney to his mother . . .'

'Dammit! He thought of everything, that dungheap!' And that made him furious as well. Léon really had planned everything. And now the solicitor was proving just how he had underestimated his adversary, and just how formidable this little scrap of a woman Mathilde was – perhaps even more dangerous than her brother, because she was better educated.

'You see,' explained the lawyer, 'Mathilde explained it all to me. When he left, Léon gave her the task of surveying everything being sold in the neighbourhood and buying the best. So, you can imagine that she's keen to do business, and she's persistent.'

'A girl doing a man's business! It's scandalous,' grumbled Jean-Edouard. 'All right,' he made a sudden decision, 'go and tell that little worm that I'll go to 2,250. I don't want to go and see her myself or argue with her; I'd box her ears, just to teach her about life! Who does the little pisser think she is? A man? Tell her 2,250, we'll see who wins in the end! I'll see them back in the hovel they should never have left!'

'Listen, I'll give you some advice; let her have the land. Don't get worked up, let me speak. I'm telling you how it is, I've just come from her place. Believe me, that little Mathilde will go to 2,500 if need be, further even, but she'll get the land.'

'Then I'll go higher!'

'She'll match it at the last moment, and that poor Duroux woman will choose her rather than you.'

'What do you know about it? My money is as good as hers, isn't it?'

'Yes, only I have to admit to you . . . Mathilde has written to her, to the widow; she told me so. And she told me that the Duroux girl would prefer to sell to her, she has a right to choose . . .'

'She dared do that! She dared to write! Oh my God!' Jean-Edouard exploded; he was beside himself.

'Yes, she did. My poor fellow, these women are astonishing, and when it comes to agreeing things behind our backs . . . Well, there it is. You're free to continue, but you won't win. Oh, but she agrees to let you have the three acres which lie between your fields.'

'Oh, good!' said Jean-Edouard sarcastically, 'now she's dividing it up! In God's name, what does she take me for? Just a minute, I'm beginning to think that you're advising her!' he shouted suddenly. 'That's it! Did you think we had forgotten your wife is her godmother? It's true, isn't it? She *is* the godmother of that suicide's daughter?'

'My dear friend, you're talking absolute rubbish,' the solicitor interrupted him drily. 'So, will you buy that field?'

'No; I don't want any favours from that slut!'

'You're wrong, it's not a favour. You see, she knows how to read a land register, that little one does. That land is enclosed by yours, so it's of little interest to her, as she'd have to cross yours to get to it . . . But it's up to you if you want to let Léon settle down in the middle of your property!'

'All right, all right.' Jean-Edouard was beaten, and white with anger. 'I'll buy that patch, since they're so keen to let me have it. But I'm buying it right away. And you can tell that little bitch and her dungheap of a brother that I won't forget them. One day I'll make them regret all their double-dealing . . .'

The deeds were signed next day. Mathilde immediately wrote to Pierre-Edouard to announce that Léon had just bought three hectares of land for her dowry, those fine fields on the plateau, stretching up to White Peak, where they had met during his leave, their own land . . . Then she wrote to her brother to inform him, and to thank him for his generosity.

Neither of them received this news. On 11 June 1918, Léon was mown down by a volley from a Maxim gun, during the battle for Piave on the Italian front. The first shot broke his right fibula, the second his left tibia, just below the knee, and the third tore off his left hand.

23

MATHILDE was terribly shocked when she learned that her brother had fallen on the Italian front. However, the fact that she knew he was alive was a comfort to her, however badly he might be injured. Yes, he was wounded, but from now on he would be protected; the war could no longer kill him.

The next day she received another dreadful blow, delivered by the postman in conversation with her mother:

'What a massacre!' he said as he put down the newspaper. 'Yesterday your poor Léon, today the Vialhes' boy . . .'

'What about him?' asked her mother.

'I'm not sure; you know old Vialhe, he's not very forthcoming. It was poor Marguerite who told me, seems he's almost done for. At least according to what she was saying . . .'

Mathilde almost ran to the Vialhes' house to find out, to relieve the weight of anxiety which was crushing her. But she was sure that they would throw her out; they would be rude to her and would not tell her anything.

So her long wait began, every minute a torture, made more painful by her mother's remarks. The poor woman had known right from the beginning that her daughter was seeing Pierre-Edouard. When the letters appeared, sometimes as many as four a week, she understood that this was a serious, lasting attachment and she was worried, nervous at the thought of how his parents would react.

'I told you that he wasn't for you,' she bleated as soon as the postman had gone. 'People like the Vialhes don't marry the daughters of smallholders! You see, even God doesn't wish it . . . If you knew how we lived before . . . before Léon started earning some money! And to them, we'll always be poor. You'll see, they'll start talking about your poor father . . .'

'I don't care! Pierre-Edouard doesn't need them!'

'That's what he says . . . Suppose his father were to disinherit him! Look what he did to his daughters!'

'Too bad! Léon will help us, I know he will. But as long as . . . How do we know . . .'

She had to be patient for five more days and nights of fear and despair. She watched for the postman every morning, ran to him as he took out the letters, and then returned like a sleepwalker to endure the endless wait while in her mind she became convinced that her fiancé had died. But, she told herself, she would have heard that. The Vialhes would talk about it! Unless they were so madly proud that they kept their grief to themselves . . .

At last, on the sixth morning, the letter arrived. A few words, practically nothing, just what had to be said.

She ran to the church and lit ten fat candles in front of the statue of the Virgin Mary, ten in front of Joseph, and ten more for Saint Eutrope. And there, seated amidst all those flames, she let herself go and cried for the first time in six days, half crazy with happiness in the warm flickering light of the candles.

Pierre-Edouard had only vague memories of his first days in hospital; he remembered distant conversations without knowing who was speaking, nor where they were. Who was the seriously injured person they were discussing at his bedside? Only later did he realise that the first conversation had taken place on the day he arrived. A strange argument . . .

'I tell you we must amputate . . . look at this mess.'

'Cut, cut, that's all you know about! There's no question of amputating!'

'But look, my dear fellow . . .'

'Fellow? You must be joking! I'm not your fellow-butcher!'

'I order it! I shall refer the matter to the authorities!'

'Get out, or I'll write to Clemenceau!'

'Do you know him?'

'Of course! He was talking to me only this morning, he said: "Fernand, I am relying on you not to turn all our wounded men into legless, armless cripples! Don't listen to the army doctors, they round up their pay with commissions from all the artificial limb makers in France . . ." '

'You and your stupid jokes! Do you think this is the time for a laugh? This lad will get gangrene; we must amputate, and quickly . . .'

'Out of the question. I'll take full responsibility.'

'Sister, you are witness to this. And you too, my dear?'

'But of course they're witnesses, and if you want a signed bit of paper, tell them I'll put it into verse for them. Go on, sister, prepare this chap for theatre; I'm in charge here.'

'Fine, I wash my hands of it.'

'What an excellent decision, I've been waiting two months for this hygienic result! . . . Now, just between us two, my boy . . .'

And later a strange awakening, a sort of rebirth, to the sound of a warm voice.

'Right, to sum up. We'll say: simple fracture of the right tibia, no problem. Simple double fracture of the left femur with tearing of the right anterior quadriceps and the vastus externus, and perforation of the vastus internus. Small tear in the large sartorial muscle. That's all. You know, my boy, you've been very lucky! Just a fraction higher and you'd be a capon singing soprano!'

Pierre-Edouard opened his eyes and looked at the man seated beside him, gently stroking his forehead. He was immediately reassured by the grey-blue eyes smiling at him through pince-nez, by the curved mouth beneath the little moustache, and by the sound of the voice continuing its monologue.

'Just imagine, they wanted to cut off your leg! Can you credit it! What idiocy, a lovely leg like that, with such strong bones! No, no, don't worry, it's still there, really well mended, a miracle! And in a few months you'll be able to gallop about — and without limping, I've laid a bet on it

328

with my eminent colleague, the local butcher . . . So tell me, is the Diamond still full of crayfish and trout?'

'At home? You know it?' gasped Pierre-Edouard in one breath.

'Of course I know it. And good Doctor Fraysse too. It was he who showed me the Diamond, what a fine stream! And I know his colleague very well too, my friend Doctor Delpy. He used to send me patients a long time ago, to be x-rayed. No, don't talk. Later on you must tell me where you lost your l. No, not your elbow.' Pierre-Edouard was looking anxiously at his arms, so the doctor repeated it: 'The l in your name. You see, I'm called Vialle as well, but with two 'ls; Fernand Vialle, of Brive, currently on holiday in the Amiens area on account of a war . . .'

A wave of warmth and happiness flooded through Pierre-Edouard and overwhelmed him, his eyes filled with tears of gratitude. He knew, for certain, that the doctor was not making it up; one day soon he would be running up the mountains, just as the man had said.

Who in Limousin hadn't heard of Doctor Vialle! A man not yet fifty whose reputation had spread throughout the département; a man who put his inspired talents as a bone-setter at the service of medicine, for whom no fracture held any mysteries or was too complicated to deal with!

'Now don't get excited, I'll come and see you tomorrow. And then we'll talk patois, I'd like that. *Ora, chaut durmir.*'

Pierre-Edouard nodded agreement, smiled and shut his eyes. Twenty-five years earlier, his mother had told him nearly every night: '*Ora, chaut durmir.*'

St Libéral, bled white by four years of massacre, was subjected from July onwards to a vicious attack of the illness which had already hit the whole of Europe. Old Antoine Gigoux was the first victim. He was carried off within three days; he was just beginning his eighty-first year.

His death was swift, but it did not alarm Doctor Fraysse;

he was very upset to lose his old friend, but consoled by the thought that now Antoine Gigoux could at last rejoin his son. The doctor had witnessed just how much the loss had affected the old mayor, when his only son had been killed on the Eastern Front in 1917. He was consumed by a grief which no one and nothing could relieve, and as the months passed he had slipped deeper into lassitude and depression. So the doctor did not pay too much heed to the cause of death.

But the death of the miller did alarm him; made it clear to him that this was a real epidemic. This man was sixty-three years old, still in his prime, healthy and strong as an ox, yet he was laid out in less than a week by this illness they called the Spanish 'flu, but which was really a sort of plague.

'That's all we needed!' exclaimed Jean-Edouard when the doctor informed him. 'What should we do?'

'Who knows? Plague, you see . . .' muttered the doctor, shaking his head. He was tired and discouraged, as he felt each time after closing the eyes of one of his patients. Besides, although he was in excellent health the years weighed heavily now; he was already eighty-three.

'What do you want me to tell you?' he murmured at last. 'Epidemics, believe me, I've seen some! But to know how to stop them . . .'

'Well, we can't leave it like that! We must warn people, there must be precautions that can be taken!'

'You're a real fighter, aren't you?' said the doctor with genuine admiration, 'and you're right. And how's Pierre-Edouard?'

'All right, coming on better than we could have hoped.'

'What good luck that he landed with my friend Doctor Vialle, eh?'

'Yes, indeed. But what do we do about this plague, then?'

'All right,' the doctor decided, 'you must publish a warning. Everyone must read or hear it. Go on, get writing . . . Start how you like, but don't put them in a panic. I'll give you the treatment, if you can call it that . . . Avoid getting chilled or overheated, especially after heavy work. Drink only water which contains a weak solution of permanganate to disinfect it, or brandy — that's right, use what you've got! Every morning on waking, after each meal, and at night on going to bed, rinse the mouth with half a glass of lukewarm water containing five or six drops of Thymol, I'll send for several bottles of it. In the morning on rising, put a little dab of Goménol vaseline in each nostril, I'll get some of that too. Finally take a gentle purgative every two weeks. That's it. Strictly between you and me, I don't really believe in it, but as you say, we have to do something . . .'

By evening the proclamation was made public, and many women came to the Mairie to read the order, then went to the doctor to obtain the drugs prescribed. But in the following months the Spanish 'flu claimed four new victims, among them a child of six.

Caught between the plague and the never-ending war, the community of St Libéral slipped into apathy and despair. The weeds and bushes gained ground on all sides.

Just as the end of peace had seen a mass departure of all the young people of the village, the end of war was greeted by the return of the wounded to the fold — at least, of those who were in a condition to come home.

From mid-October onwards they began to reappear one by one from the various hospitals; those whom death had disdained to take and the army no longer wanted either, now they were so badly injured, crushed, gassed, useless . . .

Léon arrived at St Libéral station one evening at the end of October. He had not informed anyone of his return and, limping a little, turned to walk home alone. He stopped several times on the way to catch his breath and to relieve his right arm of the weight of his suitcase. He could not change hands; he had only one.

Peace had finally arrived, but it had been so long in coming, and had cost so dear, that it did not inspire the excitement in the village that it did in the towns. In St

Libéral, a community where everyone knew everyone else, where everyone was a neighbour, there were too many missing, too many losses, too many families in mourning — those who had been spared could not decently express their pleasure.

Of course there was happiness; some songs, some hugs and kisses, and the wine flowed freely; but joy, pure joy with warmth and peals of laughter, no. That was masked by the shadow of the forty-three men the war had cut down, stifled by the black skirts and shawls of the twenty-seven widows, proscribed by the grave faces of the forty-nine orphans.

Pierre-Edouard had to wait until 22 November 1918 before he was finally discharged. He had been convalescing for two months at a hospital in Treignac, slowly learning to walk again. But if he still had a slight limp, he knew that although the broad, deep scars on his legs would not disappear, this uneven gait would; Dr Vialle had assured him of it, and he believed him.

At Treignac he had received a visit from his parents. It was a strange interlude: a father who did not know what to say and a mother full of lamentations. His father had hardly dared to speak of the future except in vague conditionals: 'If you come home, there's plenty of work . . . If you were there, we could clear the land; it's dreadful how the brambles have taken over . . .'

As for his mother, she spent her time listing all the dead in the village, telling him about the widows and orphans, the sadness of the times.

He had said nothing. What was the use . . . He had not spoken of any of his plans, nor had he tried to get them to understand that if he returned to the farm it would be organised according to his ideas; everything led him to believe that this would lead to immediate and serious conflict with his father.

Neither had he spoken of Mathilde; she was his secret. Besides, he could guess what his parents' reaction would be, how they would oppose the addition to the Vialhe family of the daughter of a good-for-nothing, the sister of a lout. He had no desire to start an argument which he knew he could not win. He had a plan with regard to Mathilde, and he would keep to it.

His parents only came to see him that once, and he had to admit that it was better so; they had become strangers to him.

He got out at Brive station towards three o'clock in the afternoon; as he was still in uniform, with all his fine medals, the other passengers kindly helped him down from the compartment. He thanked them, and limped towards the connecting train for St Libéral.

Then, suddenly, he saw her – Mathilde. She was there, ten paces away, so small, so beautiful, a miracle. Mathilde, running towards him and throwing herself into his arms. And he, overcome by happiness, stupidly repeating: 'You came, you came . . .'

And her replies merged, got muddled up and overtaken by the questions, for there was so much to say, to explain, to listen to!

'You came . . .'

'I wanted to be the first to welcome you.'

'But how did you get here, there's no train at this time!'

'By cart, Léon let me . . .'

At last they came out of the station and climbed into the trap, all the while talking, touching, holding on to each other.

'Give me the reins.'

She smiled, snuggled up against him and let herself be driven.

It was dark by the time they at last reached St Libéral.

'If your parents are expecting you on the train they'll be worried; it came in an hour ago!' said Mathilde.

'It doesn't matter, I didn't tell them I'd be back today.'

'But you told me.'

'Of course. If you hadn't come to Brive, I wanted to visit you first. That's why I didn't say anything to my parents.'

He directed the cart down the main street and set the horse into a trot.

'Where are you going?' she asked, suddenly anxious.

'To my house.'

'But . . . what about me?'

'You're coming with me.'

'But your parents, they'll . . .'

'No, they won't,' he reassured her. 'I'll bring home whoever I like.'

He guided the horse right up to the front steps and got down, pulling a face at the stabbing pain from his scars.

'Give me your hand,' he said.

He felt her trembling, so he put his arm around her shoulders, pushed open the door and went in. As he had expected, his mother and father were seated at the table.

'Here I am again,' he said. 'There's no need for me to introduce Mathilde to you, you know her, but I brought her this evening to tell you that we'll be getting married before Christmas.'

Nothing which followed surprised him – he had foreseen it all. His parents' cold welcome, their silence whilst Mathilde was there. And his father waiting for him by the fire when he came back alone at midnight, after taking her home and enjoying a drink with Léon.

'You can't have believed that we'd agree?' cried Jean-Edouard as soon as he stepped in.

Pierre-Edouard carefully filled his pipe and lit it with a spill. 'No,' he said at last. 'I knew all along you'd be against Mathilde. But I don't give a damn.'

'You don't give a damn? Really? The war and your wounds don't give you all the rights, you know!'

'The right to tell you to stuff it? Yes they do!' he said calmly, sitting on the settle.

'Bloody hell! You're making a mistake, if you think in this family – '

'No; you're making the mistake about your son, and about your daughters too! Talking of them, Louise wrote to me; she's well, and so is Félix.'

'Damnit, don't try to get at me with that old story! We're

not talking about that, but about this girl you want to bring into my house, this daughter of – '

'Take note of what I am going to say,' interrupted Pierre-Edouard gravely. 'One single insult, just one, and this time it'll be me that lashes out . . . And you can tell mother that, too . . .'

'You wouldn't dare!' Jean-Edouard taunted him, rising.

Pierre-Edouard sighed, and pushed a few twigs into the fire. 'Yes I would,' he said quietly. 'What do you think? Do you think I've come back from my first communion? Of course I'll slap the face of the first person who shows any disrespect to my wife!'

'Your wife? Already? Well, you bastard, you haven't wasted any time!'

'Think what you like, I don't give a damn about that either. Not a damn.'

'All right,' cut in Jean-Edouard, 'you don't give a damn about anything! Well marry the kid, I wish you joy! Marry her, but don't count on my roof for shelter. There's no question of that. I'll never let her live in my home! Never, do you understand? And if I'm not mistaken your mother will agree with me! What did you think, that we would let a Dupeuch lay down the law here, in our house?'

'Don't worry, I never believed that. I know you too well.'

'So then, it's settled; you can marry her tomorrow if you like, but you'll never bring her over the threshold. I'll fling her out if you do!'

'Fine,' said Pierre-Edouard, getting up, 'I wanted to hear you say it. That way we know where we stand . . . Goodnight.'

He picked up his case, limped towards the door and went out into the darkness.

Léon was still sitting beside the fire, waiting for him.

'Right, it's all sorted out, don't let's talk about it any more,' Pierre-Edouard announced. 'Tell me, what did that?' he said, stretching a finger towards the stump under his friend's left sleeve.

'That? A bloody Maxim gun. And you, what was it?'

'One of those stupid one-fifty-millimetre jobs!'

They were still talking at dawn, when Léon's mother got up as usual to light the fire.

The return of the survivors brought an increase in activity and work, which the whole village was in sore need of. First of all the men who had left school between 1892 and 1897 returned at the year's end, then in the following months came the younger ones.

Life began again; St Libéral finally emerged from its dangerous sloth. Everything seemed to return to normal, everyone tried hard to resume the old pre-war habits, but no one was fooled. They all knew that the customs, the mentality, the general climate had changed to such an extent that it was practically impossible to take up the old life they had left behind on 1 August 1914.

It was not only 1,300,000 men who had died in the war; it was a whole epoch, a century. It became obvious through thousands of little instances, and every day brought proof that they were entering a new era.

The young soldiers returned in a very different frame of mind from that which had previously been the great strength of rural society; this civilisation had been based on, even constrained by, a patriarchal system, whose legitimacy very few had ever questioned. Now disputes broke out on all sides, for the old guard felt they held authority almost as a divine right, while the young men not only questioned their autocracy, but ridiculed it unmercifully, made a joke of it and, since they lacked the power to change it, fled it.

This war had been their first opportunity to leave their little world, and they had learned more than just how to kill; they had also discovered that beyond their village or canton there was the world, with other ways of working and living. So there were many who repacked their bags and left, refusing to bow to the dictatorship of the head of the family. The company and the friendship of a whole variety of townspeople had taught them that there were other ways of earning your bread than by ploughing; they had exchanged ideas as well as wine and tobacco, compared their work and their wages.

As for the older combatants, those who had already been their own masters before the war, they also found it hard to adapt to new ways, to accept the idea that women could fill their places and manage the farms as well as they had. A new way of thinking had emerged there too, a different mentality, and if many wives stepped back and resumed the position they had occupied four years earlier, it did not fool anyone. No one could forget that they were capable of filling the men's jobs if necessary. And the band of widows was there too, to remind the men that they were not indispensable.

The years of shared misery created a close bond amongst all the former soldiers in the village. Everyone was amazed to see how warmly those who had been at the front now greeted Father Verlhac. Even the schoolteacher was not pretending when he expressed admiration, respect and friendship for him. They all knew that the priest had been a stretcher-bearer for four years, but only those who had seen combat could appreciate the importance, the self-sacrifice and the courage of the stretcher-bearers.

Jean-Edouard felt pushed aside, isolated amongst these men who had faced the guns together, but he continued his work as mayor with undiminished vigour. No one challenged him for the sash of office bequeathed by Jean Duroux; they knew that he had made good use of the power it gave him.

Nor did anyone criticise his attitude towards his son. That quarrel was of no further interest; it was no longer a boy set against his father, but simply two men who chose to differ. And such a disagreement concerned nobody but the parties involved, like an everyday dispute between two neighbours; it was wiser not to take sides.

The young woman leaned against her companion's shoulder and shivered. She raised the fur collar of her coat against the keen wind which whipped across the gangway of the big white steamship; there were few passengers prepared to brave the cold of this arctic region.

Only the announcement that an iceberg was drifting by not far from the ship brought a few of the curious out of the well-heated saloons; they rushed to the rails, admired the sparkling mountain of ice and then returned, numb with cold, to their bridge or whist tables, their conversations, their cups of tea and glasses of champagne.

The young woman and her companion reached the poop-deck and gazed in silence at the ribbon of silver created by the wake, stretching to the horizon. The man stroked her face, pushing aside the wild curls which the wind drove across her eyes.

'Then you're sure, you don't want to marry me?'

'No, I don't.'

'But why not?'

'I've told you a thousand times.'

'I'll end up believing that you hate men!'

'Idiot!' she murmured. 'You didn't always speak like that, but I'll make you suffer for having said it. No, I don't hate men, but what they can become. Husbands, for instance . . .'

'And what if I make you a nice little baby, handsome and charming like me?'

'All the more reason not to marry! First the husband, then the father! No, thank you very much! Let's go in now, I'm cold.'

That was just an excuse. She wasn't going to tell him everything, explain the whole tale to this kind Canadian doctor whom she had known for six months.

Besides, would he believe it? Probably not. Who could imagine that the young milliner who kept a shop in the rue du Bac, who employed eight workers, designed hats for all Paris and was now going to present her models in America, was young Berthe Vialhe? What was left of the peasant from the Corrèze who had spent her childhood and adolescence minding the flocks, cleaning the stables, doing the washing, working like a slave?

There was nothing left. Berthe Vialhe no longer existed, swallowed up by the famous label sewn in her hats. It was a madly chic signature, with a good ring to it, like a tinkling mountain stream: Claire Diamond.

Louise gently tucked in the child who had just fallen asleep, kissed him and left the bedroom.

Quietly she slipped down the corridors which wound between the attic rooms of the castle, and went down the servants' staircase to the first floor. Here she took the grand staircase to the first floor, and entered a long corridor of shining parquet which smelled deliciously of wax. On either side the heavy panelling was decorated with trophies of death, with stags and roe deer, boars' heads, wolves and foxes.

The surroundings no longer impressed her; she had grown accustomed to them, accustomed to the splendour of the private town house in the rue du Passy, the palatial hotels in Biarritz and Deauville and Nice. It was three years since she had become the companion to the old baroness, and luxury no longer astonished her.

She had Jean to thank for this position – or rather, his disappearance. At his death, mad with grief, she had wanted to leave the castle, to draw a veil over the past for a second time. But then the young baroness took an interest in her future. Perhaps she was troubled by this first death amongst her employees; perhaps it was to relieve her conscience, to redeem herself in the eyes of her servants – her husband had been declared unfit for military service and had not changed his way of life one iota, everything continuing as it had before the war; she needed to prove that he really was concerned about the fate of his people . . .

So it was that the young baroness suggested she become lady companion to her mother-in-law. Not a very demanding old lady; she did not ask much, just to be able to talk to someone, to have her cups of verbena or lime tea served at set times, to have a few pages read to her each evening from *The Imitation of Christ*.

Louise had accepted. Since then her life had flowed by smoothly and silently, without great joy but without great pain. She expected nothing from life, but accepted it without bitterness, because of Félix.

Félix didn't pay any attention to his mother's mourning attire, and wasn't surprised by the first white hairs, not knowing that she was only twenty-seven. Only Félix still knew how to make her laugh.

PART SIX

Coste-Roche

24

IT was snowing thick and fast when they eventually reached the dilapidated building on the night of Saturday 21 December. It was a two-roomed thatched cottage about three kilometres from the village, just past the cutting leading to the old mine-workings, on the edge of the parish, on the south slope of the plateau, at the place called Coste-Roche.

It was part of the tiny farm Pierre-Edouard had rented from the solicitor for a token sum – fifty francs a year. Five years ago fifty francs would have been the price of three sheep, but since the war you could get that much for four hens! However Pierre-Edouard had insisted that Monsieur Lardy accept the money; the solicitor was only too glad that someone was prepared to take on the cottage and the two hectares surrounding it, and was prepared to let it for nothing, as a wedding present to his wife's god-daughter.

He was a little embarrassed, really, for the house had been empty since 1914 and was in a very poor state; apart from the half-hectare field which lay close to the building and could be ploughed, the rest of the land was covered in weeds, scrub and wood.

Pierre-Edouard fixed up the house within three weeks, helped by Léon and his two labourers. Once it no longer rained through the rye-straw of the roof, the doors and shutters closed firmly, and the two rooms were scoured with lots of water and lime-washed, so that they were clean and neat, it was just right for a young couple.

Pierre-Edouard thanked Léon, who was already turning his cart, pushed open the door and went in. The huge oak-stump he had put on the hearth at the beginning of the afternoon was only half burned. The fire ate slowly into it, with tiny flames, opening out wide holes in the heart of the wood where scarlet embers threw out a lasting warmth.

He hung up the oil-lamp and turned down the flame, for the light of the fire reflected by the whitened walls was almost enough in itself. He looked at Mathilde, who was taking off her heavy black cloak, on which the snowflakes were already melting.

The snow had begun to fall just as they were going into the Mairie. Gaston, the deputy mayor, was waiting for them, confused and ashamed at having to stand in for Jean-Edouard, who had not been seen since the previous evening. Gaston was torn between his friendship with his neighbour and sympathy for Pierre-Edouard and Mathilde, but he managed it all very well, despite his embarrassment. He didn't make any mistakes; he kissed the bride and reassured Pierre-Edouard that it would all come right in the end.

In the church the ceremony was quiet but full of happiness, conducted by Father Verlhac, who obviously approved of the young couple's behaviour and rejoiced to see them happy. He even accepted their invitation to the inn, to drink the health of the newly-weds, and once more wish them much joy and happiness.

Pierre-Edouard and Léon had invited several friends to dine with them at the inn afterwards. The meal was simple, light-hearted without being boisterous; there were none of the rude jokes and coarse laughter which often punctuated wedding banquets. There were too many absentees that evening, and André Chanlat looked down on them from his frame of black crêpe.

'You're not cold, are you?' worried Pierre-Edouard.

'No, not at all, it's very cosy,' she said, holding out her hands to the fire.

He moved nearer to her; put his hands on her hips and kissed her on the neck, just below the ear. 'Are you happy?'

Yes, she was happy, but she asked: 'Will you sit with me for a moment on the settle?'

'Of course.' He took the ledge opposite her in the deep inglenook.

'Well, here we are . . .' she said, pushing the log which threw off sparks.

He saw that she was tense, a little sad and worried. 'Are you frightened of me?' he asked jokingly.

She shook her head in dissent, and blushed a little.

'No, it's not that; I don't know how to say it. It's a strange feeling, knowing we're married at last. And then . . . I want you to know that . . . if . . . Well, if you had wanted to, that's to say . . . Well, you could have, before this evening, you know . . . I wouldn't have minded, I would have understood . . .'

'I know.'

'Well, why didn't you want to? I'd have done whatever you wanted . . .'

'I know that.'

'So it's right what I thought, it was my fault if . . . well, if I deprived you, because I didn't have the courage to ask. And now you resent me for having made you wait . . . And I . . . I don't know what to do, anyway . . . so.'

She was frustrated and tense, close to tears.

'You know, you are a funny little girl! But you've got it wrong. Of course we could have, ever since I came back, and it's been hard watching you and waiting, believe me . . . But one day on the White Peak you said to me: "I'm not a little girl, I trust you". You were right to say that.'

He poked the log, pushed several bits of bark back into the embers. 'So,' he continued, 'that was it. I'm like that. If – well, if we'd taken in the harvest too early, I'd have enjoyed it, of course, just at that moment, but I would have been sorry later. And you too; you'd have been disappointed that I couldn't wait a month. And today, you and I would both have known that your white dress wasn't quite white . . . Whereas now it's different; we're married, we're not putting the cart before the oxen, it's all proper, just as it should be. Do you understand? Now we'll always remember that there was a before and after this evening.'

She gazed at him intently and smiled, her eyes dancing with happiness.

'I knew you'd say that. At least, I was hoping, and I'm so pleased you did. And that we waited till this evening. Everything's perfect.'

She got up, hesitated a moment and then continued. 'I have something else to tell you. I've got a birthmark, not a bad one, but a mark, on . . . well, on my chest. You see, it's not very nice, and I wanted to tell you, so that you wouldn't be surprised . . . . . . It's not funny! It's true! It's not something to laugh about, you idiot!' she insisted, seeing that he was shaking with uncontrollable laughter.

'Oh, you, you really are something!' The words tumbled out as he wiped the tears of laughter from his eyes. 'I know you've got a mark! I've known since you were born! What's more, everyone in the village knows too. A mark like a crescent moon. But I have to admit that I don't remember which side it's on!'

She stood for a moment in amazement, a little annoyed; then she smiled and crinkled her eyes mischievously at him.

'Oh, so it's like that! Everyone knows! Well in that case, it's time you saw it, and found out which side it's on . . .'

The snow fell all night. In the morning Pierre-Edouard pushed the door half open and saw that the drifts were up to fifteen centimetres. He closed the flap silently and made up the fire by throwing a big bundle of broom onto the still smouldering embers; they ignited instantly, blazing like a torch. Then he filled the fireplace with several hefty logs and turned back towards the bed.

Mathilde was still sleeping. He tenderly watched her gentle breathing, admired her delicate face, still so young, so fresh – the delicious curve of her half-open mouth, the mischievous snub nose, the fine tracery of long eyelashes against her cheeks. Then he thought of the little shape like a crescent moon which lay there beneath her left breast, two fingers from the nipple.

So, because it was Sunday, because it was such bad

346

weather you wouldn't put   dog out in it, because he was happy as never before, and life was beautiful, he slipped gently back into the warm bed.

Mathilde did not wake, but instinctively stretched her arm towards him, as if already used to him being there; she touched his chest and her body came to rest confidingly against his.

The snow lasted for two weeks, making any outdoor work impossible, keeping people by their firesides. Pierre-Edouard and Mathilde, completely cut off in their cottage, experienced the happiest time of their lives.

Despite the cold they climbed several times to the plateau, for the pleasure of looking down on that fine expanse below, of surveying their fields, the ones Mathilde had stolen from under Jean-Edouard's nose and which Léon had given them, the deeds signed by the solicitor, on the day of their marriage. The three hectares had lain fallow for years, but only needed hard work and proper treatment to turn into good rich plough-land again.

'And down there,' Pierre-Edouard pointed, 'those are our fields. Well, my father's . . .'

'The Long Field, with its twenty-eight walnut trees . . .'

'No, thirty-one! I should know, I planted them with my father in 1901!'

'Twenty-eight,' she repeated. 'Three died in February 1917. The frost . . . And,' she continued, outlining the other fields from above, 'then there's the Peuch, the Malides, the Perrier, the Great Field! I know each one! Léon set me to watch them when you wrote for news . . .'

'So, he didn't bother at all, that peasant! When I thought all the information came from him!'

'What an idea!' she laughed. 'He didn't have time for that. But I know your father's fields. And I can even tell you which ones he's growing grain on for three years out of four.'

'Yes, I'm aware of that,' Pierre-Edouard frowned. 'It's so stupid, it exhausts the soil. Well, that's his business . . . Tell me if I remember it right; these plots here are called Monteboeuf, la Combille and au Bourdelet?'

347

'Yes, that's what it says in the land register.'

'Well, we'll give them new names, to remind us. That one we'll call "Léon's Letters", this one "Mathilde's" and over there, below the White Peak, "The Meeting Field". Would you like that?'

'Of course,' she replied, laughing, 'and one day our grandchildren will say we were crazy to give the fields names which are quite meaningless. How funny!'

He smiled, kissed her on the nose, and pulled her down onto the vast white sheet of the plateau.

He took long paces but strode slowly and smoothly in a perfectly straight line, governed by the straw markers which divided the ploughed field.

He was sowing, with broad regular sweeps which produced a fine golden lace springing from his wide palms as they opened; the waves of grain twisted and rustled as they settled on the ground, then seemed to take flight again with the next full swing of his arm, shooting out against the blue sky.

March had come in warm and damp; conditions were right earlier than usual for the spring sowing. Pierre-Edouard had lost no time since borrowing Léon's plough and oxen ten days ago. Already the Meeting Field was a beautiful sight, a fold of brown furrows where it now rained barley seeds.

What a joy to rediscover the technique of ploughing again, the movements and habits coming back to him instantly, without hesitation. What a pleasure to hear the coarse, gritty song of the earth again as it cracked, opened and curled over, hissing behind the mould-board. With complete happiness he contemplated the stretch of shining furrows he had created, one moulded to the next; neat, straight, perfectly cut.

Of course it had taken time to get his eye in again, adjust his stride to the size of the fields and the pace of the oxen, so much slower than the horses on Moureau Farm. The earth was harder, tougher, less giving and less uniform than the rich provident earth of old Ponthier. But he had known that for a long time. And here it was all better, because he was at home, on his land, in his realm, and the barley he was to harvest would be his own.

And in the evening, instead of the table of twenty-five men, waiting in silent attention, watching the movements of their employer, ready to rise at the click of a clasp knife being snapped shut; instead of the fatty, burnt soup of Ma Ponthier, the old warhorse; instead of the huge shed and revolting nests from which rose, from time to time, one of the scullery-maid's clientele, already undressed – instead of all that, he would be with Mathilde again.

He would have soup lovingly prepared by her, the intimacy of a meal alone together, and then, when the door and shutters were closed, the fire stoked up for the night, he would have her, fresh and soft as a spray of lily of the valley, impassioned and twining like a tendril of honeysuckle; the spontaneous welcome of her warm body, so well known already, yet rediscovered each time.

They needed all that – the complete understanding, harmony of purpose, and a taste for hard work– to overcome together the daily trials. There were plenty of them!

Gradually the little nest-egg saved from four years' wages melted away, but it allowed them to equip their household and live for three months.

The money vanished in the purchase of fifteen hens: 150 francs. A two-month-old piglet to fatten: 135 francs. The bran and grain needed for these animals: 100 francs; the barley and potatoes for sowing: 250 francs. In everything – in the sacks of fertiliser which he needed this year for lack of manure, in the modest outlay for food, the bread at two francs twenty a kilo, the milk at eighty sous a litre, the vegetables and occasionally meat.

These days, 1000 francs was no longer an enormous sum. Fifteen to twenty years earlier it would have bought him three fine cows: now, for the same amount, all he could buy were three eight-month-old piglets! What madness!

Sometimes, when Mathilde saw him looking worried,

she reminded him of her savings book. 'You know, I was given seventy-five francs when I was born!'

'I remember, everyone talked about it at the time. It was a good sum then, but . . .'

'Wait! There's interest added in the book, and then Léon kept it up for me, before the war. By now I must have 345 francs. With that we could buy two six-week-old calves, keep them for eighteen months and sell them ready to breed, and . . .'

'I can tell you're related to a cattle dealer! No, keep your savings, you never know . . .'

'Well then,' she continued, 'I'm sure Léon would give us a loan. Would you like me to ask him?'

'No, he's already done enough for us. Think of the land he gave as your dowry! I don't want to borrow any money from him, nor anyone else. It's me who's got to feed you, not your brother.'

The worry about money made him touchy, but the land too was a constant source of concern. There, only an arm's length away, stretched the Vialhe holdings, his land: all those beautiful fields which his father could no longer maintain as they deserved, which he was depleting with his inefficient system of crop rotation. But the Vialhe land was forbidden to him. The best he could hope for was that one day, in ten or fifteen years perhaps . . . Just so long as his father had not sold it all by then.

Although normal life had resumed in St Libéral, there was a feeling of stagnation and depression. As mayor, Jean-Edouard was made aware of this almost every day.

His son had not been the only one to leave, slamming the door behind him. Plenty of other young people had copied Pierre-Edouard, but instead of staying in the parish they had moved to the towns, and for good; there was no doubt of that.

This exodus had diminished the ageing, dispirited population. In 1900 there had been 1,092 inhabitants; in 1914 there were 979 and now, 701 . . .

Already one of the two grocers had closed down. Before

the war there had been four carpenters; now there were only two, and they had just as much difficulty making a living as the three remaining stonemasons and the last slater. No one had come to replace the old miller, and they knew that the solicitor would be closing his office at the end of the year. The tenants of smallholdings were disappearing everywhere, no longer able to survive on a farm of three or four hectares. Weeds and bushes took over where they left.

The buying syndicate was moribund. As for the fortnightly markets, Léon had fought to get them going again, but they did not attract half the numbers who had flooded into St Libéral before the war. He had to do away with the special markets, and it looked as if they might soon be down to one market a month . . .

Nothing was going well anywhere else, either! The newspapers spoke of nothing but strikes, demonstrations, those Bolsheviks who were upsetting everyone. And to make matters worse, someone had tried to assassinate Clemenceau! What a disgrace, what depravity!

For Jean-Edouard life grew more difficult. He was assailed by lassitude, not so much physical as spiritual fatigue. Marguerite's grumpiness and bad temper increased daily; she was growing old ungracefully, and hated her isolation and solitude. Since she could not vent her anger on her own daughters, who now seemed to have disappeared completely, she turned all her bitterness on her daughter-in-law. That little serpent, with her air of innocence, she must have displayed all her charms to turn Pierre-Edouard's head – the fool, preferring to live up there in the wilds at Coste-Roche, instead of down here, working the farm. Huh, they would come to no good, those two . . . !

Jean-Edouard was basically in agreement with his wife, but the daily repetition of these complaints exasperated him. Of course Mathilde was worthless, it ran in the family, didn't it? Of course she'd gone the whole way to get that idiot Pierre-Edouard to marry her; she had her eye on his land, that was obvious, clear as the Diamond!

He knew all that, he was convinced of it, but, unlike Marguerite, he did not chew it over constantly. What good did that do? The damage was done, they had made the break; why harp on it, why stir up anger and bitterness? He didn't need that; it came back to him anyway, every time he saw his son or daughter-in-law – that kid! A week earlier, she had called out to him like a challenge, in front of everyone, a ringing: 'Good morning, Mayor!' and it had echoed defiantly along the main street. Then she had walked away, perfectly well aware of the impression she had created, confident of her youth, her cheeky little face, her hip-swinging walk. He would have liked to hit her!

He preferred his son's attitude to her defiance. At least he didn't speak. He said nothing, except when he had the gall to come and get supplies from the syndicate, and even there he found an opportunity to teach his own father a lesson: he criticised the seed varieties on offer, made a face over the heaps of phosphates, demanded some unknown fertiliser, talked of products with unpronounceable names – in short, behaved as if he alone knew more than all the farmers in the community; more than his own father, what's more! It was disgusting! After that, Jean-Edouard let one of the employees serve him and answer his questions!

But it was all so tiring and depressing; and the farm work was getting more difficult and demanding. He did it without wanting to, it gave him no pleasure. He was in his sixtieth year and felt his strength and drive fading; even that urge and need for a fight, which had supported him for so long, was going. His sash of office as mayor weighed heavy, too; he was tempted to lay it aside for good at the next elections, which were due to take place at the end of the year.

Pierre-Edouard was absorbed in his work, earthing up the potatoes he had planted six weeks earlier in the field next to the little cottage, and he did not notice Mathilde at first.

She was just tackling the final bend which led steeply up to Coste-Roche, and would be home in five minutes. He was suddenly aware that she was loaded up like a pack-mule; besides two big rounds of bread and the week's groceries, she was carrying the twenty-five kilos of buckwheat seed he had ordered. He thrust his hoe into the ground and ran down to meet her.

She saw him leaping and zigzagging through the broom bushes; relieved to put down the load which she had carried for almost three kilometres, she sat down to wait for him. She was worn out and perspiring, for the June sun was beating down.

'Bloody hell!' he shouted as he reached her. 'I didn't tell you to *bring* the buckwheat, I told you to order it. I would have fetched it! That was a bit silly of you, in this heat!'

'So, now you don't have to go to the village! And anyway, I've carried loads like that before!'

'Just content yourself with carrying that,' he said, gently placing a hand on her stomach.

Pierre-Edouard had been very attentive for the last fortnight, since Doctor Delpy had confirmed that the child would be born in January; he made sure she didn't do the heavy jobs – and that wasn't easy, because there were plenty of them.

'Anything new down there?' he asked, sitting down beside her.

'I saw your father.'

'And of course, as usual, you said "Good day, Mayor!" to him.'

'Naturally,' she giggled, 'except I nearly said "Good day, Grandfather!" After all, he is going to be a grandfather, isn't he? Perhaps that will make him happy.'

He filled his pipe and lit it. 'I doubt it. Don't forget he's been one for a long time, and it doesn't seem to have changed anything!'

'I saw Léon too, guess what he told me . . .'

He pulled on his pipe and shrugged his shoulders.

'Do you remember the Treilhes? The ones at Ayen?' she asked.

'Yes, the carriers.'

'They're selling their farm. Since she's been widowed,

poor Marie can't find a tenant for the land. Just think, twelve hectares ... You know what we must do, don't you?' she asked, and carried right on. 'We must buy the two hectares on the plateau, close to our land.'

'Have you gone mad? You know we haven't a penny!'

'We'll have to find it,' she insisted, 'and we must buy. That way we'll have five hectares, a nice little farm!'

'No,' he said drily. 'Don't talk to me about a nice farm! No house, no cowshed, no livestock, not even tools to work with! That's all we need to be ruined. You'd better forget that idea.'

He was aware that he was dashing her hopes, and was sorry for it, but the facts were plain to see: they had no money left. Apart from the 345 francs in Mathilde's savings book, and his grandfather's napoléon, the tiny sum still available would just tide them over until they got some small returns from the sale of the barley, maize and vegetables they were growing. There were also the hens and rabbits Mathilde was rearing and the small pension awarded for his war wounds, but even all added together it didn't come to much.

'All the same,' she replied stubbornly, 'we have to buy. Léon told me so.'

'What business is it of his! No, listen, instead of dreaming, why not agree to what he suggested to me?'

'You're going to borrow from him?'

'Not at all! But two months ago he suggested I go and help him on market days. Well, I'll go and do that. That way I'll earn a bit, we'll save, and one day we'll be able to buy land.'

'And the fields on the plateau will have been sold long since,' she replied bitterly. 'Well, you never told me that Léon suggested you work for him! Why didn't you say anything?'

'Because it depressed me,' he said. 'Really, I can't bear the thought of it. I'm not a cattle dealer, I don't enjoy swindling people! But I've got to put my mind to it. Soon there'll be three of us, have you thought of that? And even if I work myself to a standstill we can't survive on our thirty miserable strips of land. When I think that just next door my father is leaving half his land fallow, dammit all!'

She saw that he was downcast and demoralised, and snuggled up to him. 'Well, there you have it, that's why we must buy! I don't want you to go running round the markets four or five times a week! I don't want that, do you hear? We have to buy those two hectares, and we're going to!'

'And how much do they want for the land?'

'They're rather expensive,' she spoke softly. 'Prices are rising fast . . .'

'How much?'

'Three and a half thousand a hectare, but perhaps if you haggled a bit . . .'

'Okay, don't let's talk about it any more. Come on; it's past midday and I'm hungry.'

Mathilde had been in bed for more than an hour when he finally returned to the house. He had been taking advantage of the long June evening to work in the vegetable plot. It was late, and already the setting sun was giving way to stars, which outshone the last rays on the horizon and accentuated the dark of the night sky.

Before going into the house he drew up a full bucket of water, undressed and washed himself. The water ran down his body, fresh and delicious, after that stifling day. He filled another bucket and tipped it over his head, shaking himself. Then, having washed off the accumulated dust and sweat of twelve hours' labour, he went in and shut the door.

It was dark, but he did not light the lamp; he moved noiselessly towards the bedroom and slipped into bed. Mathilde had thrown off all the covers because of the heat, and only the coarse linen sheet lay partly over her. He felt her bare back and shoulders, worried that she would catch cold, for the night would be cool if it stayed clear. Gently, he pulled up the sheet.

'Leave it, it's too hot!'

'You're not asleep! I was being so careful not to wake you . . .'

'That was kind of you. I'm thirsty . . .'

'Now you tell me!'

He sighed, but got up and walked to the sink. She heard him feeling around for a glass.

'You could have lit the lamp . . .'

'So that we can feed the mosquitoes? Anyway, I've found it,' he said, coming back. He stumbled into a stool, and swore like a muleteer.

'Have you hurt yourself?' she asked, though a chuckle escaped.

'What do you think? I like stubbing my toes, you know that! Here, have a drink. All right, can I get into bed now? Anything else you need? Sure you wouldn't like a few cherries? I could go and fetch some for you from the plateau, it's only a couple of kilometres . . .'

'Don't be silly! Come to bed.'

He kissed her and stretched out beside her. Outside, the barn owl which nested in the loft above the stable gave a long screech.

'Why does it do that?' asked Mathilde.

'That must be the male,' he explained seriously. 'I think the female has sent him for a glass of water, and he's knocked into something on his way back.'

She pinched him unexpectedly on the behind, then sat up.

'Where are you going?'

'Nowhere,' she said, drawing up her legs and winding her arms round her knees. 'You know, I've been thinking about what Léon told me, this morning . . .'

'Oh no! Not at this hour of the night! I'm fond of your brother, but I don't want him in my bed!'

'Listen to me,' she insisted, 'and consider the way he's done things.'

'What now? He's sold a milch-cow without an udder by swearing that she gives twelve litres a day?'

'No,' she continued, 'I'm serious. Listen; before the war, when he bought all the grazing land he could and had the house built, you know what he did? He borrowed. He told me this morning . . .'

'Your brother took a loan? Well, well! and I thought he earned enough to pay for it himself. The devil, pretending to be rich on other people's money!'

'Don't be stupid! You're talking like an old man, you sound like your father! It's not a sin to borrow, is it? And anyway, he's paid it back!'

'All the better! Since the money isn't worth anything now, he hasn't been wasting his time, the crook!'

'That's true,' she admitted frankly, 'but he told me it's going to go on like that . . .'

'What is?'

'Money will lose value each year . . . You don't see gold coins any more now, he told me that was a bad sign. Well, according to him, this is a good time to borrow, and if you want to he'll stand guarantee for you at the Crédit Agricole. He knows the people in Tulle . . .'

'My God! You plotted all this with him this morning, didn't you?' he groaned, wanting to sound angry, but a note of admiration crept in.

'And why not? He's my brother, isn't he? He's got a right to talk to me!'

'Bloody hell, you make a fine pair! My word, if I hadn't got you out of there you'd have ended up worse than him!'

'No, I wouldn't. Anyway, you can't be cross with me for worrying about how we're going to manage, someone has to . . .'

'Oh no, tell me right out then, I'm a spendthrift!'

'It's not that, but Léon says that you're not interested in money . . .'

'Your brother is beginning to annoy me! Anyway, what does he know about it? Has he been to look in my wallet?'

'No, but he told me that you once made him throw away more than five francs' worth of birds for no good reason! And he hasn't forgotten. To him, that's proof enough!'

He burst into laughter, sat up and hugged her to him.

'Five francs!' he repeated with a hiccup, 'Five francs!

And for no good reason, he tells you, the idiot! Well, if I remember rightly, we had the wolves on our tail. If you'd seen him run! He'd have been glad to pay a couple of guineas to get away!'

'Don't laugh!' she struggled in his embrace and beat him with her fists. 'It's serious, what I'm talking about. Light the lamp!'

'Look, it's late; I want to sleep, I've been on my feet since four!'

'You can sleep afterwards; light the lamp!'

He sighed, fumbled for the matches and struck one. Very soon the flame of the oil lamp flickered across the room. Mathilde got up and grasped the lamp; its slender shadow danced on the white walls.

'Shut the window to stop the mosquitoes!' he suggested.

He smiled as he watched her trot across the room, admiring her body, which was improved by the rounding of early pregnancy. Later it would look ungainly, out of proportion, but at the moment her shape was changing day by day; the slim, graceful girl was growing confidently into a complete woman, in harmony with herself. It showed in the slight swelling of her breasts, the enveloping, protective curve of her hips, in certain gestures even: the instinct which led her to place her hand on her stomach as a protective wall – although it was still quite flat, a smooth soft stomach like a pigeon's breast – where their son, or their daughter, was growing, the baby who was going to be born for its mother's twentieth birthday.

She went to the sideboard, opened it, took out a sheet of paper and a pencil, and sat down at the table.

'I want to go to sleep!'

'Wait, it will only take a minute,' she replied, starting to write.

She came back to the bed. 'There,' she explained. 'That's what we need to borrow, and that's what it will cost us in repayments each year . . .'

He took the piece of paper, read it, and choked.

'Eleven thousand francs! Are you out of your mind? And why eleven thousand francs? You told me that they were

358

selling at three and a half a hectare; there are two hectares, that makes seven thousand! What's the extra for?'

'Simple; it's to buy two sows and eight ewes, and for tools; Léon will still let us borrow his oxen.'

'But look what we'd have to repay each year!'

'Well we'll have twenty years to do it!' she said, and twined her arms around his neck. 'And after all, the repayments are only four good piglets each year! And if we have two sows, we'll have at least a dozen piglets to sell!'

'Stop it, sweetheart!' he said seriously, 'we're not there yet. Let me look at your sums . . .'

He picked up the paper again and studied it. She saw he was hesitating, that he was not yet convinced, so she tried tenderness, taking his hand and placing it on her stomach.

'Look, think of this too.'

'I am! I don't want him to have a father who's imprisoned for debt!'

'There's no danger of that. If necessary, I'd sell my land! So, you've decided? You agree? We can't let this one get away! So it's yes?' she whispered, leaning closer to him.

He gazed at her for a long time and considered the two hectares which he could perhaps own, thanks to her. Those two hectares were their chance, a lifebelt thrown to the drowning; they needed them. She had done it all, she had taken the lead with firmness and energy, as in everything she undertook. So he didn't feel outwitted and beaten by her charm and her deliciously persuasive weaponry; he knew that it was thanks to her, to all the things he loved in her, that he would achieve his goals and fulfil his potential.

'I'm very proud of you,' he said at last.

'It's yes?' she asked, kissing him.

'I'd like to meet the person who could say no to you at this moment. I couldn't . . .'

25

THE sale and division of the Treilhes' farm aroused little interest. The business dragged on, for the heavy burden of summer work interfered with the discussions and calculations which are a vital precursor to every transaction. Then came the preparations for the elections to the town council and to the chamber of deputies in the autumn; this distracted everyone, so that the various purchasers managed to buy all the fields close to the village without actually tearing each other apart.

Thus Jeantout's son, Maurice, got his hands on several plots which lay within the family land – he was one of the few young men who had not fallen out with his father. Léon bought meadows for grazing; other farmers divided the remainder between them.

No one coveted the two hectares Pierre-Edouard and Mathilde wanted; the land was a long way from the village, had lain fallow for years, and lay directly between the property of old Vialhe and his daughter-in-law – in other words, right in the middle of a family quarrel. No one wanted to be involved in that!

Everyone knew that Jean-Edouard had easily enough money to push up the price by bidding for it; but no one had forgotten, either, how Mathilde had won the first round with her masterly purchase eighteen months earlier. So they were anticipating a really good feud.

Marguerite rinsed the potato with a twist of her hand, dispatched it brusquely into the bowl of water, seized a fresh tuber and peeled it nervously. Jean-Edouard noticed how tense and edgy she was, and anticipated a fresh attack.

But the more agitated his wife became, the calmer he

appeared. He carefully divided the thick slice of bread into tiny strips and let them fall into his bowl, then poured in the chicory coffee and a little milk and stirred it.

'So you're going to let them do it to you!' griped Marguerite.

He tipped a spoonful of sugar into the bowl and stirred again. 'Let them do it? No one's bothering me!' he said, without raising his voice.

'Oh, so you think that, do you? You're going to let them set up right in the middle of your property! So that every time they go to work on their land, that little slut can make fun of us and show off. You've got to buy that land, do you hear me!'

'No,' he said, and sucked in a noisy spoonful of coffee and soggy bread.

'And why not?'

'Because I can't even cultivate all the ground I've got now. I'm ashamed enough of that, without adding to it!'

'You only have to find a worker, or even two, if that's what it needs!'

'No I don't; it's nice and quiet since old Abel left to hang about somewhere else!'

'Well I'm telling you that it has to be bought, whatever you say!' she shouted suddenly, banging the table with the handle of her knife.

'You still haven't got enough land? Tell me, don't you think there'll be enough space to bury us in? My God! What do you want with another two hectares! I'd be better off selling than buying!'

'You must take them, do you hear,' she repeated. This had been her obsession for several years now – to acquire. It didn't matter what – land, money – just to hoard it, for the satisfaction of being able to say that they were rich; richer than their neighbours, and therefore more respectable.

He had shared this passion in his time, but at least when he bought land it was to increase the Vialhe holdings; for the honour of the Vialhes, to leave a substantial property for his descendants, larger than the one he had inherited from his father. But Louise had left, Pierre-Edouard had left, Berthe had left; so what was the good of buying land of which they now had no need? So that his son would get it back when he died? No, thank you, that was too easy, it went against the grain. If Pierre-Edouard wanted the two hectares, let him take them, but at least he'd have to pay for them out of his own pocket.

'If you don't buy them everyone will say that the little slut has made a fool of you again, and no one will believe that you never intended to acquire them. Or they'll say that Pierre-Edouard has got you on a tight rein!'

'Well, let them talk! I don't give a damn!' he swore, swallowing another lump of bread.

And it was true, he didn't care. He didn't care because in his view none of that mattered any more; because manners, ideas, principles even, all the ways of doing things since the war, had nothing in common with what he had known and revered for more than sixty years. In this new world children had no respect for tradition, or authority, or filial duty; in this world money, good money in fine gold coins, had been replaced by worthless paper. This mad world threatened by social revolutions and political struggles, this world turned upside down, no longer interested him. He felt like a stranger who had lost his way.

And Marguerite could go on wailing and moaning and raging as much as she liked, he would not listen to her. Just as he did not listen to those (and there were many of them) who clamoured for him to seek a further term of office as mayor.

The general election in November 1919 and the municipal elections which followed it did not unleash any strong feelings in St Libéral. It was a far cry from the fights, manipulations and struggles of former times.

There again the climate had changed. Even Father Verlhac did not hide his preference, although he did not go so far as to suggest voting for anyone in particular; he was even seen discussing politics with the teacher, and without them coming to blows! Nobody took offence. Why should the priest have to keep quiet? After all, they'd allowed women to speak, very nearly given them the right to vote!

This idea had been rejected by the Senate, who had no doubt that the Church would take advantage of the opportunity to influence its female devotees, but the women did not hesitate to express their opinions and defend their candidate just the same. And it was they who placed Jean-Edouard Vialhe first on the list of candidates at St Libéral. They had seen him at work during the war, knew how he had devoted himself to his mayoral duties, and vigorously encouraged the men to vote for him.

Two old hands were re-elected with Jean-Edouard, Léon and Jeantout, but the majority were young ex-soldiers, like Jeantout's lad, Maurice, and Jacques, the grocer's son; even Dr Delpy was elected. Everyone knew he was not convinced that he wanted to be a councillor, but they knew that he had done his duty and more during the war.

As for Jean-Edouard, he was surprised to find himself elected with such a majority; surprised and deeply moved. Although he believed and felt he had been overtaken and tossed aside by a new era in which he had no role, they had nevertheless chosen him; they wanted him to lead the community. Him, the old man, the patriarch.

He saw the electors' decision as an affirmation of his whole life and all his decisions; he was astounded, but elated too, and felt his strength return in a way he would never have believed possible. He was re-invigorated to fight on and to prove to everyone that they had been right to choose him.

He had only one regret, which no one would have guessed but which Marguerite never failed to remind him of. He regretted having once dropped his guard, not having taken up the challenge and affirmed his power as head of the family, when he had allowed his son to buy those two hectares, which he had undervalued through weariness and weakness.

But it was too late to go back, to undo what he now saw

as a humiliation. Pierre-Edouard and Mathilde were already the owners. They had signed the deeds of purchase more than a month earlier, in one of the last transactions undertaken by Monsieur Lardy. Since then his office had been closed, and Saint-Libéral had no solicitor.

Once more the wave of pain lanced her lower body, spreading out like a tongue of flame to the base of her stomach; seared her kidneys and left her short of breath, waiting for the next agonising current to flow through her.

Despite this, Mathilde did not wake Pierre-Edouard. He was sleeping the deep sleep of a man broken by the effort of a whole day spent clearing the land, their new land up on the plateau. The night before, a violent pulling in her loins had driven her to shake her husband awake; but that had been a false alarm, just a warning, and she had been cross with herself for disturbing his rest. But tonight . . .

Then she considered how she had taxed her own strength during the previous day. She had been seized by a frenzy of activity, heightened by annoyance that she had mistaken the signs of labour, and thrown herself into cleaning their little house; attacking their few pieces of furniture until they were gleaming; scrubbing out the crib which had lain ready for two weeks; sweeping the floor of beaten earth with a fierce care; hunting down the spiders in their webs who played hide and seek with her between the thick beams blackened by centuries of smoke. Yes, perhaps she had done too much.

She calculated furthermore that, since it was the night of 6 January, the baby wasn't due yet, although it would be coming soon. Tomorrow, perhaps . . .

She placed her hands on her stomach and noticed immediately that a change had taken place. The warm ball of life which distended her skin and an hour earlier had pushed against her breasts, had sunk down. It was no longer perfectly oval in shape, soft and relaxed; it was humped in the middle, like a huge misshapen fist, hard and knobbly.

A new pain shot through her like electricity, from her

feet to the nape of her neck; so she gently shook Pierre-Edouard. He woke up straight away, instantly alert.

'It's the real thing this time?' he asked, as he lit the oil lamp.

'I think so, yes. I'd like you to go and fetch Doctor Delpy.' She raised herself painfully on to her elbows and sat up, her back against the wooden headboard. They distinctly heard a rustling like torn tissue paper, followed by the sound of an egg being cracked on the corner of a table and dripping onto the floor.

'That's it; the waters are about to break, I can feel it. Hurry, go and get the doctor.'

'Good God,' he said, hurriedly dressing, 'you should have woken me earlier!' He did not panic, but an insidious fear gripped him and tightened his chest.

'But I'll have to leave you here all alone, with no one for three kilometres in any direction. Are you sure you wouldn't rather I stayed?'

He was aware that he was asking a stupid question. They had discussed this birth for long enough, and he had been the first to admit that he did not feel equal to the task alone. This time it was not a cow or a ewe to be helped through labour. It was Mathilde, his love; her softness already changing and opening for the delivery. And in that, he really did not know how to help her.

He dressed carefully, for the frost was biting outside. 'Lie down,' he suggested as he tried to cover her.

'Leave me alone, I'm all right as I am; go quickly!'

'I don't like to leave you alone . . .'

'Hurry up, it'll be okay.'

He stoked the fire with four enormous blocks of oak, then lit the big hurricane lantern and rushed out.

The burning sensation was overwhelming her stomach, cutting off her breath; her face and breast ran with sweat. It went away; it returned, allpowerful, all-consuming.

Instinctively Mathilde regulated her breathing, perhaps because she had seen so many ewes in labour: she deliberately changed to short rapid breaths which increased in tempo, until the pain blurred and settled down in the centre of her being, like an animal pretending that it was tamed, but ready to spring out again. She watched the clock anxiously, the big copper pendulum scything away each second with a broad stroke.

Pierre-Edouard had left twenty minutes ago; he would have run all the way along the track, he must be knocking on the doctor's door by now. Perhaps he was already on the way back with him, and soon she would hear the sound of the motor. Miraculous car, which could drive right up to the house bearing someone who would take away this fearful burning which was tearing her apart, destroying her!

A fresh flame of pain lit up in the small of her back. She bit her thumb in order not to cry out and she didn't cry, but she tasted her own blood through her teeth.

And the pain returned, settled in and did not leave her. Then she cried out for Pierre-Edouard, all the time, in the plaintive tones of a lost child calling for help, stubbornly repeating the name, trying to banish her fear with the sound of her own voice; talking, talking, as if to keep away the beast of death she sensed lurking nearby.

Pierre-Edouard ran like a madman; at least, he tried to run. Less than two hundred metres from the house an evil patch of ice had sent him rolling head over heels into a ditch full of brambles. He wasn't much hurt, but the glass of the lantern had exploded like a miniature grenade, leaving him in complete darkness.

There was no moon, no stars, nothing to help his dash down to the village. He ran on nevertheless, now mad with worry and overwhelmed by the certain knowledge that Mathilde needed help; up there she was alone, quite lost, and needed him more than ever before.

He tripped on a bump, fell full-length again, and slid three metres. He was up in a bound, without heeding the dull pain from his scarred legs. He set off again, ice and stones from the path embedded in his palms; he wiped them on his jacket as he ran.

At last he reached the first houses of the village. Everyone was asleep, but suddenly the dogs gave voice, alerted by the sound of his steps echoing in the alleyways. In the main square he quickened his pace and threw himself on the doctor's door, pounding it with his fist until a light appeared.

'Who is it?' demanded the old maidservant through the closed door.

'Open up, in God's name! It's me, Vialhe, my wife is having a baby! We need the doctor, quick!'

'Oh, you poor man, you'll have to wait. He left less than an hour ago to deliver Madame Bonny's baby up in the hills, not far from Perpezac . . .'

'But, good God! What shall I do?' he cried.

And suddenly he saw himself as a widower, saw himself returning to the cottage to find lifeless she for whom he would have given his life . . . But four years of war had made him into a fighter, and a decisive man. He clenched his teeth and ran towards Doctor Fraysse's house.

The door was opened almost immediately.

'What's the matter with you?' asked the old doctor, as he wrapped himself in his dressing-gown. 'Was that you yelling just now?'

'Yes, Delpy's not at home and Mathilde is in labour up there, all alone!'

'All right,' commented the old man. 'Well, go and fetch Madame Traversat, she's a good midwife.'

'No, I don't want her! She's the one who pulled Gaston's little girl about, she even dislocated the baby's shoulder, I don't want that butcher! *You* must come. You can't refuse!'

The doctor sighed, and objected mildly: 'Look, I'm eighty-five, it's not right at my age to be running about at two o'clock in the morning, especially when it's as cold as this!'

'You must come! You wouldn't leave her like that!'

'Of course I wouldn't. Well, it'll make me feel younger to help a woman I delivered twenty years ago. Besides,' the old man murmured, as if to himself, 'I owe it to her. No, you wouldn't understand, that's an old story, from your father's time. Go on, find a cart for us while I get dressed. And don't worry; a first birth always takes a long time.'

Pierre-Edouard rushed off into the darkness, ran to his brother-in-law's house, and hammered on the door fit to wake the dead.

'Who's the idiot who wants a blast from my shotgun?' shouted Léon suddenly from behind the shutters.

'Shut up! It's me, Pierre, I need your horse. Hurry up, it's for Mathilde!' he yelled, as he ran towards the stable.

Despite the darkness he found the horse and brought it out. He was already putting on the horse-collar when Léon arrived with a lamp.

'What's going on?'

'It's a mess! Mathilde is giving birth and Delpy's devil knows where! He promised he'd be there, the old cheat! So I woke up Doctor Fraysse. Lift the shafts! And you, back, back!' he directed the horse. 'Go on, back!'

'Do you want me to follow you? Do you want me to tell my mother to come?'

'No, no! What use would that be? Your mother's ill, what could she do! Bye!' He jumped into the cart, and whipped the nag into a gallop towards Doctor Frayssse's house.

The doctor was waiting for him, bundled up to the ears. He held his little black bag tightly, as if it were an object of great value, and the sight of it comforted Pierre-Edouard a little. The old doctor heaved himself painfully into the trap and tucked the cover over his knees.

'Off you go, young man. I'm ready, I'll hold tight.'

Pierre-Edouard lashed the horse's flanks and urged it on; the noise of the iron wheels grinding on the cobblestones echoed through the village. But he was forced to slow down a little when they reached the rough track which climbed up to Coste-Roche.

'Don't tip us out!' cried the old man. 'That wouldn't help. And calm down a bit!'

'Me, calm down? My God! It's almost two hours since I left! Tell me, what do you think . . . Is she in danger?'

'No, no, your little Mathilde is well made, just the right size; the child will come easily, I'm sure of that. But tell me, why didn't you ask her mother to come and stay with you? That's the usual thing.'

'I know! But my mother-in-law had some trouble with her heart a week ago, she's in bed!'

'Oh, I didn't know that. Slow down, I tell you, we've got time.'

'No we haven't! Mathilde is alone up there! All alone, remember that!'

'Of course. But you know, at moments like that you're always alone, even when the room is full of people . . . Well, that's what I feel, anyway. Take care, this curve is deceptive . . . So which would you prefer, a boy or a girl?'

'Oh, I don't care about that! All I want is to help Mathilde! Good God, if you knew . . . Oh, you wouldn't understand!'

'Yes, I know what she is to you, and you to her. You don't need to say it. You only need to look at you two to know that you're like the fingers of a hand; better still, like the eyes in a face; one never moves without the other. Don't go so fast, we'll tip over.'

'I'm frightened,' Pierre-Edouard admitted, without reining in the horse, 'frightened we'll arrive too late. Like I was afraid in the war; I'm scared to death like when they were firing on us, and I'm not ashamed to admit it.'

'I'm glad to hear it; only fools have no fear. But it's no good getting in a panic.'

'I'm not in a panic, that's not my way! But to think of her alone up there . . . Tell me, do you think she'll be in a lot of pain?'

'Maybe, but she's brave, your Mathilde.'

'I know, but that doesn't make it all right. Oh Lord, let us get there in time!'

'We will. And you'll see, she may keep us waiting all night!'

Mathilde called once more for Pierre-Edouard, over-whelmed by pain and tormented by the living thing which she sensed was there, by the lump which was tearing her apart, which she could not expel. But he had been gone an hour already, and anxiety gnawed at her: something must have happened. Perhaps he had tumbled into the ravine, perhaps he had broken his leg again . . .

So she was going to be alone there all night. Nobody would come to help her, no one would rescue her from this tearing pain which seemed to be splitting her in two; she felt herself opening like an over-ripe melon which bursts in the sun.

She repeated her cries, gasping, perspiring, exhausted; but they were growing weaker.

Pierre-Edouard encouraged the horse, urged it up the last slope.

'We're coming, we're coming, we're there,' he spoke gently, as if to his wife.

'Did you think to heat any water?' asked the doctor. 'No, of course not! Well you must do that as soon as we arrive. Damn it, what an idea to live so far away from everyone else! When I think . . .'

'I know, I should be in the village, with my father! Well, we're not, that's all there is to it!'

'I'm not blaming you, it's none of my business. Ah, we've got here anyway!' The old man could just make out the low outline of the cottage.

Pierre-Edouard jumped to the ground, grasped the rug which had protected them and threw it over the horse's back; the poor animal was sweating. He should take it out of the harness and rub it down, but there was no time; he hoped the rug would prevent it from catching a fatal chill, and rushed towards the farmhouse, dragging the doctor with him.

They went in. The house was warm and quiet, an uncanny silence hardly disturbed by the tick of the pendulum and the crackle of the fire. At the back, in the bedroom, by the flickering light of the lamp, they saw the little figure lying still in the middle of the bed, curled up beneath the covers.

Pierre-Edouard ran to her and stopped, petrified by the sight of her wan face, her closed eyes shadowed with fatigue, her pinched nose and pale lips. He did not dare stretch out his hand to touch her forehead, where her hair lay in damp wisps, stuck down by sweat.

'Push,' commanded the doctor. He brushed Mathilde's cheek with his finger, then pulled back the covers.

'Oh my God!' he exclaimed in a low voice.

The baby was there, all plump and shiny with dampness, stretched out calmly on its stomach on top of its mother. Its sticky head nestled almost between her breasts, and in that narrow cleft a little turned-up nose snuffled happily. But the reddish cord still twined beneath the baby's legs and joined it to its mother.

The doctor grasped the child by its feet, and saw the torn hanky which the young woman had managed to tie to the cord low down on her belly. Then he laid the little creature down between Mathilde's legs, and began to attend to her.

'Is she. . . ?' asked Pierre-Edouard weakly. He looked just as pale as she did, and was quite unable to move.

'No, of course not! What do you think! She's sleeping. Well, almost. But I shall have to get her working again,' the doctor explained as he prepared his syringe. 'Go on, go and heat some water, find some clean sheets, make some coffee. Get a move on!'

'Are you sure. . . ?'

'Don't worry, just do what I tell you. And get the cot ready for your son.'

'Oh, it's a boy,' he murmured, as he gradually became aware of his surroundings again. Transfixed by the pallor and stillness of his wife, he hadn't even thought to look at the child when the doctor picked it up.

'Get going, everything's all right. Look, she's already stirring.'

The burden which had weighed him down, almost crushed him, during the preceding two hours now disappeared. He crouched at the head of the bed and whispered into his wife's ear, his face close to hers, speaking a thousand sweet nothings which only she could hear. And his hand stroked her forehead and warmed her icy cheeks.

Mathilde tossed restlessly; her hands reached to her stomach and felt around there, searching; she panicked when she found nothing, and awoke with a start.

'Where is he?' she cried, lifting her head a little.

She saw the two men smiling at her, felt Pierre-Edouard's caresses. Then she sank back onto the pillow, exhausted.

'He's handsome, isn't he?' she sighed.

'Beautiful!'

'I want to see him.'

'See, here he is,' said the doctor, resting the child on her breast. He had finally divided the child from his mother, and a crêpe bandage was tied around its belly. The baby was upset and howled in rage, its tiny fists clenched and beating clumsily on his mother's breasts.

'He cried a little while ago,' she explained in a weak voice. 'I called for you, and he answered. That gave me courage. He was born at a quarter past two. You're not cross that I didn't wait for you?'

'Are you mad? It's my fault,' he apologised.

'I couldn't keep him in, he wanted to come, he pushed. I felt his head with my hands, I wanted to help him. He came, and yelled angrily straight away. I remembered that you're supposed to tie the cord, so I used what I could find and then I laid him on my body and he calmed down. After that I can't remember any more.'

'You worked like a heroine,' the old doctor reassured her. 'I congratulate you. Pierre-Edouard should be proud of you.'

'But I was a bit frightened,' she admitted, 'I thought you'd had an accident. Then I thought I'd be all alone . . . But next time you must be there, all right? Promise?'

'I promise, I'll be there. I was really frightened too.'

Pierre-Edouard marched down towards the village whistling in time with his steps like an artilleryman, despite the frosty night and the aches in his legs.

He was madly happy, ready to stop the first person he saw to relate what had happened that night; to tell of his wife's courage, to describe his fine son, a strong fellow of three kilos! To measure his weight Doctor Fraysse had wrapped him in a napkin and hung him from the hook of the spring balance Mathilde which used to weigh the rabbits and chickens.

Yes, he was ready to hug the whole world! But what a nightmare, what a fright! Now all that was over, finished, there was nothing but joy.

Towards seven o'clock Doctor Delpy had arrived, apologising to his colleague and to Pierre-Edouard, who could no longer feel cross that he hadn't been there during the night. All that was forgotten, banished by the little cries which emanated from the crib, and by Mathilde's smile. After accepting a cup of coffee, Doctor Delpy had taken Doctor Fraysse back down in his car. Pierre-Edouard did not know how to thank him enough, and the old doctor kissed Mathilde as if he were her grandfather, congratulating her.

'It's I who must thank you, my children. This is definitely my last delivery, and what's more I've done nothing! But I am glad that I came to welcome this baby. You've given me the nicest of presents. I'm very, very pleased.'

Shortly after they had left Léon arrived, all worried, not knowing what he was going to find. He knocked discreetly on the half-door with the metal claw which had replaced his left hand six months since.

What a pleasure to open the door to him, to drag him into the bedroom, to invite him to admire the mother and baby! He was going to be the godfather of this child; just as Louise had earlier chosen Pierre-Edouard in place of Félix's grandfather, Pierre-Edouard and Mathilde had asked Léon and his mother to be godparents to their son. Jean-Edouard would doubtless have refused anyway.

Then Léon had gone back down with his horse; once Pierre-Edouard had emerged from his trance he had taken it out of its harness, led it into the stable, and rubbed it down vigorously to warm its blood and dry the lather of sweat which had frozen in a hard layer on its coat.

Pierre-Edouard reached the village at about eleven o'clock, and realised straight away that Léon had announced the good news. He thanked all the people who congratulated him, bought a round of drinks for three or four friends, then marched toward the Mairie.

26

PIERRE-EDOUARD had not spoken to his father for several months. This was not out of rancour or bitterness; he simply had nothing to say to him. But the breach did not worry him, and he was ready to forget all about it on condition that his father recognised once and for all that he was no longer a little boy . . .

Anyway, as time passed he felt more inclined to smile at his father's attitude, the image he had of his role as head of the family. All that was so outdated, and so confounded by the paths chosen by his own children, that it was almost laughable.

Just one thing prevented Pierre-Edouard from contacting his parents again: their hostility to Mathilde. He would not accept that, he would not forgive that, and nothing could be done so long as his father and mother refused to recognise her as a full member of the Vialhe family.

But these thoughts did not oppress him, that morning of 6 January, and he was still whistling as he walked into the Mairie. 'Wow, you're here already?' he said, a little surprised to see his father.

He had thought he would find the secretary, then remembered that it was Tuesday, and the teacher would be busy with the children.

'Does that surprise you? I am the mayor, aren't I?'

'I know. Well, here I am, I expect you've heard the news. You know why I'm here?'

'I've been told. Anyway, it seems you made so much noise last night that the whole village heard the news . . . The whole village apart from us.'

'It's not my fault you live a long way from the main square.'

'All the same, you could have come and fetched your mother . . .'

'I didn't think of that,' he admitted.

And it was true, the idea had never even occurred to him. He took out his pipe and filled it, hoping that his father would not make a scene about a little thing like that. Besides, what would he have gained by bringing his mother to Mathilde's bedside? Nothing, except possibly a long list of complaints and bitter comments.

'Well, one could say that you were at fault . . .'

'Okay, if that makes you happy,' he said between puffs.

His father shrugged his shoulders, looked down at the register, grasped his pen and dipped it carefully into the ink.

'Let's get on; notify me about this child,' he said, starting to write: 'Today, 6 January 1920 at . . . at what time?'

'Quarter past two,' said Pierre-Edouard, and continued: 'Jacques Pierre Léon Vialhe was born.'

'Bloody hell!' said his father. He laid down the pen and briskly pushed the register away. 'Hell and damnation! You're renouncing your ancestors now, eh?'

'Which ancestors?'

'Dammit! Your great-great-grandfather was called Edouard Benjamin, your great-grandfather was Mathieu Edouard, your grandfather was Edouard, your father Jean-Edouard, and you're Pierre-Edouard, and you want to baptise him Jacques Pierre Léon! Are you ashamed of the Edouards? Huh, I've seen it all, now! And calling him Léon, like a Dupeuch!'

'So what? You don't want me to call him Mathilde, do you? He's as much Dupeuch as he is Vialhe! And it's just too bad if you don't like it!'

'No, I don't like it! A Vialhe son should be called Edouard!'

'You're beginning to annoy me with your Edouards. He'll be called Jacques Pierre Léon, and that's that, dammit, that's it! And if you don't want to write it, I'll wait till the secretary is here!'

He found the whole scene grotesque, all the more so because none of it was intentional. It had not occurred to him to christen his son Edouard, simply because his second name was rarely used now: Mathilde simply called him Pierre. And perhaps it was a subconscious decision too, because Edouard signified first and foremost his father, with his impossible character, his moods and his stubbornness.

'Well, it wouldn't cost you much to add Edouard!' Jean-Edouard persisted.

'And why should I do that? For what reason? The Edouards, all the Edouards, were born down there, at your place, in the house where I was born! They were born at home, under their own roof, on their own property! But this one, my son, was born all alone on the edge of the parish, because of your damned stupidity — yes, your stupidity! And if his mother had died, it would have been because of you! So don't give me your Edouard Vialhes; all they're good for is throwing children out of the house, and what's more they don't even bother to look after their land properly! The Edouards are finished! So you write: Jacques Pierre Léon!'

'You little bastard,' his father swore, 'you're getting rid of Edouard and putting Pierre instead of it, eh? That's it, isn't it?'

'Exactly!' Pierre-Edouard agreed, without thinking what he was saying, 'you've got it right! I'm doing that so that all my descendants will remember it, so that they'll know that you have to wait for a Pierre to come along before anything changes in this damned family!'

'Very well,' Jean-Edouard spoke quietly, and picked up the pen again: 'you can go on behaving like an idiot, but you'll do it alone. I've heard enough.'

Pierre-Edouard looked at him and noticed how he had aged. He seemed to have shrunk, and his hand trembled as he formed the letters.

'Oh, what the hell!' he recovered his previous euphoria suddenly, and began to laugh. 'Add Edouard, if it makes you happy. It's all nonsense anyway! Wait! After Léon, first add Libéral, then Edouard last of all. Perhaps the one will calm the other down. There: Jacques Pierre Léon Libéral Edouard Vialhe – and if the Edouards raise their ugly heads after all that lot, I'll be very surprised!'

'Don't be so full of yourself,' said his father, as he carefully applied the blotting-paper to the page in the register. 'Don't think you're so wonderful, or so clever. We'll see what you manage to do, you and your kids . . . We'll talk about it again some time . . . If they're as bloody-minded as you and your sisters, they'll lead you a merry dance. And when that happens I shall have a good laugh, believe you me!'

Pierre-Edouard skilfully manipulated his hoe to raise a little mound of earth around the young green shoot; then he looked behind him and thought once again that he had set himself an impossible task, far too great. He had overestimated his strength, and that of Mathilde.

However willing and strong, she could not work at his pace. But she was determined, got down to work and always appeared slightly apologetic that she could not keep up with him. And he, anxious and distressed to see her straining and exhausting herself, tried to relieve her by moving even faster; by earthing up the greatest number of tobacco plants as quickly as possible, doing the work of two men all by himself.

Despite that, the ridging of this field seemed to last an eternity; it ate up all their time and forced them to work fifteen hours a day. For tobacco was not the only crop which needed attention; there was maize too, potatoes, beets and all the other vegetables.

Added to that there were the animals to care for; feeding the two sows, the hens, ducks and rabbits, watching the eight ewes and their lambs; and for Mathilde there were the demands made by the baby, nursing it, washing its nappies, mending and preparing the meals. Pierre-Edouard was now regretting starting to grow tobacco.

As a former soldier with a war wound, he had obtained permission to plant 3,800 seedlings; he had thought he could manage that many. That way they would improve their finances and relieve the worry caused by lack of money and rising prices. Tobacco growing brought a good return, but what a drudgery it was!

First of all he had prepared a bed of good fertile earth beside the barn, where the spring sunshine warmed it; he had to sieve it and lightly enrich it with horse manure. Then he had sown the minute seeds – he had been told that a gramme weight held 12,000 of them – which he had to mix with ash to spread them at the correct density.

Then came the supervision of the seed bed; watering it, protecting it from night frosts, the first thinning of the seedlings. Later he had meticulously divided the field into strips with string and had transplanted 3,800 plants: no more, no less, for the inspector of the tobacco department was not joking when he said he inspected the plantations rigorously. The official measure was 38,000 plants to the hectare; he was cultivating a thousand square metres, so he must have 3,800 plants.

Now that the stems had reached fifteen centimetres he had to earth them up, to make them stronger and promote the development of ancillary roots.

What was worrying Pierre-Edouard was all the other work this crop would require. It was high time he started on the first thinning, cutting back the small, worthless leaves which would weaken the plant. After this first tidying-up came the pruning, during which he had to choose the seven best leaves and cut off all the rest. Then followed the pollarding, which severed the main stalk, the one carrying the flower; finally, when the leaves measured twenty centimetres, it was necessary to disbud the whole plant once more. And each of these painstaking processes had to be repeated for 3,800 plants . . .

Later, during the winter, when the tobacco was quite dry, there were other tasks which were physically less demanding because they could be carried out indoors, but still it was slow, laborious work. He had to grade the leaves by size, colour and quality, tie them into bundles of twenty-five leaves each, and finally into bales of a hundred bundles. Then, and only then, would he and Mathilde get any reward for their trouble, would at last be paid for their broken backs, aching kidneys, their hands stained yellow and stinking from handling 26,600 leaves.

He turned once more to look at Mathilde. She was far behind him but kept on doggedly, bent over the soil, bowed down with weariness and the heat. So he called to her: 'Hey, time's up!' although the sun gave the lie to this.

She straightened up, and it was pitiful to see her face so red, running with perspiration. Like him, she looked up at the sun and shook her head.

'No,' she said, wiping her forehead, 'I've still got some time to go. Anyway, he's not crying.'

'Time's up,' he insisted, walking towards her. 'Go on, go and sit over there, go and feed him. Go and rest.'

'But there's no need!'

'Don't argue,' he replied, taking her hoe. 'You're working too hard, you'll lose your milk.'

'I'm no weakling! I've got milk and your greedy son knows it! How do you think he puts on so much weight, by feeding on air? Everyone takes him for ten months old, and he's only six months!'

He took her arm and drew her to the edge of the field, towards the huge chestnut tree which sheltered the baby. His basket hung from the low branches of the tree and there he lay, gazing at the shimmering leaves, entranced to see them move in the wind, lulled by his own movements as they swayed the light crib.

'You see how good he is!' she said, bending over him. The baby, happy to see his mother again, wriggled; he trembled with happiness and blew several large bubbles.

'Now that you're here, stay here,' he said. 'You should rest, you're doing too much; let the tobacco go to the devil!'

'You won't say that when it affects our income!'

'Oh, money! No, I've taken on too much for us two. Years ago my father grew tobacco, but there were at least five or six of us to take care of it! Everyone joined in, and the work got done! Whereas here . . .'

'And that's why you've made me sit down!'

He looked at her, delighted to see her still so petite, so young. She had not lost her figure through the pregnancy; she was good enough to eat, like a bunch of cherries.

'Don't argue,' he said, pointing to the baby. 'He needs you and your milk, and he comes before the tobacco, and before any other work too!'

'I'm not made of glass! Years ago my mother had to do a man's work and . . .'

'Yes, I know; mine too, years ago. But that was a long time ago and now it's different. I don't want you to look like your mother – nor like mine, for that matter. Go on, rest a bit, and if I see you out in the field before half an hour is up there'll be trouble.'

'You'll beat me up, eh?' she teased.

'Of course,' he assured her as he walked back to his work. 'That's the only tradition which should be preserved.'

Pierre-Edouard re-counted the 725 francs which he had just received from the sale of six lambs. The animals were really not bad looking, and he had managed to dispose of his lot quite well. He would certainly have gained more by keeping them three or four weeks longer, but it was September and the acorns were dropping: he had no way of controlling the ewes and lambs. As soon as the barn door was opened the animals tried to escape into the woods to stuff themselves with acorns; they devised a multitude of tricks to escape Mathilde's watchful eye, to dash over to the oak-wood and indulge themselves. A small quantity of acorns did them no harm, but too large a dose could poison them as surely as a handful of arsenic. That was why he had just sold six of the ten lambs his ewes had produced; the other four were ewe-lambs, which he wanted to keep to increase his flock.

He came out of the bar where the buyer had been dealing with his customers, and looked around for Mathilde. She should be at the other end of the square, with the women who were selling their chickens and vegetables. Mathilde had nothing to sell this morning, but he would bet she was over there anyway, showing off her son to a bevy of soft-hearted housewives.

He walked up between the lines where the calves were lowing, and noticed how few there were. Really, the market was nothing like it had been in days gone by! On the other side, the cows were just as scarce. Only Léon and one of his colleagues had brought in some heifers, but buyers were few and far between.

Pierre-Edouard greeted and talked to the men he knew as he made his way to the lot of animals offered for sale by his brother-in-law.

'Well, you old devil, still looking for a sucker?'

'I don't want to talk about that,' retorted Léon, giving him a friendly cuff. 'It's a real misery, nobody's buying!'

'Are you surprised? With the prices you're asking?'

'It's not that, it's like this everywhere. You'd think the whole world was as mad as that poor fellow, who is president, Deschanel.'

'Is it true he's resigned?' Pierre-Edouard enquired. He didn't come down to the village very often, and didn't take a newspaper.

'You're a bit behind the times! That was a week ago! Wait, it was market day at Seilhac, the twenty-first, that was it. Huh, that'll show the cowards, they should have elected Clemenceau! My God, when I think that they preferred that simpleton to him! It was incredible! Can you wonder that things aren't going well?'

Pierre-Edouard agreed. He didn't take much interest in politics, but he shared his brother-in-law's sense of outrage. Clemenceau, Foch, Joffre, Pétain, those were real men. But the others, all the others — what a pack of good-for-nothing opportunists!

'Have you seen your godson?' he asked, as he offered his tobacco-pouch.

'Yes,' smiled Léon. 'Beautiful, isn't he? A sturdy boy! You know, my colleague here told me he looks like me!' he added, pink with pride.

'Now that has upset me!' exclaimed Pierre-Edouard

with a laugh. 'That's all we need! One of you is quite enough in this area!'

Still laughing, he turned suddenly, for someone had just tugged his sleeve.

'Well, well, Jeantout, what brings you here?'

'Your father wants to see you.'

'My father?' he mumbled. 'What does my father want me for? . . . Answer me, what for!' he insisted, noticing now the old man's haggard expression. 'What's happened?'

'It's your mother . . .'

'What about my mother?'

'Go home, go!'

'No, you explain,' ordered Pierre-Edouard, suddenly anxious, 'I wasn't expecting – What's the matter with my mother?'

'She's dead.'

'Oh my God!' he cried out, quite stunned by the news. 'But how can that be? Mathilde saw her only this week!'

'They had to take her down to Brive last night, she had perimonitis . . .'

'Peritonitis. And?'

'Well, it was too late . . . She died in the night. They've just brought her back to your place.'

He nodded to show that he understood. He felt infinitely sad, sad enough to cry. But the tears had been left behind, somewhere at the front; the well had run dry after the death of too many comrades.

In a flash he saw his mother again. Not the old embittered woman of the final years, but as she was earlier, in the good times, when the whole family sat around the dining table every evening, with Louise teasing and joking, Berthe telling tales and himself laughing in his corner. He saw her young again, gentle and attentive, and was sorry that it was too late to tell her that he loved her very much, despite everything; that Louise and Berthe loved her dearly as well, that it wasn't her fault that they had all three left home. It wasn't anything to do with her, she wasn't responsible for the Vialhe character, she was only the intermediary; they had inherited it from their father.

'I'll go there. But I must tell Mathilde.'

He moved through the crowd, which parted for him in silence, for the news had flown from mouth to mouth. Already everyone knew that Jean-Edouard Vialhe was now a widower, and alone . . .

They handed over little Jacques to his godfather and climbed the main street, walking towards the house which they were going to enter for the first time since their marriage. But without happiness or rejoicing, only in sadness and affliction.

'There she is,' said Jean-Edouard, opening the door to the bedroom. He was crying, silently, discreetly, almost as if he were ashamed of it.

Marguerite looked younger; her severely lined face was smoother, only the finer wrinkles etched by her smile remained. She was wearing an old nightdress, dragged on hastily by some nurse. She looked pitiful lying there, all dishevelled, her arms spread out, her feet bare.

'Leave us, Father,' said Mathilde, as soon as she could gather her thoughts. 'Leave us, we'll take care of her. I'll take care of her,' she repeated. 'It's my job.'

And she steered him towards the door, gently, leading him to the settle where she made him sit down.

'You're not cold, are you? Shall I warm you up a bit of coffee?'

He shook his head and fixed his gaze on the dead fire. He did not move when she furtively took out her hanky to wipe the tears that formed droplets at the end of his white moustache. Then, softly and silently, she returned to the bedroom.

'Pierre, go and fetch Jeantout's wife, she'll help me. Then after that you can be with your father.'

'No, there's no need for Jeantout's wife. I've seen more of death than you'll ever see. Come on, you help me; we'll dress her in her Sunday best. The clothes used to be in here,' he said, as he opened the big wardrobe.

They were still there.

For four days Pierre-Edouard and Mathilde took over the management of the house and the stock, received the neighbours and distant cousins, and organised the nightly vigil.

On the first morning, as soon as they had dressed the corpse, prepared the bedchamber, covered the mirrors and tidied the house, Pierre-Edouard ran to the post office and sent a telegram to Louise. He could not tell Berthe, for he had no address.

Louise arrived by train the following morning. She was so deep in the grip of sorrow that she could scarcely draw breath, yet as she walked across the village her heart softened, for at each step she rediscovered the world of her youth; the church square which had changed so little, the inn where once Octave . . . the main street where the hens pecked about as always, and the ducks still dabbled in the pools of liquid which flowed out of the dung heaps.

She saw several women she knew by name, but she did not stop. Who would recognise her? She had left twelve years ago! And yet, as soon as she passed, the whispers and stifled exclamations burst forth:

'Louise is back! Yes, yes, we recognised her easily! She's a lady now. She's well-dressed and all that, but you can tell, it's still Louise Vialhe! You see, she's not a bad girl after all . . .'

'You should have brought Félix.' Pierre-Edouard was rather reproachful.

'No, he's had enough of death for his age. And after all, he didn't know her,' whispered Louise.

They were both at their mother's bedside, but they still kept on talking in low voices. They had so much to say to each other!

'And how is my Félix?'

'Very well. And your son?'

'Oh, him; nothing worries him! You'll see, he's a true Vialhe. He's with my mother-in-law; I'll take you there.'

'And your wife?'

'She's resting at her mother's home too, she wanted to take the whole of the night vigil.'

'When I think that it's little Mathilde! She was just a kid when I left.'

'Well, yes . . .'

'So, did you manage to come to some arrangement with Father?'

'No, you know what he's like. He didn't want to see Mathilde, so that was it!'

'Poor old man, he's completely lost. I don't even know if he recognised me when I kissed him just now.'

'Of course he did, don't let it worry you. I'm sure he's very pleased that you've come back. But he won't say so . . . and I'm sure he would have loved to see Berthe again too, but I couldn't tell her; I don't know where she is, the tearaway! I would have loved her to have been here, for all three of us to be together . . .'

'I told her.'

'You know where she's staying? How the devil – ?'

'We write from time to time. She began it, during the war.'

'Oh yes,' he remembered, 'I gave her your address when I left here. Do you think she'll come?'

'I don't know, but at least she's been told. She knows that mother has gone.'

That same evening, soon after the train had passed, the door of the Vialhes' house was pushed open, but no one recognised Berthe.

Even Pierre-Edouard wondered for a minute who the beautiful young lady could be, dressed in the latest city fashions, with an elegant feathered hat perched on her short blonde hair, her face delicately made up and her hands fine. She walked without hesitation towards the bent old man by the fireside, and leant over him.

Jean-Edouard recoiled instinctively, then hesitated and examined her face steadily, narrowing his reddened eyes.

'Well, well,' he said, 'if your mother could see you!'

But he allowed her to kiss him, and they all saw him grasp his daughter's shoulders in return.

'There,' said Pierre-Edouard, the day after the funeral, 'everything's sorted out, it's all tidy. I've asked Ma Coste, and if you like she'll come in each day to make your supper and do the housework.'

He held Mathilde close to him, and little Jacques stretched out from her arms and babbled, waving his tiny fists at the fire.

'So you're leaving again, you too, like your sisters . . .' murmured Jean-Edouard.

He said it without bitterness; his tone of voice was not reproachful. He was stating a fact. As he had been forced to state that Louise and Berthe were free to act as they saw fit, live as they pleased, with whomsoever they wished.

'Times have changed,' he said, following this train of thought. 'So you're going back up there, to Coste-Roche? All right . . .'

He hesitated and cleared his throat. 'I just want to say, your wife, now I know her – she's a good daughter . . .'

He could not bring himself to speak to Mathilde, his voice failed him. He had reiterated for far too long that his daughter-in-law was worthless to be able to change from one day to the next, and speak to her without constraint. Even now he could not express, even to his son, all that he wished to say. He tried to start a conversation, but half-heartedly, knowing that he was avoiding an argument.

'If you wanted,' he tried again, 'if you wanted . . . Now, you could stay here, in this house, on our land . . .'

'I know, but we won't be doing that.'

'Well, I'm sure . . .'

'Don't think that we hold it against you, that's not it at all. Let bygones be bygones – that's how I see it, anyway, and Mathilde too.'

'But you're leaving all the same?'

'Yes, we're leaving.'

Pierre-Edouard sensed that his father was within a hair's

breadth of giving in, that he was weakening, almost broken; it would take very little to defeat him, to extract all the concessions he could demand and to push him into the abyss of despair. But that would be to humiliate him, to trample on his pride. That pride which still held him back, prevented him from saying: 'I would like you to stay; I ask it of you. I need you, your wife, your child too; please stay. From now on you are head of the family.' It would have been easy at that moment to crush the old man with the tear-filled eyes forever . . .

Pierre-Edouard looked at his father, saw that he was beaten and miserable, took pity on him and tried to explain.

'You must understand – I know we could move in here now, right away. But if we did that, sooner or later you would think that we'd taken advantage of you, when . . . Well, of mother's death, of the whole situation, you see. That we imposed the decision on you and made use of your . . . of your pain . . .'

Jean-Edouard nodded his head slowly and spat into the fire. 'Yes, you know me well now,' he admitted at last. 'Perhaps better than I thought . . . You're right to want to go. But if one day – well, we'll see, all right?'

'That's right,' murmured Pierre-Edouard, as he gently pulled Mathilde to him. 'One day perhaps, later . . . We'll have to leave it a bit, let time decide, as always . . .'

Jean-Edouard did not move as the door closed behind them.